QUILLIFER

QUILLIFER

BOOK ONE

WALTER JON WILLIAMS

QUILLIFER

SAGA PRESS

LONDON SYDNEY **NEW YORK** TORONTO NEW DELHI

SAGA PRESS
AN IMPRINT OF SIMON & SCHUSTER, INC.

1230 AVENUE OF THE AMERICAS, NEW YORK, NEW YORK 10020

For information address Saga Press Subsidiary Rights Department, 1230 Avenue of the Americas, New York, NY 10020. † SAGA PRESS and colophon are trademarks of Simon & Schuster, Inc. † For information about special discounts for bulk purchases, please contact Simon & Schuster Special Sales at 1-866-506-1949 or business@simonandschuster.com. † The Simon & Schuster Speakers Bureau can bring authors to your live event. For more information or to book an event, contact the Simon & Schuster Speakers Bureau at 1-866-248-3049 or visit our website at www.simonspeakers.com. † Jacket design by Greg Stadnyk; interior design by Brad Mead † The text for this book was set in Scala OT. † Manufactured in the United States of America † First Edition † 10 9 8 7 6 5 4 3 2 1 † Library of Congress Cataloging-in-Publication Data † Names: Williams, Walter Jon, author. † Title: Quillifer / Walter Jon Williams ; maps illustrated by Robert Lazzaretti. † Description: First Edition. | New York : Saga Press, 2017. | Series: The adventures of Quillifer ; book 1 † Identifiers: LCCN 2017011751 | ISBN 9781481489973 (hardback) | ISBN 9781481489997 (eBook) | Subjects: | BISAC: FICTION / Fantasy / Epic. | FICTION / Fantasy / General. FICTION / Action & Adventure. | GSAFD: Adventure fiction. | Fantasy fiction. † Classification: LCC PS3573.I456213 Q55 2017 (print) | DDC 813/.54—dc23 † LC record available at https://lccn.loc.gov/2017011751

To Kathy Hedges

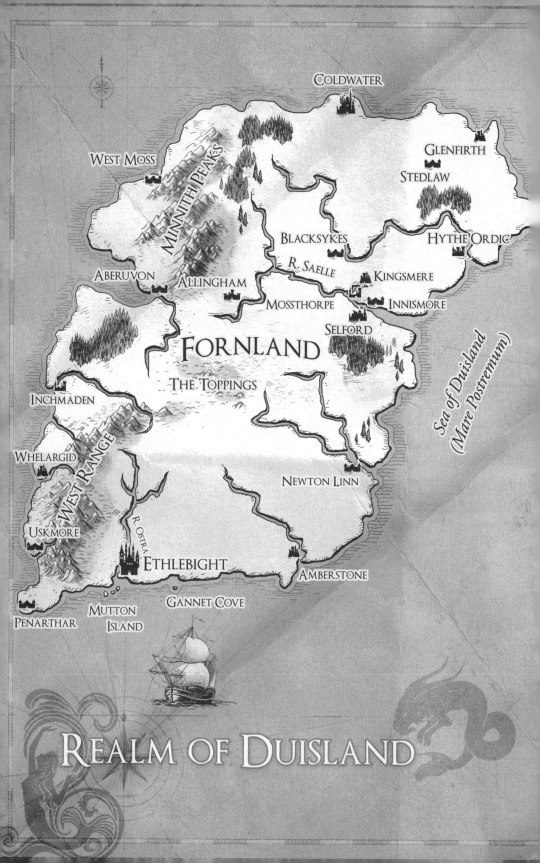

COLDWATER

WEST MOSS

GLENFIRTH

STEDLAW

MINNITH PEAKS

BLACKSYKES

HYTHE ORDIC

R. SAELLE

KINGSMERE

ABERUVON

ALLINGHAM

MOSSTHORPE

INNISMORE

SELFORD

FORNLAND

THE TOPPINGS

Sea of Duisland
(Mare Postremum)

INCHMADEN

WHELARGID

WEST RANGE

NEWTON LINN

USKMORE

R. OSTRA

ETHLEBIGHT

AMBERSTONE

GANNET COVE

PENARTHAR

MUTTON
ISLAND

REALM OF DUISLAND

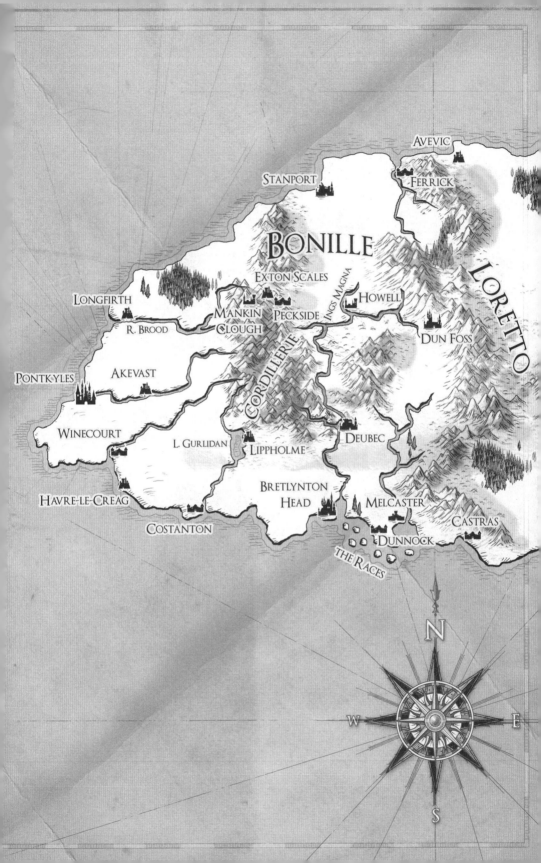

CHAPTER ONE

I can hear the waters of the Dordelle chuckling against the hull of our boat, see the silver moonlight glow on the rim of our little window, taste the warm night air. Your lilac scent floats in my senses. By the light of the moon I can see your open eyes, fixed on the dark corner of my cabin, but in truth staring into your future. For you are beginning a new life, a life apart from everything you knew, and you are anxious on that account.

I would help you sleep. I have begun life over more than once, and perhaps I can ease your concern by narrating my own tale. So, come back to bed, my heart, and rest your head on my shoulder, and I will stroke your hair and tell you how I came to become what I am.

I fear that my life may reveal more folly than wisdom. I will begin with an act of folly, then, as I hang upside down three storeys above the street, and reflect on the workings of Fate. The wheel had come full circle, and all in a flash: naught but two minutes ago, I had been sharing a warm feather bed with Annabel Greyson, the surveyor's daughter; and now I was outside the house, three storeys above the street, hanging near-naked in a brisk wind, while Annabel's father raged within, seeking the villain who had debauched his child.

Who, of course, was me.

This is amusing now, and you laugh, but it was no laughing matter to be thus caught up in some moralist's tale. I resolved to avoid the moralist's last scene, which would almost certainly involve judgment, whips, and the pillory.

What is it about fathers, and brothers too, that sets them so firmly against the course of true love?

The Greyson house was like most houses in Ethlebight, narrow and deep, with the ground floor built of solid masonry, and the upper half-timber floors projecting over the street. From the topmost gable a roof beam extended, and on the end of the beam was a large black iron hook, used to help lift furniture or supplies to the upper storeys.

I hung from the beam with the iron hook a few inches from my face, and hoped I would not find myself hanging from the hook itself within the next twenty minutes.

The beam was slick with pigeon droppings. I tried to claw my fingers into the beam like a badger digging after a burrowing rabbit.

I made my exasperated-bailiff face. *All because she asked me to adjust her Mermaid costume.* I had complied out of a spirit of pure chivalry—I had complied with *all* Annabel's requests—and now I found myself in this doleful condition, hanging above a shadowy abyss.

It has to be said that Annabel's generous nature had surprised me. I had been paying more attention to Bethany Driver, another of the Mermaids, but Annabel had broken a lace and asked for aid, and my fate had lurched onto a new path.

Some hours earlier, I had entered the house via this same gable, to avoid the groom that slept by the door. Annabel had assured me that her father and his apprentices were away on a survey, her mother was visiting relatives in Amberstone, and the only servant besides the groom was the deaf old lady who lit the fires in the morning.

Perhaps the old lady wasn't as deaf as she seemed. Someone, at any rate, had to have sent a message to Anthony Greyson the surveyor, who must have ridden half the night to show up at his own door just as the dawn was beginning to brighten the eastern sky. The city gates wouldn't even have opened yet; Greyson must have bribed his way past the guards.

Hearing the pounding and roaring at the front door, I reacted in an instant—I must admit that I was not a complete stranger to these sorts of emergencies. I dashed up the stairs and left the house by the same route I'd entered, though without all my clothing. In the dash up the stairs, I'd been able to tug on only my shirt. My shoes hung around my neck by their laces, and I held my belt and leather purse in my teeth. On my head was the cap, black velvet with the red piping and the brim turned up all around, that marked me as an apprentice lawyer. My hose, doublet, and tunic were clutched in my hands or piled in a disorderly bundle on my chest.

My situation was made worse by the fact that two of Greyson's apprentices sat on their horses directly below me. I did not wish to fumble my belongings and make the two men wonder why it had suddenly begun to rain clothing. Nor could I stay where I was: Greyson had only to look out the window to see me hanging there, presenting to the viewer the most unflattering view imaginable.

Carefully, I sorted through my possessions, and threw my loose clothes over the beam in hopes they would remain there for the next few minutes. I looked down and saw the broad hats of the apprentices below, then rolled myself, as silently as I could, atop the beam. Pigeon droppings smeared my front, and my hair, which I keep long because you ladies find it so pleasing, fell in my face. The coins in my purse rang, as loud as an alarm bell at such close range. I made my screaming-infant face, froze in place, and tried to look down without actually moving my head.

If anyone had heard the pennies sing, apparently they hadn't thought to look up. Shuddering with cold—or possibly terror—I managed to rise to hands and knees.

My pulse crashed in my head like a bowling ball thundering into an array of pins. Father Greyson continued his roaring progress through his house, accompanied by the pleas of his daughter and the toothless jabbering of the old woman. I decided it was probably time to leave my perch, and looked around me.

The Greyson house had a tile roof. I had managed to cross it in reasonable quiet earlier, but if I accidentally kicked a tile to the street, I would alert the waiting apprentices.

The house across the street, however, was thatched, and since both houses had been built to jetty out over the street, the jump was perfectly possible. It wouldn't be completely silent, but it would be quieter than a clattering tile, and once I landed, I'd be invisible to anyone below.

The difficulty would be that the opposite house was a bit taller than the Greyson place, and the jump would have to be made with great care and sure footing to avoid falling short.

Yet the leap was feasible. I am tall and big-framed and, after spending much of my youth on my father's killing floor, strong even for my size.

I considered whether or not to draw on my clothing before making the leap, and decided at least to belt on my purse. I was finishing this task when I heard a bang behind me, and suddenly I was illuminated with pale light as a lantern moved into the gable room.

A surge of alarm brought me upright, loose clothing in my arms and my bare feet planted on the beam slippery with pigeon droppings.

I heard a cry from behind me as Greyson glimpsed me through the window, and I launched myself for the roof across the street. My foot slipped in the droppings, and fear clutched my vitals as I realized I was going to fall a little short. I threw my long arms out wide to seize as much of the thatch as possible, and I landed with a great crackle and thump as my clothes spilled from my grasp. My legs kicked out over the abyss, and I grabbed great fistfuls of straw to keep from plummeting to the brick lane below.

"Thief! Thief!" Greyson's voice boomed out into the street, roaring the word that was most likely to bring the neighbors awake—if he'd shouted *"Seducer!,"* the result might have been laughter, plus of course the besmirching of his daughter's name. Greyson was at the window, pointing at my bare legs and buttocks visible in the light of his lantern. There were cries from the apprentices below, the sound of clattering hooves as they wrenched their horses about.

I had lost my clothing. I considered myself fortunate that Greyson was unlikely to recognize my backside, heaved myself to safety, rose to my feet, and ran.

"Catch him!" Greyson bawled. *"Break his ribs! Then bring him to me!"*

I took flight. By the time the apprentices' horses jangled into life, I had vaulted to another building and sprawled on tiles with a clatter. Heart leaping in my chest like a mad animal, I scrambled to my feet and ran over the ridgepole to the next roof. Jumping from one roof to another was a sport I'd enjoyed when I was younger—I would race across rooftops with my friends, trying first to reach the gun platform on the North Gate, or ring the bell on the roof of the Pilgrim's monastery, and all without setting foot on the ground.

Though it had to be admitted, I'd always done this in full daylight, and that I was long out of practice. I'd let my rooftop adventures lapse after I'd become apprentice to Lawyer Dacket—it wouldn't do for a lawyer's apprentice to be taken for trespass.

Out of practice I may have been, but pursuit lent me inspiration. Hurling myself over lanes and alleys, landing on my feet or hands and knees or flat on my belly, I outpaced my pursuers until I came to Royall Street, a grand thoroughfare too wide to leap. There, a shadow behind another shadow, I took shelter behind an elaborate carved brick chimney, caught my breath, quelled my hammering heart, and listened for the sounds of pursuit.

I heard horses gallop through the streets, and then the sound of hoofbeats slowed as the pursuit failed to find its quarry. One horse came trotting down Royall Street, but I stayed motionless behind the chimney, and the horse passed on its way. Eventually, the sound of pursuit died away altogether.

The rising sun began to gild the chimneys and rooftops of the city, and I again considered my situation. There was vast Scarcroft Square and too many wide, un-jumpable streets between me and my father's house, and at least some time on the ground was inevitable. And if I had to descend, it was best to do it now, before it was full daylight.

Three sonorous strokes on a bell sounded through the still air. The Dawn Bell from the Harbor Gatehouse, the signal for Ethlebight's gates to open.

There was little time to lose. I plotted a route that involved the least amount of time on the ground, rose from my hiding place, and made two leaps across narrow streets, leaps that were much easier in the dawn light. Making the second leap, I dislodged a colony of kitlings that had been perched on the eaves. You have perhaps not heard of these, as they have but recently flown over from the Land of Chimerae, but they are plump, furry, and winged creatures that have appeared in Ethlebight in just the last few years. They are a little larger than rats, and they like to perch above the street until they observe a mouse, a bird, or some other small animal below, and then they glide down on their furry wings and pounce.

The name "kitling" is misleading, as the creatures best resemble a large dormouse, but they kill vermin as cats do, which may account for the name. As they are small and useful, we have made no effort to eradicate them, but we are wary. I am told that dragons too start small.

As I made my leap, I heard Greyson's call of *"Thief! Thief!"*—the surveyor had waited silently in the street below, hoping to see me flying overhead, and the pack of dislodged kitlings had warned him to look up, so there was another mad scramble over the roofs until pursuit again died away.

By now it was full daylight. The only advantage of the sunrise was that the wan autumn sun was warmer than the chill autumn night, and I placed myself against the eastern side of a chimney, where the sun might warm me, while I recovered my breath and my wits.

At least Greyson was chasing me through the city, and not at home thrashing his daughter. I preferred not to think of Annabel trapped at home with the old roaring tyrant.

Soon there would be people on the streets, and to blend with those people, I would need clothing. I decided to make a search, leaped to a large building, landed in a rattle of roof tiles, and looked down into a courtyard. No laundry waved in the shadowed court, so I jumped to another building, rose in a cloud of straw dust, and then saw my opportunity below: laundry strung on lines, an empty washtub lying on its side in a pool of water, and no laundress visible.

Employing fingers and toes, I used a crow-stepped gable, a cornice, a soffit, a bull's-eye window, an architrave, and a trellis to lower myself to the ground. Shaking a cramp from my fingers, I walked barefoot across crumbling old brick and plucked a tunic, hose, and a doublet from the lines. I pulled on the hose, and was about to draw the tunic over my head when I considered the state of my shirt. There was nothing wrong with it, other than its being soiled by sweat, chimney soot, straw dust, and pigeon droppings, but its condition would have degraded my new wardrobe, so I exchanged it for a clean shirt from the line.

I would find a way to pay for the clothes. Stealing, I reassured myself, was beneath me.

Renewed, I began to walk toward the large gate that opened onto a lane behind the house, but stopped when I saw I was observed by a boy-child who stared at me from a door. The boy was dressed in a dirty smock and a single stocking on the left foot, and he gazed at me with vast blue eyes. I approached him.

"Who is your mistress?" I asked.

The child wiped his streaming nose on his sleeve. "Mum's name is Prunk." At least to my ears it *sounded* like Prunk.

I opened my purse and did some calculation. The hose were worth sixpence when new, and the shirt perhaps a whole crown, save that I'd exchanged my own shirt, which was of finer cloth. The doublet was battered, the tunic worn thin in places. And then of course there was the trouble I'd put the household to. Say a crown.

I gave the child a crown. "Give this to your mother," I said. I added a halfpenny. "And this is for you."

The child stared at the silver in his palm. "Apple-squire," he said, and wiped his nose.

I had been called thief, which I was not, and now I had been called a pimp by an infant. I decided I'd had quite enough abuse for the day. "For your *mother*," I said with finality, and walked briskly to the gate, oaken-beamed and twelve feet tall. I climbed it easily and rolled over the top, then dropped down into the lane.

In two minutes I was in Royall Street, walking at my ease.

As I walked along I gloried in my home city of Ethlebight, the great jewel at the mouth of the River Ostra. The houses were built on the same pattern, with upper floors jettied out over the street. Gables were crow-stepped, or rose in gentle curves to pediments or wooden towers or belfries. Bull's-eye windows or narrow leaded glass panes glittered in the rising sun. Half-timber beams were carved in the shapes of jesters, acrobats, gods, and fanciful animals, or with the solemn, respectable faces of the burgesses who owned the buildings. The city was built on the soft ground of the delta, and the houses tended to tilt or lean against one another, or rear up over the street like a bear about to fall upon its prey.

By now, the city had come fully alive. Sailors surged up the road as if carried on a tide, legs spread wide, straddling the pavements as if walking along the heaving deck of a ship. Knife sharpeners, sellers of whelks and oysters, rag-and-bone men, pie and chestnut sellers, all moved along the streets behind their handcarts, each giving out the distinctive, high-pitched cry peculiar to their trade. Monks in undyed wool, servants of the Pilgrim, walked in disciplined silence on rope sandals. Servants bustled on errands, the wealthy bustled in chairs or coaches, children bustled to school, and apprentices bustled to the nearest source of ale. Dogs and pigs, which devoured the waste, wandered freely; while cats perched on high gables and viewed all from a position of superiority. Drunken men sang, drunken women screeched, drunken children darted underfoot. Carters rode in the press, their wagons piled high with goods, surging along like galleons in the human flood.

My long legs carried me easily through the throng. I delighted in the familiar sights of my city, not to mention the fact that I'd survived the night unscathed. My black velvet apprentice cap had remained on my head through all the night's adventures. The tunic I'd acquired, striped in faded green and thinning white, was stretched to the limit by my big shoulders; and the quilted doublet, originally the deep red color called cramoisie, was a pale ghost of its original self. I was beginning to think I had overpaid for my new clothes.

Still, having survived pursuit, I was in charity with all: I walked with a smile, greeted friends and acquaintances, while with practiced skill I dodged small children, pigs, and filth.

I paused by the shop of Crook, the printer and bookseller, but the door was closed. Inspired perhaps by the bound verse that he imported from the capital, Crook the businessman kept poet's hours. I would try to visit later in the day.

"Hoy! Quillifer!"

I turned at the cry, and saw the urgent signal of Mrs. Vayne, the greengrocer. I avoided the rumbling handcart of an oyster-seller and crossed the street to join her.

Mrs. Vayne was a large woman in a starched white apron and a boxy hat that covered her ears. Her cheeks were red as the baskets of pippins piled about her feet. I saw at once the distinctive white-green apples nested in straw, and I felt my mouth water.

"Pearmains!"

The grocer smiled with crooked teeth. "Ay, the first pearmains have come down the river. And you know how your mother dotes on them."

"Can you send two baskets to the house?"

Mrs. Vayne nodded. "I've already set them aside."

I leaned over a tub of cresses and kissed Mrs. Vayne's cheek. She drew back in mock surprise.

"A forward creature you are," she said. "But for all that, you may have a forelle."

I picked the spotted pear from the greengrocer's hand and took a generous bite. I chewed with great pleasure and dabbed at my lips with the faded sleeve of my doublet.

"Best send a basket of these as well." I took another bite, and my free hand snaked a pearmain from its den of straw. Mrs. Vayne saw and pursed her lips in disapproval. I made my wheedling-infant face, and the greengrocer shrugged.

"The gages should come in two or three days," she said.

"Then I shall return in two or three days." I kissed her again, and she wiped pear juice from her cheek.

"You're not dressed for Dacket's office," she said.

"It's a sea dog I am today. I'm going sailing."

Mrs. Vayne crooked an eyebrow. "Does your master know?"

"I am on my master's business. Which I should no longer delay." I raised the stolen pearmain, inspected it, and took a bite of the white-green apple. I crunched the pearmain happily, smiled, and said, "Best make it *three* baskets sent to my mother."

"They will keep all winter," said the pleased grocer. "Provided you keep them in a cool room."

I looked over my shoulder and saw a pair of broad-shouldered men striding through the crowd. Was it Greyson livery they wore? And were they bearing cudgels?

It was time to depart. I gave a wave, kicked away a pig that was investigating the beetroots, and continued my walk, eating from either hand as the fancy took me.

Royall Street opened into Scarcroft Square, with its fountain surrounded by marble allegories, and the glory of Ethlebight brickwork shone bright in the clear morning sun.

Ethlebight, sitting on its swampy delta, had an excess of clay, with more delivered every spring by the flooding river; and the merchants of the town had made the most of this bounty. The city produced bricks, millions every year—plain red brick for plain buildings, but also bricks of mellow gold, of blue and purple, of black and brown. Some bricks were glazed with bright colors, pinks and yellows and green.

Scarcroft Square was a fantasia of masonry, all built of the brick that formed the town's main industry. The ivy-covered town hall, the guild halls, the grand mansions of the burgesses and the local lords, the Fane, the Court of the Teazel Bird, the New Castle, the Grand Monastery of the Seven Words of the Pilgrim . . . all blazed in the morning sun with color and light, red bricks and gold, black bricks and blue, pink bricks and green, all the glazed, bright hues. These colored bricks were laid in patterns, rose in spirals to support upper storeys, or twisted high to hold aloft the chimney pots. The square itself was paved in brick, set with spirals, quincunx patterns, or pictures of fabulous animals—mosaic done in enormous scale, with bricks instead of tiny tesserae.

We also produced glass, and the glazier's art was fully displayed: leaded glass, glass stained to produce triumphalist pictures of the city's history, glass cut into cabochons or faceted like gems, glass opalescent, etched, and enameled. The result was a square that glittered in the morning sun and winked sunlight from a thousand faceted eyes.

A temporary theater was being built on the square, to support the players during the Autumn Festival, and it was the only wooden structure in sight.

Another impermanent structure was the effigy of our much-married King Stilwell. His statue stood on a plinth, and he wore armor and carried a sword, looking like the young warrior that had triumphed in his wars against Loretto.

It was a tribute to the city's burgesses, who counted every penny, that the King's statue had been made of some kind of plaster, then painted to look like marble. There was no point in cutting a figure in stone, or casting it in bronze, when the King would sooner or later die and the image be replaced by that of the next monarch. I had to admire the canny sense of thrift displayed by our aldermen.

In fact, I delighted in everything I saw. I felt my chest expand at the sight of the square, straining the fabric of the borrowed tunic. I had spent all my eighteen years in Ethlebight, with only a few trips to other cities, and I adored the city that had raised me, and also admired the bustling inhabitants who lived within its walls.

Scarcroft Square was magnificent, but I knew I was seeing it at its height. The city was fading, doomed by slow strangulation as silt choked its harbor. I pictured it fifty years hence: the grand houses empty, windows empty, roofs sagging, colors faded, the square filled with windblown trash . . .

It could not be prevented. Best not to think about it.

I tossed the remains of my pear and my apple onto the street for the pigs, then crossed the square to a tall, narrow building with a crow-stepped gable. The glass in the tall, arched windows was stained with figures of a warrior battling a dragon, this representing Lord Baldwine, an ancestor of the current Duke of Roundsilver, who owns the building. Roundsilver is a wealthy peer, and owns a great many buildings around the city, as well as his own grand house on the square. He spends little time there, devoting his time to being at court along with all the other great nobles.

I admired the stained glass, with Baldwine holding up the severed dragon's head, and went up a tall, narrow stair to a cramped office that smelled of paper, dust, ink, and vellum.

Lawyer Dacket, my master, stood in the center of the room, a paper in either hand. Dacket was a spare man with a pointed beard, a melancholy, lined face, and the black fur-trimmed robe of his profession. He wore a velvet hat like mine, but with gold tape and a gold pompon to show that he practiced before the bar.

"Pearmains are in!" I said in joy.

My pleasure seemed only to deepen Dacket's gloom. "That would account for the juice on your chin," he said. I hastily wiped it with my sleeve.

"Mrs. Vayne was generous with her samples," I said.

"You are dressed for holiday," observed Dacket. "I wish you joy of it, and of your apples." The planes of his face shifted slightly. "May this office then hope you shall not return?"

I put on my learnèd-advocate face. "Loath though I am, sir, to stand in an abnegative posture and contradict my learnèd colleague in any way," I said, "I desire the jury to observe, *inicio*, that while your humble apprentice shall be *absent* today, that he is not in *absencia*, for though my mind may be *absent*, my *corpus* shall *absent* be on the business of the court, *videlicet*, preventing Sir Stanley Mattingly from being *absent* at the Assizes, and that *absent* evidence of jurisdiction, I pray the jury to declare evidence of dereliction *absent*, and the Crown *nolle prosequi*."

This is an example of what my father would call "flaunting my knowledge like a vainglorious peacock," forgetting that peacocks have no knowledge to flaunt, vainglorious or otherwise. Yet I find that I must continually remind people of my gifts, for they are inclined to forget my education and acuity. I expect it's because I am not impressive in my person: granted that I am tall and have broad shoulders, and long dark hair admired by the ladies, but I am not handsome like my schoolfriend Theophrastus Hastings, or as rich as the Duke of Roundsilver, or possessed of any degree of fame like the Emperor Cornelianus when he was called to the throne. My father is a Butcher, which causes some people to discount me. And of course, I am young and have not the authority that comes with age, like that of Judge Travers.

And so I must offer my gifts to the people, and offer them continually, and without cease, so that I may be something other than a nullity in their eyes.

My master, Dacket, listened impassively to my appeal. "The plea would receive a better hearing were there not apple skin between your teeth," he said. "And what is this of Sir Stanley?"

Dacket's office had been pursuing Sir Stanley Mattingly in an attempt to serve him with a writ to bring him to the Autumn Assizes, which would begin in two days. But Sir Stanley was not to be found at his town house, or at his house in the country; and unless the writ were served, Lawyer Dacket would be unable to prosecute him on behalf of his client, Mr. Morton Trew.

"And yet," I said, "Sir Stanley cannot be far away, as he stands as honorary master of the Guild of Distillers, and must ride on their float in the Autumn Festival that follows the Assizes."

"You have found his bolt-hole?" Dacket inquired.

"I remembered that Sir Stanley's sister is married to Denys Buthlaw, and—"

"Buthlaw is moved to the capital, and his house here is closed. There is no guest lodged there; we have investigated."

I raised a hand. "But sir, Buthlaw has *another* house, on Mutton Island."

Again the planes of Lawyer Dacket's face shifted. "Is that so?" he murmured.

"Remember that Sir Stanley is known as a great hunter and is ever trampling the fields of his own tenants in pursuit of the fallow deer. And bear in mind also that Mutton Island is connected to the mainland at low tide, and that directly across the channel is the Forest of Ailey, in which Sir Stanley could ride and hunt to his heart's content."

A tenuous gleam appeared in Dacket's eye. "You have evidence that Sir Stanley is on the island?"

"Nay, sir. But Mutton Island seems worth exploring, if you can but provide me with a writ and spare me for the day."

All traces of pleasure vanished from Lawyer Dacket's countenance. "Spare you for a day of sailing."

"On Kevin Spellman's boat. And I shall bring Kevin along to serve as a witness, should I find Sir Stanley."

Dacket adopted an air of saturnine amusement. "I could do with a day on the sea. Perhaps *I* should venture to the island on Goodman Kevin's boat."

I acknowledged this possibility with a gracious nod. "The sea air would serve to balance the humors," I said, "and bring an attractive pink flush to your ears. But I urge your worship to bear in mind Sir Stanley's history of violence—he is a dreadful man when his choler is up, and if you find him with his hounds, he may incite them against you, not to mention what damage he might do with his whip or his gun."

"Nay," said Dacket. "I applaud your devotion to justice, so great you are willing to fall beneath the fangs of a pack of ravenous hounds. And yet"—holding out his hands with the papers in them—"there are so many writs and other documents that must be copied before the Assizes."

"You have a clerk," I pointed out.

The clerk in question, bent over a desk, lifted his head to give me a basilisk stare from beneath his skullcap.

"Goodman Dodson is fully occupied," said Dacket. "As am I." With a sniff, he viewed one of his papers, then waved it in my direction.

"You may begin with a draft of a plea," Dacket said, "the formal plea for mercy on behalf of Alec Royce, who cut a fern tree in the Crown Forest. Cutting the King's timber calls for death, but if the judge is merciful, we may hope for prison or a fine."

I considered this. "Did you say it was a fern tree?"

"Ay." Dacket's attention had already moved on, as he browsed through a stack of through papers.

"Then there is no need to plead for mercy," I said. "The charge is baseless."

"*Base-less?*" Dacket mouthed the word as if he were tasting something foul.

"It's a new word. I invented it." Which, for the record, I had.

"We have a perfectly fine phrase, 'without foundation,' which will serve—and if it won't, we have as well 'unfounded,' 'unsubstantiated,' 'unproven.' There is no need for this *base-less*." Dacket gave me an austere look. "I advise you not to use these neologisms before a judge."

"Sir, I shall dispunge these innovations." Dacket gave me a suspicious look, and I spoke more quickly. "Sir, our client is innocent."

Dacket's gaze firmed. "Royce has admitted the charge," he said. "He has been in the cells of the New Castle for two months. There are no facts in dispute."

"Save whether the King's timber was cut at all," I said. "Timber is defined in law as 'that sturdy vegetable matter which may be used in construction, to-wit: in a house or other structure, a bridge, a boat or ship, a stile, a fence, et cetera.' A fern tree is too small and weak to be used in construction, and therefore is not timber in the meaning of the law. The fern tree was mere superfluous growth, like a vine or a periwinkle, which Royce removed in order to allow a proper tree to grow in its place."

Dacket remained motionless for several seconds, then spoke slowly. "I believe your argument may serve," he said.

"If you desire," I said, "I will undertake the defense myself, under your supervision."

"Before Judge Travers?" Dacket waved a hand thoughtfully, a paper still in it. "I think not. To put such an argument before Travers requires more tact than I have yet observed in you."

I put on my dutiful-apprentice face and bowed. "As ever," I said, "I defer to your wisdom."

Dacket nodded. "You may have the day for Mutton Island," he said. "But tomorrow, you will apply yourself to your pen." He added the paper to a pile, then put the pile on a black, ancient desk already covered with documents. "Tomorrow, you will not leave this office until you have copied every item on this desk."

I nodded. "Of course, Master."

Dacket opened a narrow drawer and produced a sealed paper. "Your writ, signed by Justice Darcy. Do not lose it: I would not vex the justice on the eve of the court by asking for another." He raised a hand. "And don't get pear juice on it!"

I bowed. "I shall in all such matters obey."

"Then be off," said Dacket. "And if you are rent by a pack of dogs, you will have only yourself to blame."

"So, what is this case about?" asked Kevin Spellman.

"Theft," said I. "The theft of a body of water."

"One can steal a lake?" Kevin asked. "I hadn't ever considered the matter."

Kevin was a sturdy, fair-haired youth, a friend of mine from our days at the grammar school. He was dressed in brilliant blues and yellows, and gems winked from his fingers. He wore a broad hat with the brim pinned up by a silver medallion, and an ostrich-feather plume. Even at leisure, even on his boat, he wore the splendid clothing that befit his status, as the son and heir to a Warden and present Dean of the Honorable Companie of Mercers.

The Mercers traded up and down the coast, and often abroad, delivering the wealth of Ethlebight and the River Ostra to the rest of Duisland and to the world. Ethlebight's bricks and glass made up much of their profit, but by far the most valuable cargo was wool.

The flatlands of the Ostra were ideal grazing country, and the river's headwaters ran through mountains where sheep browsed in high meadows throughout the summer. Thanks to arrangements made in antiquity between the craft guilds, the wool was bought from the shearers at a fixed price by the Worshipfull Sodality of Washers, who washed the raw wool in the waters of the river. The Washers sold their product to the Honorable Companie of Carders and Combers at a price arranged centuries ago, and the Carders and Combers sold to the Benevolent Sorority of the Distaff, a guild composed entirely of women, who spun the yarn in their homes, after which the wool found its way to the Dyers, the Clothmakers, the Fullers, Scourers and Stretchers, the Nappers, the Burlers, the Drapers, and the Taylors, and so on—but unless the product was sold locally, it all made its way to the Mercer, who—unlike all the others—sold it for whatever the market would bear, provided they sold it to another Mercer.

Kevin's father, Gregory Spellman, was the owner or part owner of eleven companies or corporations, which in turn owned barges, ships, warehouses, and the piers at which the ships and barges moored. And thanks to the profits of wool, the elder Spellman lived in one of the most brilliant houses on Scarcroft Square, and was able to keep his son in the brightest, most fashionable clothing, a walking advertisement for his wares.

"Water is a commodity like any other," I said. "It may be hoarded, sold, lent, and of course stolen."

"And Sir Stanley Mattingly is alleged to have stolen—a lake?"

"A river. And there is no 'alleged' about the matter; he *did* steal it, though there exists a bare possibility he may have stolen it legally."

With practiced tread, Kevin and I avoided wash-water hurled from an upper floor, then turned onto Princess Street, where we danced around the barrow of a gingerbread-monger. We passed, and then Kevin, enticed by the odor of the gingerbread, returned to buy a loaf.

While the transaction went on, I eyed the street for men in Greyson livery, and continued my exposition. "Sir Stanley Mattingly," I said, "sold a piece of grazing to a gentleman named Morton Trew. The transfer was in livery of seisin—seisin in law, yes?—wherein the two parties went to the land together, and Sir Stanley performed the rite of turf and twig in sight of two witnesses."

Kevin paid for the gingerbread and turned down the street. "Sir Stanley actually gave the man a stick and a clod of dirt?"

"He did."

Kevin looked dubious. "I've never heard of anything like that, and I've been present at any number of transfers of property."

"These rites are not common in the city," I said. "But in the country, folk hold with old traditions in transferring a freehold."

"And in the country, apparently they steal rivers."

"They do. Or at any rate, Sir Stanley does—because when Mister Trew came later to his field, he found that his land no longer had the river that had originally flowed through it. Sir Stanley had dammed the river and turned the water into a leat to power his new stone-cutting mill. As grazing land is worth little without a source of water, Mister Trew desires to take Sir Stanley to court to overturn the sale."

Kevin was thoughtful. "The river was dammed *after* the rite of rock-and-hard-place, or whatever it's called."

"Yes."

"Then I don't see how Sir Stanley can possibly defend his action."

"Ah." I made an airy gesture and put on my pompous-magistrate face. "That is where you fail to perceive the supreme suppleness and flexibility for which the common law of Duisland is justly famed."

Sniffing the gingerbread. "Apparently, I do not."

"Sir Stanley maintains, first, that the deed does not mention the river or any other water source—"

"And does it?"

"Alas," said I, "the river is not mentioned. And furthermore, Sir Stanley maintains that it was perfectly clear he never intended to sell Mister Trew rights over the water, as is proved by the fact that at the sale he did not perform the rite of water and porringer, where—"

"Where he would have given his poor victim a porringer of river water," said Kevin, "to go along with his lump and his branch."

"Just so."

"I say it's fraud," said Kevin, "and to hell with the porringer."

"And Judge Travers at the Assizes is likely to agree with you, which is why Sir Stanley is careful to avoid his summons. As Judge Travers is retiring, the next quarter's judge is likely to be Blakely, who is some kind of cousin to Sir Stanley's wife, and who bears a reputation for sharp practice of his own, and who therefore may appreciate the ingenuity of Sir Stanley's argument."

"One fraudster to another."

"Just so."

Indignation lifted Kevin's chin. "I shall tell my father to avoid any dealings with Sir Stanley. If anyone in the Mercers' Guild behaved in such a fashion, he'd be disciplined or expelled."

"Alas," said I, "there is no Worshipfull Guild of Landowners to enforce honest behavior."

A large, old house loomed on our left, the first floor of plain Ethlebight brick, the upper storeys carved wood that projected over the street, with a thatch roof that projected farther still. My heart warmed at the sight of my home, a friendly welcoming sanctuary after my cold night on the rooftops. I turned inside and was followed by my friend.

The ground floor made up a butcher shop owned by my father, and the family lived in the storeys above. My father shared my name of Quillifer, and I had been named after his own father, and his father after his, the name stretching back into antiquity.

For all that I was wary around my father's weighty authority, it has to be said that I greatly admired my senior. My father was not only Dean of the Worshipfull Societie of Butchers but a respected alderman of the city, entitled to wear a gold chain on formal occasions, and often mentioned as Ethlebight's next lord mayor. He shared my height and the broad shoulders developed from years of wielding the cleaver and pollaxe. He kept his hair short, and shorn up around the ears, which kept it from being spattered with blood. He wore the cap and leather apron of his profession, though in fact he made most of his money from moneylending, speculation, and land-dealing.

My paternal grandfather had been the first in our family to learn to read, and my father was the first to learn to write. I myself had been to a dame school for my letters, and to a grammar school for writing and recitation, after which I apprenticed with Master Dacket. I was raised with books and the beauties of poetry and the sonorities of ancient languages—for now with printed books, education was no longer the domain of monks and nobles with private tutors. What would come of that change, I felt the whole world would soon see. The profession of the law would allow me to travel, perhaps to the capital and the court of the King. For our family was rising, and I intended to rise as far as my talents would take me.

At the moment, my father was serving a well-dressed Aekoi, an older woman who had powdered her golden complexion white and painted on her face an expression of fey, perhaps even malevolent, interest. She had come with a human girl servant, who stood in the center of the room and stared down the long hall behind the counter, the hall that ended in the open courtyard at the center of the big house. I, standing behind her, could see a calf that had been slaughtered and hoisted head-downward by a chain. Its blood was draining into a large basin even as two apprentices, naked from the waist, were taking off the hide.

None of the calf would be wasted at the House of Quillifer. The hide would be sold to a tanner, the bones to a button-maker or handle-maker. The hooves would become glue. The meat would be sold, to become roasts or steaks or chops, and miscellaneous organs put into pastry for kidney or umble pie. The tripes would be cleaned and turned into sausage casings or fried chitterlings or white tripe for soups and stews. The stomach would become rennet and would be sold to a cheesemaker. Tongue would be roasted, lungs poached or stewed. The edible parts of the head would become a gelatinized loaf known as brawn, and the bladder used as a container in which other parts of the animal would be cooked. The heart would be cut into strips and cooked on skewers, the liver fried or made into pâté, and the blood itself cooked down with spices to make a kind of pudding, or mixed with oats and turned into blood sausage.

None of which was likely of interest to the servant girl, who probably ate meat only rarely. Instead, she watched the apprentices at work, the fit young men, nearly naked, who worked up and down the carcass with their sharp skinning knives.

I didn't interrupt the girl's reverie, or my father at the counter. Sweetbreads were wrapped in paper, the result weighed, and the Aekoi woman's payment accepted. The Aekoi woman turned to the daydreaming servant, observed her woolgathering, and slapped her briskly across the face. The painted expression on the Aekoi's face did not change. The girl yelped an apology, took the package, and followed her mistress out.

I waited for the customers to walk out of earshot. "That fair painted face charmed me not," I said.

My father shrugged. "Well. Not human."

"I've known humans to behave worse," Kevin offered.

My dad nodded in the direction of the departing Aekoi. "Her

name's Tavinda. Her daughter's the mistress of Lord Scrope, the Warden of the New Castle—the daughter may be earning the family's living on her back, but it's Tavinda who looks after the pennies." He tossed the coins in his hand. "She's always trying to barter me down."

Kevin was curious. "Have you seen the daughter?"

"Oh, ay. Fetching enough, if you like 'em golden."

"I've never"—Kevin searched for the word—"*experienced* an Aekoi."

"They are as other women," said the older man, and then—hearing his wife on the stair—added, "or so I am told."

My mother, Cornelia, came down the stair, her white apron starched stiff and crackling, and she stood on her toes to buss me on the cheeks. Graying blond hair fell out of her cap in corkscrew curls. I basked for a moment in the warmth of maternal affection. "Why are you dressed like that?" she said. "Are you not in the office today?"

"I'm delivering a writ to a man who would run if he saw me dressed as a lawyer's apprentice," I said. "Kevin's taking me in his boat." I smiled. "And I arranged for Mrs. Vayne to send you three baskets of pearmains, just come down the river!"

"Pearmains! Oh, lovely!" She kissed my cheeks again, and I allowed myself a moment of pleasure in my mother's benevolence.

There was a clattering on the stairs, and my two younger sisters, Alice and Barbara, appeared. They were twelve and fourteen, and had inherited the Quillifer height: both were beginning to overtop their mother.

They were both attending the grammar school, the first women in our family to learn to read and write. My father had initially been opposed to this innovation, but my mother had convinced him that it would get them husbands from the better classes.

"We're going to the Fane to help decorate for the festival," Cornelia said.

All the fruits of the year were to be laid at the feet of the god. "Don't give him too many of our pearmains," I said.

"He gets a basket of sausages," said Alice.

Actually, the god Pastas got two baskets, which my father handed to the girls. He kissed his wife and daughters, and sent them on their way, then looked at his son in an expectant way.

"Are there any sausages for us?" I asked. "Sailing is hard work."

"Help yourself," said my father.

From the pantry I took some smoked pork sausages, slices of ham, a loaf of bread, a brined goat cheese, and a hard yellow cheese. The food went into a leather satchel. I took also a jug of cider from the buttery, and carried it and the satchel into the front room.

"I hope you find your quarry," my father said. "Otherwise, I'll have been looted for nothing."

"Charity to the wandering sailor is accounted a fine virtue," I said. "No doubt the god will reward you."

"Just possibly he may." My father regarded me with a careful eye. "Though I hope you have been doing your duty to Pastas as well."

I looked at Kevin. "We have learned our lines."

"Let's hear them, then."

"Ta-sa-ran-geh," I recited obediently, and then Kevin joined me in the next part of the chant. "Ta-sa-ran-geh-*ko*."

The chant was ancient, so ancient that no one any longer understood the words or their meaning. But it was known that the words honored Pastas Netweaver, god of the sea and principal god of Ethlebight, whose great round temple stood four leagues above the town.

The temple of Pastas had once crowned the center of the city, but as the muddy River Ostra filled in its delta, the city had followed the water and crept downstream over the centuries, and eventually the huge temple was stranded in the country. Major ceremonies were still conducted at the great old building, but a newer, smaller temple, called the Fane, had been constructed on Scarcroft Square for every-day use.

The Autumn Festival, coming just after the Assizes, was one of the great festivals of the city, and featured a ceremony at the old temple featuring the Warriors of the Sea and the Mermaids, each impersonated by young folk from the city's leading families. Both Kevin and I were Warriors this year, and obliged to wear antique bronze armor, carry weapons, dance, and chant the incomprehensible words that honored the deity.

My father listened to the chant, nodding his head to the rhythm, and when we were finished, he clapped his big hands once.

"Very good!" he said. "But look you, it's ren-far-el-den-sa-*fa*-yu, not ren-far-el-den-sa-*sa*-yu."

"We are corrected," said I. "Thank you."

His father pointed a thick finger at me. "The god knows when you care enough to make it right."

"Yes. Of course."

"Pastas has always had the best people in his service," said my father. "His priests are the most important citizens of the district, who give their time and money freely." A look of scorn crossed his face. "Not like those monks who serve the Pilgrim, and who are supported by our taxes no matter what the King claims. Let King Stilwell but stop his gold one day, and those monasteries would be deserted the next."

I had heard these opinions before, and Kevin too. But the recollection of the festival and its Mermaids brought an uncomfortable memory to my mind.

"Father," I said, "I should forewarn you of the possibility that you may receive a call from Master Greyson."

The master Butcher frowned. "The surveyor? What's the trouble?"

"A misunderstanding. You may remember that Greyson's daughter Annabel is a Mermaid this year and . . ." My poise faded under my father's cool eye. I put on my innocent-choirboy face. "She asked me to adjust her costume," I said.

"And you adjusted more than that, I suppose."

"It is possible Annabel will refuse to give my name," I said. "In which case your peace will not be disturbed."

My dad had received fathers on my behalf before, and did not seem unduly disturbed. "Greyson, eh? I had thought the next would be old Driver, Bethany's father."

"It fell out otherwise," I said. I looked at my father. "At least I may be saved by my reputation as a steady, sober young fellow, walking the streets with his nose in a book of law."

He answered only with a sardonic laugh, just at the moment when Mrs. Vayne's boy arrived carrying the first basket of pearmains, and I took the opportunity to say good-bye and make my exit into Princess Street. I and Kevin turned toward the Harbor Gate.

"Annabel Greyson," Kevin said. "I thought she fancied Richard Trotter."

"His name did not come up."

"And her father caught you? What happened?"

I preferred not to relive my moments hanging off the roofbeam. Instead, I looked at Kevin. "Are you well shod?"

Kevin glanced down at the glossy boots that rose to his calves. "I believe I am."

"Those boots are too heavy," I said. "They'll slow you down." I smiled. "Remember, when Sir Stanley sets his dogs on us, I need not run faster than the dogs, but only faster than you."

"The boots serve as armor against their bites," Kevin said. "These are good leather."

"We'll see." I passed among the carts and wagons that labored through the great River Gatehouse, and from the paved apron outside I looked up at the great red brick city wall, thirty feet high, with fifty-foot towers at regular intervals. The wall's outlines were blurred with vegetation, grass, and bushes and even a few small trees growing through cracks in the masonry.

"Look at all that rubbish," I said. "Time for another Beating of the Bounds." In which packs of the local children were gathered together and marched to every important point of the city, then beaten with willow withes until they could remember Rose Street from Turnip Street, the Gun Tower from the Tower of the Crescent Moon. After which they were lowered on ropes from the battlements to clear away all the vegetation that had grown up since the last cleaning.

I still remembered the whipping I'd received from old Captain Hay, when at the age of ten I'd been driven from one tower to the next. Hay had laid on as if he were flogging a mutineer.

That had been eight years ago. There hadn't been a Beating of the Bounds since.

I would speak to my father about it. It wouldn't do for the city to look so unkempt—and I was happy the cleaning job would be undertaken by a different generation.

CHAPTER TWO

The lugsail rattled overhead as the sailboat came across the wind, and then it filled and the boat surged forward, cutting the water with a fine, crisp murmur. Sunlight glittered from wavetops, shone gold on the tall reeds that surrounded the channel.

I leaned against the weather gunwale and smiled up at the sun. Loafing about in boats is perhaps my second-greatest pleasure, and my pleasure was only increased by the knowledge that I was sparing myself a day copying documents.

Kevin tucked the tiller beneath his arm. "Do you think the god truly cares whether we sing *sa-sa* or *sa-fa?*" he asked.

I squinted into the bright morning sky. "I think if the god truly cared about his worshipers and his city, he wouldn't let the harbor silt up."

"True."

"My father hopes that we'll be struck by a strong-enough storm to blast open a new deepwater channel. Perhaps he even prays for it." I looked at my friend. "Does your father pray for such a thing?"

"My father owns ships. He does not pray for storms."

"In any case, let us pray there are no storms today."

Kevin surveyed the brilliant blue sky, the small clouds perched high in the inverted azure bowl overhead. "I hardly think prayers are necessary."

"Pray, then, that when we meet Sir Stanley, he isn't carrying his gun."

The sailboat raced along the channel, carving a perfect silver wake behind. Tall reeds rustled on either side. *Doomed*, I thought.

The city of Ethlebight had at last come to the end of its centuries-long crawl down the banks of the Ostra. Below Ethlebight the river spread into dozens of small fingerlike channels separated by reefs of silt, each islet crowned by golden-brown reeds. The once-open bay had filled with alluvium, and even the strong tides couldn't keep it clear.

The winding channels, surrounded by reeds taller than a man, were a daunting maze that required an experienced pilot, but it was the silt that would choke the life out of the city. Already there was no passage deep enough for a galleon, and with the galleons gone, Ethlebight had lost its deep-sea trade with foreign nations. Only barges, pinnaces, hoys, flyboats, crumsters, and other such small craft could now hope to gain the port, and ere long Ethlebight would become a city of ghosts. This sad truth was why my father had encouraged me to adopt the law as my profession, as a lawyer could work and lodge anywhere.

I loved my home city, but perhaps my fantasies were beginning to overleap its walls. I could feel another world beckon, a world with more scope.

The tide had started to ebb before Kevin and I had set sail, and the current helped draw the boat out through the vast, rattling sea of reeds. The channel split before us, and we bore right and were at once confronted by a pinnace aground. She was a handsome little vessel, with a vermilion hull and a broad ochre stripe, and on her canvas shimmered the waves' reflection. She had backed her sails and put out a kedge anchor in hopes of towing herself off, but was almost certainly stranded till the next high tide.

"Eighty tons," Kevin judged. "Too big for the port." There was sadness in his voice.

The pinnace flew the ensign of Loretto, the kingdom with which Duisland had been at war at least as often as it had been at peace. In times of conflict, my city's merchants abandoned their countinghouses for their quarterdecks, and sent their ships to seize the commerce of Loretto, or the Armed League of the North, or Varcellos, or any other nation declared an enemy by the King. The harbor of Ethlebight filled with their captures, the warehouses were stuffed with plunder, and the pockets of the sailors grew heavy with silver. The privateers of Ethlebight were famous for bringing the wealth of other nations to their city.

But now, in time of peace, no stirring action beckoned, and any large prize would run aground trying to make the port. I waved to the stranded sailors as we passed, and the sailors waved back. Within minutes the sea of reeds fell away, and our little boat pitched on the open sea. Sun-dappled spindrift flew over the bows and stung my face. Kevin swung onto the new tack, southwest, and the lugger raced along under a freshening wind. I stretched out along the thwart.

"The sun above, the sail full, the horizon boundless," I said. "Is it so strange that I prefer this to the practice of law?"

Kevin looked at me from beneath the broad brim of his hat. "You don't care to be a lawyer, then?"

I considered this, and shrugged. "It is a path superior to many," I said. "And I must walk some path, a path to take me into the wide world."

"Your father said, did he not, that you enjoyed argument so much, that you might as well do it for a living?"

I made a broad gesture and invited fantasy to fly into my words.

"I could become a famous advocate in the courts of royal Selford, or a member of the House of Burgesses in water-girdled Howel, or a judge whose wisdom echoes down the generations. . . ."

Kevin grinned. "Why not all three?"

"Why not?" I echoed. "But yet, on such a day as this, I find myself stifled by the thought of spending my life in dusty legal chambers, or pleading the case of some poacher or profiteer before a drowsy judge—or for that matter drowsing on the bench myself, listening to advocates monotonize their cases."

Kevin laughed. "Monotonize. You just made that word up, didn't you?"

"Ay." I shrugged. "It's a little unrefined, I admit, far from my best." I looked at Kevin. "Your father already sends you to sea, to do business abroad and meet with his affinity."

Kevin made a face. "And to encounter young ladies, with whose fathers my own father wants a connection."

"Your plight does not stir my sympathy."

"You have not met the ladies in question. Either they simper and say nothing, or they demand to know how much money I can expect to inherit, and how much of it will be spent on *them*." Kevin shivered, then looked out to the blue horizon. "If you cannot abide the law, you know, you could run away to sea. After twenty years, provided you survive war, pirates, and tempest, you might find yourself the proud captain of a crumster, carrying tubs of tallow from port to port."

I made my sad-clown face. "It is a mournful picture you draw, cousin."

A gust heeled the boat, and Kevin drew the tiller toward me to keep the boat on the wind. I leaned out over the rail to keep the boat in balance. The gust faded, and as the boat righted, Kevin's look turned thoughtful.

"My father and I need lawyers now and again," he said. "Contracts must be drawn up, debts collected, defaulters pursued. We might be able to employ you—not in Ethlebight, where old Clinton handles our needs, but in other ports."

I sat up with sudden interest. "Boats and the law!" I said. "Delightful duality!"

"I'll speak to my father. But when does your apprenticeship end?"

"Eight or twelve months, though it's really up to Master Dacket."

"And of course, you'll have to avoid jail or the pillory for seducing the Mermaid."

I preferred not to discuss Annabel. All too well could I imagine her beneath her angry father's belt, or rod, or him hustling her off to a nunnery. There was nothing I could do to prevent it, for a father possessed absolute legal authority over his daughter. If I could some-how break into the Greyson home, free Annabel, and run with her, we might flee far enough to avoid her father's wrath—but only to starve to death in some distant country, without friends, support, or money.

Again it occurred to me that fathers, as a breed, are unreason-able. Greyson had turned his own house upside down, pursued me over half the town in the middle of the night, and doubtless now was straining his imagination for ways to punish his daughter—and all because of a harmless dalliance. What mad fury had possessed him, and why? He was doing far greater damage to Annabel's reputation than ever I could have.

Why, I wondered, *are the young denied the opportunity to be young? Why should we not love, and be carefree, and enjoy our pleasures before age and care ruin them?*

I thought of Annabel again, and considered that if I were a character in a poem by Bello or Tarantua, I would be in agonies of shame and worry, perhaps rolling like a dog on the floor while weeping and calling Annabel's name—and yet I was not weeping.

Was I deficient in some crucial element of character, that I did not feel such extremities of anguish? Should I now be rending my garments, or hurling myself into the sea to drown?

Yet I could not see how my drowning would improve the situation in any way. Annabel would be no better off for my death, or my torn clothing would make no impression on her father, nor for that matter any loud displays of anguish. He would simply thrash me with the same fury with which he had threatened his daughter.

I had not meant to do any harm. Surely, intentions should count in these matters.

Because I did not wish my thoughts to dwell on Annabel, or on my own lack of merit, I turned the conversation to admiralty law, and so discoursed on jetsam, merit salvage, carriage hook to hook, inherent vice, and laches, estoppel, and actions *in rem*, or "against all the world." Kevin listened patiently—he probably knew much of this already—but if he were to trust me with some of his family's business, I wanted to demonstrate my own thorough knowledge of the subject.

To leeward of us were islands with prosaic names: Cow Island, Pine Island, and Mutton Island. At high tide, the islands were surrounded by a turbulent sea, but when the tide raced away, the retreating waters revealed mucky causeways that connected the islands to the mainland. The low isles were a lush green and dotted with flecks of white, the flocks of sheep that formed most of the islands' population. Mutton Island was well named; there were many more sheep than cows on Cow Island, and more mutton than pines on Pine Island. The salt grass that grew on the flat country around Ethlebight was perfect grazing for sheep, and produced a distinct flavor and tenderness in the meat that had made Ethlebight mutton famous throughout all Duisland.

Kevin and I shared the jug of cider and bites of gingerbread as we passed the first two islands. Kevin wanted to talk about Annabel, and I kept diverting him until we took the channel into Mutton Island. We moored at the pier, and I left behind in a locker the cap that marked me as an apprentice lawyer.

I did, however, take the jug of cider, and Kevin bore the satchel of food.

We gave the mooring line enough slack so the boat could ride the tide up and down, then walked along onto the island. A shepherd, wearing a big straw hat and carrying a staff over his shoulder, gave us an incurious look from amid his flock. His dog, far more interested, stood alert on stiff legs, eyes fixed on the intruders.

We took the only path inland. White clouds of sheep drifted around us. The island was mostly salt-grass meadow broken by clusters of gray stone, and ahead I saw quickbeams and maples planted as a windbreak, the maples already scarlet in the early autumn, and the green leaves of the quickbeams right at the cusp of going gold.

We passed into the trees and saw in a glade a modest country house of red brick, probably intended as a summer retreat for Sir Stanley's in-laws. Brown brick outbuildings and empty paddocks for sheep stood dark in the shadows of the trees. I paused in the shade of a maple and considered my approach.

"If we go to the front door," I said, "Sir Stanley could go out the back. Or he could have the servants bar the entrance."

"We should hide and wait," Kevin said.

"The shepherds already know we're here."

I considered that it was unlikely that the lower servants would ever have been told why Sir Stanley was hiding here, or indeed that he was hiding at all. I turned off the path and moved through the grove. The first of the outbuildings was a woodshed, the second a stable with empty stalls, but with a scent of horse that had not faded. Past this was a paddock with sheep still in it, and beyond a brick creamery with a sagging thatch roof. I paused for a moment with my nose in the air, and thought I scented a whiff of warm, fresh milk. I walked to the door of the barn, looked in, and saw a young woman sitting by a milking stand, drawing milk from a sheep while other ewes, impatient for their turn, flocked around her.

"May I beg a sip of milk?" I asked.

At my unfamiliar voice, the dairy maid turned on her stool, though her hands remained at their work. She was about my age, and had a heart-shaped face under a blue cap. Her lips were full, her eyes dark, her complexion rosy. I felt my interest quicken.

I nodded at the grandly dressed Kevin standing uncertainly in the creamery door. "I've taken the young gentleman to the island in my boat," I said. "And it's thirsty work."

She looked at the jug in my hand. "Have you emptied your own jug, then?"

"It's variety I seek," I said. "That and a few words with a lovely maid such as yourself."

A few moments' light conversation with a pleasing young maid, I thought, *will do no one harm.* Annabel Greyson was beyond my reach, perhaps forever. Surely, I had the right to seek a balm for my wounded heart.

The woman's hands continued their work, twin streams of milk foaming into the pitcher. I eased myself through the sheep clustering about the milking stand, and leaned against the wooden gate to the pen.

"I'm willing to share my cider, if you like," I said. "I imagine you see enough milk around this place."

"I'm paid mostly in beer and cider," said the dairy maid. "Cider is nothing to me."

"I'd give you wine, if I had it." There was a pause. "I could bring wine tonight, if you'd care to meet me."

She gave me a look from under her cap. "You would come all the way from town to bring me wine?"

"I have a boat, so why not? I would bring you a moscatto from far Varcellos. A wine as sweet as the finest peach, as sweet on your lips as your smile." At the compliment I saw the smile tugging at her lips, and I pointed. "There!" I said. "Sweetness itself."

I am not, I think, handsome, though some I believe find my countenance amiable enough. Were I as pretty as my schoolfriend Theophrastus Hastings, say, I would scarce have to speak to women at all; they would simply tumble into my arms as they tumble into his.

But because I have no great share of beauty, I must call upon other resources, chief among them the art of conversation. I strive to amuse.

I also listen. It has been my observation that many who can declaim with the greatest actors of the age are not as facile when it comes to hearing what others are saying.

The dairy maid finished with the ewe and brushed the animal off the milking stand. The waiting ewes jostled one another in their eagerness to be milked, but one was quicker than the others and jumped onto the small table. The maid took the pitcher and prepared to empty it into a bucket standing by her feet.

"Ah," said I, "and may I not have a drink? The milk drawn out by your own clever hands?"

"If it's the milk you're really after, you can have some." She offered the pitcher. I took it and drew in several drafts of warm, foamy sweetness. I deliberately left myself a white mustache, and returned the pitcher. She laughed at the froth on my lip.

To use the tongue would be vulgar, I thought, and so removed the stain with a sleeve. She poured the remaining milk into the bucket, and then began to turn to the waiting ewe.

"May I know your name?" I asked.

"Ella," she said.

"I am Quillifer."

Ella looked thoughtful. "I've heard that name," she said.

I leaned closer. "Will you share my moscatto with me tonight? I will bring it, but only if I don't have to drink alone."

Ella looked at me slantwise from beneath her dark brows. "Surely, you can find drinking companions in town."

"But none so lovely," I said. "None with such roses in her cheeks, hands so clever, or lips so sweet."

The roses in her cheeks crimsoned. "If you will bring the wine," she said, her voice a little throaty, "I will help you drink it."

"The pleasure of the moscatto shall be thine. Where shall we meet, and when?"

She looked up at me, her hands jogging the sheep's udders. "Here. The creamery is empty at night."

"The hours till nightfall shall seem each a year." I leaned over her and put on my pleading-lover face. "May I have a kiss to seal the bargain?"

"Not in front of the gentleman," Ella said, tossing her head toward Kevin. "He'll gossip."

"If not your lips, like a lover," I said, "and if not your cheek, like a brother; then may I kiss your hand like a suitor?"

Ella removed her hand from the teat, wiped it on her blue wincey dress, and held it out. I brushed the taut knuckles with my lips.

"Until tonight," I said. I looked up at Kevin, still standing uncertain by the door. "My gentleman bears a message for Sir Stanley. Is he at the house?"

Ella resumed her milking. "Nay. He's gone hunting, and won't be back till the tide is out."

"That will be soon, will it not?"

Ella's lips twitched. "I know nothing of tides; I work in the creamery. But I know that my Master Golding will be here soon, back from scalding the curd, and that you should be gone before he arrives."

"I will come back tonight," said I, "with the wine, and without the young gentleman." I darted a kiss to her cheek—she gave a cry of mingled delight and surprise—and then I rejoined Kevin. We two walked around the creamery and began the stroll to the ford.

"He will come at low tide," I said. "And brother, I shall need to borrow your boat tonight."

Kevin looked over my shoulder at the creamery. "You didn't think to ask if she has a friend?"

"There comes a time," said I, "when a man should shoot his own fowl."

"Perhaps, then," said Kevin, "a man should also own his own boat."

"When I return," said I, "I'll bring you a cheese. Or a sheep. Whichever you like."

Kevin sighed. "I shall have to content myself with a cheese. Yet now I am wondering why I came."

"A pleasant sunny day on the water, and yet you complain. You should have talked to the girl yourself, an you liked her."

We placed ourselves beneath a maple on the path leading to the ford, and applied ourselves to the satchel, and its bread, meat, and cheese.

Wind whistled in the high branches. Sheep drifted across the grass like foam on water. I began to feel sleep tugging at my eyelids, and then I was started into alertness by the sound of a hunting horn.

"A recheat!" said Kevin. He was more familiar with the vocabulary of the hunt than I.

I cupped my ears. The mellow call, rich as cream, came from the north. I rose to my feet, then jumped onto one of the lower branches of a quickbeam. Riding over the rich grass on the northern horizon I could see a party of horsemen.

"Ay, they come," I said. "You might wish to take cover, stand at a distance; you are too brightly colored. And hand me the satchel."

Kevin passed the satchel to me and withdrew farther into the glade. A dove flapped away as I climbed higher into the tree. I could see the hunters coming on, hear the dogs calling—not the baying of the hunt but a pleasant gossip within the pack. The hunting party was coming at a slow walk, the horses and men tired with their morning exercise.

The quickbeam's berries were turning red with autumn. The wind chuffed overhead, rattling the dry leaves. I pulled the writ from my pocket and took a firm grip on my leather satchel with its cargo of meat and cheese.

The horn blew another recheat. I heard a door bang from the direction of the house, as the servants bustled out to assist the hunting party.

The staghounds scented their home and bounded into the lead, barking amiably as they arrowed for the kennels. Like a gray-brown river they poured along beneath my feet, followed by some of the grooms. The hounds, grooms, horses, and hunters were all spattered with mud from crossing the causeway.

Sir Stanley rode in the middle of the party, a big man with a thick neck and long gray mustaches that reached halfway down his chest. He wore heavy boots and hunting leathers and a goodly coating of mud, and he held the reins in one hand and a braided whip in the other. His horse was heavy-framed and yellow where it wasn't spattered by ooze. Behind came the grooms, one bearing the straight sword their master used to kill the stags once the dogs had cornered them, and another with the gun used for hinds, who were less sport because they had no horns with which to defend themselves, and therefore could be shot instead of attacked on foot. Behind came sumpter horses bearing the bodies of the kill, already cut up and packaged and ready for the kitchen or the smokehouse. The trophy heads were carried in a basket: a red stag and a fallow buck, and a small but angry-looking boar.

My pulse beat high in my throat. I calculated my moment, then made my leap and landed in a crouch just ahead of the rider, and to his left, on the side away from the whip. The big horse reared and bellowed in surprise. The rider clutched at the reins.

"Sir Stanley! Sir Stanley!" I called out. I waved the satchel near the horse's head and provoked more rearing. The hooves lashed out. Sir Stanley cursed, sawed the reins, and finally backed the yellow horse down. Rage turned his face a brilliant scarlet. He turned to me and roared.

"What do you mean, waving that damned thing, you jack-in-the-box!"

"Hold this, sir. You may have broke the martingale."

I held out the writ as I feigned an interest in the horse's bridle; the yellow horse backed away again, and out of exasperation, Sir Stanley snatched the writ from my hand.

"No, I see the martingale is all right," I said. I gave the knight a brilliant smile. "And sir, that is a writ in your hand, and you are commanded by the justice of the peace to the Assizes."

Sir Stanley stared. The hounds had seen me appear as if by sorcery and came bounding back; they surrounded me in a rough, boisterous crowd, as if in admiration of the trick I'd played on their master. I am fond of dogs, and they of me, and I laughed and scratched their ears. Sir Stanley lashed at the dogs with his whip.

"Down!" he said. "Down, you bratchets!" He snarled. "Stop that fawning! Tear him, tear him! Ahoo! Ahoo!"

I danced away from the whip, the excited hounds still bounding around me. I pointed at the grooms who were starting to gather, themselves equipped rather ominously with whips, guns, or bright boar-spears. "These gentlemen are all witnesses!" I said. "And if they are not enough, I brought a witness of my own!" I brandished the satchel in the direction of Kevin, who—with what seemed a degree of embarrassment, or perhaps well-grounded reluctance—emerged from behind his tree.

One of the grooms blew on his brass horn to call the dogs but was ignored. Sir Stanley made a few more slashes with his whip before grooms rode into the melee and deftly separated me from my pack of admirers. I ghosted away from the trail, found a groom behind me, as if to cut me off, and ducked under the horse, which snorted and lashed out with its rear hooves. The hooves were no threat to me, but they kept the other horses clear.

"I have done my duty, Sir Stanley!" I said, backing. "I will forego the customary tip an it please you, and wish you good day." I waved. "The Compassionate Pilgrim save you, Sir Stanley!"

"Damn your Pilgrim!" The knight shook his whip in the air. The staghounds bounded and gave excited voice. The groom blew another useless recheat.

"Good day, Sir Stanley!"

The knight propped his fist on his hip and glared after me.

"Who in hell art thou, thou impertinent louse?"

I left the question unanswered as I turned and made for the landing. Kevin joined me. We walked briskly.

Kevin adjusted his broad hat. "Dare I look over my shoulder to see if he's taking aim with his gun?"

"It is a lovely gun," I said. "I saw it in the hands of his bearer. Wheel-lock, the lock and barrel chased with silver. Rifled, I daresay. And we know he is a good hunter."

"You offer no comfort."

"There is no comfort till we are out of range."

We left the shade of the grove and returned to the green, sunny domain of the sheep. Shepherds and sheepdogs watched us with professional interest. Another recheat sounded from the grove.

"They summon the dogs," said Kevin. "Walk faster, thou impertinent louse."

I said nothing but increased the pace. Then from the grove, instead of the barks of excitement and interest, came the baying of a hunting pack, and it was time to run.

Alarmed sheep gave their staccato bray and scattered before us. Sheepdogs barked warning. The sound of the baying pack came closer.

Surely, I thought, *he does not mean to kill us.* If he wanted that, he would have used his gun. A few ounces of flesh torn by the fangs of his staghounds should satisfy him.

Not wanting to be shredded, I ran and fumbled with the straps of the satchel. I heard oaths from the shepherds, who feared the dogs would savage their charges. I considered lunging for one of the shepherds and seizing his stick to use in my own defense, but decided that this was no time for the pack to catch me wrestling a herdsman.

My throat ached as the cool air froze my gullet. I dared to cast a glance over my shoulder and saw that the lead staghound was a mere twenty yards behind.

I reached into the satchel, retrieved a piece of ham, and hurled it into the air. I didn't look back, but the tone of the yelping behind me changed: there was a short cry of interest as the lead bratchet saw the offering and changed direction, then a peremptory bark as she challenged another dog for possession of the treat. I heard a scuffle as a number of hounds disputed possession of the ham, and excited barking as other hounds stayed to watch. I was surprised how long it took the dogs to remember their business and begin their baying again.

Another slice of ham delayed the dogs a second time, and then a third; and after that, I was out of ham, and resorted to the sausages. After the sausages were gone, I broke off pieces of cheese and tossed them, and found they interested the dogs equally. By the time the pier was in sight, I was out of cheese. I began flinging bread.

"Run for the boat!" I gasped at Kevin. "I'll keep them busy."

Tossing bread over my shoulder, I ran straight into the water, the cold so shocking that I would have stopped dead if momentum hadn't carried me on. A wave heaved me up, and I plunged in, the water a salt slap to my face. When I was chest-deep, I turned to face the pack of gray-brown staghounds baying at me from the shore. I reached into the satchel and heaved a chunk of waterlogged gingerbread into the midst of the pack. They were habituated to food flying to them by now, and the bread disappeared into a seething gray-brown mob.

I heard the brass hunting horn tootling closer, and the sound of horses. I tossed bread. The first of the grooms appeared just as I heard the crack of the filling lugsail.

"Behind you!" Kevin called.

I turned, saw the boat's bow approaching, and tossed the satchel aboard. I seized the larboard gunwale as it went past, and rolled aboard as Kevin shifted his own weight to starboard to prevent capsize. Kevin shoved the tiller and the boat swung its nose to the sea.

On the shore, Sir Stanley Mattingly was cursing and whipping his dogs. I rose to my feet, dripping. I put a foot on the gunwale and grasped a shroud for balance.

"Sir Stanley, I thank you for your kind hospitality!" I called.

Vigorous obscenity pursued me across the water.

"Sir," I said, "you asked my name, and now I am pleased to answer. I am Quillifer, son of Quillifer, the apprentice to Lawyer Dacket, and in two days' time, I shall have the pleasure of seeing you at the Assizes!"

I offered an elaborate bow, and straightened in time to see Sir Stanley snatch his gun from his bearer. I decided it was time to take shelter below the gunwale, and to pull Kevin down likewise.

The shot put a neat hole in the sail. By the time the knight had reloaded, the boat was well out of range.

The lugsail rattled overhead. "Friend," said Kevin. "May I trust you no longer to mock armed, violent men? At least till I am safe at home?"

"We were in no danger," said I.

"Safe as long as the sausages held out, and Sir Stanley's aim remained poor."

I waved a hand. "He was aiming at the sail, not at us. He wouldn't want to be hauled up on a charge of manslaughter."

"You have more confidence in his moderation than I."

"I'm hungry," I said. "The orgulous Sir Stanley has deprived us of our dinner."

"Orgulous?"

"A new word I invented. From the Lorettan, *orguilio*, pride." I stared unhappily at the horizon. "I should invent a new word for hunger."

"You are welcome to catch a fish."

"And you left the cider behind! For shame, Master Spellman."

I removed my soaked, chill clothing, and stretched naked across a thwart, in the sun. The brisk wind dusted my skin with gooseflesh, but I was comfortable enough. I had been far colder when I was hanging upside down from Master Greyson's roofbeam.

"Pity you won't be visiting the fair Ella tonight," Kevin said.

I gave him a surprised look. "Why would I not?"

"What?" Kevin laughed. "You want another race against Sir Stanley's pack? Or his bullets?"

"Sir Stanley is unlikely to march up and down his pier with his gun on his shoulder—he will be asleep in his bed, or in the hall, draining the wine and brandy of his brother-in-law. The dogs will be in their kennels, and the sheep in their pens."

"And Ella in the creamery, screaming for help and earning a reward for catching you."

I shook my head. "Friend, your skepticism is alarming in its degree."

"We've upset the whole household. Ella might be frantic in her desire to keep the others from knowing about your arrangement, and the best way to preserve her innocence will be to denounce you."

"The lovely Ella? I can't imagine such a thing."

We argued the matter, and then found other matters to argue. By the time we arrived at the Ostra's many mouths, the tide was rushing in, and carried us to the city with fine efficiency. The Lorettan pinnace was still aground, but the crew were heaving at the capstan, and the hawser leading to the kedge anchor was taut as a bowstring, tension shooting water from its fibers.

"Now," I said, as I began to draw on my still-damp clothes, "I pray you go to my master Dacket's office, and there sign a paper that you witnessed my delivery of the writ."

"You won't go yourself?"

"He'll put me to copying documents, and I'll miss the meeting with Ella. I've already promised tomorrow to the work, and I see no reason for an early start."

Kevin was skeptical. "And what excuse will I give for your absence?"

I tugged my tunic over my head. "You may relate the tale of our escape from Mutton Island. Recount our heroism, the attack by dogs, the shot through your sail. And you may inform Dacket of my injuries—embroider them as you like, but tell him how manfully I am bearing up, even though the doctors have been called and my mother despairs of my life. You may then say how I expect to be early at the office tomorrow."

"You are the expert in such embroidery, not I."

"You underrate your ingenuity. Remember that story you told Professor Mitchell, when we were at grammar school and caught out of bounds."

"We were caned," Kevin said. "He didn't believe us."

I drew hose onto my legs. "But the *story* was a marvel! Were there not tritons, and some kind of monster from the Land of Chimerae that flew overhead and darkened the sun?"

"Very well," Kevin said. "I will tell Lawyer Dacket you were taken by tritons."

Kevin found a place near the quay, dropped the sail, and tied the boat. I jumped onto the quay and helped Kevin disembark.

"Are you truly mad enough to visit the maid tonight?"

"Oh, ay. 'Twill keep me out of trouble in town."

"Ethlebight will take comfort from that, but I will rest uneasy."

We marched beneath the great River Gate blazoned with the shield of Ethlebight, crenellated towers and ships supported by the hornèd rams that represented the wool that remained the foundation of the city's wealth. Kevin departed for Lawyer Dacket's office, while I carried my empty satchel home to Princess Street. I changed my clothes, got more bread, meat, cheese, and a few of the pearmains. Then I went to the buttery for a bottle of the moscatto, and another jug of cider for the journey.

On my return to the quay I tarried by a barber's shop, and there sought a preventative for parturience. My last packet of sheaths I had left with Annabel Greyson, and I could but hope her father hadn't found them, proof of her perfidy.

I returned to the boat, repaired the hole in the sail, and as soon as the tide shifted set out through the cane, past the handsome pinnace that had finally won free of its mud bank, and was now creeping up the channel under sweeps, with a leadsman in the chains calling out the soundings.

I am young, I thought, *and a man; and whyfore should I not act the role of a young man? Enjoy my pleasures before age and care ruin them?*

No guard marched along the Mutton Island pier. Ella I found in the shadow of the creamery door. We kissed for several long, fair moments, and then she took my hand and led me beneath rows of ghostly round forms that hung from the roof beams—pendulous muslin bags, filled with curd and dripping on the brick floor the last of the milky whey-drops. Beyond was a room with stalls intended for sick animals. No ailing sheep were in residence, but there was straw to make a bed.

Make a bed we did, and stretched out our cloaks to fashion an inviting couch. I opened the moscatto, with its flavor of sunnier, drier climes, and we drank and then licked drops of the sweet wine from each other's lips. For some hours we dallied on the straw, sharing our pleasures, and then I kissed Ella good-bye, plucked straw from her hair, laughed, and kissed her again before wrapping myself in my cloak and setting off for the pier.

The fortified wine burned in my veins, and I felt a pleasant loose-ness in my loins. I found the boat, cast off, and raised the sail. The moon soon set, and I found myself alone on the dark water, where I nibbled bread and cheese, drank cider, and sang to myself as the brisk wind blew the boat along.

> *Youth will needs have dalliance,*
> *Of good or ill, some pastance.*
> *Company me thinketh the best*
> *All thoughts and fancies to digest*
> *For idleness*
> *Is chief mistress*
> *Of vices all;*
> *Then who can say*
> *But mirth and play*
> *Is best of all?*

I put on my apprentice cap and pulled the brim down over my ears against the cold wind. I would have an hour or two of sleep, I supposed, before reporting to Lawyer Dacket's for my day of copying.

I judged the harbor entrance by the stars, turned the boat for Ethlebight, and only then noted the glow some distance inland. It wasn't the moon, which had set; and the sun would rise east, not north. I had seen the aurora on cold winter nights, but the aurora was shifting color, massed spears of light that advanced and retreated, and this light was steady. I stood, but could see no detail over the sea of reeds that stretched between my boat and the city.

Fire, it was fire. Anxiety gnawed at my mind.

The tide was coming in: water gurgled beneath the counter as the boat flew toward home. The glow grew brighter as I neared the city, and I saw red reflected on the undersides of scattered clouds. In growing fear I sped from channel to channel. I thought that in the blustering wind I heard clattering, and screams, and I hoped the sounds were only my own fancies.

At last the reed curtain fell away, and I saw my city on fire, flames silhouetting the towers and battlements of Ethlebight's wall, and the main channel of the Ostra black with an enemy fleet.

CHAPTER THREE

The ships of the invaders were black on the black water, with black flags and drooping lateen yards. The piers were black with enemy, and the black night rang with screams.

I stared in amazement so complete that it left no room for fear. I had been gone eight or ten hours, and in that time, a fleet had poured like the tide into the harbor and the city had fallen.

Screams. Shots. A sudden rising spout of fire so tall that it over-topped the walls, the flare as a roof fell in.

There was a hissing in the air, a splash beyond. I realized I'd come too close to the enemy, and someone on deck had loosed an arrow. The fear that had been delayed came rushing into my head, and I put the tiller over, and heard the lugsail bang overhead as the boat lost way.

Enemy ships crowded the piers, had grounded on the shore. There was no place where I could land.

Another arrow buzzed overhead and then skipped away over the water like a stone. I fumbled for the sheet, the sail filled with wind, and I raced back into darkness, away from the consuming red light.

My family. My city. On fire.

Panic flayed my nerves, and my mind seemed to chatter like a broken cog in a decrepit mill. I couldn't imagine what to do. I had no weapons, no armor. Nothing but a small knife to cut bread and cheese, that and a boat I'd borrowed from a friend.

I looked more closely at the enemy ships. *Chebecs,* I thought, *with two or three masts and a raking, jutting bowsprit, capable of traveling under oar or sail, small enough to get up the channel that guarded the city.* I had seen chebecs come in and out of port all my life, most bringing wines and silks and spices from the old Empire of the Aekoi.

But never in these numbers. What was moored in the port was a pirate fleet, manned by gold-skinned reivers from the edges of the empire, cities ruled by warlords and brigands, sometimes with the support of the emperor, sometimes without. Pirates such as these had raided the coasts of Duisland in the past, but not in years, not since well before I was born.

And never had Ethlebight fallen to a raid, nor had the city even been menaced in decades, not since the harbor had begun to silt and the entrance become too difficult for a stranger to navigate. Half the attacking fleet should have run aground within a quarter mile of the bight's entrance.

Screams. Shots. Another gush of flame. I could not sit and watch, not while my family was in danger.

A passage opened in the reeds and I took it. I knew most of the channels, having boated and fished in them since I was a boy, and I was reasonably certain this one led to the salt marshes southeast of the city. The salt marshes were empty at night save for flocks of sheep and their shepherds, but they would also be empty of reivers.

I ran the boat aground on mud, threw out the anchor, and then slogged through reeds and calf-deep mud till I came to the boggy meadows south of the city. The effort had me straining for breath by the time I reached something like solid ground, and then I moved as fast as I could force my limbs. Ooze spurted from my shoes at every step. Urgency dragged me on. The air smelled of salt grass and smoke.

Red light winked through the South Gate, the smallest gatehouse on the wall, built for the convenience of the shepherds and fishermen who lived in or near the marsh. The gate was open, and I increased my pace.

I slowed again as I saw firelight glint on swords and pikes, and I realized that the gate had been opened from the inside by the reivers, who had gathered outside and hoped to tempt desperate citizens to run out and be captured.

Captured to be slaves. For the reivers were here for loot, certainly; but as far as they were concerned, most of the city's wealth walked on two legs.

From somewhere in the city came the cry of shrill whistles. I retreated into the darkness, then began a circumnavigation of the walls, loping eastward in hopes of finding an unguarded rampart. Fantasies clawed at my brain: find a reiver alone, knock him on the head, take his weapons. Kill more reivers, free the captives, put together an army and retake the city . . . I knew perfectly well the fancies were absurd, but I couldn't stop them from flooding my mind.

I remembered Captain Hay's willow whip on my shoulders during the Beating of the Bounds eight years before: here before me was the Broad Tower, the Blue Tower, the Tower of Prince Peter. Beyond the Blue Tower, I thought, there was Sheep Street, which led at an angle into the city and intersected Princess Street. If I got into Sheep Street, it would take me almost all the way home.

As water squelched from my shoes, I dragged myself across the boggy ground and approached the base of the wall. I saw movement on the towers, though I could not be certain whether the people I saw were friends or slavers. There was no indication that anyone on the walls saw my approach across the dark ground. I came to the rampart and raised a hand to touch the cold, wet, dark brick. The wind whistled around the battlements far overhead. Another scream rose on the air, and I leaned my forehead against the wall, closed my eyes, and hoped that the sound was only the wind.

The fantasies that bled into my brain had grown lurid and horrible, graphic accompaniment to the sound of screams and the crackle of burning. My head snapped up and my eyes opened. Whatever the truth was, it could not be as horrible as my imagination. I needed to see for myself.

I looked up and desperately hoped to see something that would help me scale the wall. I could see the dark silhouettes of plants and shrubs growing out of the brick face, and I moved back and forth along the wall, in hopes of finding something like a vegetable ladder that would help me rise. In the darkness, I couldn't see well enough to choose a path, and so I cast off my heavy cloak, reached for a small bush overhead, seized it with both hands, and hauled myself up. The bush bent under my weight and showered my face with a spatter of frigid dew. My right shoe found lodging somewhere in the courses of brick, and I pushed myself up, the rough brick scraping against the front of my doublet. One hand groped upward, found a fingerhold, pulled until the left foot could prop itself against the bush and propel me farther up the wall.

The wall was thirty feet high, and the battlement on top jutted out over the wall. I tried not to think of how far I had to go, and instead clawed upward with both hands. I found grass and moss growing out of the wall, and it tore away before it would support me. Then I found another grip for my fingers, and pulled myself up just far enough to reach with my fingertips the bole of a small tree. The hard leather sole of my right shoe found a purchase and helped me climb a few inches more.

The masonry was old, and the ground beneath it soft: the wall was no longer perfectly vertical, and the bends and waves in the brick bulwark helped fingers and toes gain a lodgment. Rain had eroded mortar from between the courses of bricks and provided holds. Blood made my fingers slick, and the pain in my arms and shoulders was agonizing. My breath seared in and out of my throat.

After a cold, black eternity, each minute measured by inches, I found myself beneath the battlement, a stone ledge outstepped from the wall by eighteen inches, with the crenellated rampart built on top. I reached out with bleeding fingers, found a handhold, and measured it carefully. It was long enough for both my hands, and I would need both for what followed.

My heart beat in my chest like a hundred trip-hammers. I propped myself as carefully as I could, moved my second hand to the ledge, and then kicked my legs free and swung out over the gulf.

Now there was no going back. If I couldn't climb the parapet, I would fall thirty feet to the ground below, and lie broken until I was found by reivers or rescue or frozen death.

I pulled myself up, reached a hand up, then fell back to full extension as strength fled my arms. I took a breath, then another, then another. Air flooded my lungs. I closed my eyes and concentrated only on the necessity of climbing the last few feet, but no matter how high I groped, I could not find a handhold.

I needed to reach higher, but I couldn't pull myself up by a single hand while reaching with the other. Futility warred in my brain with useless, desperate plans, and then I thought I might swing myself like a pendulum, and at the top of the rise reach higher. I began to sway my legs left and right, building momentum with each swing but terrified that my impetus might grow so great it would tear me from my fragile handhold. Puffing like a breaching whale, I swung to the right and at the height of the movement snatched up with the right hand, reached an eroded course of brick, pulled myself up farther, snatched again. Hand over hand, one breath after another, I drew myself up again and again, mere inches each time . . . and then I was able to curl myself so as to get a foothold, and then with one great uncoiling motion I kicked myself up and through a crenellation, to land in a disordered heap on the cold flagstones of the rampart walk.

I surrendered to blackness. My senses fled, and I could only pant for breath like a beaten dog. Agony shrieked through my tormented muscles.

Gradually, through the torment, the world returned, a world of blazing fire, of clashing weapons, of breaking glass, of sobs and screams. I rolled onto my side and stared at the city with dull eyes. Silhouetted by flame, I could see the belfry of the Seven Words Monastery, the fantastic tower at the Court of the Teazel Bird, and the battlements of the New Castle. From somewhere—from everywhere—came the sounds of terror and pain.

I got an arm beneath myself and propped myself up on one elbow. The New Castle, the source of royal authority in the city and the home of the Lord Warden and his garrison of royal troops, had fallen—black flags waved from the tops of the towers. Lost with the castle was any hope of organized resistance. There was no army for me to join, and all that remained for me was the hope that I could somehow rescue my family.

I sat up and gazed around me. In the light of all the fires, the roofs of the buildings were bright as daylight, but the streets below were in deep, black shadow. The result was a perfect map of the city, black streets on a shining background. I found Sheep Street easily, the one lane that failed to follow the city's gridiron pattern because it took flocks of sheep straight from the South Gate to the Sheep Market just off Scarcroft Square.

The corsairs had fired the thatch of many of the houses, presumably to drive the occupants out into the street where they could be taken; but not all roofs were thatch, and not all thatch buildings were alight. Just below the rampart was an old, crooked building with a thatch roof, easily reached, but with a fall of perhaps fifteen feet. The thatch was thick, however, new spar-coating simply laid on the old until it piled up centuries deep. I rose to my feet, gasped at the pain in my limbs, and then launched myself at the old house.

I made a soft landing on thatch ten feet thick, dropping down on my front, limbs spread wide. From there it was an easy climb to the next building, which had a tile roof, and then I began a run along the south side of Sheep Street, jumping from one building to the next and managing to dodge around the structures that were on fire. The roofs were so well lit that my progress was much faster than it had been when I was running from Greyson's horsemen.

Because of the light, I was able to orient myself and run as directly for my own house as all the arson permitted. Hope began to die as I saw flames licking around the familiar carved chimneys, and suddenly I felt the weight of my own limbs, my own exhaustion, the smoke burning in my throat. I slowed, and my last steps dragged across the roof tiles as despair clawed at me.

My father's house had been set alight—hours before, to judge by what little remained. The roof and upper storeys had fallen in, and there was nothing left but embers, charred beams, and blackened brick. The fire had spread to the thatch-roofed house next door, or perhaps the other way—both had fallen in. Bodies lay before the front door of the butcher shop, and in the ruddy light I could see the dead were Aekoi reivers. My father and the apprentices, then, had given a good account of themselves before their luck had run out.

But were they still alive? The fire might have forced the defenders into the street, where they could have been captured.

I didn't believe it. In my heart I knew that my father would have fought to the end, wielding his pollaxe and calling on the Netweaving God.

Still, I needed to know. I was still standing in stunned stupefaction when I heard, a short distance away, the clash of arms and a shrieking of whistles.

My father, I thought, might still be alive and fighting. At once I was running along the tiles, leaped over Princess Street at a narrow place, then charged on.

My heart gave a leap as I saw a group of my countrymen, armed with pikes and swords and whatever other tools they could find, pushing toward the East Gate. There were men and women both in the crowd, thirty or forty all told, all shouting, all driving a crowd of Aekoi before them.

Shrieks went up from Aekoi whistles. They were calling to other reivers, bringing them to the fight.

I knew the band had to move quickly or they'd be overwhelmed. I cast about frantically for a weapon, then saw the roof tiles under my feet.

I heaved up a tile, threw it at one of the Aekoi, and missed. The second one missed as well. The third struck a reiver between the shoulder blades and knocked him down long enough for the defenders to reach him and trample him into the brick street.

In the meantime, the whistles shrilled, and the reivers gathered, at first hovering around the resisters, firing arrows from their short bows; but then, as their numbers rose, rushing in with swords and short naval pikes. I hurled more roof tiles, but the pirates were swarming in, the resisters' advance had slowed to a crawl, and I felt a rising despair clutch at my vitals.

Then I looked up from levering another roof tile, and I saw one of the reivers standing on the roof across the road, aiming an arrow directly at me. I gave a startled leap just as the pirate loosed his missile, and the arrow missed me by inches, struck the tiles, and bounded off into the dark.

The pirate reached for another arrow, and I scrambled away, over the ridgepole and into the shelter of a bulky brick chimney. There I found myself staring right into the startled face of one of the reivers come to the call of the whistles. In the light of the flaming city I could see the reiver's gold complexion, the bottle of incendiary fluid used to fire thatch, the quilted leather jacket, a hard leather cap with flaps tied down over the ears, and the curved bone-and-sinew bow in his hand.

I smashed the reiver in the face with a fist. I felt the impact jarring up to my shoulder, and the pirate went down in a tangle of limbs. The tiles clattered beneath me. I dropped onto the man, a knee planted on his midsection, and smashed my fist into the face yet again. I batted away the hands raised in defense and kept hammering at the face until the corsair lay still, face threaded with blood. I looked for a weapon and drew a short sword from the reiver's waist. It was badly made, its surface pitted, its cross section a *T* to stiffen the badly forged steel.

Still, my spirit leapt as I held the cheap sword in my hand. At last I had some means of striking back.

And then I heard tiles rattle, and I turned to see the first archer, the one who had shot at me, crossing the ridgepole twenty feet away.

The reiver drew the bow, and I skipped away in mad flight over the rooftops. Arrows whistled through the air near my head. Behind me I could hear the band of survivors dying, baffled by packs of invaders as the red stag had been by Sir Stanley's hounds.

Other archers saw me and fired, and I ran, carrying the useless sword, until I could see no more Aekoi silhouettes on the rooftops, and then I fell gasping to the tiles. I could hear no more fighting, no sounds of whistles, only the crackling of flame and the sigh of wind. Swirls of ash flew over me, and the smell of burning clogged my throat.

After a short, bleak eternity, I dragged myself to my feet again, sought the shelter of a chimney, and looked about me. In my flight from the archers I had taken no bearings, and now that I peered around a crow-stepped cornice, I found myself overlooking Scarcroft Square.

I ghosted forward to the cornice to get a better view, and peered through the ivy that massed over the building's front. In the light of

torches and burning buildings, I saw that the square had been filled
with a vast mob of prisoners, all forced to sit or crawl by the reivers
who stalked among them with swords and whips. The prisoners were
all women and children, many only partly dressed, and they were in a
continual, horrible, hobbling motion, as if the square were occupied
by a flock of crippled lambs, none able to lie still, none permitted to
rise. A constant sobbing and wailing hung in the air—no individual
voice could be heard, but only the ululating rise and fall of a massed
lament.

I realized where I was—atop the hall of the Honorable and
Worshipfull Companie of Fullers, Scourers, and Stretchers, one of
the wool guilds that flaunted its wealth and position on the square.
Many was the time that my younger self had climbed its ivy-covered
facade, pretending to be Sir Brigham of Hookton climbing the Tower
of Doleful Visage, or Antinius leading the imperial storming party
over the walls of the capital of the Felerine Republic, thus ending the
Fifty Years' War.

Antinius, I remembered, who was an Aekoi general, and who had
led his men over the walls and into a sack, a sack such as the one I
now witnessed. And yet Antinius had been a great hero, and the boy
I had been wanted nothing so much as to emulate him.

For a brief, intense moment, I hated Antinius, all heroes, and
my own younger self. By what right had I evaded death or capture?
Because I was clever? Because a milkmaid had loved me?

If I were truly clever, I told myself, I would have saved my family.

I glanced around and saw the eastern sky already pale with the
approaching dawn. The silhouettes of archers prowled the rooftops,
and I knew they would be far too dangerous in full daylight. I needed
to hide.

I did not particularly doubt my ability on that score. I knew the city
far better than the reivers—there would be some alley, some courtyard, some alcove where I would escape notice.

And then I recalled a place only a few yards below my feet. The guild hall was covered in ivy, except for some niches with statues of celebrated patrons of the guild. Above the entrance was a portico with a pitched roof, and behind the pitched roof was a deep niche that had once held a statue of old King Emmius. But the ivy that draped the hall kept falling over the niche and obscuring the statue, and the obscurity was deemed an insult to royal dignity. The statue had been moved into the guild banqueting hall, where toasts could be offered in the good King's memory; and the ivy was allowed to obscure the niche completely.

When I was a boy, the niche had seemed a great cavern, with the ivy leaves pouring over it like water over a weir. It was shadowed, private, and completely invisible, at least until the ivy turned yellow in the winter and began to die back.

And more important than anything else, it would give me a view of everything below. I still did not know the fate of my family, and if I saw any of them in the hands of the reivers, I would know to try to raise a ransom.

I peered far out over the cornice to make sure no one was looking in my direction, and saw no faces raised to view me. I rolled over the cornice and dropped down the front of the building. It was far easier to climb down the ivy than it had been to climb the courses of brick, and within a few seconds, I passed through the green curtain into the niche. There I gave way to exhaustion, dropped to the floor, and slumped against the wall, my useless sword dropping from my fingers; and as the cries and moans of the captives echoed in the small chamber, I slowly, one teardrop after another, let my hope slip away.

I did not sleep, but I fell into a kind of waking trance that had every quality of nightmare. I watched the Aekoi as they went about the business of sacking a city—and business it was, for all was aimed at generating profit for the attackers. Loot was brought in sacks or carts from all quarters of the city, and piled in the center of the square, around the fountain and its allegorical statues. The guild halls and town hall were pillaged for plate and other valuables— even King Emmius was carried off. None of the plunder was taken by individual reivers; it was all collected to be distributed later. One reiver who appeared laughing, dressed comically in a bolt of valuable silk, was viciously clouted by an officer and the silk taken away.

Weapons were taken to the New Castle, where the enemy commander had apparently established his headquarters. The pigs that roamed free on Ethlebight's streets were killed and butchered, and the meat taken to the castle. Other food was also brought into the castle, and soon the scent of cooking wafted from the gates.

New groups of prisoners were harried into the square. All bedraggled, some wounded, they were kicked into place and then ignored. Punishment was savage if any protested, or if any so much as tried to stand. The prisoners were otherwise not molested—their captors were far too busy sucking the city dry of wealth.

The women and children were herded right before me on the west side of the square, and the men on the far eastern side, behind the piles of plunder, their position partly obscured by the half-built wooden theater. The men were all shackled, but only a few of the women had been chained. Perhaps the reivers had succeeded beyond their dreams and run out of fetters, or maybe they considered women less prone to rebellion if they had the lives of their children to consider.

My body was a mass of cramp and pain. I was desperately thirsty. My torn fingers oozed blood. Exhaustion reached rude, clammy hands into my mind and tore away everything but despair.

Harsh commands, barks of laughter, and crude jokes echoed up from the reivers. In the grammar school, I had been taught the classical Aekoi authors, all famed for their balanced, elegant rhetoric—I had learned nothing like the crudities that came from the square, that sounded little more than the yapping of terriers.

At noon, the reivers were called by groups into the castle for their meal. The captives were given nothing. And after that began the complex business of moving the captives and the loot out of the city.

The women and children went first, kicked to their feet and marched to the square's central fountain, where they were allowed to drink. Each was then given a bag of loot, a bolt of costly fabric, or a basket of food, and marched away in the direction of the River Gate.

I sat up, wringing my torn hands in anxiety as I peered through the ivy in hopes of viewing my mother or sisters. I failed to see them, but I felt a cold spear enter my heart as I saw Annabel Greyson bent weeping over a bolt of cloth as she shuffled along in a nightgown and bare feet. With her I saw other young women I had last seen gaily clad as Mermaids, along with their mothers and sisters. I saw girls I'd flirted with at market stalls, young boys I'd seen running in the streets, dignified grandmothers I'd met at the temple or the Fane. And I saw Tavinda, the Aekoi woman who'd always bargained with my father for a better price, leaning on the arm of her concubine daughter, both dressed in soiled finery, their captivity a demonstration that the Aekoi had no objection to enslaving their own race.

By the time the last of the women had passed, my heart had been wrung dry of sorrow. I was as bereft of feeling as the stone and cold brick that shaped my hiding place. I could only watch, observe, and keep a mute tally of the tragedies below.

After the women and children had been marched away, the men were given the same treatment, save that their burdens were heavier. They shuffled along, chains ringing, backs bent. I saw aldermen, the Mayor, and the Lord Warden Scrope, who with his band of royal troops had so signally failed in his duty to defend the city. Lawyer Dacket shuffled along with his two sons. I recognized many of this year's Warriors of the Sea, and though I didn't see Kevin, I saw Kevin's father, the Mercer Spellman. I saw monks in their robes, their sacred character having proved no boundary to enslavement. I saw Anthony

Greyson, the wrathful father who had pursued me the previous night. Greyson was badly battered, having resisted captivity, and I found no joy in this enemy brought low.

The long, anguished procession took hours. By late afternoon, the square was empty save for the corsairs, who carried away whatever loot remained. Last of all, the reivers carried away the god Pastas, his azure skin and green hair shining in the sun as his statue was carried from the Fane to join the Thousand Gods of the Aekoi.

As the eastern sky began to darken, trumpets blew from the New Castle—*a recheat*, I thought—to signal any reivers remaining in the city to depart. In armor that glittered of captive gold, the commander marched away, shadowed by half a dozen black flags, and was followed by a few scurrying stragglers.

After which I was left to emerge from my cave into the new, ravaged city, a new world that smelled of cinders, of death, and of blackest misery.

CHAPTER FOUR

Y ou know what it is to feel loss, a loss so great that you feel sick, and your head swirls, and your limbs turn to water. That is how I had felt that day, with the loss of everything I had known.

My little sword stuck through my belt, I climbed down from my hiding place just after sunset. Red stained the southwestern sky, but the square was in deep shadow, as if to hide the horrors that had taken place there.

My muscles had stiffened, and my arms felt as if they'd been drawn from their sockets. It had been three days since I'd slept. Hunched with pain and faint with thirst, I walked to the fountain, caught the edge of the basin with my hands, and drove my face into the water as if I were diving into a lake. I took two swallows so prodigious that they pained my throat, then came up gasping for air, throwing back my head and my hair. I dunked my head again, swallowed again, and kept swallowing until the taste of ash was gone from my throat. I hadn't had anything to drink since the cider on my return journey from Mutton Island.

When I'd had enough water, I found my apprentice cap floating on the surface of the fountain. I washed the blood from my hands and the soot from my hair, then put the cap back on my head. Water coursed down my face.

I was not alone on the square: a few ghostly forms drifted through the big open space, some coming for water, others hoping—or fearing—to find their friends or relatives among the bodies the corsairs had left strewn on the brick pavement. I wiped my face, and tried with dulled mind to decide what to do.

Not all the fallen were dead. I heard voices calling out for help, saw a hand wave in the air. I walked to the fallen man and crouched by him, and saw that he'd been stabbed, his shirtfront red with blood.

"Water," the man said. I didn't know him. He was elderly, with a lined face and white hair and thin sticklike arms. The corsairs had probably thought he was too old for slave work, and not worth enough money to bother with ransom.

I rose to my feet and wondered where I could find a vessel for water before I remembered my cap. Most of the water drained through the fabric before I could return to the wounded man, but I managed to dribble a small stream onto the man's parched tongue.

"Thank you. Thank you. More water, please."

"It will not help," I wanted to say. "You're dying." But I didn't say it; instead, I went back for another capful of water.

I wanted to go to my home on Princess Street and find out what had happened to my family. But the old man was not alone in wanting water, and others were calling out, and people who were not wounded were wandering out from their hiding places. No one seemed to know what to do, so I decided to pretend that I was in charge. I led a group to a tavern, not to drink but to find cups for water. Those made of valuable metal had been stolen, and those made of glass smashed for the sheer sake of destruction; but the old pewter drinking vessels were still there, and these were carried out to succor the injured.

After this, it occurred to me that the wounded shouldn't be allowed to lie in the square all night, and I sent people into the Grand Monastery for blankets and the simple beds on which the monks slept, and the injured were carried in blankets to the guild halls and laid on the beds. There was no doctor or surgeon to care for them, but I saw that their wounds were bandaged.

At midnight, an armed group of young men arrived, carrying pikes and led by one of the Warriors of the Sea in his antique bronze armor. I sent them to the Harbor Gate to keep watch on the enemy. Their leader soon came running back.

"The corsairs haven't left. They're still on the docks and in the harbor, trying to carry away all the ships."

I could only shrug. "Let us know if they come back to town, will you?"

The Warrior peered past the visor of his ancient helmet. "Do you want us to fight them?"

"I don't think that would be advisable."

Toward dawn, another armed party arrived under the command of Sir Towsley Cobb, whose park and country house lay a few leagues north of the city. He was a small, bustling man in armor, with a little smear of a mustache and a youthful countenance. He and his sons rode chargers, and with them marched the men of his household, armed with clubs and spears.

"Who is in charge?" he called.

I was with a group by the fountain, trying to organize a party to round up food supplies, and I walked to the baronet and his party. Sir Towsley looked me up and down and seemed unimpressed.

"What exactly has happened in the city?" Getting straight to the point.

I told of the Aekoi attack, the looting of the city, the fires, the captives carried away, the corsairs still busy in the harbor, the injured being carried to the guild halls.

The baronet nodded. "And you are organizing things? Who are you again?"

"I am Quillifer, Sir Towsley."

"Ah." The mustache twitched. "The Butcher's son." The baronet's tone was dismissive, and my assumed authority twisted and vanished like smoke in a breeze.

"I shall take command, then," the baronet said. "I shall establish my post in the New Castle." He turned to his sons. "Set these people in order, and have them do something useful."

I tried to explain to the sons what had been done and what still needed doing, but they ignored me and did whatever suited them—and they rarely agreed about anything, so amid the fraternal anarchy only the loudest voice prevailed, and that temporarily.

I decided there was no reason to stay, and went to Princess Street in search of my family.

In the wan light of the rising sun, I found them all. My father and the apprentices had held the door with their pollaxes and killed at least three Aekoi, whose bodies still lay stretched on the pavement. The reivers then fired the thatch, and my father had known that to fly into the street would mean nothing but their execution at the hands of pirates angered by the loss of their mates; and so he had stayed at his post till the smoke overcame him. He and the apprentices were unwounded, and had died before the floor above collapsed. Their weapons were still in their hands.

My sisters and mother had locked themselves behind the stout door of the buttery, and lay with their arms about one another under a shelf, where they had probably crawled in search of fresher air. They had smothered, and were not burned at all, only covered with a fine silver layer of ash.

I knelt by the bodies in the cramped, ruined space, and I saw the fine ash tremble in the lashes of my sister Alice, and at the sight I felt my heart swell in my breast until there was no room left for breath. I staggered out of the house sobbing, and a few doors down the road crouched beneath the overturned cart of a tinsmith, and surrendered for a long black hour to despair.

When I next crawled into the light, the sun, behind a low listless blanket of cloud, had risen well over the ramparts of Ethlebight's useless walls. Limping, muscles an agony, I returned to the ruins of my home, and I picked my mother and sisters from the ruin of the buttery and brought them out into the street, where I laid them as best as I could on the bricks. I dragged out my father and the apprentices and laid them out as well. The pale, waxen faces of my family gazed sightlessly into the sky, and suddenly I knew I couldn't leave them like that.

I turned up the street and walked through a broken door into the shop of Mrs. Peake the dressmaker. All the expensive fabric had been looted, but I found a bolt of unbleached muslin, and there I made simple shrouds for my family, which I draped over them. I weighed the shrouds down with broken brick at each corner, then went back into the ruins and took my father's pollaxe.

"I will come back to you," I told them, then turned and limped away down Princess Street.

I turned into the broader lane that led to Scarcroft Square. Others walked in the same direction, and I looked to see if I knew them. I saw a grim-looking barber-surgeon named Moss, a frightened boy called Julian, and a stout, furious, red-faced woman with clenched fists, who looked ready to give the corsairs' admiral a box on the ears.

And then I saw a man in faded, soiled blues and yellows, and my heart gave a leap.

"Kevin!"

My friend lurched into sight, fair hair uncombed and straggling over his unshaven face. He stared, slow to recognize me, but I rushed to Kevin and embraced him.

"I saw your father!" I said. "He's taken but alive!"

"Praise Pastas," Kevin said. His voice was a coarse whisper. He licked swollen lips, then said, "I need water."

I took his arm and led him to Scarcroft Square and the fountain. Kevin drank greedily, then washed his face and blinked at me with reddened eyes.

"My mother?" he asked. "My sister and brother?"

"I didn't see them," I said. "They were probably taken."

"I must go to the house."

The Spellman house was one of the grandest on the square, with walls patterned with bricks of different colors, its chimneys carved with mythological beasts, and its many windows brilliant in the sun. The windows were less brilliant now: faceted glass panes built to dazzle in the sun's rays had been knocked out, possibly under the impression they were gemstones. The door stood open, its lock smashed. Kevin walked into the hall and called out. There was no answer.

With heavy, reluctant feet, Kevin trudged up the steep, narrow stair. He turned his face away from a streak of blood on the upper step.

"This is where my father tried to fight them," he said. "I came from my room to see what was causing the commotion, and he turned to me and told me to run." He closed his eyes. "The Pilgrim help me, I obeyed."

"You could not have fought them," I said. "You would only have been caught or killed."

"I should have tried to save my brother," Kevin said. "Or my sister. But the pirates were right on my heels." He looked down the upstairs hall. "I ran up to the servants' floor, and bolted through the grooms' room to the dormer, and out the window. I was shouting for everyone to run, but I don't think they understood." He turned to me. "I was the only one who got out. I heard more fighting in the house, and there was a swarm of pirates in the square in front, and some took shots at me." He raised his hands. "I ran across the rooftops. And when I saw they were sending men up on the roofs, I hid. I burrowed beneath the topmost layer of thatch between two dormers, and stayed there until just a while ago." He gave a forlorn look down the hall. Tears overfilled his eyes and spilled down his cheeks. "I should have stayed," he said.

I took a step toward my friend and put a hand on his arm. "You did the right thing," I said. "Someone must remain in Ethlebight and manage the business, and make up the ransom to save the rest."

Kevin stood silent for a moment, and then his chin rose and a hard light caught his eyes. "The ransom!" he said.

He ran down the stairs past me and through the door into his father's countinghouse, and there looked for the door, hidden in the carved paneling, where the ready money was kept. The door had been torn open and the contents looted, and many of the remaining panels had been torn from the walls in an attempt to find more hidden valuables. The heavy ledgers, with records of the Spellmans' affairs, were scattered on the floor. Without a word Kevin turned, and knocked shoulders with me in his haste to dash again up the stair. From there he ran to his parents' bedroom, where he beheld the strongbox torn from the window seat where it had been hidden. The strongbox was nearly three feet long, two broad, and a foot high, made of thick oaken panels strapped with iron, and with a complicated geared mechanism that, on the turning of a stout key, would shoot no less than eight steel bolts into place to secure the contents.

The reivers hadn't tried to find the key: instead, they'd hacked the box to bits with a halberd or some other heavy weapon. With a groan, Kevin threw himself on the floor and searched the wreckage, and found nothing. He rose and turned to me. "The silver's gone, of course," he said. "But also the *contracts*! Loan agreements! The deed to the house! Deeds to other properties!" He looked at me. "Of what use would any of that be to pirates?"

The loans might be sold at a discount to brokers, I supposed, but the usefulness of the rest was obscure.

"They could not read or write," I judged. "So, they took all." I looked over the wreckage of the room, saw the drawers pulled from the bureau and emptied, the closets emptied of all fine clothes, the looking-glass smashed. The Aekoi had even carried away the feather mattress.

And then the sight of the broken strongbox brought to me a memory erased by hours of pain, fatigue, and misery.

"My father's strongbox!" I said. "I'd forgotten it."

Kevin's expression mirrored my own surprise. "And I had forgotten your family entirely," he said. "Are they—are they taken?"

"Dead."

Kevin looked stricken. "All?" he said, and I nodded. Kevin stepped to me and embraced me. "I had thought only of my own kin," he said. "Yet how much better my parents are in captivity than yours in the grave."

Not in the grave yet, I thought. I returned Kevin's embrace, and said, "We have survived, and now we must rebuild. We have nothing with which to reproach ourselves." I hoped this last statement was true.

We returned to my house, and found the strongbox where it had fallen to the ground amid the burning ruins of an upper story. I searched my father's body to find the key on his belt, where he had always carried it. Inside the box were three gold royals, enough silver to make up twenty-four royals in value, a few pennies, and some foreign money of uncertain value—hardly enough to rebuild the house. There was also the gold alderman's chain belonging to my father. Documents—property deeds, records of money owed to Alderman Quillifer, agreements to deliver sheep and beeves—all had burned to ashes when the box baked in the fire.

There will be many suits at law over all this, I thought. I would put

Lawyer Dacket on retainer, if I could; but since my master was lost, I should hire the first surviving advocate I could find.

The strongbox was too heavy to carry with me, so I found a box with a broken lid that the reivers had thrown away, and put the money and the chain in it, then bound the lid with twine.

Kevin and I returned to Scarcroft Square, where a surviving alderman, an apothecary named Gribbins, was arguing with Sir Towsley Cobb over who was in charge. I could not bring myself to care about the outcome, and Kevin and I went into the Spellman house, where we found some cheese in the servants' pantry and made the best meal we could, after which I went to sleep on a groom's pallet, lying on bundles of sweet-smelling rushes. My last memory was seeing Kevin, who had got pen and paper from his father's study, staring at the paper and murmuring to himself as he made a record of all of his father's transactions that he could remember.

In the morning, I found Kevin asleep in his father's countinghouse, his head on the desk, the ledgers stacked around him, the candle burned out, his fingertips black with ink. We finished the cheese and walked to the square, where we found Gribbins and the Cobb family still arguing over the proper course of action. Gribbins should have been overwhelmed by sheer numbers, but the Cobbs could never agree with one another, and the arguments looked like every man or boy for himself. Nevertheless, some things seemed to have been accomplished—there were regular companies of men drilling with pikes and firelocks, and enormous cauldrons had been set up to make porridge out of whatever grains could be brought to the square. At least one bakery was delivering loaves of bread, but these were promptly confiscated by the Cobbs and doled out to whoever they saw fit. Sir Towsley and his sons dismissed me without a word, but Kevin's social prominence rated a loaf, which he shared with me as we considered what next to do.

Smoke hung again in the air. The Aekoi had towed off whatever ships they could from the port, and burned the rest along with the looted warehouses. They had not left the Duisland coast, but moved most of their power to Cow Island while small squadrons of chebecs patrolled the coast in search of fresh prey.

Kevin's family concern had lost one pinnace set afire and another carried away, and Kevin fretted after a third ship that was expected soon to return from Varcellos, and might sail right amid the pirate fleet before they knew they were in danger. He paced in agitation, but I was too weary and sore to keep pace with him.

While prowling the square, Kevin overheard Gribbins arguing for building a funeral pyre for the dead, an idea which the Cobbs, for the moment, declared premature.

"They're going to wait till carrion bursts the crows' bellies," Kevin said in disgust.

"I am not going to burn my family on a common pyre," I said. "Nor wait for the crows. Or that quarrelsome oriole Sir Towsley Cobb."

Kevin and I returned to Princess Street and confiscated a cocking cart from a neighbor who kept fighting birds—all the cocks eaten now, it seemed, and the neighbor carried away. I threw the cages off the cart, and made further space by removing the rear seat intended for the groom. The cart was pulled to where my family had been laid on the bricks. I saw that the bodies of the two apprentices had been carried away, I presumed by their families.

Kevin mutely assisted as I lifted my family into the cart, and in the absence of a horse, we two set ourselves between the shafts and pulled the cart out the North Gate, and to the city of the dead that stretched north from Ethlebight toward the old, abandoned city upriver.

The necropolis was deserted, and a fitful north wind sighed and muttered among the half-sunken tombs and tilted, lichen-crusted slabs that stood as the silent guardians of the worm-eaten dead. Cows and sheep grazed upon the grass, and had cropped away the underbrush to reveal old mounds, broken urns, and a few old bones that had worked their way to the surface. Here, in the shadow of the gray tomb of an extinct noble family, was a section of ground owned by the Quillifers, where Quillifers dating back to the foundation of new Ethlebight were buried. I had taken a pair of spades from a shop on Royall Street as I passed, intending to bury my family in a single grave atop my grandfather until more proper burial could be arranged. But on the sight of the old tomb, I paused for thought.

The outlines of the tomb's irregular blocks of gray stone were revealed by crumbling plaster. For some reason, there were geometrical objects standing on the four corners: a sphere, a cube, a tetrahedron, and a cone.

I smashed the tomb's rusted padlock with three swings of my spade. Because the tomb had partly sunk into the soft soil, there was some digging before I could wrench open the iron door. Ancient hinges shrieked, and birds took flight from nearby monuments.

The tomb smelled of damp earth. Lying on their slabs, beneath moth-eaten shrouds, the sad remains of a noble house gazed blankly at the sun for the first time in generations. My spade cleared away skeletal rubbish from a pair of the slabs, and then Kevin and I carried my family into the darkness that was their new home. My father was laid to rest on one slab, with little Alice lying under his arm; and on the other slab, my mother, Cornelia, with Barbara. I draped the unbleached muslin over them for shrouds.

"I will raise you a tomb of your own," I told my family. "I swear it."

Kevin nodded. "I am witness to the oath," he affirmed.

And then I heard the sound of hoofbeats outside the tomb, and I froze, my mind alight with the absurd possibility that after all this I would be arrested for tomb-breaking. Cautiously I peered out the door.

A carriage rolled past on its way to the North Gate, drawn by four weary horses. Burly footmen rode atop the vehicle, and I could see a heraldic badge on the door.

"That would be Judge Travers," I said, "come for the Assizes. A fine mess will he find, with the Cobbs and Gribbins at odds and the docks still smoldering."

"Ay," said Kevin. "There's more for him to do than to judge whether or not Sir Stanley Mattingly stole a river."

We left the tomb, and I closed the door and stopped it with turf and stones. My body ached, and I rolled my shoulders against the pain and looked at the silent tomb with its geometric figures. My eyes lifted from the rusted iron door to the name carved above the lintel, and I read, SHAYPE.

I smiled. From somewhere a warbler called.

I cleared my throat. "Ta-sa-ran-geh," I chanted. "Ta-sa-ran-geh-*ko*."

Kevin was surprised, but then quickly joined in the chant of the Warriors of the Sea. We circled the tomb as the chant rose in the air, the chant so old that no one knew what it meant. But well I knew the words had meaning for my father, and so with the chant I sent my father on to his blue-skinned Pastas, the god he had served all his life, and with whom he had shared food on the last day of his life. Nor did I forget my father's correction, "Ren-far-el-den-sa-*fa*-yu."

Five slow revolutions of the tomb brought the chant to an end. Here the Warriors of the Sea, at the festival, would have started over, but I felt a single repetition was enough, and fell silent. The necropolis was still. I felt my spirits rise, and a strange stirring in my soul, as if I had in some way been touched by the divine, perhaps a blue-skinned god who whispered some half-heard affirmation, and now welcomed my family to their new home.

I wiped the stinging tears from my eyes, blew out my breath, and turned toward the town.

"Shall we bring the cart back?" Kevin asked.

"It may be useful still," I said. "Our lives are full of ruins that yet need to be shifted." So, Kevin and I stood in the traces again, and brought the cart back to Ethlebight.

I limped as I walked, a hamstring protesting with every step. Pain wracked my arms and shoulders, and my back was a torment.

There was nothing, I thought, to keep me here. My family was dead, my house destroyed, my master taken prisoner. Kevin had offered a chance of employment, but that was before his own family trade had been brought to the edge of ruin.

I would take the money I had found in the strongbox and go to the capital at Selford. What I had in my box was enough to live on for two or three years, if I were careful, and surely I would find employment in that time, and be on my way to becoming an advocate at the court, or a member of the House of Burgesses, or a judge renowned for my wisdom . . . or all three, as Kevin had said.

Though what I most wanted now was to be the admiral of a fleet, to bring fury and destruction upon the Aekoi.

On the way we passed by Crook's bookshop. The place had been broken into, and books hurled from their shelves by reivers in search of money, but nothing had been destroyed or burnt.

Without a word exchanged, Kevin and I began to move the books to the cocking cart. I had browsed the shop regularly, and knew the contents well. I chose only the best—tomes on law, rhetoric, and history, the epics of Bello, the entire cycle of the Teazel romances, the love poems of Tarantua, the comic verse of Rudland, the tales of Erpingham. We piled the cart so high that it could hardly be moved.

If Crook were ever ransomed, the books would be returned. And if Crook were never released, the books would form the core of a fine library.

After unloading, we put the cocking cart in the courtyard behind the Spellman house. I had seen Judge Travers's heavy coach standing in Scarcroft Square, and it occurred to me that my storied legal career might as well begin now as later. I left Kevin with his lists of debtors, and returned to the square to find the judge in conference with Gribbins and various Cobbs. I did not approach, but went to the narrow house where my master Dacket had lived, and climbed the stair to the office. There, amid a riot of destruction, I found my master's fisher fur–trimmed robe with the reivers' footprints still on it, and cleaned the robe as well as I could. I cleaned myself as well, and my apprentice cap, and then found some wax tablets in a cupboard and put them in the pockets of the robe. I donned the robe—very narrow in the shoulders, but it must do—took a stylus, and then returned to the square again to approach the judge with as much gravity as I could manage.

Travers was a tall, solidly built man in a judge's robe of black watered silk trimmed with glossy otter fur. His posture was military, and he took immense care of his own dignity, which was enhanced by his white pointed beard, a curling halo of white hair, and his commanding blue eyes.

"There should be an informal census as soon as possible." His trained rhetorician's voice spoke with the accent of Bonille. "Those bringing relief must know how many souls are in need of help."

Gribbins and the various Cobbs seemed impressed by this argument. Their own thoughts had not reached so far as a census.

"And there should be a fire watch set," Travers said. "New conflagrations may yet be brought to life by smoldering embers."

"We have no lack of volunteers," said Gribbins. "We can set watches—and should, to prevent looting."

I waited patiently at Travers's elbow, my stylus poised above a wax tablet, until the judge became aware of me.

I donned my learnèd-advocate face. "My lord," I said. "I wonder if your lordship is in need of anyone to keep a record of these decisions."

Travers's blue eyes surveyed me from cap to shoe, and back again. "Who, sir," he said, "are you?"

"The Butcher's son!" called Sir Towsley Cobb in mockery. "The Butcher's son dressed up like a lawyer!"

I ignored the baronet. "My name is Quillifer, my lord. I'm apprentice to the advocate Dacket."

"And where is your master?"

"Taken by the reivers, my lord, and his family with him."

"I already have a secretary," Travers said, and frowned across the square at a young man—dressed in satins, bejeweled—who was amusing himself by brandishing a pollaxe borrowed from members of a militia company. Laughter trickled from the group.

"Well," Travers said, and turned back to me. "You may prove of use."

I made notes of the day's actions: watches posted, surveys made of all granaries, of all available weapons, of cannon and gunpowder. Plans made for an informal census. Scouts set to keep a watch on the Aekoi. A search made for all surviving doctors and surgeons. Clothing and blankets to be distributed to those without homes. Bakeries to be operated through the night. And bodies to be brought out of the city early the next day, and burned. Gangs were set to work taking apart the temporary stage set up in the square, to be used in the pyre.

I learned much from Travers as I trailed the judge through the afternoon. Not so much about the proper response to a catastrophe, but about how to make oneself heard and, having been heard, obeyed. Outside the boundaries of his courtroom, Travers had no authority in Ethlebight—he wasn't an alderman, or the Lord Warden or the Lord Lieutenant of the County, or an important noble. But he carried himself with a quiet, erect air of authority, and he spoke quietly and with finality, and what he spoke made sense. His success was aided by the accent of Bonille, which carried with it a suggestion of urbanity and sophistication and the air of the royal court, with its subtle, unspoken promise of patronage and power. By the end of the afternoon, even the Cobbs were eager to run Judge Travers's errands.

This in contrast with the apothecary Gribbins, who shared a great deal with Travers—the white beard, the blue eyes, the distinguished profession—but who despite his status as alderman seemed unable to get anyone to listen to him. He made some good arguments, but more bad ones, and he tended to wander from one to the other. His ideas clattered with each other and sometimes collapsed in hapless confusion. By contrast, Travers raised his ideas one at a time, reached a decision, and then offered the next.

More people arrived over the course of the day, nobles and gentry with their personal following, among them a pair of aldermen who had been at their houses in the country during the attack. So, a rump town council was able to convene, and once they assembled in the city hall and declared themselves in session, Travers told them what to do.

Apparently, not every pantry had been looted. The day ended with a dinner of spit-roasted meats, bread, and beer, which my famished stomach accepted with gratitude.

Afterward, I made my way back to my groom's straw bed at the Spellman home, and paused in the square for a moment to sniff the fresh, cool wind hunting down from the north. For a moment, I felt a sensation of soaring delight; and then I thought of the wind muttering around the Shaype tomb, and the scent of ash as I laid my family to rest, and for a moment the wind seemed to blow bitter through the empty hollow of my chest, and to freeze to my eyelids the tears that rose unbidden to my eyes.

I had always known that I would leave Ethlebight, but I had been in no hurry to do so—I had been content to live with my family, amuse myself as an apprentice lawyer, and spend my free time in pursuit of women and love.

But now my boyhood had gone in a single blazing night, and with it the security and support of my family and city. The catastrophe had thrown me into premature independence, reliant in the war-ravaged world entirely on my own gifts. To my former self, my talents had been toys, baubles for my own amusement; but now the game had turned grim, and the stakes were life and death.

If I did not seek my fortune, fortune would abandon me in the ruins of my past.

The Warriors of the Sea did not dance on the first day of the Autumn Festival, and the Mermaids did not sing. The actors didn't perform their plays, and the guilds did not parade. Instead, a small crowd watched as a pair of priests prayed outside the great old temple north of the city, and sheep were sacrificed along with a white heifer. The rump council and the members of the Embassy Royal, followed by me, came into the temple for a personal interview with the god.

The temple was built in the old annular style of the Empire: round, with a double row of columns, a dome, and a peaked portico. Embedded in the white limestone were remains of the god's own creatures: skeletal fish, sea lilies, sharks' teeth, the spiral shells of nautili. The dome was covered in bronze scales that had corroded to shades of sea green, and looked as if a piece of the ocean had been captured under a glass bowl.

The azure-skinned god stood atop a plinth in his sanctuary, five yards tall, pieced together of ivory, bronze, and a glittering array of blue stones: lapis, kyanite, turquoise, blue sunstone, chalcedony, iolite, and aquamarine, with eyes of blue opal that shifted subtly in the light, at times bright, at times somber, at times pensive and withdrawn. A net of copper wire dangled from one hand, filled with jeweled fishes; and the other held a gold-tipped trident.

The light of sacrificial fires glimmered in the eyes of the god as I entered on the heels of the Embassy. Standing quietly behind the others, dressed in my robe and cap, I bowed to Pastas on his plinth, and politely voiced to the deity my hopes for a journey to the capital.

The grandly named Embassy Royal would travel to the capital of Selford, and petition the throne for aid for survivors, protection against the reivers, and ransom for the captives. If, that is, they were able to catch King Stilwell before he departed for the winter capital of Howel.

The embassy consisted of the alderman Gribbins, who had somehow dithered himself onto the delegation, and Richard Hawtrey, who
because his father was the Count of Wenlock, bore the courtesy title
Lord Utterback. Utterback was a saturnine young man of twenty-four
years, dark-browed, scant of speech, and careless of manner. He had
ridden into Ethlebight two days after the sack, leading a company of
thirty men, all well equipped out of his father's armory. And though
his martial bearing had won a degree of popular regard, he hadn't
been nominated to the delegation on account of his ability to command men, but rather the letters patent that ennobled his father,
which would guarantee him a hearing in the capital.

If, that is, Utterback could be persuaded to speak at all. So far, he
showed little inclination.

Judge Travers, alas, would not make the journey. He had assizes
to conduct, not just in Ethlebight but elsewhere in the southwest, and
he held no real authority in the city. He did, however, provide me with
a letter of introduction to an advocate in Selford, from whom I might
be able to find employment.

There was certainly none to be had in Ethlebight. Even if I were
willing to act on behalf of Lawyer Dacket's clients, none were left. Mr.
Trew, whose river had been stolen by Sir Stanley Mattingly, was now
a captive on Cow Island. So was Alec Royce, who had cut a fern tree
in the King's forest, and had been freed from his jail cell not by the
judge but by the reivers who had come to enslave him.

The council and the delegates bowed their heads before the statue
of Pastas, and the priests asked for the god's blessing on the journey.
Their voices echoed beneath the dome. Sacrificial firelight ran up the
golden trident as the Embassy Royal promised to conduct their business for the benefit of all, without partiality or favor. After which the
formal part of the ceremony was over, and the group broke up. I saw
Utterback and Gribbins together, and approached.

"I have arranged for us to travel in a carriage of some magnificence,"

Gribbins said. "We shall not be out of place in the capital, I assure you."

"Didn't bring a carriage myself," Utterback murmured.

"I hope your lordship will approve of my choice. It is the carriage used by the Court of the Teazel Bird to carry their King, and is ornamented with allegorical carvings and the armorial bearings of the court's members." Gribbins smiled with the pleasure of his own self-regard. "We will have no reason to be ashamed of our equipage, my lord, not in the capital or anywhere else."

"It's very fine, I'm sure," Utterback said. "You will excuse me?"

He turned, took a pace, and encountered me, who stood as ever with my stylus and wax tablet ready, and my attentive-courtier face fixed firmly to his visage.

"I beg your pardon," I said, and took a step away to allow Utterback to pass. As the count's son walked on, frowning at the floor, I followed.

"My lord," I said, "it's clear that the mission of the Embassy Royal will require a large correspondence, both with the court and with those here in Ethlebight. I wonder if you are considering a secretary to manage these affairs."

Utterback's frown deepened, and he halted. He looked at me briefly, then returned his gaze to the floor.

"I write my own letters," he said.

"Of course, my lord, but—"

Lord Utterback looked up again. "Write my own letters," he said, with more emphasis, and turned to walk on.

I saw little point in pursuit. Instead, I turned back to Gribbins and asked the same question.

"So irksome will be your correspondence," I said, "I wonder if the Embassy should employ a secretary."

Gribbins smoothed his beard with ringed fingers. "The town has not seen fit to vote the Embassy a secretary," he said, "greatly though it would add to the dignity of our emprise. Alas, we will have to write our own petition to the throne."

"Ay, you must," said I, "if you know the form."

Gribbins looked up sharply. "The form?" he asked.

I put on my pompous-magistrate face and affected a sniff. "Boors and rustics may scrawl their petitions on scraps of paper and push them through the crack beneath the palace door," I said, "but the Embassy of a great city would be expected to know the proper form for a royal petition, the modus sanctified by protocol, usage, and the custom of centuries. Everything from the choice of the calfskin to the arrangement of the seals must respect the proprieties." I looked at Gribbins in alarm. "Surely, you do not want the petition rejected because some chamberlain turns up his nose at deficiencies in the punctilio, or a lawyer points out infelicities in the phrasing!"

Gribbins clutched at the purfled border of his robe. "Indeed I do not!" he said. "Where can I find this form?"

"Many lawyers would know," I said. "But of course, we have few advocates left in the city, and these are consumed entirely in preparation for the delayed assizes. I myself may claim a clear proficiency in the art of the petition, as Master Dacket drilled me ceaselessly in the praxis." I drew closer to the apothecary. "Do you know, sir, that the wording in the induction is drawn from Mallio's *Rhetorica Forensica*, and in the Rawlings translation, not in the Delward as you might expect?"

"Not the Delward," Gribbins muttered, "but the Rawlings." His voice sounded like a blind mouse scrabbling in its nest of paper.

Within another two minutes, I had secured my post as the secretary for the Embassy Royal.

The Embassy left not the next day, for an astrologer hired by Gribbins had declared the day inauspicious, but on the afternoon of the day following, which the occultist declared ideal.

"A pity that this magus, so perfect in his auguries, did not fore-warn the city's sack," I said to Kevin.

"He could not scry the stars," Kevin said. "Remember the night was cloudy."

We stood in the square and watched the loading of the expedition's grand carriage. The carriage was a great, heavy object, tall and stately as a galleon, and like a galleon festooned with ornaments and carv-ings painted gold, knights and monsters twined in battle. A smaller, much plainer carriage, like a light, agile pinnace, carried the baggage.

The Court of the Teazel Bird, whose King the great carriage bore in procession, was a fraternity of wealthy burgesses who dressed as knights and lord of ancient times, and named themselves after the legendary heroes of the Teazel romances. They feasted regularly in their towered palace on Scarcroft Square, and sponsored jousts and other entertainments on days of festival. But now most of them, including this year's King, had been carried away by the corsairs, and the survivors were content to loan their carriage to the Embassy.

"That great heavy thing will take forever to reach Selford," Kevin said. "Wouldn't a fast messenger serve better?"

"A messenger will not serve Gribbins's vanity," I said. "He wishes to make a grand entrance into Selford, and become a great figure at the court."

"And Lord Utterback does not check this?" Kevin said. "He puts up with this preening fathead?"

"Utterback can't be bothered to oppose or propose. He can barely be bothered to speak."

"Ah, well." Kevin made a sour face. "Ethlebight will then be on its own for the winter."

"The winter will at least drive the corsairs from our door. Those little galleys of theirs will never bear our winter gales."

A small group came from the broken doors of the city hall, Gribbins and Utterback, Judge Travers, the Cobbs, and Sir Stanley Mattingly clanking in armor. When the reivers had occupied Cow Island, Sir Stanley had brought the entire household away from Mutton Island, marching them along the mucky causeway at low tide, and with as many sheep and goats as his shepherds could bring. The dependents now lived in the Forest of Ailey, feasting on mutton where the corsairs were unlikely to find them; and Sir Stanley had donned armor and come riding on his big-framed yellow horse to Ethlebight, where he anointed himself the savior of the city.

In my capacity as secretary to the council, I had transcribed the great debate between Sir Stanley and Sir Towsley Cobb over which would be appointed Deputy Lord Lieutenant and placed in charge of the county's defense. The two had shouted and roared and proclaimed, and in the end, Sir Stanley had outbawled both his rival and his sons and secured the appointment. Sir Towsley had to be content with becoming Deputy Lord Warden, an appointment meaningless as the Lord Warden commanded only royal troops, and the royal soldiers in the New Castle had all been taken or slaughtered.

In any case, the appointments would have to be confirmed by the King.

I appreciated the scene as a kind of low, earthy comedy; but otherwise couldn't help but note that one candidate for commander of the military despised me as a Butcher's son, while the other had shot at me only a few days earlier. I kept my eyes on my wax tablet when Sir Stanley glanced my way, and decided that, under the circumstances, I was not destined for martial renown.

At least I was pleased the milkmaid Ella was safe. I pictured her lying on a bed of moss in the Forest of Ailey, her heart-shaped face turned up to the night sky, the moonlight a shimmer in her dark eyes. *Did she think of me,* I wondered, *as she lay there, and wonder how I fared, caught in the fall of the city and perhaps killed? Did she mourn me, without knowing I was alive? Did she long for me, alone on her verdant couch?*

Gribbins began to speak from the steps of the city hall. The alderman had prepared a farewell address, and he was determined to read it even though my audience consisted of perhaps a dozen bystanders, plus the footmen and servants atop the carriage. I stood in an attitude of respect while my mind returned to midnight thoughts of Ella, languorous on her bed of moss. A voice murmured in my ear, one with the accent of Bonille.

"Ambition is laudable in its way. But advancement comes in its season, and a man who grasps at a passing opportunity with such desperate fervor runs the risk of becoming ridiculous."

I turned to Judge Travers and bowed. "You refer to our vaunting embassy?"

"Not at all." Amusement played about Travers's lips. "If anyone, I refer to *you*, and to your great petition." He reached out a hand, not unkindly, and touched my shoulder. "I trust you have acquired a copy of *Rhetorica Forensica* in the Delward translation, and not the Rawlings?"

I felt heat rise to my face. "My lord, I have so provided myself." The Delward was part of the booty from Crook's bookshop.

"That is well. I have assured Alderman Gribbins of your ability, but he will want to check your work."

"I hope that he shall." I realized that I spoke a bit more defiantly than I intended, and I lowered my voice. "I thank you, my lord, for your kind interest."

"I think you may do well in the capital," Travers said, "particularly if you learn to mask your ambition behind a pretense of humility."

I felt my lip curl in anger. "Sir, I have lately encountered much in my life to keep me humble."

Again the judge touched my shoulder. "I believe, young Goodman Quillifer, that I did say *pretense*." And with a smile, he turned away. Kevin's voice came into my other ear.

"That seemed unnecessarily cryptic."

I let out a breath, then turned to Kevin. "Nay," I said. "Not cryptic enough."

Judge Travers had warned me against grasping for advantage; but that grasping was what I saw all about me, a greedy rush for vacant offices and honors, the candidates all a-froth with vaunting and vanity. Why should I refrain when everyone else was clutching with both hands?

At last the Embassy Royal left the stairs and went into the carriage, and I gave a farewell embrace to Kevin and followed Gribbins into the carriage. The scent of leather and polish rose to my senses. I took the little sword from my belt, tucked up my lawyer's robe around me, and prepared to sit next to the alderman. I became aware that Gribbins was staring at me with his rheumy blue eyes.

"What mean you here?" said the alderman.

"I, sir?" I was surprised. "I mean to sit. Would you rather have this place?"

"Young man," said Gribbins, "you are a servant. Admittedly, a secretary is a superior sort of servant, but still your place is atop the carriage, or with the luggage in the servants' conveyance."

I was too startled to be offended. "As you wish, sir."

I opened the carriage door and prepared to step out, but Gribbins put me another question.

"Quillifer," he said, "have you recovered your father's chain? His alderman's chain, I mean?"

I had given up my seat, and was not inclined to give up anything else. "It was lost in the fire," I said, the truth as far as it went.

"The chain belongs to the office," Gribbins said, "not to the bearer. If you were to find it, you should return it to the council."

Judge Travers had begun a fund to pay the ransoms of the corsairs' captives, and in a spasm of anger, guilt, and frustration, I had donated half the money I'd recovered from my father's strongbox. The chain I fully intended to keep as a memory of my father—or, if necessary, to sell it link by link to support myself in the capital.

"The house was burned," I said. "And my family with it."

The apothecary made a fussy little tilt of his head. "Can't be helped, I suppose." And then he frowned. "I see you carry a sword."

"I took it from one of the corsairs, sir."

"Did your father have a grant of arms?"

I blinked. The pertinence of armorial bearings escaped me.

"No," I said. "He didn't."

"If your father did not have a grant of arms," Gribbins said, "he was not a gentleman, and neither therefore are you. I do not mean to say anything against your condition, but nevertheless you are not entitled to bear a sword in public."

"Ah." I considered this, and put on a dutiful-apprentice face. "May I keep the sword until we are out of range of the enemy? I should prefer not to be without a weapon."

While Gribbins gnawed on this matter, I glanced at Lord Utterback, and saw a glint of sardonic amusement in the young man's eyes.

"Keep the sword," Utterback said.

Gribbins chewed his lip. "Are you certain, my lord?" he asked. "I wish to be most observant of all the regularities, so as not to bring disrepute upon the dignity of the Embassy."

Utterback closed his eyes and leaned his head against the plush velvet cushion. "He may keep the sword," he said.

"Keep it *now*? By which I mean, for the present? Or also in the capital? Would that not be irregular?"

I did not stay for the answer, if there was one, but instead climbed onto the carriage roof, where my fellow drudges welcomed me with the smirks plain on their faces. There were four of them: the coachman, reeking of brandy, and three footmen, each armed with a hardwood truncheon and a blunderbuss. I sat and looked out over the square to see if Travers had witnessed this valuable lesson in humility, but apparently, the judge had left the scene.

The driver snapped his whip, the postilion kicked his lead horse with his special reinforced boot, and the great carriage groaned into motion. It swayed across the square and onto Eastgate Street, nearly deserted, and with burnt-out buildings gaping amid the others like the black stumps of broken teeth in a prizefighter's smile. I couldn't help but compare this dispiriting sight to the bustle that had carried me down Royall Street only days before, the great pulse of sailors and hucksters, carters and shopkeepers that had flowed through the veins of the city.

Soon enough, the carriage passed beneath the gatehouse and out into the country. It was a fine autumn day, the sun bright and the air cool, and it was no hardship to be in the open.

I looked past the two footmen on the rear seat and watched Ethlebight lurch out of sight. Before the raid, the city held eight thousand people, with another six or eight thousand in neighboring villages, farms, and estates. The reivers had taken four thousand at least, according to Judge Travers's inexact poll, and could have taken more if they wished—and probably they hadn't so wished, because their raid had been successful beyond their most ambitious dreams. They had as many captives as their ships could carry, and no need to seek more.

And for the most part, they had taken the best. After scaling the harbor wall on ropes and rope ladders—for sailors climb well—and then taking the River Gatehouse, the invaders had split into several groups, each with its own mission. The New Castle was taken as easily as the gatehouse, and the other gates were secured. And then groups set to work rounding up loot and captives, attacking first the wealthiest districts of the town, then expanding outward.

The Lord Mayor had been taken, most of the aldermen, the Lord Lieutenant and the Warden of the Castle, and the chief merchants like Gregory Spellman. Countinghouses had been plundered, taking even the contracts and deeds. A few hundred were killed when they resisted, and a few hundred more when they proved unworthy of ransom.

With the best folk gone, survivors now squabbled over what remained. The Cobbs and Sir Stanley, Gribbins and the supine Lord Utterback. Picking through the ashes, preening over the prospect of new titles and new dignities.

And none of them speaking aloud what to me was perfectly obvious: that the city had been betrayed. Someone who knew the way had taken the enemy fleet through the twisting channels that separated Ethlebight from the sea, and directed the corsairs to where they could find the most plunder and the richest hostages. The raid had been planned by a mind that knew the city intimately.

Perhaps it was wise for the city not to consider this at present. A hunt for a traitor would be a distraction, especially as the turncoat had almost certainly sailed from the city with his new friends and his share of the loot. At best, they would find a scapegoat, hang him, and the real villain would go free.

But still, that traitor had killed my family, and I groped in my own mind for a name that seemed just out of reach. Someone who hated the city, or who had suffered a reversal of some sort and taken this obscene way to fill his empty coffers . . .

No name presented itself. And the carriage lurched and shuddered its way east, and left the plundered city and its mysteries behind.

CHAPTER FIVE

even days later, I sat at a table at the Men and Mayds Tavern
by the waterfront in Amberstone, and scratched with a quill
on a piece of paper.

*To the Worthy and Esteemed Mercer Kevin Spellman,
from his schoolfriend, the unproven ambassador Quillifer,
Greetings:*

  *The Embassy Royal stayeth a third night in Amberstone,
as Master Gribbins hath not yet received the worship and
acclaim of every single inhabitant thereof. There will be
another banquet tonight, in the guild hall, & a breakfast tomorrow at the expense of the Worshipfull Guild
of Apothecaries, & because the splendor & gravity of the
Embassy knoweth no limit, Master Gribbins will wax
full of rhetoric & windy addresses, all of which will be
placed in his mouth by his suffering secretary, who feeds
the Ambassador's vanity with bonbons verbal, as ladies
feed their spaniels. Surely no more ridiculous progress has
been seen in the nation, at least since the Fool Pretender*

marched to his execution, while thinking he marched to his throne.

The logomania of the apothecary is met by the silence of Lord Utterback, who endures the prattle all the hours of the day & utters barely a syllable in response. His lassitude is remarkable to behold, and sometimes I wonder if he is simply an imbecile. (Do you like "logomania?" I made it up.)

I suppose you will have heard of the death of good King Stilwell in Bretlynton Head, of a sudden illness on his progress to Howel. We encountered the messenger three days ago, riding post to Ethlebight. The gods rest our King, sith the Pilgrim will not care.

The King had crossed the sea before the corsairs attacked Ethlebight, and our embassy would not have caught him even if we had ridden the fastest horses in the kingdom. But the rider told us the princesses are still in Selford, and will remain there until our new Queen Berlauda is enthroned on Coronation Hill. As monarchs often mark their accession by acts of generosity, I hope we may move her majesty to render aid to our city, at least if we arrive before our backsides are shaken to bits by the coast road.

It is the worst road in the kingdom, I am told. Anyone moving east or west along the coast would take the faster journey by sea, so the road exists only for the convenience of those who live along it, & their labor, or their sense of duty, is insufficient to keep it in repair. The great carriage of the Embassy Royal heaved itself along the road like a bull seal wallowing on a beach, lurching from rock to rut to pothole, & every toss & roll & pitch rattled my teeth & shivered my brains. After the first day I shifted my aching backside to the lighter baggage coach, which travels with more ease.

The coast road does not always run within sight of the

coast, but when it did, I saw the corsairs' dark chebecs on the sea, cruising for new captures. I wondered if they were laying ambushes along the road, and whether I might actually need to use my ridiculous sword.

More likely my legs. I have run from the reivers once, and I could do it again.

Because the astrologer had insisted on the Embassy leaving in the afternoon rather than morning, we didn't reach the first posting inn until after midnight, & found the gates locked against corsairs. Eventually the landlord was roused, & the gates unlocked. There was no food. The Immodest Apothecary informed me I was not entitled to a bed, & so I rolled myself into my overcoat on a bench in the bathhouse, which at least was clean.

On the second day of our long, wrenching journey we climbed a series of stony hills and came out above a lovely bay called Gannet Cove. D'you know it? The water is deep, & protected from southeast storms by a pine-fletched peninsula, & from the west by a skerry crowned with a perfect hemisphere of darting sea birds. There is a village of fisher-folk there, but when they saw the chebecs of the reivers offshore, they fled above the cliffs behind the beach & built themselves drystone shelters, like the shepherd people do. Gannet Cove would make a fine port if those cliffs did not cut it off from the commerce of the country, & if there were a broad river like the Ostra or the Saelle to bring in the produce of the hinterland. But because the cliffs wall them off from commerce, the fishers live in driftwood huts & marry their cousins.

That night the Great Embassy got to the posting inn after dark, but there was some kind of village meeting going on, & the place was full, & the spits charged with meat. The

August Personage was distressed that he shared the dining room with common folk so ignorant they knew not to worship him, & he wanted manchet-loaves of white flour instead of the cheat & raveled bread served by the landlord. (Milord Utterback, as if he were a Person & not an Eminence, ate the cheat with what an objective eye might have deemed pleasure.)

I was not deemed worthy of sharing a table with the Personage, but making friends with a serving-girl, Lucy of the bright eyes & scarlet hair, I had the better meal, to-wit, a fine pottage of onions, peas, and carrots, with bits of bacon and firm whitefish; and after, a roast quail, followed by a joint of venison which I carved myself, and lastly a cheese. Plus a jack of spiced wine that had grown steamy by the hearth. That great-gutted luxurious gastrologist the Emperor Philippus had no better, I vow, for all his bustards stuffed with ortolans. (Do you like "gastrologist?" I just made it up.)

Again I was not allowed a bed, but told to sleep in the stable with the other servants; but my new friend Lucy had a little cottage nearby, and there we kept warm all night long, with a little help from the mulled wine. I arrived at breakfast happy & refreshed, but the two Ambassadors had spent a v. uncomfortable night, having less pleasing bed partners than I—they came downstairs fleabit & lousy. I was very pleased not to share their carriage and their scratching, & I felt v. righteous in that pleasure.

The next three days' journey to Amberstone was a wearisome repetition: the wretchedness of the road, the poverty of the inhabitants, the dreariness of the company + clouds & rain to snuff out all remaining joy. No Lucy appeared to assuage my boredom, & no beds, with or without vermin.

Yet straw in the stables has its simple country virtues, & is warm enough I believe.

And now we will spend our third night in the city, guests of Count Older, cousin-german of my lord Utterback. I sleep beneath the eaves, in neither the best nor the worst bed I have enjoyed this journey. The Ambassadors spoke with the Lord Warden in hopes that he would send some of his soldiers to help secure Ethlebight & the New Castle, & I believe progress has been made there, so our travel has not been a complete waste. And the grand abbot said he would send monks!—so you will not be without your philosophical comforts, be ye ever so poor and hungry.

The Ambassadors are also taking a great many baths & being deloused generally. I and the monks shall pray for their success.

Now that we have reached the city, I have abandoned the coaches and bought a horse. It is a chestnut gelding & is agèd but not completely dilapidated, or so the dealer informs me. It is a palfrey & on the little ride I took yesterday ambles with a v. easy gait. Its name is Toast, after its favorite food.

I had hoped we might be able to sail from here to Selford, but the Aekoi blockade extends even this far. Captures have been made within sight of the town, one so close that the forts fired their great guns, but managed not to hit anything. But I see Irresistible, a great high-charged galleon, is being fitted out in the town, a private vessel owned by the Marquess of Stayne. It has four masts, with demicannon on the lower deck, culverins on the upper, & an array of sakers, minions, falconets, and such other mankillers on the castles fore and aft. Soon it shall be "busked and boun," as the saying is, & I cannot imagine the corsairs could stand against it, even their whole fleet together, so long as there

was enough wind to keep steerage-way & prevent the che-
becs from rowing up under the stern to rake her.

There are also some royal vessels being brought out of
ordinary, & they should cross their yards within the week.
So possibly it will be the reivers who are blockaded on Cow
Island, so may it please the gods.

But I have forgot to tell you the good news! Your ship
Meteor *hath come into Amberstone, laden with olives, figs,*
pickled fish, & pipes of wine from Varcellos! I know you were
worried that the corsairs would take her, but she came in just
before the chebecs appeared off the port, & is quite safe. You
may rejoice, & may this be the restoration of your fortune.

There is now discord among the Ambassadors concern-
ing our next step: should we continue along the coast road
four or five days to Newton Linn, & there hope for a boat to
take us the three days' journey to Selford, or should we go
overland direct for Selford by way of Mavors' Road, which
is the shorter way but goeth over the Toppings, which is said
to be "all hill and no broad," & will be difficult for the big
carriage to traverse & take at least twelve days. I spoke for
Newton Linn & the sea-route, and my lord Utterback agreed
in his barely audible way; but the Personage has not yet
given up his vision of a grand entrance into Selford, with
all falling on their awestruck knees at the sight of a coach
worthy of a god, & so I fear it we will be swaying up and
down hills ere long. But what care I?—I will be on my hon-
est palfrey! The coach may sink into a bog for aught I care,
and the Personage with it.

You do not mind that I look at other women, I hope. I desire to be
honorable in my conduct toward women, and part of that honorable
conduct is to speak frankly.

My dalliances are harmless, and indeed are more the matter of comedy than of romance. As you shall discover in due course.

I looked up from my letter at the sound of shoes clacking on the paving stones of the quay, and saw a dark-haired, striking young woman walking along with a basket of turnips slung over her shoulder. The brilliant leafy greens bobbed behind her head like a soldier's plume. Her eyes met mine, and held them pleasantly for a moment, and then the woman looked away and kept on walking. I felt it unjust that a young woman of such pleasing aspect should be obliged to shoulder her own turnips, and gathered my writing material between cardboard covers with the intention of carrying the turnips on her behalf—and then I saw, pacing along behind, Lord Utterback.

Utterback was dressed as befit his station, in brilliant blues and yellows, with swags and purfles, pinks and braid, and a doublet slashed to reveal the satin shirt beneath. A brass-hilted rapier glowed at his side, and he wore a tall hat with a plume and a diamond pin. I had become used to the plainer clothing Utterback wore on the journey, and seeing him in his role as lord caught me a little by surprise.

But Utterback was not reveling in his status, or strutting in his finery, but frowning down at the pavement with his hands folded behind his back, beneath a cape trimmed with black crow feathers.

Utterback paused, as if working at a thought that had just occurred to him, and then looked up with an air of faint surprise, as if he only now realized where he stood. Then he saw me, and gave a start of recognition.

I approached and put on my respectful-courtier face. "My lord."

Utterback blinked. "Do you bear a message for me?"

"No, my lord. I was at the tavern, writing a letter, when I saw you walk past."

Lord Utterback seemed to consider this for longer than the

information deserved, but then asked a question which showed his mind was far from the quay, letters, or taverns.

"Goodman Quillifer, do you agree with Eidrich the Pilgrim that human purpose is to be found only in the mind's acceptance of Necessity?"

I, more than a little surprised, took a moment to compose my answer. "I think perhaps that depends strongly on the definition of Necessity—and, I suppose, its opposite."

"Some do call that opposite Freedom."

"My lord," said I, "I should find it hard to despise Freedom."

"Walk with me," said Utterback. I fell into step with him, and the count's son returned to the troublesome matter of doctrine.

"The Compassionate Pilgrim said that Freedom was an illusion. That the first motion brought the world into being, and that this creation itself created more motion, and yet more motion, until in time that motion created us, and created also our compulsions and desires, and created as well the world about us with its people, and their appetites and so on, and that to win free of all this is impossible."

"And yet," said I, "should I stoop to pick up a rock, and throw the rock into the water, the rock then flies into the water. The rock has no will in the matter, but it seems to obey my will, as do my arm and hand."

Utterback stopped in mid-stride, took my arm, and brought me close. His level brown eyes gazed into mine from mere inches away.

"Do you desire women?" he asked.

At this surprising intimacy, I found unwanted speculation flew through my mind on agitated wings. I resisted the urge to take a step away.

"I do, my lord," I said.

"So do I," said Utterback, to my relief. "Yet do we desire women through choice, or by Necessity, compelled by our natures? And do we somehow achieve Freedom by enslaving the desires that are natural to us?"

I adopted my innocent-choirboy face. "For myself," I said, "I follow the Pilgrim's advice, and act in accord with the dictates of Nature."

Utterback smiled and released my arm. He continued his progress down the quay, and I again fell into step beside him. My mind whirled with the strangeness of it all. Utterback had spoken scarcely a dozen sentences to me on this entire journey, and now it seemed that he wished to debate philosophy. Were these the sorts of questions that occupied Lord Utterback's thoughts on the long journey? Was philosophy how he endured Gribbins's company?

"Necessity made me a lord," Utterback said. "It is due to no special virtue of mine that I am my father's son. But are lords themselves a Necessity? And it is Necessity that I behave as a lord behaves?"

I began cautiously. "Do you not have more Freedom than most men? You have wealth, you have access at court, you have liegemen and noble kinsmen to support you, you have your privileges . . ."

"And yet in some ways I have less Freedom than most men. I will marry a woman of my father's choosing. I may go to court, but only to labor on my father's behalf. If I go to war, it will be because my father sends me, or brings me to war with him. I will enlist in the cause of other nobles, as my father chooses, and conspire against cliques of nobles who oppose him. Even my friends and enemies are chosen for me."

"It is no disgrace to obey your father's will. All custom commends it. And of course you will inherit, and then need obey no will but your own."

"Ah, but then it will be worse!" Utterback offered a laugh. "I myself will be creating these allies and enemies. I myself will be conspiring for power, marrying my children for advantage, trying to send my enemies to prison or to the hangman."

"I cannot believe those are your only choices," said I.

"Then we return to my question. Is it Necessity that great lords behave as great lords behave?"

Utterback had come to the end of the quay, where a great wooden jetty sagged on ancient pilings. The great galleon *Irresistible* moored there, its forecastle and steeply pitched poop shadowing the pier, its gangplanks filled with men bringing aboard stores.

"Hast seen Stayne's ship?" Utterback asked.

"I was just writing of it to my friend. I should think it might drive the corsairs from our shores all on its own."

"If it fights the corsairs at all."

I was surprised. "What else should it do?"

Utterback fingered his dark pointed beard and narrowed his eyes as he looked down the quay. "*Irresistible* returned a fortnight ago from a voyage to the north, with a cargo of lumber, pitch, and turpentine. Eight days ago, a rider arrived from the marquess ordering the ship to prepare for war. Most of the great guns had been struck into the hold to make room for cargo, so these were brought up to fill the ports—sixty-two guns on three decks. Powder, shot, and other supplies are brought aboard, and they are recruiting a fighting crew— over six hundred men. Stayne himself is expected within the week, to sail aboard her."

I had been calculating ever since I heard that *eight days.* "Where is Lord Stayne's seat?"

"Allingham. Over the Toppings, then four or five days' journey northwest."

"So," I said slowly, "he ordered the ship made ready for war before he could have known of the attack on Ethlebight."

A smile twitched across Utterback's lips. "Just so."

"Could he have foreknown that the reivers were coming?"

Utterback gave a shrug. "I doubt they would have sent him notice of their intentions."

"He could have employed a scryer, perhaps?"

"And told him to scry the whole wide ocean on the chance that a fleet of corsairs might be bound for our shores for the first time in over a generation? I think Stayne, in his highland home, is not so concerned with the safety of the coasts."

"So, he intends to attack someone," I said. "But who? We are at peace."

"Perhaps we should ponder what a great nobleman might consider Necessity."

I duly pondered, and was able to reach no conclusion. I spoke cautiously. "You have not described a noble's behavior in flattering terms. You have said that the great nobles form cliques that conspire against one another, and I believe history supports this—but I don't recall history supporting a naval attack from one clique against another, at least not in peacetime."

Utterback's answer was quick. "And is Duisland at peace?"

"Not with the corsairs."

"But within its own borders?"

I hesitated. "The King is dead," I said.

"Stilwell is dead. Leaving behind?"

"The two princesses." A startling idea gripped me. "Do the princesses war with one another?"

"There's more in the world than the two princesses, Goodman Quillifer." Utterback raised a slinkskin-clad hand and began to count off the gloved fingers. "The princesses. Young Queen Laurel. Three former Queens, all still alive, and all with their noble relatives and their affinity. There are three or four bastard daughters; I know not how many, but they do not matter because their families do not matter. Then there is the bastard son, Clayborne, raised at court, whose mother is Countess of Tern confirmed in her own right, and who has but lately married the Duke of Andrian and all his land and wealth in Bonille. Clayborne is popular at court—a pleasing young man, quick of wit, handsome and charming, and resembling his father in many ways, save that he is lazy. He has always denied any ambition, but there are many who say he would make a good King. The princesses have been raised by their mothers, in exile from court, and are not well-known, and are not popular."

The tally of this list had taken all fingers of both hands. I looked at the gloved hands for a moment. "You imply that Clayborne may try to seize the throne?"

"He may, or may be pushed into rebellion by his mother, who was deprived of a throne by that inconvenient first husband of hers, who would not oblige her with a divorce even when the King himself asked it of him. My Lady of Tern has deeply felt the lack of a throne ever since."

My eyes turned again to the high-charged galleon waiting at the wharf. "So, Lord Stayne readies for a civil war. On which side?"

"He is a friend of the Countess, and a sometime ally of the duke. A companion in the bastard's revels. I know nothing of his relationship with our new Queen, if he has one."

I contemplated barrels of supplies rising in a net, and floating over the galleon's hold at the end of a yardarm. "If Stayne wished to pledge his loyalty to Queen Berlauda," I pointed out, "he needn't ride all this way to board a warship; he could ride from his home to Selford in three or four days. And neither would he sail if Clayborne were any- where that could be reached by road."

"A telling point," Utterback said. "I had not considered that. The bastard must be in Bonille, or abroad."

"Have you spoken to the Lord Lieutenant? He could close the port and prevent Stayne from leaving."

Utterback waved a hand. "Of what party is the Lord Lieutenant? I know not—Stayne might be permitted to sail free, while I am tossed in a dungeon." He frowned. "Would that I knew my father's mind. He is well disposed to Clayborne, I know, and has been one of his mother's lovers, but I cannot say whether any such sentimental attachment will lead him to rebellion." He looked again at the galleon. "Would he wish me to go aboard with Stayne, I wonder?"

"What," I pondered, "would a great nobleman consider Necessity?"

"Hah." Utterback was darkly amused. "The secretary grows impudent, to turn his master's words against him."

"The master grows careless," returned I, "to speak of rebellion before the secretary." I stepped closer to Utterback, and spoke into his ear. "We know nothing of this matter, whether there be rebellion or no, because the corsairs blockade us here, and keep the news from sailing to us. Let us then take horse and ride to Newton Linn—I cannot imagine the Aekoi will have sailed so far north, and there will be tidings waiting us."

Utterback gave him a look. "Are you so reckless? Or so determined on adventure, that you would venture rebellion?"

"I have already lost all," I said. "Family, fortune, prospects. One prince is as good as another, so they be generous to their followers."

Utterback regarded me closely. "Have you the stomach for more than one Ethlebight? For if we have a civil war, plundered cities will be common as spots on a leopard."

I felt my stomach turn over. I could find no words. Utterback put a hand on my shoulder.

"Nor am I so bloodthirsty," he said in comfort. "Nor am I." He sighed, and turned to walk heavily down the quay. I joined him.

"The Pilgrim offers as his philosophy," Utterback said, "that a dispassionate submission to the dictates of Necessity is the first of all virtues. And so I shall resign myself to fate, and continue this sad, useless embassy until Necessity compels me to another course." He shrugged, and looked over his shoulder at me. "Thus shall I be a dutiful son, or failing that a dutiful subject, or if both objects fail, the dutiful citizen of a dungeon, as fortune wills."

"As my lord wishes," said I. "Though the humble secretary wishes to remind his master that there are still courses of action that have not been considered."

"Ay. I could join a monastery!" Utterback grinned, and made a mocking bow with a swirl of his feathered cape. "The master thanks the secretary, and will release him to finish his letter, though he also hopes the secretary will be discreet regarding the substance of this conversation."

I bowed. "Of course, my lord. The secretary knows better than to argue the merits of rebellion in a message that anyone could open."

But even without a description of my conversation with Utterback, I had a very long postscript to add to my letter to Kevin.

I could describe Clayborne's possible rebellion as a rumor I had heard on the docks, and suggest that the *Irresistible* might be intended for fighting the war, and not the corsairs after all. If any of this were true, no help would come to Ethlebight this winter, and precious little in the way of sympathy.

I was beginning to realize how little the country cared about my city, and how small its concerns were against the intrigues of the great powers of the land.

The Embassy Royal set out at midmorning, after the long breakfast at the Guild of Apothecaries. Clouds opaqued the sky, and by afternoon the cold rain pelted down.

I had brought a long overcoat that, like the rest of my clothes, I had looted from an abandoned house. It was a thick cheviot tweed, very warm, and had a cape that I could pull over my head as a hood. I remained reasonably comfortable, but still I wished I'd bought oilskins. The rains continued on and off all day, and made the journey miserable.

My new chestnut, Toast, with his palfrey's gait, floated with ease over the road, and would have delighted me had the weather been more reasonable. I bribed Toast with his favorite food and consoled myself with the thought that I no longer had to put up with the lurching carriage, even at the cost of being wet and cold.

I am not a natural rider, and after the first day I was near-hobbled with pain But as the journey continued, the pain faded, and I believed that the animal and I were forging an understanding, one based on bribery if nothing else.

Mavors' Road was in better condition than the coast road, but the weather made it more trying. And for five days the coach lumbered through wet weather, its big wheels throwing up sheets of water as it careened through ponds, lagoons, and fords. It bogged down frequently and had to be shoved and worked and coaxed out of the mud. Then the road began to ascend the Toppings, one after another of steep-sided hills crowned with hardwood forests. Here the road was in poor repair, and sometimes washed out. Creeks and rivers ran between the hills, and though some were bridged, most had to be forded, and the water was high and the crossings difficult. Old castles loomed above the track, most of them deliberately torn open so they wouldn't become the haunts of bandits. The towns were small and mean, and the inns mean and wretched. Soon, Gribbins and Utterback were scratching again, and I rejoiced on my clean bed of straw.

No messengers came galloping down the road, shouting out news of war, rebellion, or the death of kings.

Sometimes the hills were so steep that the passengers had to leave the great carriage and walk in the downpour, which vexed Gribbins greatly. His high, peevish voice carried far along the road, and I was happy to trot ahead to where the only sounds were birdsong and the clop of Toast's hooves echoing off the surrounding trees.

On the third day in the Toppings the weather broke, and thick golden sunbeams swept like pillars of light across the green country, while mist scudded between the leafy, brilliant crowns of the hills. The ridges ahead did not seem as tall as the ridges behind, and I felt my heart lift as I sensed that soon we might win free of the Toppings and descend into the lush country that fed the River Saelle.

Late in the morning the road descended into a long coomb, with a clear, lively stream running alongside the track, and willows overhanging the water. The leaves were just beginning to turn, and in the bright sun gleamed gold and scarlet flashes along the stream's green banksides.

I rode a few hundred yards ahead of the Embassy, enjoying Toast's easy glide over the ill-maintained road, and taking pleasure in the rich abundance of life in the coomb, the birds singing in their trees, the river's laughter as it scurried over stones.

The road made a curve, and I pulled up short at the ancient willow that had fallen across the track, and an instant later saw that the tree had not fallen in its own time, but been sawn. I realized that the birds had fallen silent, and I scented a faint trace of smoke in the air—not woodsmoke, but smoke with the slight taste of brimstone, like that of a slow-match.

My heart began to thunder like a kettledrum, and I sawed Toast's head around and banged my heels on the chestnut's sides. The elderly horse paused for a moment of astonishment at this unprecedented treatment, then jolted into belated action as I kept kicking him. Soon, Toast was flying down the track at something like a canter, while I waved an arm and shouted.

"Ambush! Bandits! Ambush!"

On the grand carriage, the three footmen, coachman, and postilion stared at me with identical expressions of imbecilic surprise. My blood turned cold as I realized that the Embassy Royal was essentially defenseless—the three footmen were armed with blunderbusses, but the rains had doused their slow-matches days before, and they hadn't been relit. Instead of terrifying weapons of close-range combat, the firelocks were now little more than awkward clubs.

Shots cracked out, white gunsmoke plumes gushing from the green bank above the road, and what seemed a host of wild men rose from concealment and dashed down onto the track, hot on my heels. The ambuscade had been laid just at the fallen tree, and because of my warning the attackers now had to sprint to the coach instead of finding it right in their net, but they were no less dangerous for having to run a hundred yards. I cast a glance over my shoulder and saw there were about a dozen, all armed with swords, pikes, or pollaxes.

Calculations sped through my mind, and they all led to the same sad conclusion: the Embassy was about to be waylaid and robbed, its delegates perhaps beaten or killed. I, with my little sword and superannuated gelding, could not affect the issue one way or another, and it was therefore only sensible that I preserve my life.

Someone, after all, still had to carry the Embassy's message to the capital.

Toast raced past the great carriage at an accelerating canter. The baggage coach, with its servants, was only now slowing down, its driver standing on his box to peer in bewildered curiosity at the fast-unfolding disaster ahead of him. I left the baggage coach behind, and for a moment my heart lifted at the sight of a clear road ahead—and then a man stepped onto the path to block my way.

He was an old, white-bearded character in a flat-crowned hat. He seemed to be wearing a faded blanket over his shoulders; and a pair of heavy boots, like buckets, engulfed his skinny legs. He carried a spear in his gaunt, thick-knuckled hands.

I reasoned that if the bandit was going to stand in the road like that, it was my clear duty to ride him down. So, I dropped my head behind the gelding's neck and kicked the horse into greater effort.

The old man stepped forward, waving his spear up and down like a flyswatter, and shouted, *"Hai! Hai! Hai!"*

Toast, confronted with this scarecrow apparition, found himself burdened with a number of choices. Apparently, he decided to contemplate his own advanced age, and the kicks and shouts and unearned abuse he had suffered from me in the last few moments, and the lack of toast evident in this unfolding scenario . . . and in an act of stubborn insurrection decided no longer to play a part in the action. The horse stopped dead in the middle of the track.

The world revolved about me as I catapulted forward over the horse's neck to land on my back in the middle of the road, the wind completely knocked out of me, I could only gasp for breath as the elderly bandit approached on his huge boots and brandished the spearpoint at my neck.

"Will you yield?" said the toothless mouth. "Or shall I slice out your tripes?"

Unable to breathe or speak, I mutely threw my hands out to the side, and gave myself up as a captive.

CHAPTER SIX

I thought the journey to the bandits' camp took two or three hours. My hands were tied behind my back, and to keep me from learning the path, my head had been covered with a baize bag. The track led up and down, and forded streams. One of the bandits was detailed to stay by my side to steady me and guide me over the obstacles, but the man amused himself by letting me stumble and fall, once full-length in a stream, and by the time I staggered into camp, my clothes were sodden, my scraped knees were bleeding freely, and there were bloody cuts on my face from branches that had whipped me through the baize hood.

The last part of the journey was alongside a stream, and I could hear the chatter of water and smell the fresh, free air of the brook. Then I was hauled up some stone stairs and shoved into an area paved with cobbles that I could feel through the soles of my boots. The sound around me—horses clattering, shoes scraping, rude laughter, and ruder greetings—seemed to have a slight echoing quality, and I suspected that I was in an enclosed space.

I had a few moments to catch my breath. And then the baize bag was pulled from my head, and I shook my hair from my face to discover myself in one of the old forts that crowned the hills in the Toppings. To make the place useless as a bandits' lair, the walls had been torn down in two places, and the keep ripped open; but the bandits had moved in anyway, and built their refuge amid the ruins.

I gasped in air tainted with woodsmoke, and stood in a rough line with the prisoners. Lord Utterback, I saw, seemed to have suffered no injury, and looked about himself with a distracted air. Perhaps, I thought, he was consoling himself that all this was Necessity.

Around them prowled the robbers, looking at the prisoners as wolves might stare at a lost calf. The outlaws were more ferocious at close range even than they had seemed charging along the road, as now it was possible to see the mutilations that had been inflicted on them for past crimes—cropped ears, cheeks burned with the King's brand, fingers missing joints or twisted by the thumbscrew. Despite the mutilations, they all seemed fit and hardy, and they were well armed with swords, bucklers, pistols, spears, and firelocks, and some wore bits of armor. Almost all were young, for few seemed older than five-and-twenty—the great exception being the old scarecrow who had taken me hostage, and who swaggered around the court with his spear on his shoulder, toothlessly cackling along with his fellows.

There were also women in the company, for the most part looking worn and well-used, though some carried weapons and seemed as lethal as the males. Others made a brazen parade in looted satin finery, rings glittering on their fingers, as if to leave no doubt they were willing to barter their persons for a share of the loot that was to come.

Most surprising were a pair of monks, dressed in dirty robes, with their tonsures growing out. They carried no weapons, but otherwise looked as disreputable as the others.

And as for the loot, the baggage had been brought up on horses, along with Gribbins, who when his legs had given out had simply been tossed across a horse.

The bags and Gribbins were unloaded in a pile, and then two of the bandits jerked Gribbins off the baggage pile, and stood him up with the other captives. When the bag was taken from his head, he blinked about him with milky blue eyes, and seemed not to know where he was. There was a bruise over one eye, and his nose had been bleeding.

Of the prisoners, only Gribbins had been damaged. Perhaps he was the only one who had resisted: none of the stout footmen, whose job it was to protect us, seemed to have suffered at all.

Under the direction of a tall, narrow-shouldered man, the luggage was opened and ransacked. Lord Utterback's fine court clothes, with their bright velvets and silks, occasioned both comment and laughter. His purse and a bag of silver were emptied into a large wooden bowl produced for the purpose, as were the purses of Gribbins, myself, and the others. Rings taken from Gribbins and Utterback were added to the bowl.

I didn't feel sorry for my lost clothes—they were loot to begin with, taken from empty Ethlebight houses to replace the clothes lost in the fire, and now they were being looted again. But I winced as the tall bandit unwound the twine on the narrow box that I had found in the ruins my father's house, and emptied out my entire fortune. The man stared down at the bowl, then fished out the alderman's gold chain that had belonged to my father, and held it out for the appreciation of the crowd.

"Lo!" he cried "It is a great official we have before us! Give a proper welcome to the liegeman of the King!" The crowd bayed in response.

I couldn't help but cast a look at Gribbins, who was staring at the chain. The apothecary's dazed look faded, and for the first time since he had been thrown off the horse, comprehension entered Gribbins's eyes. He looked at me, then back at the chain, and then at me again.

"You are a liar, sir!" he hissed. "You assured me the chain had been destroyed! You are a liar and a thief!"

I was about to ask if he hadn't other things to worry about besides

a lost chain, but one of the bandits, who thought Gribbins was referring to his chief, clouted Gribbins on the head and knocked him to
his hands and knees.

Hearing the apothecary's moans, I decided to hold my tongue.

The tall robber continued to rummage through my bag, and came
up with the two books I had brought with me. He opened the first,
and glanced at the title page. "Corinius, is it?" he said. "The *Satires*—
strong stuff! And though he was an Aekoi, he had the measure of
Man well enough." He stuffed the book into a pocket, then looked at
the other. "Mallio!" he said, and his voice was full of scorn. "Know
you not that the Delward translation is superior to the Rawlings?
Rawlings barely knew a fee tail from a defeasible estate!" He looked
up at the captives. "A beef-witted, folly-fallen stinkard of a lawyer you
would make if you depended on this *Rawlings*!" He threw the book
onto the pile, then continued to sort through the baggage until he
lifted Gribbins's gold chain from the apothecary's trunk.

"Another magistrate!" he proclaimed. "Should we bow before their
glory? Should we tremble in terror before these representatives of public order! Surely the gewgaws on their coach proclaimed their majesty!"

The grand coach, after having been looted—and after the bandits
had assured themselves that the ornaments were gold paint and not
gold leaf—had been declared useless and tipped into the stream. I
had last seen it lying on its side, grinding over stones as the current
carried it away.

It might see Selford before any of us, I thought.

Interestingly enough, the carriage horses and postilions had been
allowed to leave. The horses didn't belong to the Embassy, but to the
last posting inn, and the postilions were the inn's hired men who
returned the horses to their home after each stage. I guessed that the
inns probably paid blackmail to the bandits in order to not lose their
horses time and again—and also likely tipped the robbers to any rich
travelers passing through.

The bandit leader finished rummaging through the baggage, then mounted a stair that led to the gaping keep and turned to his prisoners. He was tall and lean, and wore a brilliant green doublet and trunks, yellow hose, and tall jackboots—all looted from travelers, I assumed. The man's dark, pointed beard was shot with gray, and his hair straggled down his back. An overcoat, gray as the sodden morning light of the Toppings, hung to his ankles, and he wore a tall-crowned hat. He turned to his captives.

"Lord, magistrates, and other suchlike blockheads!" He spoke in the rolling tones of north Fornland. "I am Sir Basil of the Heugh. Perhaps you know of me!"

He said this with a sharklike grin, and in fact I *did* know of him, though all I knew was that Sir Basil was an infamous bandit.

In a purposeful, theatrical way, Sir Basil reached behind his back and drew out a long dirk, bright steel blade and a black iron handle with an acorn-shaped pommel.

"This is my dirk!" he told the captives. "This weapon has been in my family for two hundred years, and was crafted by the dark enchanters of the Nocturnal Lodge of the Umbrus Equitus. Twelve necromancers prayed over the iron for twelve nights, twelve virgins were entombed alive to guarantee the steel's purity, and twelve captives were sacrificed to provide the blood that quenched the blade." He drew the blade slowly through the air above his head, as if cutting the throat of an invisible giant.

"Because of its origin in the Nocturnal Lodge and its use in ritual sacrifice by depraved and murderous sorcerers, this dirk *lusts for blood*." Sir Basil laughed out loud as his dark eyes sought out each of the captives, one by one. "It is all I can do to keep a firm grip and prevent my knife plunging into your livers! And so"—with another flash of the knife—"I will need your help in restraining my dagger. You must *help me to help you to survive*! And the best way to help me"—again that sharklike grin—"is to urge your kin to pay me a *generous ransom! That* is the best and only way to impel me to restrain my weapon's appetite for blood."

The grin remained, though the dagger was returned to its hidden scabbard. "I shall first speak with Lord Doubleback, or whatever your name is. Come this way, young sir."

Utterback declined to move. "I should like my hands untied," he said. "You need not fear me, as your men have seen I'm unarmed."

The bandit affected surprise and amazement, then took off his hat and offered a sweeping bow. "I fear my courage may not be up to the task of facing such a foe as an Unarmed Crumpleback, or whatever you claim as your title." He rose, smiling. "Yet I shall summon up what little valor still attaches to my debased knighthood, and dare to meet with you, tremble though I may!" He made a sweeping gesture. "Cut him free. Cut free them all!"

Utterback's lashings were cut, and he stood swaying for a moment as he contemplated his crabbed, swollen, empurpled hands. Then, his useless hands at his sides, he walked up the stair to the ground floor of the gaping keep, where a table and a number of chairs waited before the keep's ancient carved fireplace. The bandit and his captive sat, and for all appearances began what seemed to be a civil conversation.

In the meantime, my bonds were cut, and I looked down at hands as swollen and useless as those of Lord Utterback. For the first few moments they were numb, but as soon as the blood began to beat through my veins, the numbness was replaced by piercing pain. I was determined not to be an object of mockery to my captors, and I tried not to cry out, and attempted not to hunch protectively over my tortured hands—I stood with my hands clasped in front of me, and clenched my teeth, and blinked back the sudden sharp tears that filled my eyes.

My eyes cleared, and before me I saw one of the outlaws, a young man in a slouch hat, with a scarred face and a contemptuous sneer. I straightened, and returned a defiant look. The outlaw laughed at my pretensions, and walked away. I busied myself with brushing away mud and gravel from my skinned knees.

Utterback and Sir Basil concluded their conversation, and both stepped out onto the stair. The outlaw grinned broadly and addressed the crowd. "I am pleased to record that Lord Smotherback has agreed to pay us a generous sum in return for our hospitality!" The bandits raised a cheer, followed by a moment of polite applause for Utterback's magnanimity. Sir Basil paused to join in the applause, then turned back to his audience. "So generous was he that my lord shall be quartered in the Oak House, where he shall enjoy all the rude comforts the Toppings can provide, and where he shall be given writing materials so that he can write to his father, the Count of Shylock."

A stoic, ironical expression lay on Utterback's dark face as he listened to the mangling of his father's title, and he was then led away by a pair of bandits through one of the gaps in the fort's curtain wall. Sir Basil surveyed his remaining captives.

"Perhaps I shall have one of the magistrates now?" he said. He pointed at Gribbins. "That one, then, who crawls like a dog. He and I had best make an arrangement before he succumbs to his honorable wounds."

Gribbins, who had been wheezing on all fours since being hit by the robber, was picked up by a pair of bandits, rushed up the stair, and dropped into a chair. Sir Basil jauntily swung a leg over another chair, and the two began to speak.

I watched the conversation while I massaged warmth and feeling into my hands and arms. The outlaw spoke, and Gribbins replied, and then the outlaw spoke again. Gribbins's high, peevish voice answered. "Sirrah, I am an *ambassador*! An ambassador to the *royal court*! You shall release me at once, or the King shall hear of this!" He gaped a moment as he realized his error. "The Queen, I mean!" He waved an admonishing finger. "The Queen shall hear!"

I winced. Everyone but Gribbins could see where this was bound.

Sir Basil, for his part, affected surprise. "You call upon royal protection?"

Gribbins seemed very pleased with himself. He folded his arms. "Ay! In the Queen's name, you must release me at once."

Sir Basil rose from his chair and turned to his audience. "The gentleman calls upon the Queen!" he said. "And well must he be situated between her fine white thighs, to call upon *her* instead of his royal majesty!"

There was a laugh from Sir Basil's claque. The toothless old bandit in the big boots raised quivering hands. "Nay!" he cried. He quaked in mock terror. "Not the Queen! Call not upon the Queen!"

"Not the Queen!" cried the bandits. And they all began to moan and wail, and stagger about as if in bewilderment and terror. Their pleas echoed from the fort's mossy stone walls as they beat their breasts and begged Gribbins for mercy.

I could imagine the sequel all too well. I tried to think of something that might alter the course of events, but my inspiration failed me. I clenched my teeth and tried to resign myself to Lord Utterback's god of Necessity.

Gribbins reddened, but maintained his attitude of defiance. Sir Basil watched his men with a leer of approval, and then made a gesture, and they fell silent. He cocked an eye at the apothecary, and put a hand to his ear.

"Sir Ambassador, I hear not the Queen. Nor the King. Nor their armies. Perhaps Their Majesties have abandoned you? Or should you call louder?"

Gribbins's answer was firm. "I will not bandy words with you, sirrah. I am an ambassador and you must release me."

Sir Basil turned back to his audience. "Despite his ambassadorship, this gentleman is by profession an apothecary, which is to say a mountebank. What fine have we established for a self-confessed mountebank?"

"Ten royals!" came the answer.

"Ay, ten royals. And the gentleman is also an alderman, which is to say a man who lives well on money he has taxed out of the people. What is the fine for a self-confessed tax collector?"

"Twenty-five royals!" shouted the bandits.

I winced at the numbers. A skilled workman might earn twenty royals in a year, and Gribbins doubtless earned more, but he would not earn it all at once, and I guessed that it would be rare for an apothecary to have thirty-five royals lying about in cash, even if his home hadn't been looted. And if he didn't have the money, then whoever raised it on his behalf—wife? brother? son?—would go to a moneylender and agree to an interest of a hundred or hundred fifty percent, perhaps more, considering how scarce cash would be in Ethlebight at the present.

Sir Basil spun and threw out an arm toward Gribbins. "And the gentleman is also an ambassador!" he said. "No ambassador has ever enjoyed our hospitality before, so I know not what fine to ask. But I understand that the task of an ambassador is to lie to the King, and then to send the King's lies back home, and to carry such lies back and forth, and to otherwise be a procurer for lies. So, what should be the fine for pimping lies?"

"Twenty royals!" said one bandit.

"Thirty!"

"Fifty!"

"Fifty!" Sir Basil laughed. "Ay, make it fifty!" He stepped toward his audience and leered at them knowingly. "And the gentleman ambassador has called upon royal protection." He spread his hands. "What, my friends, is the penalty for calling on royal protection?"

"*Double the fine!*" they all shouted in joy.

"Ay! Double the fine!" Sir Basil swung toward Gribbins, who only now was beginning to show comprehension of his situation. Sir Basil held out a cupped hand, as if asking for a tip. "That is a hundred seventy royals, master apothecary. How do you intend to pay?"

Gribbins's face was a mask of horror. "I cannot pay," he said.

"Have you no friends?" Sir Basil said. "No wife? No sons?"

I knew that Gribbins owned a house, with his shop on the ground floor, but it couldn't be worth more than fifty royals. And even if he mortgaged it, it would pay only a fraction of his ransom, and leave his family in debt. He probably invested in merchant ventures, but these would only pay off at the end of a voyage, and very possibly had gone up in smoke during the corsairs' attack.

Doubtless these same calculations were whirling through Gribbins's mind. His mouth opened and closed, as if he were trying various arguments and rejecting them before they quite got out of his mouth. If only, I thought, he'd tried that approach earlier.

Again I tried to think of a way to intervene, something clever that would save Gribbins from the consequences of his own vainglorious folly. But I could not imagine anything that could stop the onrush of events, not unless I was willing to rush onto the bandits' swords, run myself through, and hope my death provided enough entertainment to satiate Sir Basil and the other outlaws.

"I do not have the money," Gribbins said. "Though if the ransom remained at thirty-five, I could raise it."

Sir Basil snarled. "Do you *bargain* with us, sir?" He stepped to Gribbins's chair, took his arm, and pulled him to his feet. He dragged Gribbins to the top of the stair, where he could view the bandits growling up at him, shaking weapons and fists. "Do you bargain with *them*?" he demanded.

Gribbins made an effort to control himself. "Sir," he said, "I am heartily sorry if I impugned your—"

"Do you bargain with *this*?" Sir Basil asked.

I tried to turn away, but I was too late. The dirk was swift as a striking serpent, and flashed from beneath the outlaw's cloak and into Gribbins's side before I could so much as blink. And then, unable to turn away, I saw Gribbins's look of shock, saw his knees begin to give way, and then saw Sir Basil withdraw the dagger and kick Gribbins down the stair, where the apothecary disappeared behind a wall of robbers.

The bandits bayed their approval, their weapons brandished overhead.

Sir Basil flicked the dirk several times to shake off the blood, then re-sheathed. His restless eyes prowled over the courtyard, then lighted on me. He made a gesture.

"You are next, Goodman. Come."

I slowly walked through the mob of bandits, which parted only reluctantly. There I saw Gribbins dying at the bottom of the stair, his watery blue eyes blinking as they stared into onrushing darkness.

My stomach turned over. Many were the times in the last two weeks when I had cordially wished the apothecary dead, but now that it was happening, I found no pleasure in the sight.

To mount the stair, I would have to step over the dying man. I contemplated this action and found myself unable to do it, so I stepped to the side of the stair, reached up to the crumbling floor of the keep, and pulled myself up.

Sir Basil of the Heugh looked at me with mild surprise as I popped up in front of him, and stepped back to invite me to sit in the chair that Gribbins had just occupied. I seated myself cautiously, but Sir Basil threw himself carelessly into his own seat, the skirts of his overcoat flying. He crossed one booted foot over his knee, and looked at me with bright black eyes.

"You're a lawyer, I see," he said.

I was surprised to realize that my apprentice cap had stayed on my head through the whole adventure.

Sir Basil narrowed his eyes. "I don't like lawyers," he said.

"I don't care for them myself," I said. I had decided to agree with the outlaw whenever I could.

"My own advocate was no use at all," said Sir Basil. "He thought I was guilty. He served me up to the jury like a mincemeat pie."

Apparently, Sir Basil felt his fame was such that I would know this detail. I thought it impolitic to correct him.

I donned my learnèd-lawyer face. "The advocate must have been unfit."

"*I* unfitted him," said the outlaw. "I slit his nose and burnt his house."

I nodded what I hoped Sir Basil would view as approval. "A resolute action, Sir Basil."

"I failed to catch the judge," the outlaw added, "but I robbed his wife."

A flush burned in Sir Basil's cheeks, and his black eyes flashed. The murder had stimulated him, and he shifted restlessly in his chair and spoke with restless, rapid animation.

"I was innocent of that theft," he said. "I was a devoted priest of the goddess Sylvia, and 'tis true I had a key to the treasury under the podium of the temple. But it was another who opened the lock and took the money and the temple offerings!" He snarled. "I will admit to any deed I have committed—I will own to killing that blockhead a few moments ago—but I will *not* admit to a crime of which I am innocent!" He jabbed an angry finger onto the table. "They found not a single stolen article in my house—they had no evidence at all—and yet I was convicted!"

"It sounds like a monstrous injustice," I said.

"I prayed to the goddess," said the outlaw. "But she was as useless as my lawyer." He snarled, and brandished a fist to the sky. "Damn all lawyers! Damn all gods! Damn the Pilgrim, and the King with him!"

I nodded, and began to think it a good idea to change the topic. "One item of your program is complete. King Stilwell is dead."

Sir Basil raised an eyebrow. "So, that is why that imbecile called upon the Queen?"

"Yes. We have Queen Berlauda now."

The outlaw made a noise of disgust. "She won't last. Women can't rule. Some ambitious knave will chuck her off her throne, or marry her and keep her so stuffed full of children she won't think to say 'boo' to him." He ran his fingers along his jawline, thoughtfully smoothing his beard. "And yet women are sentimental and foolish—would she be inclined to offer pardons, d'ye think?"

"Many pardons are issued after coronations." I considered for a moment, then decided to seize the slight opportunity this seemed to open. I put on my respectful-apprentice face. "I could be your advocate in the capital, if you like."

Sir Basil gaped at me, then laughed. "My *advocate!*" he scorned. "That is precisely what I need, *another advocate!* And further, one who reads his Mallio in the Rawlings translation, hah!" He pointed a finger at me. "Look you—how would you translate the following: '*Quatenus permittit aurum prodit lex*'?"

I was a little surprised to find myself at school again, but rose to the challenge. "'Laws goeth where gold pleaseth.'" Though there was no way to translate "*prodit*" in all its subtlety, with its hint of betrayal, and of keeping the subject on a short leash, and bound by strict Necessity.

"Ay, plain but serviceable enough," Sir Basil judged. "Yet Rawlings has it, 'Howsoever gold and laws goeth ever in company.' He understands not even that *prodit*, which is plain as—" He made a fist. "As the corruption of the common law by the judiciary!"

"I have the Delward translation at home," I said. "But I preferred not to risk it on the journey."

"That is the first wise thing you have said." The outlaw laughed again, and shook his head. "My *advocate!*" His glittering black eyes regarded me for a long, unsettling moment. "So, you are not an ambassador, I take it?"

"I am a drudge," I said, "a mere secretary. Nor am I an alderman, nor a magistrate. Nor will I call upon the Queen of Duisland when I am in the power of the King of the Toppings."

The outlaw gave a thin smile. "Flattery may win the favor of royalty, but not Sir Basil of the Heugh. We have yet to determine your fine, Goodman . . ." He reached for a word and failed to find it. "Goodman," he said, "I know not your name."

"Quillifer, Sir Basil."

"Is that a forename or a surname?"

"It is my only name," said I. "It is one of the ways in which I am singular."

The outlaw laughed. "And the gold chain?"

"A keepsake in memory of my father. He was an alderman, and was murdered with the rest of my family two weeks ago in an attack on Ethlebight by Aekoi corsairs."

Sir Basil was not moved by this story, but entertained. "So, you plead that you are an orphan? A penniless orphan?"

"I was not penniless until this last hour, Sir Basil."

"The fine for penniless orphans, Goodman Quillifer, is five royals."

I had expected worse, though five royals was bad enough. Perhaps my drolleries had encouraged Sir Basil to lighten my ransom.

"I will write to my friend," I said. I knew Kevin had no money, but could probably raise five royals if he needed, especially as his ship *Meteor* had come into Amberstone.

The thought of *Meteor* brought to mind the galleon *Irresistible*, and suddenly I realized how I might save myself the debt, and perhaps do the new Queen a good turn. I leaned back in my chair and looked at the outlaw.

"Sir Basil, I wonder if I could beg a pardon from you on condition."

The outlaw's eyes turned cold. "On condition? *Condition?* When I hear the word *condition*, I hear also my dirk crying for blood."

"I can put you in the way of a ransom larger than any you have collected," I said. "If my information is correct, will you let me go free?"

"You wish to turn informer?" The outlaw was darkly amused. "Certainly I can foresee for you a glorious and successful career before the bar."

The man was probably a traitor anyway, I thought. In any case, he owned an estate and a high-charged galleon, which he could afford better than I could afford five royals.

"The Marquess of Stayne will be riding south on Mavors' Road in the next few days," I said. "He will be joining his galleon *Irresistible* in Amberstone for a voyage abroad."

Sir Basil's cynical look faded, replaced by one of calculation. "How do you know this?"

I explained while the outlaw listened carefully. "I know not whether he will ride a coach or come on horseback," I concluded, "but he will probably have an armed company of men with him. Yet such an expert in ambuscade as Sir Basil of the Heugh need not fear such a troop."

"No, I need not fear them." Sir Basil's tone was not defiant, but thoughtful. Abruptly he lunged to his feet, overcoat swirling. "You will be given pen and paper, and you may write to your friend. Whether the letter is sent or not depends on whether your information proves sound."

He broadly gestured me to the stair, then looked balefully over the crowd, to his remaining captives, all servants. "Come, then," he said. "All of you."

I saw Gribbins still lying at the foot of the stair, and rather than step over the corpse, chose to leap down from the keep to the court below. I slowed as I passed the white-faced body, the eyes blank yet still somehow conveying the bewilderment that so often filled them in life, and knew that Gribbins's vainglorious journey to the capital had finally reached its end.

A pot of ink was presented by one of the bandits, along with a piece of paper and a board on which to write. I penned my brief letter to Kevin, and included as well the information that Gribbins had been killed for trying to barter over his ransom. I also suggested that another embassy be sent to the Queen, as it might be some time before Lord Utterback and I were released to deliver their message in person.

While I wrote, the party's loot was disposed of. The money in the wooden bowl was counted, then returned to the bowl along with the gold chains and any jewelry with valuable gemstones. The bowl was carried away, presumably to be added to the bandits' hoard and divided up later. The rest—the clothing, luggage, weapons, and the less valuable jewelry—was given away to the robbers by a method they all seemed to judge fair. The bandits sat on the ground, facing away from Sir Basil, as he held up one item after another and said, "Who wants this?" Whoever shouted first, or raised a hand, received the article. Afterward, there was a great deal of merriment as the bandits tried to trade away unsuitable items.

My letter was taken to Sir Basil for his approval. Apparently, the outlaw had no objection to my message, and so put the letter in a pocket. Sir Basil by this time had finished interviewing the servants, and announced that one of the footmen along with Gribbins's body-servant had decided to join the band of robbers. The other bandits roared their approval, and hooted at the others as they returned to captivity.

There followed a formal initiation ceremony, in which Sir Basil had each of the new recruits swear a horrible, godless, bloody oath on the dirk that had just killed Alderman Gribbins. I thought the business of the oath ridiculous, but the bandits themselves took it very seriously indeed, and so while the oath was pronounced, I kept my face composed in an attitude of awed respect.

By the time this was all over, the sun was burning red through the western trees, and the shadows were long.

"To supper!" Sir Basil proclaimed. "And let's drink to our new companions!"

The company filed out through one of the gaps in the curtain wall, and I saw that the fort had been built to guard a corrie surrounded by a great semicircle of cliffs. The hidden green valley had a dimple in the center filled with a small lake, a limpid blue eye which emptied into the small fresh stream along which I had marched on the last stage of my journey.

By the lake was a corral with the troops' horses, which now included my traitor chestnut, Toast. I also saw milk cows, goats, and a great many dogs.

In the corrie the outlaws had built their camp, a clutch of buildings clumped against one of the cliffs. I saw that the bandits' huts had been built of old, worn dressed stone, and I concluded that the robbers had built their settlement atop the ruins of a much older town, and made use of what materials they'd found.

One of the bandits had killed a roe deer that morning, and this had formed the basis of a stew with parsnips and carrots, wild onions, mushrooms, thyme, rosemary, and other herbs found in the area. There were also flat oatcakes with butter and homemade cheese, which argued for a very well-organized commissary. The bandits and their new recruits pledged each other in wine, but I and the other captives were given sour ale.

After returning my wooden bowl and spoon to the ramshackle kitchen, I went to the lake to wash the cuts on my knees and face. I was wincing through this procedure when a man approached, a man of middle years. His beard was long and untrimmed, and his clothing soiled and worn.

The man was, in fact, another captive, a man named Higgs. He had been held for five months, a merchant captured on the road with two wagons of goods. Higgs had applied to his brother for his ransom, but the money had not arrived, and now he was beginning to suspect that his brother had betrayed him.

There was another merchant here, Higgs reported, who had been abandoned by his partner, and who had been captive even longer, since before the band had moved to the Toppings from their former range to the north. The two captives were used by the bandits as slaves.

"I begin to think I may have to join them," Higgs said. "I begin to think it may be the only way to survive."

I, shaking the cold water from my hair, had little comfort to offer. "Join them, then. Gain their trust. Then run away when you can."

"That is not as easy as you might think," said the captive.

Higgs showed me over the camp, pointed out the Oak House, a small building in a field, with barred windows and an entrance through the roof. There Lord Utterback had been locked away, a privileged prisoner but with a guard who prevented him from speaking to anyone.

Utterback, I thought, *would have plenty of leisure to contemplate Necessity, and to cultivate the proper attitude of resignation.*

Higgs took me past the armory, which was locked and in a very public place, and the dairy, which along with the kitchen were under the command of an Aekoi woman named Dorinda. In contrast to her species' usual gracile form, she was broad and powerful, her golden complexion darkened by exposure to the elements. She stood before the kitchen and glared at everyone with strange, fierce eyes, irises small and dark and surrounded by white, each like a black pearl in the middle of an oyster shell.

"Is she Sir Basil's lady?" I asked, for her fierceness seem to sort well with that of the outlaw knight.

"She's her own," said Higgs. "And you do not ever want to be her kitchen slave."

"I shall try to avoid her," I said, though I knew that, as long as I remained here, that choice would not be mine.

"And that," Higgs said, pointing out a building, "is the treasury. Your money lies there, and my goods, those that haven't been sold."

"It looks like a temple," I said. It was a sturdy, square building, with a portico and four pillars. What had probably been a tile roof had been replaced by the same crude thatching used in the rest of the camp.

A roughhewn wooden fence surrounded the building, with gaps between the pickets, so that no one could hide there. A large padlock secured the timber door. I saw something slither along behind the pickets, and I felt a cold hand touch my spine.

They undulated across the ground like thick-bodied snakes, their scales lawn green and midnight black, but when one of the beasts seized a picket the best to view me, I saw that it had small, clawed hands. Malevolence and hatred glittered from its eyes. I could not bear its stare, and turned my own eyes away.

"Ay," said Higgs. "Wyverns. Sir Basil raised them from their eggs, which he found up in the Peaks. Stay clear from them, for they breathe fire." He pointed out another structure. "Their master lives in the next building."

There was the clop of hooves on the turf, and the master himself came trotting up on a dapple gray courser. "You, Quillifer!" said Sir Basil of the Heugh. "Come up to the keep! Your master's body needs burying!"

Dogs had to be chased away from Gribbins's body. I and the other servants of the Embassy Royal carried the body in a blanket to a sward below the old fort, where four graves already lay in a row. It was full night by the time we began to dig, and the only light was that of the stars and the slow-matches of their two guards, who each carried a sword as well as a blunderbuss so kindly provided by their captives.

Afterward, sweating and dirty, we were taken to confinement, locked in the echoing dungeon of the fort, surrounded by massive great stones at the base of the keep. There we were shown our places by the light of a horn lantern, pointed at the slop tub in the corner, and then left alone in darkness while the sound of the slamming door echoed in their ears.

I rolled up my cheviot coat for a pillow, and wrapped myself in the coarse blanket I'd been given. I was asleep at once, and I dreamed of Ethlebight, strong and intact, the brilliant window glass of Scarcroft Square shining in the sun. I walked the streets of my city, admiring the beautiful brickwork, the ornate gables, the detailed carving on the wooden frames.

But I walked the streets alone. The city was empty, and I saw no other person, and heard no sign of life beyond my own echoing footfalls. I was walking a city of the mind, and no one shared my dream.

CHAPTER SEVEN

I woke to the booming of the door and the soft light of dawn. "Up!" cried a sour voice. "Up, eat, and ease your bowels!"

I came up the stair to see the courtyard filled with activity, the bandits cleaning their weapons, seeing to their horses, saddling their mounts, or filling their bags with supplies. Sir Basil rode about on his gray, then saw me being marched to my breakfast and rode up to me. He prodded me on the shoulder with a whip.

"Your intelligence had best prove true!" he said. "My dirk thirsts for the blood of a liar."

"I wish you the best of luck in your hunting," I said, and then one of my captors shoved me along and I staggered to keep from falling.

Breakfast was a buckwheat porridge. The latrine was a trench dug in an open field. And then we captives were rounded up and marched back to the dungeon, where we were again shut up in the darkness. Sir Basil was marching with so many of the bandits that few were left to stand guard, and so we were to be locked away till he returned.

I disposed myself on my blanket. "Does anyone know a song?" I asked.

"Shut up, ye puisny, longshanked dew-beater!" snarled one of the footmen.

"He who likes not a song lacks a soul," I said.

"*You'll* lack a soul ere I'm done with you," said the footman.

At which point, grim silence and darkness prevailed.

We were allowed up that evening, a few at a time, for more buckwheat gruel and another trip to the latrine, escorted by a pair of bandits armed with blunderbusses. The two monks I had seen earlier, and who apparently had no employment, watched from a distance and joked with each other. Then it was back to the dark hole for another night of captivity.

I had drowsed through the day, and now I drowsed through the night. Bites and itches kept me from sleeping soundly: I was now as alive with vermin as any man in the kingdom. I could no longer feel superior to the great ambassadors and their lousy bedding.

There was more gruel for breakfast, but this time made of oats, and it was eaten in pouring rain. The dry cellar of the keep was a relief after the freezing deluge.

On the afternoon of the third day I heard the thudding of hooves in the courtyard, and then the door was thrown open to brilliant sun. I blinked my way out of the dungeon and saw the bandits returned with a large number of captives, twenty at least, along with their horses, magnificent animals with expensive, jingling equipage. The prisoners were tied, and had baize bags on their heads; but the superiority of their clothing, with finely worked leather and swags of lace and silver spurs, showed the majority of them gentlemen of quality. When the bags were removed, despite a certain amount of disorder, the faces revealed were groomed, with long hair well dressed. Some bore bruises and cuts, but most seemed to have suffered few ill effects from their capture.

Apparently, I thought, one brought barbers and hairdressers when riding off to commit treason.

The Marquess of Stayne was tall and lank, with long graying hair and a trim little beard that framed a small disdainful mouth. Beneath his ornate black leather riding clothes, his silk shirt was a brilliant yellow, and falls of lace dripped from his sleeves and flowed over his boot tops. He looked about in grim silence, his eyes shifting from one bandit to the next as if memorizing every face, in order perhaps to bring retribution later.

The luggage was brought out and opened. Silks and lace spilled on the moss-covered cobbles. Money rang as it fell into the wooden bowl. There was a great deal of armor found among the captives, along with banners and weapons, all clanging uselessly onto the cobbles.

"So many swords and pistols!" cried Sir Basil. "Breastplates of proof! Tassets chased with silver! And yet they offered so little resistance!" The quality of the booty almost had him dancing in delight.

The outlaw floated up the steps to his place on the floor of the broken keep, then swung to face his audience, the skirt of his coat sweeping out behind him. "I am Sir Basil of the Heugh," he proclaimed. "Perhaps you know of me." He doffed his hat during the dramatic pause that followed, then produced his knife. I saw that he was wearing Lord Utterback's slinkskin gloves. "This is my dirk! For two centuries it has been in my family, and was crafted by the dark brotherhood of the Nocturnal Lodge of the Umbrus Equitus!"

There followed much the same scene that had been enacted three days before, and in much the same language. Lord Stayne was brought up for his interview, and then taken away to share the Oak House with Lord Utterback. The other captives were brought up in their turn, and pens and ink distributed so each could write his ransom note.

Only one servant had been captured, probably because the bandits had devoted themselves to rounding up their masters. He was brought up last of all—he looked about fifteen, with a wheat-colored shock of hair, and his arms were still bound behind him.

"Where are the new recruits?" Sir Basil called. "Where are Anthony and Little Dickon?"

The two fledgling bandits were brought forward, and stood awkwardly by the captive. Anthony was a burly footman with curly hair; and the other, small and sharp-faced, had been Gribbins's varlet. Sir Basil clapped them on the shoulders, and looked deliberately at the boy captive. "This boy stands where you stood just days ago, does he not?" he asked.

"Ay," said Little Dickon, and his companion nodded.

"But since that time some days ago, you have sworn to be of our company!"

"Ay."

"You are sworn to be true brothers to those of our emprise, to be bloodthirsty and resolute in action, and to obey without question the orders of your captain?"

The two men nodded. Sir Basil pointed at the captive boy, and said, "Take then your knives, and kill me that fellow."

The two were so surprised they only stared, while the captive gave a cry and tried to shift away from the others. Sir Basil caught him by the collar and dragged him back. He looked at his two recruits.

"Do you defy me, then?" he demanded.

"No, sir, no," said Anthony, and he drew his little dagger. Little Dickon fumbled at his scabbard, and drew out his own knife.

"No, sir, no!" echoed the captive. "I have done nothing! Nothing to deserve this!"

Sickness rose in my heart, and I looked down at the mossy cobbles of the courtyard, thinking furiously of what might buy mercy from the outlaw chief.

"Why do you delay?!" Sir Basil demanded of the new recruits. His rolling northern voice echoed in the amphitheater. "What is this hesitation? I say, death to the villain who hesitates! My dirk will drink deep of his heart's blood!"

"Sir." Little Dickon seemed barely able to express the words. "Sir, what has the prisoner done to deserve—"

Sir Basil snatched his dirk from the scabbard and brandished it over his head. His voice was full of scorn. "I am not here to be questioned! Have you not sworn obedience? Have you not been bound by the most desperate oaths a man can utter?" He laughed. "By all the discredited and useless gods, what good are you if you cannot even kill a bound captive?"

The boy began to weep and beg for his life. I felt my limbs go cold. I stepped forward and raised my voice.

"How much to spare the lad?" I called. "How much for his life, Sir Basil?"

There was a collective inhalation from the bandits as they turned to stare at me, and from the expressions on their faces, they clearly expected there would be more than one murder in the next few minutes.

"Thank you, sir!" called the captive. His face was streaked with tears. "Bless you, sir!"

Sir Basil paused for a long moment, his head cocked as he worked out how to respond, and then he stepped forward and pointed his dirk at me.

"Do you propose to ransom the boy yourself, then, Goodman?" he asked.

I strove to control the quaver I felt hovering about the margins of my voice. "You know, Sir Basil, how much money I possess." I surveyed the latest captives in their fine clothes and well-dressed hair. "But there are others among us better provided than I."

"Congratulations, Goodman!" Sir Basil affected delight. "You follow my example—in being generous with the bounty of others!"

That raised a laugh from his followers, and I felt the tension ebb, and thought perhaps I would not get a knife between my ribs. Sir Basil capered to the front of his stage, and made a wide sweep with his dirk at the captive gentlemen assembled before him.

"Fifty royals, then!" he said. "Who will save the boy's life for this token sum?"

I felt my spirits sink as low as my boot soles. Fifty royals was a rich man's ransom.

The gentleman prisoners were silent, their eyes shifting left and right, never lighting on the boy bound on the floor of the keep.

"Please, sirs!" called the captive. "Please save me!"

He was answered only with silence. "I'll work for you!" the boy cried. "I'll work for you all my life!"

I clenched my fists. "You could each pay a little," I said.

"Too late!" Sir Basil said. "Goodman Quillifer has shown himself free with others' money, and these fine gentlemen have shown all the fine compassion of a North Country jury—which was all that I expected." He turned to the two apprentice outlaws, Anthony and Little Dickon.

"Kill him," he said. "And do it quickly, or you'll join him in a shallow grave."

"Mercy!" the boy screamed. *"Mercy!"*

I turned away, unable to bear the sight any longer, and found myself facing the prisoner Higgs, who looked at me with sad, meaningful resignation. I understood that Higgs had watched this scene play out more than once, that such savage theatrical displays were common in Sir Basil's camp.

After brief hesitation, the two apprentice bandits began the execution. Neither were practiced at killing, and the business went on for some time, the thuds of the striking knives alternating with the shrieks of the victim. I pressed my hands over my ears but failed to seal out the sounds of the slaughter. But finally the boy fell silent, and I heard the thud of a body falling to the ground, soon followed by the noise of Little Dickon being sick.

Higgs approached. "I told you that it was not so easy to join Sir

Basil's company." He murmured for my ear alone. "New recruits are made to commit murder as soon as a victim can be found. It is to prevent betrayal—if any of them inform on the robbers, the others can denounce them and see them hanged."

"I shall try to win free somehow," I said.

I could not admit that Sir Basil had promised my release in exchange for the capture of Stayne's party. It would have to be managed as some kind of daring escape.

For now I, too, was complicit in the youth's slaughter. The boy would not have been taken prisoner if I had not turned informer, and the likelihood that those I had betrayed were themselves traitors was little comfort.

Blindly I walked to the rear of the court, and collapsed against the wall. The screams of the murdered boy still echoed in my ears.

It seemed my fate to blunder from one massacre to the next. I lay back against the cold stones, looked up at the brilliant blue sky, and surrendered to misery.

At least I would soon receive my traitor's bounty, and be free.

Sir Basil read the new captives' ransom letters while a lieutenant conducted the auction of captured goods, including all the finery, weapons, and armor. By the end of the distribution, I thought that Sir Basil probably led the best-armed outlaw band in Duisland's history.

After the auction, Sir Basil divided the letters and handed them to the two monks, who rode off on a pair of horses. Now I understood why the monks were in the camp—it was the monks who contacted the prisoners' families and carried the ransom—or, more likely, deposited the ransom in a local monastery, and withdrew it from another monastery closer to the Toppings. The monasteries, as well as temples to the old gods, were often used as repositories of gold and silver, kept under the gods' protection; and the monasteries of the Compassionate Pilgrim often accepted money in one place, and issued a bill allowing the money to be drawn elsewhere. In this they acted as banks, but only for deposits, for they were forbidden by law, as well as their own doctrine, to make loans or charge interest.

Sir Basil ordered some of the fine gentlemen to bury the body of their servant, and there was a moment or two of resistance before the outlaw imperiously brandished his dirk, and the captives quietly carried the victim away. All the other prisoners were marched out into the corrie and given work, for the most part that of preparing supper for the large company. Dorinda, the Aekoi cook, thumped me on the back with a wooden ladle, and in a harsh voice assigned me to bring water from the lake. I was given a yoke with leather buckets dangling at either end.

Near the shore of the lake I found some watercress, nibbled some, and picked the rest before I dipped the buckets and returned to the kitchen, where I found gentlemen cutting vegetables, building a wood fire, and leading a calf to be slaughtered, all under the supervision of bandits dressed in their captives' brilliant silks and satins, and engaged in vigorous barter over clothing, weapons, and armor.

Dorinda was standing in the kitchen compound, barking out orders, her strange, furious, white-circled eyes starting out of her head, her lashing ladle as effective as a whip in making her victims skip to their duty. *"Salvio, domina,"* I said.

She turned on me, her ladle brandished under my nose like a sword. "What do you mean with that jabber?" she barked. "I was born in this country and I speak your language as well as you!"

"I brought cress," I offered. She took the cress, sniffed it suspiciously, and ate a piece. Then she pointed with her ladle. "Put the water in the kettle."

I did, and brought more water, and with it more cress. As I returned with my third delivery, I encountered Sir Basil of the Heugh, who was riding one of the captured horses along the shore of the lake. It was a lovely bay courser, with black feet and a sable splash on its forehead, and its bridle and saddle glittered with wrought silver. He drew the horse to a slow walk beside me. I saw that he was still wearing Lord Utterback's slinkskin gloves, along with a vivid green doublet slashed to reveal a yellow silk shirt. He had put away his long overcoat for a cloak lined with scarlet satin and edged with gold brocade.

"Like you my new charger?" said the outlaw. "Does the harness not shine in the sun?"

"Truly you have chosen the best," I flattered. "And perhaps with these dashing new steeds on which to mount your troop, you will not need my venerable gelding. May I have it for my brave escape?"

Sir Basil looked down with amusement. "If you evade my men, and their shot, and the dogs that will be set on you, you may take all you like. That is the rule of our free company—any man is free to take what he likes, so he bear the consequences. But for now"—he pointed with his silver-tipped whip—"you must bear the yoke."

I shifted beneath the pole that crossed my shoulders. Smoke from the wood fire scented the air. "Bear it I will," I said, "confident in the promise you made of impending freedom."

The outlaw's black eyes sparkled. "And when did I make such a promise?"

"You said I would be set free if my information regarding Lord Stayne proved true."

"Pah." Sir Basil's lip curled with disdain. "Your recollection is imperfect. I promised nothing."

Only the knowledge of Sir Basil's celerity with his dirk prevented me from swinging a bucket of water at the outlaw's head. "But, Sir Basil," I said, "I've brought you the greatest ransom you will ever collect, a marquess along with his whole affinity. Surely, that is worth such a paltry thing as my liberty."

Sir Basil was indignant. "Do you ask me to cheat my company? They are all due their share of your five royals' ransom, and I shall see it collected." Again he pointed the whip. "Now carry the water, or I may be forced to tell the other prisoners the part you played in their capture."

My heart turned cold. I straightened under my burden, and looked Sir Basil in the face. "As you command," I said, and made my way to the kitchen.

I could not trust Sir Basil at all, I thought, not even if the five royals arrived from Kevin. The outlaw was a murderous brigand, arbitrary in his will and his whims, and plumped up with his little massacres. He'd kill me as easily as he'd killed Gribbins, and for less reason.

It seemed best to apply my mind to escape.

A monotonous *chop-chop-chop* sounded in the air as I delivered my load, took the yoke from my shoulders, and shrugged away the soreness. The wood fire burned briskly, and Dorinda shifted the kettle over the flames. The chopping grew irregular, and was then followed by curses and loud argument. I ventured toward the sound and found two of the gentlemen cavaliers squatting beneath a beech tree and trying to butcher the calf.

They'd succeeded in killing and bleeding the animal, and were now trying to hack up its joints. They hadn't skinned it—apparently, they planned to skin the joints after they'd cut them free.

"Have you never watched your own huntsmen butcher a deer?" I said. "Or do you retire after the kill to play at dice and drink the wines of Loretto?"

One of the gentlemen, a dark man with a forked beard, rose raging from the animal. He was splashed with blood from his boots to his crown, and his well-dressed hair was somewhat less than perfectly in order.

"You are welcome to try!" Fork-Beard snarled, and held out his heavy knife. "Try and be damned to the nethermost pit of hell!"

"I will perform this infernal task for you if you fetch the water in my stead," I said. "You look as if you need washing, in any case."

The cavalier and his slope-shouldered companion threw their

butchering implements on the ground and stamped away, the less furious of them dragging the yoke and buckets. I viewed the tools, found them adequate, then examined the calf. I decided it wasn't completely ruined and rolled the animal onto its back, its legs splayed toward the autumn sun. I paused a moment to remove my overcoat, doublet, and shirt, then skinned the calf's ventral half. I collected the brisket, then looked up at the beech tree overhead. Any number of its strong limbs would serve for hoisting the animal, but as I saw a block already hanging from one bough, I assumed this marked Dorinda's butcher shop. I threaded the rope provided through the block and hoisted the calf into the air.

Within ten minutes I had cut the calf into quarters, and took so long only because I had to keep kicking the dogs away from the offal, and because the saw provided was inadequate for cutting through the chine. I hesitated only once, as I thought of the boy being butchered up in the keep, and for a moment the world swam before my eyes. After which I deliberately suppressed all thought and memory, and worked on the calf like a mere machine, my hands and arms making the well-practiced movements without mindful calculation. At the finish, I looked up from the work to see Dorinda standing by, her strange eyes slitted in thought.

"Do you wish to hang any of it for later?" I asked.

"That would bring bears down from the hills," Dorinda said. "It all goes into the stewpot to feed this crew of rogues and fustilarian bellygods."

"A waste of good chops," I said. "But I will volunteer to stay up tonight and shoot any bear who come to molest us, and we may dine on bear steaks tomorrow."

Dorinda barked a laugh and thwacked me on the elbow with her ladle. A bolt of pain shot up my arm all the way to my teeth, and then the arm went numb.

When I recovered, I finished butchering the calf, and put the cuts up on the thatch roof of the cookhouse to keep the dogs off them. I knew the trick of cracking the skull to preserve the brains entire, and these with the sweetbreads I put in a bowl.

After I finished, I let the dogs have what remained, and taking my clothes walked out to the lake to wash. I made a half circuit of the water, and kept an eye on the cliffs that surrounded the corrie in hopes of finding a path to escape. I saw several routes that led to the upper rim of the vale, but none were easy, and they were all in plain sight of the well-armed bandits. It would be suicide to make the attempt in daylight. At night I would be locked into the dungeon, and nothing but a clever ruse would serve to keep me free.

Of course, at night the climb would be far more hazardous, and once I topped the corrie I would still be in the dark, and lost in a part of the Toppings that the bandits knew and that I did not. I was not a woodsman, and I knew little of how to evade the pursuit that would follow.

My wanderings brought me to the stream that fed the lake, and there I stripped off my remaining clothes and dove into the chill, clear water. Like rats from a drowning ship my fleas leapt for safety, and I cracked them between my fingernails as they struggled in the water.

The lice, unfortunately, would survive a bath, so I would have to be satisfied with eradicating only a single species of tormenter.

After my bath, I dried myself with tufts of grass, put on my clothes, and followed the stream through a grove of osiers toward the cliffs. A fresh, cool scent filled the grove, and the leaves were turning gold with autumn. At the foot of the cliff I found an ancient structure, a half circle of dressed yellow-brown sandstone overgrown with bushes and vines, and in front a deep, broad, weed-filled marble trough filled with water gushing from a spring at the base of the cliff, a trough that overspilled to form the stream. I saw fallen pillars and broken arches and realized that I was viewing a nymphaeum, a monument to the divine spirit of the spring.

I knew that such things had been built in the ancient Empire of the Aekoi. The Aekoi had never conquered Fornland, but nevertheless someone had built this imitation here.

Curious, I looked through the rubble, and found the broken remains of old marble urns and bits of shattered, elaborate carving, wreaths and flowers and vines with pendulous grapes.

The melancholy ruins set amid the drooping osiers suited my dark mood. I jumped up on the edge of the trough, then stepped over the water to what had been the central arch. The natural spring rose just behind, in a small grotto, and was brought into the nymphaeum by a thick-walled lead pipe that might have survived a thousand years. Atop the pipe were the remains of the fallen arch, the rubble overgrown with brooklime and creeping jenny. Water dripped from the walls of the grotto into the spring, the sounds echoing in the confined space.

I squatted by the bank of the spring, and stirred the cold liquid with a hand. A frog leaped from the bank into the safety of the water. As my eyes adjusted to the darkness of the grotto, I saw something pale amid the rubble, and as I leaned closer, I saw that it was a human hand.

For a moment my blood ran cold, and then I saw the hand belonged not to a corpse, but was made of rose-colored marble. Gently I pulled rubble and water plants away from the remains of the broken arch, and laid bare the statue of a woman clad in ancient drapery. She was about four feet tall, and lay on her side, her cheek reposed on her hand as if in slumber.

I freed the statue from the rubble and picked her up as if it were a child. I carried her out of the grotto and laid her in the trough to clean the marble, and afterward propped her up amid the ruin of the arch. She was posed prettily with one hand lifted to her cheek, and the other holding a bunch of water lilies. The draperies exposed one breast. Her hair waved gently down to her shoulders, and her features were so worn by time that there was only the suggestion of a face, the nose worn down, the merest outline of brow and lips. On the lips there was a trace of an impish smile.

Despite its age and condition, there was still a spirit in the old statue, a sense of coquettish mischief that lifted my mood.

"Well, mistress," said I aloud. "It seems we have both met with misfortune."

I filled a cupped hand with water and washed away a smudge of dirt that clung to the nymph's neck. Then I heard a horn blow from down in the bandits' camp, and knew it for the call to supper.

I rose and bowed courteously to the statue. "I hope to pay you court tomorrow," I said, "if the ruffians will permit it."

I made my way out of the grove feeling strangely lighthearted. The westering sun had left the corrie in shadow, with only the trees atop the cliffs still in bright sunshine. For a moment I saw a human figure outlined against the sky, and the sun winked scarlet against a red cap, or perhaps red hair, before the figure turned away and vanished. Though the figure had only been visible for a few seconds, its appearance was enough to darken my mood.

There were sentries on the cliffs, I thought. I could climb the cliffs and be shot down as soon as I set foot on the corrie's rim.

Roast meat scented the air as I approached the camp. I saw a pair of bandits carrying plates to the Oak House, where it seemed the two noblemen would sup on spit-roasted calf shank. Other bandits, mixed promiscuously with their captives, sat on the grassy sward around the lake with their plates and cups. I thought for a moment that this might be a good time to escape, with the bandits relaxed, but I looked up at the old fort and saw the gleaming helmets of a pair of sentries.

I was the last to arrive, and I found the kitchen deserted. Dorinda I saw quite alone, squatted down by the lake, and bent over her plate.

Trestle tables had been set up with bread, plates, and wooden spoons. There was little left of the veal stew, and the remains of the cooked vegetables were unappetizing, so I looked up on the thatch for any parts of the calf that the cooks had left unused. I saw the calf's brains in their bowl and fetched them down. I cleaned away the membranes and blood vessels, then blanched the brains in a pot of water that had been set boiling to clean the dishes. Once the brain was cooked, I cut it up, dusted the pieces with flour, and fried them in an iron skillet with butter, parsley, garlic, and a sprig of rosemary, and then ate while congratulating myself on enjoying the best meal in the camp.

I looked up from my bowl to see Dorinda glaring at me from across the table, her ladle poised in her fist. I put on my attentive-courtier face. "No one else was using the brains," I said.

She fetched me a stunning blow to the skull, one that set stars blazing before my vision. "*No one* in this camp uses their brains!" she cried, and then she burst out into coarse laughter and hit me again.

Under Dorinda's ferocious gaze I hastened to wash the skillet along with my bowl, and then took a brief stroll along the stream that ran from the lake past the fort. I was gazing down into a tree-shrouded vale and trying to make sense of my location when I heard a meaningful click, and looked up to see that the two guards were looking down at me from the walls of the fort, and that one of them had ostentatiously cocked his firelock. I doffed my cap to him, and returned to the corrie until the horn sounded to tell the prisoners to march to their dungeon.

As I made my way through the broken curtain wall, I looked out over the bandits' camp, and I saw a woman who stood quite by herself on the sward near the lake, perhaps a hundred yards away. She wore a dark skirt that contrasted with the bright green grass, and a dark shawl over shining red hair.

She was staring at me with shadowed eyes in her pale face. A thrill ran along my nerves at that look, and I froze, staring back in astonishment. The women of the camp looked worn, or brazen, or vicious, but this woman seemed none of these, but a vision of freshness and beauty from out of a song.

We stood there, staring wordless at each other, and then one of my captors swore at me and shoved me along, and I stumbled on toward my captivity, my mind awhirl.

After the hours spent in the open air and sunshine, the miserable, fetid, dark cellar with its vermin and its stinking slop tub was all the more intolerable, and I had to steel myself to go down the steep stair. I found my blanket where I had left it, and prepared for another night of scratching and misery.

"This blanket's soiled!" someone complained. "By the Pilgrim, I think it's blood!"

I looked over my shoulder to see the two cavaliers, Fork-Beard and Slope-Shoulder, who had so signally failed to butcher the calf. One of them, the angry Fork-Beard, was holding up the blanket he'd just been given, and I saw that it was the same blanket in which I and the others had carried Gribbins's body to his grave.

I was about to advise the man to go back up the stair and ask for another, but at that moment the cavalier looked at me and spoke. "You, there! Give me your blanket!"

I gave him a cold look. "I'm not your servant," I said.

"Listen, Butcher-boy," the cavalier said. "Do you know who I am?"

"You're a man who let himself be captured without a fight," I said. "What more need I know?"

The man gave a roar and a stamp of fury. "Are you calling me a coward?" he said. "Why, if you were a gentleman, I'd—"

"Surrender?" I suggested.

The cavalier raised a hand—I knew not whether the man intended a blow or was merely making a gesture in aid of some rhetorical point—but I had suffered enough insult for the day. From Sir Basil, out of prudence, I was obliged to endure abuse, but from this fellow not at all.

I tossed my blanket over the other's head, and while the cavalier struggled free, I punched the man full on the jaw, hard enough to send him unconscious to the floor.

"A foul blow!" said Slope-Shoulder. "That was—"

At that instant the door to the dungeon boomed shut, and complete darkness claimed the room. I ducked to pull my blanket free, and sensed the breeze of a fist passing over my head. I rose from the floor and jostled Slope-Shoulder back on his heels, then swung my own fist in a swooping backhand arc and caught the cavalier on the side of the head. Slope-Shoulder made a muffled noise and stumbled away, and I pursued, shoving and punching alternately, until I heard the cavalier's boot come up against the slop tub, a sound that sparked an idea in my mind.

I ducked, seized an ankle, and jerked it from the floor. Slope-Shoulder gave a shout and fell with a great splash into the slop tub. We captives had been locked in the cellar for three days, the tub hadn't been emptied in all that time, and it was very full.

I grabbed the other foot as it flailed near, and I turned the cavalier over and bore down with my weight, driving him face-first into the tub. The sounds of splashing, flailing, and bubbling filled the air, and a horrid stench rolled into the room. I endured the stink and bore down until I felt Slope-Shoulder weaken, and then I hauled the man out, coughing and sobbing.

I adjusted my blanket over my shoulders and stepped away from the horrid mess. My heart thundered in my chest, and hot fury raged in my veins. I felt I could thrash the whole room.

"*Does anyone else want to learn how to breathe piss?*" I said in a loud voice. There was no reply.

I went to a far wall and made my bed between two of Lord Utterback's servants. As I wrapped myself in my blanket, one of the footmen reached out and touched my arm. "I shall bite thee by the ear, my brave!" he said with great approval. "That was well done, bawcock. Those robustious younkers needed a taking-down."

Which, I thought, was the first pleasant thing any of my fellow servants had said to me.

I settled down to rest, my overcoat pillowed beneath my head, and once my fury faded, I remembered the woman by the sward, and the intent way she had looked at me, and I felt a quiet shimmer along my nerves, a memory of the thrill I had felt when first I saw her gazing at me. I wondered who she was, for if she was in the camp at all, and unmolested, she had to belong to some outlaw. Perhaps to Sir Basil himself, for she seemed so far above all the others that she might well be the consort of their chieftain.

Or, I thought, perhaps she was not Sir Basil's wife or concubine, but his daughter. The protection of his swift dirk would account for her being alone, and unmolested, and so bold in the way she stared at strangers.

For a moment, before dreams took me, I invented a charming romance, that of the captive and the bandit's daughter, and how that story might lead to love and freedom.

When I woke in the morning, I seemed to hear the singing of a mandola.

That day, I saw her again.

CHAPTER EIGHT

"The fork-bearded one, I have discovered, is a baron, and his friend a knight, and Stayne their liege-lord. Neither have spoken in my hearing since the night, and no doubt they desire revenge, if they can only imagine how to accomplish it. They have no weapons but their wits, and their wits are dull indeed. I shift my bed every night, after we are locked in darkness, so they may not find me while I am sleeping. Yet even an attack in the darkness seems beyond their abilities."

I adjusted myself in the marble trough, and raised a palmful of water to scrub my itching whiskers. More than anything but freedom, I would have delighted in a razor, to shave my week-old beard along with the vermin that lived in it. I leaned backward to duck my scalp, scrubbed at it, then sat up and shook the water from my hair. I turned to the rose-colored marble nymph and spoke again.

"It is droll to see the young gentlemen labor," I said. "Cutting vegetables, churning butter, boiling laundry, hauling the slop tub up the stairs and emptying it into the stream. They are poor cottiers indeed, but the bandits take joy in whipping them about their tasks, and Dorinda is even more fierce with her ladle! Their fine clothes are going to ruin, they are overrun by an army of lice and fleas, and they know not how to dress their hair. Sad they seem, and much reduced. . . .

"Look you, mistress," said I as I looked at the little goddess in earnest, "for here they set out, forty of them, to follow their lord in a great adventure, to overthrow a monarch and grow rich from the spoils of war, and they find themselves bested by a gang of low ruffians almost before they can set out. Half Stayne's army ran away at the first shot, and the rest, now captive, make up a village of the worst workingmen in all Duisland!" I laughed. "The world turned upside down! The cavaliers labor while the robbers parade up and down in their finery! It would amuse you, should you ever peer out from your grotto to view the fine green world."

The statue spoke no reply, but her playful smile seemed a reply to all possible questions.

It had been three days since I had first explored the old nymphaeum, and since then I'd returned every day. I'd cleaned weeds and ooze from the trough, and turned it into my own tub, where daily I bathed and rid myself of fleas. Daily I chatted with the rose-pink goddess as if she were my oldest playmate, and told her all the news of the camp, and all that occupied my mind. She was the most perfect audience imaginable, and listened to my talk and my complaints, my conceits and my jests, with all the tolerance in the world—and even approval, if the smile was anything to judge by.

I braced myself against the trough and pushed myself upright, the water cascading from my shoulders. I carefully sat on the edge of the trough, and clapped my thighs with my hands. "It is not Fork-Beard that concerns me, mistress," I said, "but Sir Basil. Each day he has sought me out. He wishes to talk—talk about his services in King Stilwell's wars, and his knighthood won on the field, and the injustices he has endured. He talks about war and women and poetry, about Mallio in its Rawlings translation, and about the plays that were seen in Selford in the days of his youth. He talks about his brave part in the Wars of the Ghouls, and all his quarrels with his neighbors, and the challenges he issued and on what grounds—for his knowledge of the common law comes from the fact that he was always being taken to court by his neighbors, or the other way around, usually for fighting." I looked over my shoulder at the goddess. "I begin to believe the jury found him guilty not because they thought he'd committed the crime, but to rid themselves of a troublesome neighbor."

I stood, shivered, and brushed cold water from my body. "A troublesome neighbor," I repeated. "Will he even let me go, do you think? Or is he so lonely for conversation—for speech with an educated man rather than another brigand—that he will keep me here forever, half servant, half buffoon?"

I reached for my doublet and turned it inside out. I took up a coil of slow-match I'd found in the camp and lit the match on a piece of punk I'd set alight in the kitchen as I left, then kept alive in a bowl covered with a lid. I blew the match to ruby brilliance, then began using the match to burn the lice running freely in my clothing.

"He has sent the ransom demand to Kevin," I continued. "But the letter must first *find* Kevin, who may be away, or at sea on a trading voyage. Kevin must find or borrow five royals in a city that has been looted of most of his money. And then the money must find its way here, to the Toppings, to Sir Basil's rude little treasury with its guard of wyverns." The scent of burning insects tainted the air. I looked up at the goddess. "Is it likely, do you suppose? And how long will it be before this happens? For Sir Basil plans to leave this place as soon as the two lords' ransoms arrive, and find shelter in another wild place before an angry Lord Stayne raises an army to wipe him out. And if I leave this camp before my ransom arrives, the money may take some time to find him. . . ." I sighed. "If I am not murdered beforehand, by some arbitrary caprice of Sir Basil, or some other wanton brute in the camp who may shoot me for his own amusement."

Water chuckled pleasantly from the trough. Wind sighed gently in the osiers. Golden leaves flashed in the air as they fell.

"I must escape," I said to the little goddess. "That is all I can think. For it is intolerable in this camp, and I do not trust Sir Basil to keep his word, and I do not wish to be slaughtered."

I pulled louse eggs from the seams of my doublet, then cast the doublet on the ground and picked up my shirt.

"Yet," I said, "I cannot escape in the day, for the bandits are ever on guard. I need the fall of night to avoid the guards and make as many miles as I can before dawn, and for this I must somehow avoid being locked up at night. But the bandits are alert to this possibility, and make a head count as they send us down the stair. And therefore, I must go forth at night *with permission*. Which brings us to the figure of Dorinda."

I let the name hang in the air for a moment as I burned a fat crab-louse. "She is rare in being a solitary woman in the camp," I resumed. "Most of the women here are married or otherwise attached to one of the men, and the rest are public women bought for the price of silver or a trinket or a fine silk shirt. I cannot speak to the first for fear of angering their menfolk, and the latter despise me for having no money. But Dorinda—"

I looked up at the goddess, as if I sensed an interruption. "You laugh at me, mistress," I said. "And truly, I laugh at myself. Dorinda, indeed!"

I cocked my head, as if listening to a reply, and then went on. "For you see, we eat well in the camp. The bandits no longer haunt the roads for fear of encountering armed parties searching for Lord Stayne, and so they amuse themselves with hunting. And since Sir Basil plans to shift his post, he plans to eat all the domestic animals we may not take with us. And I have become Butcher to the robber band, and daily prepare their meat. Because I have proved good at carving, I am even privileged to cut the collops that feed their lordships Utterback and Stayne. There is no apron, and the work can bespatter a man, so I work near naked.

"Now, I have seen Dorinda look at me as I dismember a deer or a hog, and despite the bruises she daily inflicts upon me with her ladle, I flatter myself that she thinks well of what she sees. And so, *if* I encourage her, and *if* she takes me for her paramour, and *if* I survive the encounter with my back unbroken—for she is a strong woman, and I have seen her hoist a side of beef with no more effort than Lord Stayne might employ to lift a box of comfits—*if* I survive, as I say, and *if* I please her well enough to send her into a sound slumber, and *if* I can then sneak from her lodging and away from the camp . . ." I laughed. "A long, pretty list of *ifs*! *If* I can run through the Toppings without falling and breaking my neck, and *if* I can avoid the dogs and hunting parties sent after me—I believe I am to run in a stream to lose my scent, am I not? So, another *if* presents itself—*if* I do not drown, and then *if* I can somehow escape the Toppings and beg my way to Selford, then I shall be a free man." I laughed. "And if not, a corpse. Or the concubine of a savage, half-mad cook. Or a captive, growing ever more crepuscular, like Higgs." I looked at the goddess and smiled. "Do you like *crepuscular*, by the way? I made it up. From the old Aekoi, *crepusculum*."

I finished my shirt, put it on the grass, and picked up my riding breeches. As I searched the seams for lice, I gave the statue a wistful look. "But it is not Dorinda to whom I wish to address my attentions. Nor to you, mistress, begging your pardon. But rather another—a woman I have seen only twice."

I looked up as a gust of wind rattled the autumn leaves over my head, and a golden whirlwind of leaves clattered through the grove. The tip of the slow-match flared brighter, then faded. I lifted my brows and looked at the goddess.

"Are you jealous, mistress?" I asked. "Do not fear; she is beyond my reach.

"Two days ago," I continued, "I saw her walking on the sward, across the lake, while the camp was having its dinner. And last night, at twilight I saw her standing not fifty feet away, but I was being harangued by Sir Basil about some point of law, and could not get away. And again she stood looking at me, her green eyes gazing at me, and I felt that in her eyes I might be the only man in the world. . . ." My voice drifted away as I relived the memory. And then I shook myself, and laughed as I looked at the rose-pink goddess. "You laugh at me, mistress! And yet, and yet . . ." I touched myself just above the heart. "The gaze of those green eyes stirred me to my bones. A poet would compare her skin to ivory, and call her eyes 'smaragds,' I suppose, and then have to find a rhyme for the word!" I gave a bitter laugh. "And I—a prisoner, penniless, without smaragds or anything but the clothes on my back!" My tone turned wistful. "Yet I would dare, if I could."

I had finished my task with the slow-match, ground the burnt end underfoot, and coiled the rest. I hastened to put on my clothes, and rubbed warmth into my arms and shoulders. "As your sole worshiper," I told the statue, "may I beg a favor? Will you provide a little hot water tomorrow? My baths are too cold for the season."

I offered the goddess a bow. "With your permission, I shall come again tomorrow to worship at your feet." I threw the overcoat over my shoulder, and made my way into the grove, through a rain of slender golden leaves.

I walked beside the stream, my eyes on the ground, my mind occupied by memories of the ghostly red-headed woman. And then, from somewhere above me, I heard a sonorous chord.

I looked up in deep surprise, and saw the mysterious woman above me, perched on a limb of one of the largest osiers, her feet dangling just above my head. She was dressed simply, in a deep blue velvet skirt, a blouse of the dark red called cramoisie, and a long woolen shawl of deep greens and blues draped over her head, one end stylishly thrown over her shoulder. She wore soft boots of dark suede. Behind her, the bright gold of the leaves shimmered and surged like a sun-struck sea. She held a mandola in her lap, and strummed more chords while her green eyes glittered with amusement.

"Mistress!" My heart gave a leap, and I doffed my cap. "I count myself fortunate to encounter you."

"Fortunate?" she asked. "Hardly so. I believe fortune's wheel has cast you down, sir, and cast you hard upon stones."

"Then may I rise again?" Without waiting for permission, I tossed my overcoat onto the grass, grasped a tree limb with both hands, then swung my legs up to embrace the bough. In a rattle of falling leaves I pulled myself upright, and soon sat on a bough adjacent to hers, our feet nearly touching.

Her eyes dropped modestly, and she played a short, bright phrase on the mandola. "I had thought," she said, "that my practice was private."

"You may play on, if you like," said I. "And I will pretend that I'm not here."

Her full lips quirked in a smile. She brushed at a strand of red hair that had escaped her shawl, and looked at me with her brilliant eyes. I felt my breath stop in my throat.

"May I know your name, mistress?" I asked.

Her eyes turned to a corner of the sky, as if she were making up a name on the spot. "I am Orlanda," she said.

"I am Quillifer."

She smiled. "I can see that you are."

I laughed. "Fair Mistress Orlanda," I said. "How come you to be here?"

Her answer was simple. "I climbed the tree."

"I mean," I said, "you seem to be free in the camp. You possess privilege of some kind."

"If I possess privilege, I also possess caprice," she said. "It is my caprice to stand on my privilege, and privilege not your question."

She returned my every volley, the most enticing tennis player I had ever met. I tried again. "You have looked at me, I think."

"I look at many things." She played a low trill on her instrument, four strings singing as one. I found the sound strangely melancholy for an instrument celebrated for its joyous voice.

"Are you sad, mistress?" I asked. In answer, she began to sing.

> *Ah me! as thus I look before me*
>   *Along the course of time*
> *Steals tides of pensive musing o'er me*
>   *Like sound of sad knell chime*
>
> *Now many a gentle flower, its race*
>   *All run, its sweet breath sped*
> *Its beauty wasted, hides its face*
>   *And slumbers with the dead.*
>
> *The dead of many generations*
>   *Of its own frail kindred*
> *The countless dead of tribes and nations*
>   *Who once with open lid*
>
> *Like it looked on the morning's grace*
>   *And saw the noontide glory*
> *And drank life's joy, but went apace*
>   *Ah me! the endless story.*

The last chord died away; the grove was still. Orlanda gazed at me in pensive silence. I wondered how old she was, and decided she was a few years older than I.

"A song for autumn," I said. "But see, we are young, and can kindle summer in our hearts."

"Do you offer up my heart for kindling?" she asked. "As if it were straw, or twigs?" She gave me a doubtful look. "I hope you don't mistake me for lightwood."

"I offer to fill your heart with fire. A fire like that in my own." I reached for her hand. She struck a dissonant chord on her mandola, and I drew the hand back. She offered an approving smile, and a soft melody rang from the instrument.

"Many summers were kindled in this place," she said. "And yet all ended. Many were the hopes engendered in the town that was builded here, but all hopes failed when failed the silver."

"Silver?" I was surprised.

"There was a mine—" Orlanda glanced up at the cliffs, but the limbs and leaves of the trees kept me from seeing where her gaze lighted. "The mine was why the town was built, and the castle. There was a great wooden gallery that carried the ore down to the valley."

Her fingers drew forth the melody, and somehow the strings sounded like coins ringing. "The silver pennies of the Morcants were famous, and they paid for the war that drove out the Sea-Kings. But the silver ran out centuries ago, and the Morcants faded, and it was the sons of the Sea-Kings who united Fornland, not the Morcants. When the silver failed, local lords remained in the castle, great oppressors of the people, till they too died out."

The dynasty of the Morcants, I thought, *had been eleven hundred years before, great warriors and poets and builders. According to all the histories, they had been rich, and now I know why.*

"Is the mine still there?"

"Dark tunnels half-collapsed—no silver."

"I had thought I might hide there, until the bandits ceased to hunt me."

Orlanda looked at me for a long moment, and the melody died on the strings. "You wish to flee."

I looked at her. "I wish to flee with *you*. We can go to the capital. I have an urgent message to carry to the Queen—my city was plundered and blockaded and is in sore need of aid. I must urge the court to send relief. And once in Selford, I can take up the law, I can make my way in the world. Become a judge, or a courtier, or a Member of the Burgesses. I'll put my mark on the world! My ambition is enough for the both of us."

Sorrow touched her face. Her fingers drew out a little refrain: *Ah me! The endless story.*

"The mine is no refuge, nor the court," she said, and turned away for a moment. "Speak of fire again," she said. "The day grows chill."

"I would set a fire in every part of you," I said. I reached for her hand again, and this time she allowed me to take it. "The fingers so clever," I said, "coaxing melody from wood and ivory," and kissed them, and then I turned the hand over and kissed the palm. I leaned close and brushed the hair back from her face. I slipped the shawl to her shoulders, and inhaled the scent of her hair, rich and earthy as a spring glade. "Your hair," I said, "on fire already. Your cheeks"—kissing—"smooth as cream." She looked at me, and I could feel her warmth on my skin. "Your eyes," I said, "so like—"

"Smaragds?" she said. "Or is that too poetastical?"

I stared at her, words frozen in my throat.

"Do you like 'poetastical'?" she said. "I just made it up."

I threw my head back and laughed. "You overheard!" I said in joy.

Answering delight danced in her emerald eyes.

I stared at her. "You saw me naked!" I said.

"I saw nothing," she said demurely. "I pretended I wasn't there."

I laughed again, and pressed her hand. "Mistress, we must flee this place together! Nothing can stop us, an we are together! The world will lie vanquished before us, and offer us sweet wine and Orient pearls."

"I should want such trifles?" Orlanda asked. "I am caprice and privilege, remember. What is Selford, or the world, to me?"

"A setting for your beauty. A choice audience for your wit. A playground for your caprice. And besides, mistress, will you stay here? In this camp, till Sir Basil chooses to move his band to some other desolate country?"

A cloud crossed her face. "I was content," she said, "till you came."

I raised her hand and kissed it. "Content is valued only by those who have already grappled with life, and earned their victory. Content is for old men with their mulled wine, and old women with their grandchildren, and old fat dogs who lie before the fire. Content is not for the young and dauntless, those who wish to brand the world with their mark. Fly with me! You know the country; you must know a way to evade pursuit."

"You paint a persuasive picture," Orlanda said.

I kissed her cheek. "Let me entice you further." I kissed again, and she turned to me, and was about to kiss again, but the horn blew in the camp, and she put two fingers on my lips and gently pushed me away.

"You're called to supper," she said. "Don't be late."

"I'll see you tomorrow? So I can collect my kiss?"

A smile crossed her lips. "I promise that I will see *you*."

I laughed. "We'll meet at the fountain of the little goddess. Perhaps we can bathe, and to preserve our modesty each can pretend the other isn't there."

I dropped to the ground, picked up my overcoat, and walked with a light heart along the stream, turning every so often to wave, until she disappeared behind the golden screen of the osiers. Dorinda growled at me for my tardy arrival, and beat me thoroughly with her ladle as I served stew to the bandits, and then cut up the lords' meat and handed it to the outlaw wife who carried the platter to the Oak House. I barely felt the blows.

After my own hurried meal, and the cleaning of the bowls and spoons, I shuffled down into the dungeon with the rest, and made a pillow of my overcoat. The rich scent of her hair still floated in my memory.

Smaragds, I thought ridiculously, and was soon asleep.

I awoke to the fragrance of her hair, and a soft kiss on my lips.

CHAPTER NINE

M y gasp of surprise was smothered by another kiss. I stared up to see Orlanda gazing down at me, her face softly glowing in the light of a small horn lantern. She bent close to my ear.

"Come now, and quietly. I can't set all these people free, only you."

I came to my feet swiftly, my overcoat in my hands, suddenly awake and half delirious with joy. She put a finger to her lips to signal silence, and then took my hand and led me through the room toward the stair.

Around me men snored, the rumbling filling the air. Though some stirred uneasily, none woke as I passed. I wondered if I was still dreaming, if this were all some midnight phantasie.

Orlanda went silently up the steep stairs and I followed, and then we were out of the noisome pit and into the realm of cool, fresh air, heavy with dew. The thick cellar door hung open, and Orlanda turned to hand me the lantern and push the door once again into place. I heard the heavy wooden bar nestle into its home, and then Orlanda took the little lantern and led me out of the castle, toward the camp.

"Where are the guards?" I whispered.

"In their beds. Once the prisoners are locked in, there is nothing to guard."

"We're going to the camp? Why?" I pointed to where the stream emptied into the valley below. "Why not to the vale?"

Again Orlanda put a finger to her lips, and I fell silent as we padded among the rough dwellings at the foot of the cliff. To my surprise, the dogs of the camp were silent. My heart gave a leap as she paused at the wicker gate to the bandits' treasury.

"Nay," I whispered. "The wyverns will tear you to pieces!"

She ignored me and pushed the gate open, and I readied myself to fight murderous animals trained to tear and roast human flesh. But Orlanda passed into the enclosure unmolested and walked onto the portico of the old temple. I followed, saw the monsters lying together in a corner of the yard, and decided Orlanda must have poisoned them.

I didn't see what Orlanda did to the lock, but I heard it clack open, and then Orlanda pushed into the temple itself. I followed, and in the dim light of the little lantern saw chests and bags set on tables.

Orlanda shoved a leather rucksack into my arms. "Hurry!" she said.

I opened chests and saw silver crowns neatly and lovingly stacked. I found a small coffer with gold royals, and another coffer that held miscellaneous jewelry, among which I recognized the gold chains of Ethlebight's aldermen. I first emptied the gold royals into the rucksack, then a chest filled with crowns. Overspilling, silver crowns rang off the stone floor.

"No noise!" Orlanda hissed. I took more care with the next coffer, and shook the contents carefully into the rucksack until it was nearly full. Then I poured the jewelry on top and tied down the rucksack's flap with its leather cords.

"A pity to leave so much behind," I said.

"Come." Orlanda led me out of the old temple, and as I shrugged into the rucksack, she turned to lock the door.

The rucksack was heavy, but I knew it held my fortune, and felt willing to bear it to the ends of the earth. While I was adjusting the straps, I heard one of the wyverns give a kind of snort. There was a brief flash of flame, and I almost leaped out of my boots.

Not dead, then, but sleeping. Drugged, presumably, but not to death.

I still felt as if possessed by a dream, as if freedom and fortune were a fantasy that would vanish with the dawn. Orlanda and I left the enclosure, and Orlanda fastened the gate and led me between the treasury and Sir Basil's house. I walked with care and held my breath, and I did not hear the outlaw stir. We came to the base of the cliff that surrounded the corrie.

"This path goes up to the rim," Orlanda whispered. Her light played over the stones, and I saw a narrow path I hadn't noticed on my previous investigations of the scarp.

"There are no guards on top of the cliffs?" I asked.

"Nay," she said. "Why would there be?"

I followed her and the bobbing light up the trail. The route would have been easy enough in daylight, but at night it was challenging, the path having to twist around large columnar rocks that stood like sentinels over the valley, and which sometimes had to be climbed directly. Pioneers long in the grave had cut hand- and footholds in the rock, and Orlanda was careful to shine the lantern on the hollows that would help me set my hands and feet. There was only one moment when I nearly fell, as the weight of the rucksack threatened to topple me backward while I edged around a column of basalt. One arm flailed, and vertigo clutched me by the throat as I realized I was about to fall, but Orlanda seized my arm and steadied me, and I recovered and, after a moment to catch my breath, continued the climb.

By the time I reached the top of the cliff, any sense that I inhabited a dream had vanished. My chest heaved, and I gasped in cold air scented with the pines that rimmed the corrie. My legs felt like water, held upright only by a fierce act of will. Orlanda waited, a little impatiently, for me to get my breathing in order, and then led me along the ridge that walled the corrie until she found a trail. Our footsteps were muffled by pine needles, and a gentle wind whispered through the spreading boughs overhead. Ahead of them, a grazing hind raised her head in surprise, then bounded away.

"The moon will rise soon, and we will better see our course," Orlanda said.

"Let us tarry a while," I said, and caught her hand.

She turned. "Are you still fatigued?" Starlight glittered in her eyes.

"No, mistress," I said, and took her in my arms. "I desire only to kiss you, and to thank you for my liberty."

I kissed her gently, then with greater ardor. Her body warmed mine. Her breath had a bright, fresh taste, like juniper berries, and the earthy scent of her hair swam in my senses.

She gave a gasp, then drew away. "Come." Taking my hand. "We have a long way to go, and Sir Basil will pursue you to hell itself for the sake of the silver on your back."

We walked along the ridge above a valley, then down into the vale and across a stream. The moon rose and limned the path ahead with delicate traceries of silver, and Orlanda blew out her little lamp. Night birds called, and deer drifted through the night until they were aware of the humans among them, and then fled, bounding. Agile foxes and grumbling badgers crossed our path.

The path went up, down, left, right. At times, I could have sworn that we were doubling back on ourselves. Yet the chill night was beautiful, and peaceful, and I felt an effervescence filling my veins. I carried my burden lightly, walked with ease on the moonlit path, and viewed the world with unfolding delight.

Hours were spent on the winding route, and as the path dropped from a ridge into a pine-strewn valley, I thought I heard a waft of melody on the air, perhaps a figure played on a viol. "Listen!" I said, and we paused as my ears strained the night.

The sound was difficult to hear over the sough of wind in the pines, but at last I heard it clearly: a viol, tambour, and a fipple flute, all playing a coranto.

"Hear you?" I said. "There are folk ahead."

"You need not fear musicians," Orlanda said.

"Musicians are as other men," I said, "and as greedy for silver. We may not be safe."

"Perhaps we will join them."

"In that case, I am heartily sorry that you abandoned your mandola on my account. I will buy you a new one, and a better."

We continued through the trees, and the sounds of music grew clearer. Other instruments joined the ensemble as the coranto was followed by a galliard, and the galliard by a canario. I fancied I heard laughter and the sounds of clinking glasses.

"For the revels to last so long, they must be celebrating a wedding," I said. "The charivari runs late."

Orlanda looked at me over her shoulder. "A wedding indeed."

She took my hand and drew me forward, and we advanced together. A shimmering, indistinct light flittered ahead, like a bonfire eclipsed by tossing trees. We crossed a small stream, almost dancing along the stepping-stones, and then continued until the forest died away, and I saw before us a steep, bare round hill. The hill seemed to cast off a shimmer, like an aurora, that silhouetted it against shifting spears of white light.

Every detail, every blade of grass, was perfectly visible. The hill itself was crowned by an ancient earthen rampart, and on its summit was a ruined tower of black stone, like a broken fang. The music rang on, like tuned bells tumbling joyously down the slope.

Doors thundered open in my mind, and in a moment of staggering revelation I realized who I was dealing with. I knew why the guards and monsters had slept, and why the temple doors had opened to she for whom the temple was built.

Perhaps I had been a cretinous fool, but I had not till this minute realized that I had walked out of the world and into a song.

I turned to Orlanda in astonishment. She gazed at me expectantly, her eyes dark in the shadow beneath her tranquil brows.

"My lady," I ventured. "Whose home is this?"

"Mine," she said, "and you are welcome to abide in it this night."

"And whose wedding," I asked, "do those musicians celebrate?"

Her hand tightened on mine. "Ours," she said, "should you prove willing."

"O my lady of the fountain," I said, "you have been toying with me."

The goddess then put on her full beauty, her perfect face a luminous glory, her hair a flame, her simple clothing now a silken gown sewn with pearls, the skirt embroidered with figures of animals and birds. A diamond necklace cascaded down her breast like a sparkling fountain, and a vaunting ruff framed her head like a halo. A coronet shone gold in her hair.

The radiance of her figure struck me with such weight that it bore me to my knees. For a moment, she imitated the pose of the nymphaeum's marble statue, one hand lifted to her cheek, her smile a promise of mischief, and then she dropped the pose.

"I am caprice, am I not?" she said. "Yet my deceptions have done you no harm."

"You have done me nothing but service," I said. "I owe you my liberty."

"Shall we go then to our wedding feast?" She helped me to my feet, and began to lead me toward the hill. Yet I found myself reluctant to follow; and as I began to drag my feet, she turned.

"My lady," I said, "is it true, as the stories have it, that this wedding feast may last an hundred years, and that I will come staggering from my marriage bed into the land, bewildered by a world no longer my own?"

"You need never leave," she said.

"That," I dared to point out, "is not quite an answer to my question. Should I desire to visit my friends, my city, the world at large . . . will I find the world I know, or some other, stranger land?"

She regarded me with something like compassion. "Do you know of Benat?" she asked. "Benat the Bear, Benat of the Copper Spear, Benat the Champion?"

"I do not recognize the name," said I.

"The greatest hero this country has known? Victor in a hundred fights, slayer of beasts and monsters, founder of a kingdom?"

"I know neither he nor his kingdom," said I.

"A thousand songs were made on Benat. Poets labored to create grand word-pictures for his great shoulders, his flashing eyes, his mighty laugh, his deadly spear. The epic of Benat was chanted by every bard in the land. But where is Benat now that the songs are no longer sung and his kingdom is not even a memory?"

"Under yon hill?" Nodding toward the hill, the rampart, the stone fang.

"Nay. I laid my lover a few leagues from here, in a tomb dug into a cliff, with his bright spear beside him. His monument is the golden rambler rose I planted there, and which, like my love, blooms in all seasons."

"Did he leave your bed?" I asked. "Did he wander and die in a world that knew him not?"

Orlanda slowly shook her head. "I was different in those days," she said. "I helped his rise. I aided him in his battles, I advised him in ruling his kingdom, I shared in his glory. When he finally came to my home, he came as a grizzled warrior, unbent but weary, and he left only in death." Her emerald eyes searched mine. "Death comes to all mortals, and all my aid can only postpone that end. But in my house Benat lived long, and in honor, until I laid him to rest."

She stepped close to me, her voice low and in earnest. "Hard it was to lose Benat, but harder it was to watch as he faded from memory—to watch the kingdom slip away, the great stone monuments tarnish and crumble, the songs fall from memory. That was a harsh lesson, that all earthly ambition is impermanent, and never in the ages since have I so aided the aspirations of a mortal." She drew lightly on my hand. "Better to come away from this perishable world when you can, and escape the bitter knowledge that your deeds will fade from memory, that all greatness is dust, that your aspirations were doomed before ever you came weeping into the world. Celebrate youth and joy for all the years I can give you, and avoid all sadness."

I allowed myself to be pulled forward, but came only a few steps before slowing to a halt.

"My lady," I said. "I have certain responsibilities—to bear a message from my city to Selford, and to lay my family to rest not in a stolen tomb but a monument worthy of them."

"Well do you know that Ethlebight is mortal," she said. "What difference will your message make in ten years, or twenty, when the harbor is sealed? All too soon Selford itself will crumble, and the river carry its glories to the sea. And as for your family, it is no longer in their power to care where they lie."

"I do not honor my family for the sake of the dead," I said, "but for my own self-regard, so that I can view myself in the mirror and not feel shame. If I fail them, how can I be worthy of the proposal which you have so generously offered me?"

Orlanda's eyes narrowed. "I am myself the judge of who is worthy to guest in my house," she said.

"Yet I would know—"

Orlanda turned on me with green fire blazing from her eyes. "What are these questions?" Orlanda demanded. "What is this lawyer's artful chop-logic and crinkum-crankum?" She stepped close, and cold fear chilled my blood as I felt her power surge through the air, lifting the hair on the back of my neck.

Orlanda's angry voice fell against my ears like the crack of a whip.

"You spoke very differently not long ago, when you needed my aid to flee the bandits' den! What of those loving, admiring words with which you addressed me? Were you playing me false?"

Through my terror, I managed to find my tongue. "I loved a mortal girl," I said. "I loved a mortal girl who climbed trees and played the mandola and left me in burning hope of sweet kisses. Yet now it seems that girl is something different than what I had believed."

Her anger faded. "I am that girl," she said. "I may be that girl or any girl whosoever you choose. But," she conceded, finally, "if you have questions, ask."

I composed my whirling thoughts, and of the many questions that crowded my brain, I asked the one I deemed most harmless. "Why am I bearing this load of silver?" I said. "What use will you make of it? Is there some great hoard in your house?"

"There must be an exchange," she said, "that is all. To live in my world, you must bring something of value. The silver was at hand."

I remembered the story of Menasso, and what part of himself the goddess Sylvia had demanded as a toll in her domaine, and I felt grateful for my brief stay in the bandits' treasury. I asked the question that was both of greatest import, and perhaps the greatest peril.

"How much time will lapse in this mortal world while our wedding night passes beneath the hill?"

"I hope it will be long," Orlanda said. "For its duration depends on the strength of our desire, and how long that desire may be prolonged and renewed and protracted and satisfied and re-satisfied before our love reaches its uttermost, if temporary, satiation." And, seeing me about to ask another question, she pressed her fingers to my lips, and said, "If you leave my house after that night, you will indeed be an exile in whatever world you find. No one will remember you, and no one will believe your story." She took her hand away, then raised warm lips to mine and kissed me. "Therefore do not go, and stay with me for night after night, for song and revels and dance, for raiment of rich fabrics sewn with gems, for the long span of life I can grant, and for the many long nights of mutual pleasure that will be ours beneath the eternal stars."

She kissed me again, and the taste of her lips made my mind whirl. But I forced my thoughts into the form of words.

"And if I choose to take up my worldly duties, and decline this sublime offer you have made? Will you curse me, or pursue me into the world on some mission of vengeance?"

Her eyes flashed again, and she took a step back. "I cannot answer your question," she said, "for no man has ever refused my favors."

I took her hands and raised them, and kissed the warm, fragrant skin. "I would give you anything in thanks for my rescue," I said, "anything but spending all my days as your lodger."

Orlanda's face blazed with fury and scorn. "It is your ambition that is behind this refusal!"

Against her power I could summon only the truth. "I will not deny it."

Nor would I put into words my other thought, that I had not escaped slavery at the hands of the Aekoi to become the house-pet of a capricious nymph.

She gazed at me with eyes both cold and magnificent. "Adventure and worldly power you may have," she said, "but it will be swept away. Love you will have, but it will thrive only in the shadow of death, and the grave will be its end."

My blood ran chill. "Is that your curse?"

"Pah! As if I needed to expend an ounce of my power to make this augury!" Her lip curled. "You are cursed only as all other men are cursed, to death and misery and futile striving."

I kissed her hands again, but her fists were clenched.

"I esteem you above all others," I said, "and I would give you anything but this one thing."

"The only thing that matters." She gave me a cold look from her green eyes. "There will be a price for this decision of yours."

"A dear price it is that I shall not see you again."

A smile touched the corner of her mouth. "Perhaps," she said, "that is not quite what I meant." Orlanda drew her hands away, and pointed toward the trees that rimmed the hill. "There you will find the path that will take you down into the valley. From there, follow the stream until you reach the road. Turn left, and you will enter a village where you can find a horse, and then you may go about your precious, useless, pointless errand. The errand that leads only to the grave."

"My lady." I bowed deeply, and backed away from her until I reached the limit of her radiance, and then with a last look at the beautiful figure standing before me, I turned and walked into the woods. Whole worlds seemed to be crumbling around me.

The trail was plain in the moonlight, and I made good speed through the pines, which turned to aspen as I descended the slope, and then to willows as I reached the floor of the valley. A cold stream laughed and plashed alongside the narrow trail, which soon turned to a narrow cart-track. The sky in the east was brightening, and I found my heart surge. The farther I walked from Orlanda's hill, the greater was my sensation of freedom and release; and after I found the promised village. There, I looked at the contents of my rucksack and was faintly surprised to discover that the silver had not vanished like the morning mist.

I rented a post-horse from the mean, wretched posting inn, and heard the sound of the hooves on the road, and as I felt the surge of the horse beneath me and the breath of freedom in my face, I laughed aloud.

Surrounded by a storm of falling leaves, I rode hard from stage to stage, changing horses at every stop, and paused only for the bread, meat, and beer that were offered me. None of the horses had the gliding gate of my palfrey, Toast, but they all carried me closer to the capital. And by afternoon I had left the steep, winding roads of the Toppings behind, and was in the fertile plain of the Saelle on a good road that ran straight as an arrow's flight across the country.

I rode all day and through the night, and in the morning, when exhaustion overcame me, I rented a small, light carriage, and slept as the coachman drove through the day. As I drowsed, I realized that I was not scratching, and that Orlanda had given me a parting gift: I was no longer prey to vermin. By late afternoon I was riding again, passing through rich farmland, where smoke curled from the chimneys on every horizon, and workers picked apples from the groves. I paid a penny for a pearmain, and relished the sweet remembrance of home as I rode into the night.

Again I rode on past dawn and into the morning, and passed through villages large and small. At noon of that brilliant day, as the high sun glowed gold on the stubble of the fields, and the sky dappled with silver cloud, I came within sight of the walls of Selford, and on a bluff above the river beheld the white towers of the royal palace. There was a great crowd of people outside the walls, surging under a brilliant array of flags, and on a conical hill in the center of the mass I could see a tall canopy, striped red and gold, and beneath it a throne, and around the throne an array of men and women in silks and gay colors; and at once I knew that I had come to the capital on the day that the princess Berlauda would receive her crown, and reign as Duisland's new Queen.

CHAPTER TEN

hough you say nothing, I can sense a certain degree of skepticism in you. You may have thought the preceding was a fantasy, or the concoction of a mind confined too long to a dungeon. Perhaps it is better—safer—that you think so.

But what follows is historical-factual. There are many witnesses, and if you can find one, you may consult that person.

The crowd surrounding Coronation Hill was so large it would have overspilled Scarcroft Square in Ethlebight. I eased my horse through the mass until from horseback I could see the figures standing beneath the spreading canopy in the red and gold of the Emelin dynasty. The canopy was held aloft by men in the robes of knightly orders. A little below the throne, a man in the garb of a monk addressed the crowd with well-bred sentences, while an armored man with a naked sword stood guard. Other guards, red-capped and clad in black leather, pressed with their pikes to keep the crowd well back.

A blond, rather impassive woman sat on the throne, her figure clothed in golden silk, on top of which several tabards or surcoats, all of different colors, had been placed. Two figures stood on either side of her, one a tall woman in brilliant blues and yellows whose glance, at once fierce and nervous, darted over the crowd; the other a small, dark-haired girl of about fifteen who seemed aswim in the vast embroidered acreage of her silk gown. Both wore small crowns. These, I decided, were Berlauda's mother, Leonora, one of Stilwell's divorced Queens, and the new Queen's half sister Floria, who was the child of another Queen, likewise divorced.

There seemed to be an abundance of Queens in our realm. I began to feel a degree of sympathy for Floria, who was a mere princess.

Behind the throne stood a brilliant half circle of men and women, most wearing coronets and scarlet, fur-trimmed robes, and I supposed these kin of the new Queen. Another brilliant half circle faced the throne, most of them nobles by their coronets and by the banners displayed by their followers. These, more junior than the group behind the throne, were careful to keep outside the line of pikes. While the monk's sonorous phrases floated through the still air, I searched these banners for that of Lord Utterback's father, the Count of Wenlock, but I failed to find it.

The monk came to his beautifully rounded conclusion, and called in the Pilgrim's name for prayer, which he then proceeded to lead himself, calling for blessings upon Duisland and its Queen. I knew that some of the followers of the Compassionate Pilgrim eschewed prayer as useless, and that the issue was one of controversy within their sect. By the fact there was prayer at all, I assumed that Berlauda had shown her own preference.

The prayer over, the monk gracefully stood aside, and the coronation continued. Notables detached themselves from the group behind the throne to recite a bit of antique verse and hand the Queen a pair of spurs, or place a ring on her finger, or waft her with a peacock-feather fan. To me these rituals were meaningless, for all they were performed with great solemnity. The orb and scepter were placed in the monarch's hands, and she rose from the throne so that a clutch of elderly peers could drape her in a scarlet cape trimmed with ermine, a cape so long that it took eight noblemen to carry it.

Then, last of all, the Queen's mother and the princess Floria stepped forward, carrying the crown between them, and raised it over Berlauda's head. There was a moment of unintentional comedy as the little princess had to stand on tiptoe to hold the crown fully over the head of her taller sister. I saw that all the men in the crowd took off their caps, and the nobles their coronets, and so I took off my own apprentice cap. The nobles' banners were also dipped, the flags bowing down.

Trumpets called, and the crown was lowered onto the head of the monarch. Cheers rang up from the crowd, and cannon boomed out from the city walls, white powder smoke blossoming from the embrasures. Coronets and caps were returned to heads or tossed in the air, and the flags were raised and flaunted overhead.

"The gods save your majesty!" bellowed one giant voice from the back of the crowd. There was laughter and applause from the audience.

Queen Berlauda, burdened by the weight of her crown, costume, regalia, and the enormous cape, made no movement—perhaps was unable to move at all—but a look of displeasure crossed her face at the interruption. Her supporters helped her gather her skirts and cape, and she backed herself onto the throne. Officiants carried away the orb and scepter, and someone handed her a paper.

The cheers died away, and Queen Berlauda took her oath, in which she vowed to respect the ancient rights and privileges of the nobles and commons, to do justice, to maintain the security of the realm, and to punish treason. At the word "treason" her eyes flashed, and I felt myself reappraise the scene before me. What had seemed hollow ritual now took on a deeper meaning, a monarch's reassurance to her people in a time of uncertainty.

The bastard Clayborne, I decided, had raised the standard of rebellion after all. Resulting in confusion across the realm and a very hasty coronation for Berlauda, to prove her right before the people.

For if we have a civil war, plundered cities will be common as spots on a leopard. I remembered Lord Utterback's words, and shivered.

I remembered other parts of that conversation, and wondered if I had failed to find the Count of Wenlock in the crowd because Utterback's father was off with the rebel army.

Berlauda completed her oath, and the armored man with the sword raised his voice and offered to fight anyone disputing the Queen's right. He threw down his gage, and glared furiously over the crowd, as if Clayborne might saunter out from the throng and pick up the gauntlet at any moment.

That moment of drama passed, and the ceremony grew tedious as the nobles knelt, one by one, to proffer allegiance, and office-holders knelt to kiss the royal hands in order to retain their position. It reminded me too clearly of the scramble for place and office taking place in Ethlebight, so I edged my horse toward the margins of the crowd, and then wondered where I would go next. The crowd was such that the inns were almost certainly full, and I thought that wandering a large, strange city, in the midst of what promised to be a boisterous holiday, with a fortune on my back would not be conducive to my long life or health.

Perhaps, I thought, it would be best if I could return to the country and find lodging there.

There was another blare of trumpets, and more red-capped pikemen appeared, creating a lane between the throne and the city gate. The crowd was pushed aside by a wall of pikes, and I found myself and my horse backed against the city walls. The horse snorted a warning and threatened to lash out. I was unhappy with the idea of being atop a misbehaving horse, and had very little idea how to pacify the animal, and for lack of any other idea I patted its neck in hopes of calming it.

The cannon began to fire another salute, and the horse gave a nervous leap at the first shot. I urged the crowd to keep clear and tried to find a safe way to withdraw, but the pikemen were adamant and the crowd were confused, and packed into too small a space.

I spoke soothing words into the horse's ear, and wished I had a piece of toast or some other bribe to distract it from the tumult. Its ears were laid back, and it glared at the crowd nearby and snorted, but it calmed once the barrage overhead was over. I felt a modest glow of pride at the thought that I might be on the verge of becoming a competent equestrian, and then I glanced up to see the Queen gliding along the lane the pikemen had carved for her. Though in motion, she was herself utterly motionless, the orb and scepter back in her hands. Her impassive, handsome face looked straight ahead, and she seemed to be somehow soaring in midair.

This strange motion was explained once I had straightened in the saddle and was able to see over the pikemen. Queen Berlauda was being carried in an elaborate, gilded litter by twelve gentlemen, six before her, and six after. Behind came her mother and the princess, also floating along in chairs, and then the armored man on foot, red-faced and sweating after his long hours baking in the sun, his long sword still upright as he clanked along.

Someone shouted an order, and the pikemen formed into a column and marched into the city after the Queen. I suspected that a mistake had been made, for this in effect stranded the rest of the dignitaries in the midst of the crowd.

The mass surged toward the gate on the heels of the soldiers, and I, who had decided to return to the country to lodge for the night, was unable to make my way against the press. So I remained by the city wall, and watched the throng enter, commons and nobles and dignitaries alike all knocking elbows in one great column.

I kept an eye out for the badge of Wenlock, in case Lord Utterback's father had been hidden in the crowd around the throne, but again I failed to see it. Instead I recognized another badge, the coins argent of Roundsilver, and my heart gave a leap. In addition to being Lawyer Dacket's landlord, the Duke of Roundsilver was the greatest magnate in the west country, so great that he almost never appeared in Ethlebight but followed the royal court from place to place.

Though the duke came but seldom to Ethlebight, I recognized him from his appearance at some of the large festivals. He was a slight man, a little below average height, with delicate features and gray strands in his long, fair hair. He rode a beautiful, high-spirited chestnut with a flaxen mane and tail that flashed like red gold in the sun. A spray of diamonds shone on his deep blue velvet bonnet, and more diamonds glittered on his fingers. Beneath his scarlet duke's robe, with its ermine trim, he wore a long velvet tunic of a brighter, brilliant red shade, patterned all over with swooping, intricate painted designs in radiant gold. Red and gold, the royal colors. Gems had been sewn all over the tunic, and their flashing, reflected light, combined with the soaring yellow patterns, gave Roundsilver a shimmering effect, and made him difficult for the eye to fasten upon.

I wondered if all the money in my rucksack would have bought that tunic, and I thought it would not.

Beside Roundsilver, on a matching chestnut, rode a small, dainty woman, slim and vivacious. She seemed about my age. Masses of her blond hair had been caught up in braids and coiled about her head to form a setting for her coronet, and she also wore an ermine-trimmed cloak. Her silk gown seemed to be made entirely of silver, and like the duke's was patterned with elaborate designs and sewn with gems, and covered with a cloud of silver tissue. She laughed as she rode, and spoke continuously, while the duke looked at her fondly.

I urged my mount forward. "Your grace!" I called. "My Lord of Roundsilver!"

They didn't hear me, or pretended not to; and I rode forward and bawled the name again. At this the duke turned to me, and with a quick glance of his dark eyes seemed to itemize me, add those items together, and find the sum less discouraging than it might have been. It was impossible to have a conversation in the gateway, not with the flood of human beings pouring through it, and so he gave a little wave of one glittering hand, telling me to follow.

I urged my horse through the mass and followed the brilliant couple through the dark tunnel of the gateway, and into the broad street beyond. There the duke slowed his horse and allowed me to reach him.

I pulled off my cap. "Your grace!" I said. "I have come from Ethlebight. The city has fallen."

Surprise crossed the duke's delicate features. The young duchess, hearing the news, reached for her husband's hand.

"The usurper's taken the city?" he said.

The usurper. The bastard Clayborne, then, truly had risen in rebellion.

"Nay, your grace. Reivers out of the old Empire. They have taken half the people for slaves, including the mayor, the Lord Lieutenant, and the Warden of the New Castle. I am sent to implore the Queen to send aid, and money for ransom."

Their horses walked slowly on as Roundsilver considered this, his hand still clasped with that of his duchess. "It is not possible today," he said. "The Queen is hedged about with duties and ceremony, and of course the great dinner. We shall have to do it tomorrow."

I heard "cewemony" and "tomowwow," and realized the duke either could not pronounce his *r*'s, or perhaps chose not to.

"And your name, Goodman?" the duke asked.

"Quillifer, your grace. Son of the alderman Quillifer."

The duke gave no sign he had ever heard of my father. "You come alone?"

"I am secretary to an embassy sent by the city, but we were taken in the Toppings by Sir Basil of the Heugh. The alderman Gribbins was killed, and Lord Utterback is held for ransom. I managed to escape, and have ridden these three days to the city."

Again I felt the dark eyes assess me, coming perhaps to a different conclusion than before.

"Do you have lodging?"

"Not at present, your grace."

"There is not a bed to be had in the city," the duke said. "You may stay at our house till you find a place. I will leave instructions with my steward to find you a bed and some clothes."

I tried not to smile at that *instwuctions*. "You are very kind, your grace."

"Today, the Queen provides a coronation dinner for the entire city. We must dine at her table, but you will have no trouble finding a meal anywhere in town."

"I'm sure not, your grace."

"You'll deliver your report to me tomorrow, and I will consider how best to get the news to her majesty."

"Very good, your grace."

And so, now on speaking terms with one of the great men of the realm, I rode into the capital.

Three days later, I sat in a book-lined cabinet overlooking the park in the Selford home of the duke, and completed a letter to Kevin Spellman.

> *He had said "our house," but his grace lives in a palace, one grander than anything found in Scarcroft Square. It occupies the entire west side of a park in the fashionable district just below the Castle, & is faced entirely with Ethlebight brick in all colors, the finest endorsement for our town which you can imagine. There is a great hall with a loge for minstrels, a long gallery full of paintings & statues, a*

library beneath a dome of faceted crystal, & marble pillars nearly everywhere.

The steward was a little put out to have to find a place for another guest, for the place was v. full of the duke's friends, but soon enough my horse was stabled & I was lodged, provided with water for washing, and after a little delay some clothing was found for me, belonging originally to one of the duke's musicians killed in the streets by a runaway horse. I was informed that the style was a little out of the fashion, but the shirt was of patterned silk, the doublet and trunks of brown velvet, & the linen v. fine. I was given a matching brown velvet bonnet, with a badge in the royal colors of gold & scarlet. I who had lately been captive in a dungeon was now a picture of magnificence. (And how I came out of that dungeon is a story so strange, and full of wonder, that I will not set it down in this letter, but confide it to you when next we meet.)

I felt apprehensive that I had no secure place to stow my fortune, but decided that I was unlikely to be plundered when everyone was out of the house on holiday, so I put my rucksack under the bed & went into the city with a high heart.

The city was all a-bustle with crowds & the scent of cooking. In every square were geese & hens turning on the spits, and lambs and goats cooking alongside great chines of beef. Barrels of small beer were lined up like batteries of artillery, and cheat and raveled bread piled on tables like fortress walls. For the Queen on her inauguration was determined to feed the entire city, & there are near four hundred thousand within the walls, & an hundred thousand visitors + folk from the suburbs had come to the feast as well. Acrobats tumbled for the meiny, & daring men & women performed on ropes stretched from one tower to another. Minstrels sang, & players performed on rude stages. Prizefighters battled each other with pollaxe, staff, and sword-and-buckler.

Seers and monks also preached on street corners, but were generally ignored.

This great holiday was framed in only a few weeks, since word of the King's death and Clayborne's rebellion came to the city, & though there was some confusion & shortages here and there, such was the good humor of the crowd that all mishaps were forgotten.

I ate my fill for the first time since that last absurd banquet in Amberstone, & being full of cheer decided to scale the hill to the great palace, & view the Queen at her meat.

The castle, like much of the city, is of white sandstone, and ornamented with carvings, vines & fruit & fantastical animals, all so abundant that the keep looks as if it were swathed in lace. Everywhere is seen the triton of Fornland, the griffon of Bonille, & the red horses of the Emelins. Faces of gods & zephyrs gaze down from the corners, and in one tower live a tribe of howlets, who looked down at the banqueters with their great staring eyes.

The royal party was at a great table set out in the inner ward, & the crowd of gawkers, your correspondent among them, shuffled along from one gate to another. The Queen spoke little but seemed pleased with the day, though she spared a few glances for the young man who served her, beautifully dressed in blue & silver, his doublet aglitter with diamond studs. The divorced Queen, Berlauda's mother Leonora, sat by her daughter's elbow, & "triumph sat on her brow," as the poet saith. She looked upon the banquet, the castle, & the throng as if all belonged to her, & perhaps it does.

The little princess Floria was at the Queen's left, & like her sister said little, but watched everyone with bright, sparrow-like eyes. Floria's mother, the divorced Queen Natalie, sat by her & talked without cease.

Around them were the nobility, who are of course relatives of the Queen, & amid them Their Graces of Roundsilver, who seemed friends with all, though of course I know not the relations between the members of this family, or whether or not any member, behind a pleasant-seeming face, was thinking of dropping poison into his neighbor's cup.

They were eating swans, if you please, which birds were presented roasted, but yet fully dressed in their feathers. I don't know the trick of it.

After I had my glimpse of our nation's charming family, I descended into the town again, & participated once more in the revels. I had my freedom to celebrate, & my lodging in a palace, & a fortune, & I was of a mind to let the world know of my joy.

I had found my way to a little square, & beneath the chestnut trees I met a maiden, apprenticed to a milliner, she flown in wine & inclined to be merry. I offered her the most civil attention until her brother, for some reason vexed, came & fetched her away.

Have I mentioned to you the inconvenience of brothers? Here is another example.

It was the weather, & not the night, that put an end to the celebration. For clouds had loured down upon the city, & now began to drench the streets with a great storm. Summer, which had lingered long over our country, had turned to winter in but a few hours, & I was thankful that the storm had not caught me on the road. And so I made my way back to the duke's palace & to my room, where I found my fortune where I had left it, lit a fire, and slept warm beneath a blanket of scratchy wool.

In the morning, I broke my fast with the guests of my lord the duke, friends & members of his affinity, some from the Ethlebight or elsewhere in the West. These knew nothing of the fate of our city, & it was my task to give them the despairing news. I fear I caused many of them great distress, for I knew not the fate of their friends and relatives.

The meals in the great hall are served with a magnificence I had not imagined. Before the meal, we go to the Table of the Ewer, where the Yeoman of the Ewery helps us wash our hands in clean, scented water. Then we go to the cup-board, where we are each presented with a beautiful blown-glass cup brimming with wine—we each have a cup, rather than share a cup with four or five people. And when we are seated, we each have a linen napkin, rather than have to share a surnap. We each have our own fork and spoon, though of course we bring all our own knives.

Yet there is not much to do with our knives, for there is the Carving-Board, where three Master Carvers cut our meat before servants bring it to the table. (I have to say I would have done a better job.)

The duke and his bride seem v. much in love. They are forever touching, or holding hands, or offering one another compliments. It is v. pleasing to see them together.

Afterward the duke took me into his cabinet, a room which he has filled with his treasures. There are small delicate statues carved of alabaster or chalcedony, medals & caskets in gold & silver, enameled & ornamented with mythological figures, miniature portraits set in precious frames, cameo figures of old kings, ancient coins cleaned & mounted for display, rare minerals, porcelains brought from the furthest east, & the bones of beasts and monsters. The coffer ceiling is painted a deep blue, with golden figures astrological, & beneath it hangs a stuffed cockatrice, its feathers hanging limp, its death-dealing eyes now replaced by glass.

I could have spent half a day viewing the contents of the room, but even on brief inspection I could discern the duke's tastes, which sit in the most extravagant realms of high emotion. The small statues are for the most part of naked athletes or warriors caught in the extremes of triumph or desolation, & the medallions on the precious caskets are of kings dying of mortal wounds or Queens in the final agonies of suicide. The subject matter is extravagant beyond reason, but the work is fashioned in the most perfect & exacting style, by masters of their craft.

I do not know whether this is the epitome of taste here in the capital, or merely a predisposition of my lord the duke.

The duke, for his part, showed extravagance only in his dress, which was of a brilliant green silken robe wrapped about his body & painted all over with fruits & vines & dripping red hearts. He wore also pointed slippers & a kind of turban with tassels. I believe this is a costume for the duke at home & not the fashion, for no one else dressed in this style.

His grace showed none of his whimsy or extravagance when he interviewed me, but was v. grave and courteous when he asked me for my report. I presented to him everything I knew of the attack on the city, all the names & numbers I had gathered for use by the Embassy Royal. He asked what the city most needed, and I said not food, for the corsairs plundered the warehouses but left the granaries alone, but that soldiers were needed + supplies for rebuilding +

money for ransoms. He shook his head and said that money & soldiers were going for the war, but that he would give freely from his own coffers, & urge his friends to do the same. He also said he would exert himself to create some manner of committee, or association, to raise & bring aid to the city.

I also told him of Basil of the Heugh, & how he had taken Lord Utterback and Stayne captive, and I told him of Stayne's circumstances & intentions as I understood them. (And here is another matter best not mentioned in a letter.)

Then the duke rose & said he & the duchess must dress to go to court, where he would do what he could for us, & he left me at liberty. So I took my heavy pack with me, & first thing bought a purse, & then filled it with silver. I walked through rain to the Guild Hall of the Worshipfull Societie of Butchers, where I found many of that sodality taking a blithe holiday—for it may be a festival for the multitude when a meal is given to the city, but for the Butchers it is work, & now that the city is returned to its normal life, the Butchers have a day of leisure.

As I know the passwords of a journeyman of the guild, I was admitted to that society, & met the Dean, who made me welcome. He had corresponded with my father on guild business, & gave me a proper condolence for the loss of my family, & for the tragedy that befell Ethlebight. And straight-away he arranged for a Leave-Taking, which is a ceremony of the Butchers to say farewell to one of their number, & a great honor to my father. The Leave-Taking will occur in four days' time.

I asked if I might store some money in the coffers of the guild (for we do such favors for our members) & I was shown to the strong-room, where I deposited a third of the money, & all the gems & gewgaws. I asked for a recommendation of some reliable bankers, which he gave, & I went to two of the countinghouses, & placed in their strong-rooms each a third of the money, & so I have now safeguarded my fortune, & made certain that the failure of a bank, or the looting of a strong-room, will not bring me down.

I do not wish to remain in clothing borrowed from a dead man, for I have worn nothing else for many weeks now, so from the bankers I went to a tailor, & commissioned two new suits, one suitable for court. There are colors that are forbidden—scarlet & gold, collectively or individually, may be worn only by members of the royal family and their kin, which includes much of the nobility—though different shades of yellow & red are permitted, like mustard or cramoisie—and the tailor pushed me to garb of a sober brown. So I ordered a staid brown suit, but also a more splendid array of deep blue velvet slashed to reveal a silk shirt of sky blue worn beneath, with trunks and hose to match. It should be most dashing. Perhaps I am influenced by the splendor of his grace the duke.

I returned to the duke's for supper, & found the company reduced, with many returning to their homes, & others gone for Ethlebight to see to their property there. The duke informed me that he was unable to make headway against the throng about the Queen, all men greedy for honors & office, for it is certain that the Queen will change the composition of the Great & Privy Councils, & make appointments to other offices besides, but nothing is known for certain, so all manner of people permit themselves hope. Nevertheless, he spread word of the fate of Ethlebight in the ears of the court, & spoke in particular with those who come from the West or have interests there.

In the two days since, I have found myself an apartment,

though I have not yet moved in, a place with a private stair in the house of a member of the Butchers' Guild. His kind wife offers to cook me meals. But more important than this, the private stair is off Chancellery Road, which is the principal route of business that runs up the hill to the Outer Ward of the Castle, & which is dominated by the Royal Court, the High Court, & the Moots, where lawyers are lodged, & their apprentices instructed. Should I obtain certification by one of the Moots, I may hope to lodge there & practice law within the capital.

And in my travels about the capital, & my conversations with the duke & duchess & their guests, I have come to understand much of the current state of the court & of the kingdom. For I am no longer in the Kingdom of Duisland, but rather the Kingdom of Women.

For not only is there a reigning Queen, but also the Queen's mothe,r Leonora, who has long resented the way the late King put her aside, & who, all are convinced, plans to exercise power through her daughter. While over in water-girdled Howel, the eastern capital, we find the Countess of Tern, mother of the bastard Clayborne. Clayborne, the duke confides, would never have rebelled had it not been for the ambitions of his mother, & of his stepfather, Lord Andrian, both of whom wish to rule the land between them. And there is the divorced Queen Natalie, who has v. great ambitions for her young daughter the princess Floria, but who has neither powerful friends nor an office through which she might wield patronage.

Apparently, we must also consider Marcia, the Countess of Coldwater, the new Queen's best friend. When the late King divorced Leonora, he ordered her & the princess to lodge at Coldwater House on the north coast, & Marcia became a kind of older foster-sister to the princess. And now Marcia is expected to have much influence with her, perhaps as much as her mother, for the Queen has confirmed Marcia in her father's title, one of the few to descend in the line female.

And beside these yet another woman has come into play, for the bastard Clayborne has not risen in his own name, but as regent for young Queen Laurel's unborn child, who, an it be male, is the rightful King of Duisland.

Those of Queen Berlauda's faction say that Queen Laurel is not with child, but that she is held hostage in Howel, & that five or six months hence, an infant will be produced that is in no wise the child of King Stilwell. Whereas Clayborne maintains that not only is Queen Laurel praegnatis, but that astrologers & learnèd doctors & great scholars & practicers of grammarie have confirmed the child is male and destined for a long and healthy life.

His grace the duke has said that he is not inclined to believe in the existence of this heir, as the King's attention had lately been caught by a young lady-in-waiting, & that it was she with whom the King bedded in the months before his departure for Bonille. Which affair was why Queen Laurel left in advance of the King, & also why the two princesses lagged behind, not wanting be seen compliant or approving in the business of the King and his new paramour.

Whereat her grace, hearing this, gave only a deep sigh, & said "Poor Laurel!" For it is certain that this young girl, whose only fault it was to be caught & held by a roving King, is now mewed up as a prisoner, & fated either to be used by those who care only for their own advantage, or viewed as a traitor by Berlauda's faction. She may never see the light of day again, & as one who was but lately held *prisoner myself, I feel great sorrow for her—and greater sorrow for the child, if he exists, for he is certain to fall prey to one side or the other . . .*

I, having coming to the bottom of the sheet of paper, paused for a moment to read what I had written, and began at once to feel I had been too bold. What might be an acceptable opinion spoken aloud in the intimacy of a dining room or a private closet had a fatal look when written on a piece of paper. The country was at war, and the land was filling up not only with armies, but with informers and spies. There were private companies that carried mail through the kingdom, but I had no doubt that the government could read such mail whenever they desired. What would one of Berlauda's partisans make of those words about the Countess of Coldwater and her ambitions? Or of my sympathy with the unfortunate Queen Laurel and her unborn child? And might mere sympathy be construed as treason?

I should, I thought, *tear up the pages,* and took them in hand with the intention of doing so, and then I hesitated. Perhaps, I thought, I should instead find a reliable captain to carry the letter to Ethlebight, or at least as far as Newton Linn.

But ships would not sail until the reivers were gone, and word had not yet come that they had sailed away.

I put the letter down, and looked at the two others I had penned that afternoon. One to Gribbins's widow, informing her of her husband's murder, and urging her not to pay any ransom that might be demanded of her. The other was to Lord Utterback's father, the Count of Wenlock. Wenlock had not been seen at the coronation not because he had declared for Clayborne, but because the Queen had sent him north, to his wife's native country, to be Lord Lieutenant of Blacksykes, and there raise forces to fight the bastard Clayborne.

I wrote Wenlock of the circumstances of Utterback's capture, praised Utterback's behavior before the ferocious outlaw Sir Basil, and said little about my own escape. I also informed Wenlock that I possessed Utterback's signet, which I'd poured into my rucksack along with all the other rings and jewels, and not noticed until I'd taken it out, three days earlier, at the guild hall. I would keep it until his lordship advised me what to do with it.

I had also the signets of the Marquess of Stayne and his faction, but I cared less about these. Still, I supposed I could inquire of the duke where to write his marchioness.

These letters, I thought, I might freely address and send. Though whether anyone would carry Mrs. Gribbins's letter to besieged Ethlebight was still unknown.

I folded and tucked the letter to Kevin in my doublet, and then folded and addressed the other two.

I carried them out of the cabinet and down a stair, and there found a page who told me that I was summoned for dinner.

CHAPTER ELEVEN

came into the great hall on its creaking herringbone floors, and found that the duke's great company had dispersed but for a few clustered about the head of the table. This group was composed of the duke, his duchess, an engineer named Ransome, a playwright and actor called Blackwell, and an Abbot Ambrosius, a serene, white-bearded figure dressed in the robes of the finest, softest unbleached wool, and who was introduced as the late King's Philosopher Transterrene. His tonsure, which shaved away all the hair on the front of his brow, made his head look like an egg. This small band formed the sort of heterogeneous company that was more usually to be found at the duke's than the huge gathering that had arrived for the coronation.

The duke's orchestra, in the loge above the hall, played pleasantly. The great hall featured pillars of some green stone and gilded acanthus capitals holding up a barrel-ceiling painted with mythological scenes, pink-skinned gods and goddesses roistering among the clouds. Between the pillars were statues of maidens bearing platters of fruit or skins of wine, the floor was different-colored hardwoods laid in a herringbone pattern, and above was a clerestory to let in the light. Below the clerestory was a frieze in which the coins of Roundsilver were interlinked with scenes of fantastic fish and animals, all romping along like a parade of demons holding a circle dance, and below the frieze were brilliant tapestries showing mythological scenes or Roundsilver ancestors either commanding armies or dying picturesquely in battle—it appears that war had claimed a surprising number of the duke's forefathers.

A few days in the Roundsilver palace had made it possible for me to go several minutes without staring at some wonder or other. I was doing my best not to appear an awestruck rustic—though if I were, the others were too polite to tell me.

"I have found an apartment, your grace," I told the duke as I sat. "With your leave, I'll move tomorrow, and no longer be a burden to your steward."

"You must let him know where you lodge," said Roundsilver. "For you are the man who must bear witness to the court about Ethlebight's tragedy—in fact you must testify tomorrow, for I have gained an interview with the Lord Chancellor, so perhaps you should not shift your lodgings till the day after."

I had no objection to enjoying the duke's hospitality for another day, and was pleased to say so.

"You should see Hulme while he *remains* Lord Chancellor," Ambrosius advised. "Her majesty may yet choose to replace him." He gave a deep, languid sigh. "For Hulme has made many enemies in exercising his office, as have so many of his late majesty's loyal supporters." Another sigh. "As had I, though I did not know it."

By this I guessed that Queen Berlauda had appointed a philosopher more to her liking, and send Ambrosius off with his pension.

"Sir," I said to him, "I am unfamiliar with your—your former office. Is there also a Philosopher Mundane?"

The abbot smiled, and nodded at Ransome. "I believe," he said, "they are called *engineers.*"

Ransome laughed and brushed his mustaches with the back of his hand. They were well tended, along with his glossy shoulder-length hair and his immaculate white linen. He was tall and a little plump, and offered to the company a perfect air of self-satisfaction. He was so pleased with himself, and pleased so pleasantly, that it was difficult not to be pleased along with him.

"There is only one true philosophy, lord abbot," he said. "The science that permits us to move from a state imperfect, diseased, and transient to one perfect, healthy, and everlasting. And that science exists on the earth, in metals, extracts, distillations, and essences, not in the sky, floating in your transterrene aethers."

"I shall look forward to seeing you made perfect, healthy, and everlasting," said the actor Blackwell. "But until then, I will retain a grain or two of doubt regarding the claims of your science. And to you, sir"—he bowed to the abbot—"I confess myself bewildered between the *hominem* and the homonym, your *fortiori* and your ficos, your *priori* and your priory. In either case, when you speak either of the Nurse of Caelum or the nature of Being, I find myself suspicious that the primary purpose of employing such grand language is not to better describe Nature, but to conceal ignorance."

"And yet," said Ambrosius, "you use such elevated language in your poetry."

Blackwell smiled. "I have never made the claim that my poetry is anything but itself. It describes a moment in time—time imperfect and transient, if you will—but that moment exists only in my own mind. I do not assert that I describe reality, let alone Being, whatever that is."

I was inclined to applaud Blackwell for this claim. He was about thirty and blade-thin, with blond hair and beard and eyes of startling deep ultramarine, and he wore a russet-colored suit along with a gold earring. His voice was a clear tenor.

Blackwell turned those deep blue eyes to me. "Like this man's music. Music may be texture, melody, emotion, rhythm. But to claim that music describes the world is to debase music."

I realized that he thought I was one of Roundsilver's musicians. Which was not surprising, as I wore the uniform.

"Quillifer isn't one of our orchestra," the duchess clarified.

"His grace was kind enough to lend me this costume when I was in distress," I said. "I am not a musician but an apprentice lawyer, and as such I possess a lexis more rarified and useless than all of yours put together."

This amused them. If I had learned anything in my legal career, it was that everyone hated lawyers, or at least pretended to, and were inclined to applaud when I feigned to share their prejudice.

"To which Moot do you belong?" Ambrosius asked.

"No Moot at present," I said. "I've just arrived in the city."

"Goodman Quillifer has come from Ethlebight," Roundsilver said. "The only member of the deputation to survive both pirates and the bandits that haunt the Toppings."

The monk gazed at me with sober interest. "Ethlebight?" he said. "There is a monastery in that city."

"All taken," I said.

"I shall try to organize a ransom for our brothers," he said.

Because, I thought, *what Ethlebight most needs now is more monks. Still, I suppose Ambrosius's actions will save the city money that may be used to ransom others.*

"I see now how you became distressed and in need of his grace's aid," Blackwell said. "But his grace spoke of bandits as well as the pirates?"

"Sir Basil of the Heugh and his band," I said. "Who one day I hope to see hanged, along with the rogue who betrayed Ethlebight."

The duchess was surprised at this last. "Who was that last?" she asked. "I had not heard there was a traitor."

I explained how the reivers had attacked with foreknowledge of the channel, the city's defenses, and its chief inhabitants.

"There has to have been a renegade among the pirates," I said. "A dog I hope to send to a new kennel in hell."

Blackwell frowned at his plate. "You don't know who that person would be?"

"I do not," I admitted. "Though I think that it would not be hard for a someone in the reivers' home port to find out. He would be richly rewarded, I'm sure, and that sort of money would attract attention."

The duke frowned at me. "Is it your intention to seek this traitor yourself?"

"I know not," I said. "The pirates have deprived me of all attachments and affections, and nothing holds me in Duisland. There is nothing to hinder me from crossing the seas on a mission of vengeance—nothing but the likelihood that I would fail. I'm a lawyer, not a soldier or assassin or spy."

The abbot looked at me and stroked his white beard. "He who embarks on vengeance," he said, "should first dig two graves, one for his intended victim, the other for himself."

"Before I can dig a grave for myself," I told him, "I have other duties. I must try to rally as much help to my city as I can. I must see my family properly buried. After all that, I can worry about what follows."

"I should not like to see you throw your life away on some fool-hardy adventure," said the duchess.

I looked into her crystal-blue eyes. "I am touched by your grace's concern."

And I *was* touched, too, and a little puzzled at how to view the young duchess, and from what perspective. She was attractive, bright, lively, and kind, and married to a man much older than she. It was not entirely unknown for women in these circumstances to view me with a degree of tenderness.

Were I in Ethlebight, I would understand my position. But as she was a duchess, and I a nobody far from his home, I was at a loss as to how to proceed.

And besides, I rather liked her husband, who had furthermore been very kind to me. I did not wish to abuse hospitality, nor did I wish the duke an injury. So, I restrained my gallant instincts insofar as I could.

"I agree with you," her husband said. "The identity of the renegade will come out in time."

"The Chancellor tomorrow, then," I said.

The duke nodded. "Indeed."

And then the conversation shifted to other topics. The duke was giving to the Queen's war a pair of giant bronze cannon, enormous weapons that fired stone cannonballs weighing sixty-eight pounds. Impractical on the battlefield—they would have to be drawn by trains of forty horses—these were intended for the sieges that were considered almost inevitable. Ransome had been engaged for the casting, and he discoursed at some length on the miraculous recipe for the metal. As I had guessed from the discussion of essences, distillations, and the Nurse of Caelum, Ransome held himself an expert in alchemy, and to his own private mixture of copper and tin added orpiment, philosopher's wool, magnesia alba, and ground diamonds for strength, all in combinations held in close secret.

Abbot Ambrosius, for his part, would make his own contribution to the enterprise, and would send twenty-four of his monks to pray and chant over the metal for twenty-four days before, during, and after the casting, to infuse the weapons with strength, accuracy, and the power to smash walls to rubble.

"For exalted power such as this," he said, "can only be summoned by those in a state of absolute purity, and I flatter myself that the discipline of the Path of the Pilgrim Monastery is second to none."

The monks in Ethlebight, I reflected, made no magic that I know of, so perhaps their purity was not up to standard. Certainly, they did not perform sorcery upon artillery.

I wondered what the Pilgrim himself would say about such practice. I understood his philosophy to aim at personal perfection, not the ability to knock down city walls.

As for the actor Blackwell, he was a principal of the Roundsilver Company, one of the capital's leading bands of players. The duke was sponsoring Blackwell's performance of *The Red Horse, or the History of King Emelin*, which would be performed for her majesty.

While the discussion wandered from play-acting to alchemy, from poetry to siege artillery, dinner arrived in its many courses. Herbed tarts, pies stuffed with pork belly, rabbit simmered in its own heavily spiced blood, sirloin of beef basted with orange juice and rose water, a fine mess of eels, curlews with ginger, badgers with apricots, porpoise and salmon. Every dish was a beautiful display, surrounded by fruit or flowers in a dazzling design, the pork pies topped by pastry sculpture in the shape of a hog's head, the sauces laid out in intricate patterns on the plate. Each course came with its own matched wine. Most of the dishes were highly seasoned with imported spices, a practice I find dubious. (As a display of wealth, it has much to recommend it; but a salmon hardly needs to be covered with shavings of nutmeg, or a beefsteak with sugar and cinnamon, in order to please the palate. But perhaps my tastes are hopelessly plebeian.)

The great culinary moment occurred with the Presentation of the Cockentrice—not the monstrous cockatrice such as that hung in the duke's cabinet, but a chimera of a gastronomic kind: the front half of a piglet sewn to the rear half of a capon, then stuffed and roasted till its honey-brown skin crackled. This prodigy was wafted before our noses so that we might admire it, before being taken to the Master Carver to be sliced and served.

I watched my hosts carefully, all to learn proper behavior at this elite level of our commonwealth, to discover how to eat some of the novelties, and to find an example to follow amid all this extravagance: I imitated their graces and ate sparingly. Having been in their household for several days now, I knew that even the most intimate suppers featured this kind of lavish abundance, besides which the Queen's roast swan dressed in its feathers seemed poor fare indeed.

And besides, I knew I'd have to go through all of this again for supper.

The thrift with which I had been raised protested against the waste and extravagance, but this was somewhat assuaged by my knowledge that the remains of the feast were given to the poor that daily lined the alley behind the palace. The duke's leavings fed a multitude.

I wondered what the ragged, hungry poor thought of the marzipan castles, the pastry sculptures, and the fanciful chimerae like the Cockentrice. To a pauper these bestowings must have seemed as fantastical as if they descended from the banquet-tables of the gods.

I waited till the meal was ending, with a custard served on a dish made of sugar-plate, and eaten with a knife and fork also made of sugar. I turned to the abbot.

"Reverend sir, I begin to wonder at your erstwhile title. How is it that a servant of the Pilgrim can be a Philosopher Transterrene? Did not the Compassionate Pilgrim say that the proper study of man is man? And how is that man to be studied outside the bounds of the world?"

Ambrosius considered this question with the same serenity with which he had contemplated everything, except perhaps his dismissal as royal advisor. He frowned, then spoke.

"It is true that the Compassionate Pilgrim (upon whom be peace) advised that the search for truth should begin in this world. He chided philosophers whose concept of virtue and perfection was based on their claimed knowledge of worlds other than our own. But he did not forbid the study of the transterrene—he only wished such a study to be based on a firm earthly foundation, a complete understanding of humanity and the world in which humans live. An understanding which the Pilgrim Eidrich (blessed is he) bequeathed to us."

"Did he not disparage the gods?"

"Rather famously he did, using a word that I will not repeat in the presence of a lady." Gracefully he nodded at the duchess. "For when you consider the stories told of the gods, they are shown as tyrannical, capricious, wayward, and wanton, behaving in ways that would reflect no good on any person who followed their example. The Pilgrim advised paying no attention to the gods—forgoing sacrifice, for example, and festivals—and instead build human ethics upon human reality."

The duchess spoke. "Did the Pilgrim not say that if the gods were just, they would reward human goodness whether you worship them or not; but if they were unjust, there was little point in offering worship (as there was no certainty of a just reward); whereas if the gods did not exist at all, there was no point in worship whatsoever?"

"Your grace maketh a good translation of the passage."

The abbot, I thought, might not flatter the gods, but well he knew how to flatter his hostess.

"Many followers of the Pilgrim deny the existence of the gods," I pointed out.

Ambrosius gave one of his serene nods. "In this they follow the dictates of their own reason. But the Pilgrim (may he remain a virtuous example to us all) offered no opinion as to the existence of the gods, but said only that there was no sense in building them temples or offering them worship."

"And your own opinion?"

The abbot pressed his lips together. "You presseth rather the point," he said.

I smiled. "You are a Philosopher Transterrene, are you not? Is this not your province?"

"Very well," he said, with the merest hint of ill grace. "Since you insist upon an answer. I prefer to think not of tangible, material gods or goddesses, but rather a universal divine Essence, which may be perceived by those whose senses have been refined by the gifts of Nature, or by long study fixed upon the ultramundane. By which I mean certain poets, perhaps"—this with a nod at Blackwell—"as well as musicians, great spiritual leaders, and most especially by the Compassionate Pilgrim, Eidrich (rest he in peace). And I hold furthermore that those whose senses are not attuned to the Divine can do no better than to follow these figures, the Pilgrim especially."

Which was no help at all. I had hoped to find some understanding of my encounter with Orlanda, but instead found nothing but blather of divine essences perceptible only by great spiritual leaders, among whom I had no doubt Ambrosius numbered himself.

I was still haunted by the memory of Orlanda, and the choice she offered me. In addition, I still gave a start every time I saw a red-haired woman, fearing the goddess had come for her vengeance.

"I know a man who has met a god," I said. "Or if not a god, at least a being holding some aspect of divinity."

"Many claim such things," said the engineer Ransome. He caressed his mustaches. "Most are mad, the rest deluded."

"The man was not mad," said I. "Nor was he extraordinary in any way—a respectable burgess. He was found credent by all in the city."

"Credent?" asked Ambrosius.

"It's a new word. I made it up."

"From *credentus*," said the duke helpfully.

"Ah." Ambrosius waved a hand. "Of course."

I returned to the story of my mythical burgess. "He was held, as I say, in repute. And he said that on a journey in Bonille, when he was a young man, he encountered an old well—a holy well with a nymphaeum."

"I believe I know the place," said the abbot.

The old faker. I had invented this particular well in Bonille to disguise my own in Fornland.

"Very casually he paid his respects to the nymph of the well," I said, "and was on his way when he met a woman riding along his road. A lovely, lively young woman, he said. They held conversation for an hour or so—I believe he offered gallantries, which she playfully declined—and then her path turned away, and he bade her farewell. Later, during a shower, he took shelter in an old stone stable, and the ancient wall collapsed. He was pinned beneath the rubble, very badly injured and like to die. If his injuries hadn't killed him. he might have frozen to death before help arrived.

"Yet he was rescued, and the young woman he met on the road managed it. She removed the heavy stones, an extraordinary feat, and bound his wounds, and helped him to his horse. It was night and cold, and he knew not where to travel, but she led his horse out into the country. And as the night progressed, and as she kept up a stream of diverting conversation, he began to realize that his wounds were healed.

"She brought him to her home—an old ring-fort in the hills near Lake Gurlidan, the place blazing with light and revelry—and he realized that she was the nymph of the well. She offered to make him her lover—"

"And he accepted, and was gone for an hundred years." Ransome waved a hand. "I believe we all know the story."

This cavalier dismissal spurred my anger, but I chose to make a mild reply. "On the contrary," I said, "the man bethought him of his own home and bed, and made as polite a leave-taking as he could. She was furious, but allowed him to depart. He has lived ever since in fear that the goddess might curse him for his rejection of her favors."

I saw interest kindle in the eyes of Blackwell the playwright, but Ransome and Ambrosius both spoke at that point, and together came to the conclusion that either my invented burgess was a vainglorious liar, or that he was deranged by his injuries and that the entire incident was a fantasy concocted by an impaired mind.

"I cannot swear to the truth of the story," I said, "but can only state that the man was not otherwise known as a liar, and showed no other evidence of delusion. But still"—I turned to the Abbot Ambrosius, and adopted my learnèd-advocate face—"if the gods do not inhabit this transterrene realm of yours, then what else exists there that is worthy of your attention? This divine Essence of yours may be studied here as well as in the aether, I suppose."

Ambrosius was taken aback. Perhaps no one had ever asked this particular question before.

"Well," he said weakly, "the proper study of philosophy includes that of matter, and in addition to its manifestations on our world, matter may be defined by its absence. And so far as we can tell, matter is a property entirely of the earth, and so—"

Ransome began to laugh. "You study matter by its absence? You might as well say that you can study life by looking at lumps of lead!"

"I suppose there are planets and stars and the crystal spheres," offered the duchess.

"Yet it is men with telescopes who have enlarged our knowledge of these things," said Ransome. "Not philosophers."

"There is also the Comet Periodical," said Blackwell. "Which turns all knowledge of the spheres to dust." He viewed Ambrosius with his eyebrows lifted. "You do not hold, with some of your brethren, that the Comet is the refuge of the gods?"

Since the discovery of the Comet Periodical, which returns every seventy-seven years, some of the Pilgrim's followers have claimed that the gods, having been rendered superfluous by the Pilgrim's life and thought, had withdrawn to the Comet until they were needed again. Thus they returned at regular intervals to see if the Pilgrim's doctrine was still being practiced, and then, discouraged, withdrew again.

"That is a charming myth," Ambrosius said, "though no one of any sense credits it."

"What of your transterrene philosophy is *not* a myth?" Ransome challenged. For though I in my pique had begun the questioning of

Ambrosius's transterrene pretensions, now Ransome scented blood, and was determined to finish off the quarry, all in the most pleasant, self-regarding way possible. But he was unable to continue, because at that moment a page entered, and told the duke and duchess that the dressmaker had arrived, and waited in one of the parlors.

They rose, we offered our thanks, and the party went their ways. I went in search of the steward, to give him my new address, and returning from that errand I passed by the archway leading to the parlor where their graces were meeting the dressmaker, a Master Fulke. Ransome stood partly concealed behind the arch, and on seeing me beckoned me to join him.

I stepped near the arch and was able to look into the parlor to see Fulke, with his assistants, showing their graces huge great bolts of rich fabric, embroidered silks and blazing satins, all to become new gowns for the duchess. Roundsilver spoke knowledgeably of fabrics and fashion, and his bride followed his words carefully, and looked up at him with worshipful eyes.

Ransome preened his mustaches. "His grace is playing with his new doll," he said.

I almost said that she was a doll well worth playing with, but on consideration decided the reply too vulgar for this cultivated a setting. "It is a measure of his admiration for her," I said instead.

He took my arm and drew me away. As we walked toward the front door, he inclined his head to me.

"You are not an old acquaintance of his grace?" he asked.

"We met on coronation day," I said.

He adopted a confidential tone. "I advise you not to be associated too publicly with this duke."

I cast him a glance. "May I inquire why?"

"Before the marriage," Ransome said, "this house was infamous for the degree of vice and depravity practiced here. I cannot count the reputations that were destroyed within these walls."

"I have seen no sign of dissipation," said I. "Beyond the over-luxurious dinners, I mean."

A superior smile floated across his plump, pleased features. "Her grace is still young. I have no doubt that he will corrupt her, and once again this place shall be notorious again for its wickedness. For look you." He drew me closer. "His grace only married because of a promise he gave his mother on her deathbed. And once her grace delivers an heir, that promise is discharged, and he may return to his former way of life."

I bridled at this advice, delivered as it was in a conceited, condescending tone, as from a superior to an inferior.

"His grace is the only man in the city who has been kind to me," I said.

A knowing look came into his eyes. "He has marked you, then, for one of his minions. I urge you not to become one of his degenerate pack of acrobats, actors, and mincing boys."

I found myself offended, not by the notion of the duke trying to corrupt me, but with Ransome's confiding tone and self-congratulating manner. I stiffened.

"I believe I know how to preserve such virtue as remains to me," I said.

"I offer a word to the wise," said he.

"I thank you," I said, "for the advice, insofar as it was kindly meant." *And insofar as it was a piece of malevolence*, I thought, *may you fly instantly into pieces.*

He may have sensed this meaning, for he said nothing more. I bade farewell to Ransome at the door, and then decided, in view of wine and the great meal, that I may as well sleep till supper, when another great feast lay in store.

My path took me by one of the libraries—there were at least three, but this was the largest—and there I saw the playwright Blackwell, looking at a small volume and jotting in a notebook. I wandered in, and he glanced up without speaking. His quill continued its scribbling even though his ultramarine eyes were directed at me.

"I didn't mean to interrupt," said I.

"I'm merely performing a little exercise," he said. His pen scratched on. "I'm translating this sonnet by Rinaldo into the tongue of the Aekoi. Pentameter into classical hexameters, and all this in a language known for its concision."

"Not into our own language?"

"That has already been done, very well, by Sebastian." He looked down at the paper, frowned, and finished the last lines. "That final couplet compares the beloved's hair to russet, but the Aekoi did not have clothing made of russet." He indicated his own russet doublet. "Russet appears to have been invented only a few centuries ago, here in Duisland. I could have invented a word, and called it *russum* or something, but I thought it more fair to find what an Aekoi would call such a color, so I thought of black chalcedony, which gives us *calcedonius niger*. Which as it happens, fits the meter rather well."

"Russet and black are not the same," I pointed out.

"That is why my translation is imperfect," Blackwell said. "And some imperfection is allowable in art." He smiled. "Perhaps even necessary."

"Perhaps a dark shade of agate?"

"*Achates densus?*" He frowned down at his paper. "I think it would not serve."

I was on the verge of suggesting *zmaragdachates*, but decided I'd heard quite enough of smaragds. "*Achates purpureus?*" I offered.

"I do not think it is quite the poet's intention to suggest purple hair, even in so extraordinary a lady." He put down his pen. "Well. Enough." He looked up at me with his deep blue eyes. "Your tale of the traveler and his nymph was intriguing. I am thinking of making it a play."

My first response was to ask, *You can do that?*, but an instant's reflection told me that of course he could. Any story could be a play, or a poem, or a song, though I very much doubted whether Orlanda would care to be any of these things.

"It is but an episode," I said.

"Your episode would make a fine first act. I should then have to invent further encounters between the traveler and the angry goddess, and fill the scenes with characters and clowns and a scattering of sub-stories. But the main question is whether the story is comedy or tragedy."

"Need it be one or the other?" I asked. "Can it not simply be a story?"

"People don't come to the theater for simple stories. Simple stories they can have from their grandmothers." Blackwell looked down at his ink-stained hands. "If tragedy," he enlarged, "the vengeful nymph would pursue the traveler, destroying his hopes and killing all he loves, until the traveler dies in a final blizzard of pentameter. Whereas in a comedy, she would be the cause of misunderstandings that would delay the joyful ending until the last act."

"Let it be a comedy, then," I said hopefully. In truth, I was hoping Blackwell would forget about the entire project.

I drew up a chair and sat across from the actor. "Goodman Ransome just warned me that the duke intended to debauch me."

He was amused. "Not without your permission, I'm sure."

"Has he such a wicked reputation?"

"Instead of going to war, looting cities, and scheming for high office, he stands as patron to poets and painters. That makes him unnatural."

"It would make him a poor patron," I mused, "if office were what I pursued."

"Is it?"

"This last month I have seen little beyond men grasping for office, honors, or money. It makes office seem less desirable, somehow, that it can be held in such company."

He smiled. "Instead, you can be debauched by the duke. I'm sure it would be exquisite and very likely musical."

"I wouldn't care to disappoint the duchess by taking her husband away from her."

"Well"—he waved a hand—"if *conscience* is an issue, surely we will all hang ourselves. Yet indeed they are a beautiful couple." He looked down at his notes, then cleaned his pen and stacked his papers. "I'm supposed to be writing a play, not amusing myself with translations."

"I wish you and your hexameters every success."

I rose as he put his papers in a portfolio and walked toward the door. He stopped, and turned to me with a thoughtful manner. "It seems to me that my projected play is itself an argument against the existence of the gods," he said. "Were the gods real, would they not object to the way they are treated in our entertainments? Would I not be bringing upon myself some kind of damnation by treating your friend's nymph lightly?"

"I would not chance it," I said, perhaps a bit too firmly.

His brows rose. "I thank you for your advice," he said. "And I will also reconsider the matter of the lady with her purple hair."

CHAPTER TWELVE

The next morning, wanting to get out of my musician's livery, I stopped by the tailor's and collected my sober brown suit. I was a little vexed that the grander blue velvet suit was not ready, but once I joined the duke on our trip up Chancellery Road to the palace, I was glad that I was not in my gaudy best, for that best would not have been nearly fine enough.

The women at court were aglitter with diamonds and rubies, embroidered fans and gowns of hand-painted silk, and the men, if possible, outdid them in the matter of splendor. The duke wore a cape trimmed with sable fur, a scarlet silk doublet woven with gold wire and stitched with seed-pearls set into swirling designs, a ring on every finger, shoes with gold buckles, a hat pinned up with a carbuncle the size of a hen's egg, and a large pearl dangling from each ear. Nor was this his own extravagant fashion, for the raiment of the great noblemen was equally lavish. Many dressed in the royal colors of scarlet and gold to emphasize their nearness to the throne. I looked like a poor brown hen cast among peacocks, but I was grateful that my blue velvet was not ready, for the suit I had considered very grand would have looked vulgar in this company. I would have seemed as if I were trying to ape my betters, and failing.

A very few of the men and women were dressed entirely in white silks or satin, enough to make them conspicuous. Though the color was simple, the fabrics were rich and luxurious, and glittered with silver thread, pearls, or diamonds. I turned to his grace.

"Who are the lords and ladies in white?"

"They are called Retrievers. They attempt to free the philosophy of the Pilgrim from the corruptions attached to it over the centuries." He shook his fair head. "I would find it grim work, for the Pilgrim's original philosophy was cheerless indeed."

I smiled at the duke's *We-twievers*. "In Ethlebight, the followers of the Pilgrim are too few to have fragmented into sects."

"I seem to constitute a sect of one," said the duke. "For I hold that the supreme virtue is Beauty, and I endeavor to serve and admire Beauty above all other things. For Beauty fights no wars, lays no plots, and causes harm to no one. Other virtues, like honor and fidelity and justice, are a source of endless strife, but all people know Beauty when they see Her, and worship Her in their own way."

I was on the verge of conceding the truth of this observation when our conversation was now interrupted by an acquaintance of the duke. It was the first of many interruptions, to which his grace responded with his usual charm. We had by this point advanced through the Outer, Middle, and Inner Wards, and were now in the Great Reception Room, a vast chill hall crowned by ancient timbers, dimly lit by a clerestory, and inadequately warmed by a pair of giant marble fireplaces carved with nymphs and salamanders. Tapestries of Emelins and gods circled the room, and would have shown brilliantly if the light had been brighter. Every bit of the room that could bear an ornament or carving did so, and we were regarded as we walked by the eyes of birds, animals, monsters, fishes, and grotesques. A throne stood beneath a canopy at the far end of the room, but the throne was empty, for the Queen was meeting with her Privy Council in another chamber.

This left the glittering courtiers with nothing to do but gossip and conspire with one another, and so they circulated, interrogating one another about available offices and commissions and the state of Clayborne's rebellion. Roundsilver, as a member of the Great Council and a near relative of the Queen, was presumed to know a great deal, and so was often approached. He politely introduced me to the each of his interlocutors, and I put on my dutiful-apprentice face and tried to keep straight all the peacock lords and ladies. They, for their part, were so intent on the business of politics and office-seeking that they barely acknowledged my existence at all. Probably they thought I was some kind of servant.

The throng was brought to silence as a sennet, played by trumpets hidden high in a gallery, echoed from the hammer-beam ceiling; and then her majesty entered, followed by her Privy Councillors. We all took off our hats and bowed low, and as I rose I noticed among the royal party the Queen's mother Leonora, the Queen's particular friend the Countess of Coldwater, and also the young man, still dressed in his diamond studs, who at the coronation banquet had served the Queen her roasted swan, and who had been favored with so many of Berlauda's smiles.

"Who is that gentleman?" I asked, in the duke's ear.

"Viscount Broughton of Hart Ness," said he.

I saw the scowls on the faces about the young viscount, and said, "He is not popular with the Queen's friends, though her majesty seems to like him right well."

"When news of Clayborne's rebellion first reached the capital," said the duke, "no one knew how far the conspiracy extended, or who among the peers was loyal, or whether Queen Berlauda's reign would last more than an hour before one of Clayborne's allies invaded the palace and toppled the Queen into a dungeon. Even the Yeoman

Archers, who guard the monarch, were suspected, because in Howel the other royal regiment, the Gendarmes, had declared for Clayborne. Viscount Broughton raised a troop of his friends and rode into town to declare his loyalty to the Queen, and to pledge his gentlemen as her guard. It is generally admitted that this was well and bravely done."

"And the others, no doubt, wished they had done the same?"

"The others wish they had cut Broughton's throat before he thought of it. For now her majesty favors him, and has made him Master of the Hunt and given him a place on the Privy Council, and—they say—her heart."

I viewed the viscount. He was a small man, but well-formed, with a blond beard and yellow hair worn past his shoulders. Today the diamond studs fastened a green velvet doublet stitched with silver thread, and with a neat white ruff at throat and wrists.

"He is a handsome man," said I. "Perhaps her majesty, too, worships at the feet of Beauty."

The duke smiled. "Beauty," said he, "is rather inconveniently possessed of a wife."

"Her father divorced," I pointed out. "And more than once."

The duke nodded. "It would be a sad way to begin a reign, to snatch such a play-pretty from his spouse, behavior too reminiscent of the late King. And this, too, while the realm is under threat. Arguments will have been made for a match that better secures the throne."

I observed the royal party as they made a circuit of the great room, and saw the look in Berlauda's eyes as she regarded the man by her side, as well as the firm jut of her chin.

"And yet," said I, "royalty has a way of getting what it wants."

A man with extravagantly wide sleeves approached Queen Berlauda, took off his hat, and bowed low. The two spoke, he with florid gestures, she briefly and impassively.

"The ambassador of Varcellos," said the duke. "Varcellos is burdened with a number of spare princes, and the ambassador offers them severally, or all together, according to her majesty's taste."

Another man hastened to approach the Queen, a tall fellow with a handsome, dark face and eyebrows raised in perpetual half circles. He wore a gold chain. He too bowed, and joined the envoy from Varcellos, who seemed none too pleased to see him.

"The ambassador of Loretto," I was told. "Loretto has only one unmarried prince, but he is the heir."

I gave his grace a surprised look. "Is it a serious offer? For Duisland to unite with our greatest enemy?"

"In the event of marriage, they would not be our enemies, but our kin."

"Then they greatly underestimate the sorts of quarrels that can arise in families."

Queen Berlauda listened to the two ambassadors for a brief while, then gave a nod and continued her progress around the room. She approached the duke, and the two of us bowed low and swept off our hats. Her scent, very floral, flowed over me as I straightened.

"Is her grace not with you?" asked the Queen. "We have not seen her."

"This morning, she rides in the park with friends," said the duke. "She will attend court this afternoon."

"Tell her we have missed her." A faint smile touched Berlauda's impassive face.

"I shall assure her of your majesty's kind regard." His grace turned to me. "Your majesty, may I introduce Quillifer, who has escaped both pirates and bandits to ride to Selford and alert us to the fate of unfortunate Ethlebight."

The Queen regarded me with her pale blue eyes. "We have been informed of the sad plight of our loyal city," said she. "It moves us."

"Thank you, your majesty," said I.

"And we thank you, Lord Quillifer, for your bravery and enterprise in bringing the news to us."

I decided not to correct the Queen on the matter of my being a lord. "It was only my duty, your majesty," I said.

"Would that all our subjects shared your sense of duty." And then, regally, she turned her handsome blond head and continued her procession around the room.

The duke and I bowed again, and as we straightened I observed the duke exchanging nods with one of the royal party, a very tall man dressed all in black, from his shoes to his skullcap. His raiment had none of the pearls or purfles affected by the others, though he wore a gold chain of office, and sapphires and smaragds worn over the gloves on his fingers. His face was lean and careworn, and his hair and beard streaked with gray. The duke turned once more to me.

"Quillifer, this is Sir Denys Hulme, the Lord Chancellor."

I bowed. "Sir."

"Let us go to my closet," said the Chancellor. He spoke in a deep, almost subterranean voice.

He led us out of the great room and to a different entrance hall from the one his grace and I had used earlier. This was far more magnificent, with an enormous straight marble stair ascending two storeys. It seemed a wonder of the world, for I had never seen a straight stair in my life, but only stairs that circled round, or tracked back and forth from landings. Then I realized that I had never seen such a stair because I had never before been in a building large enough to house one.

The Chancellor took us to the second story, and from there through a series of offices filled with scribes plying their quills. He took from around his neck a key, opened an iron-strapped oaken door, and brought us into a small room. There were a desk and a pair of cabinets, and everywhere a profusion of books and papers. The smell of paper and dust and ink brought a memory of my old master Dacket, and his little offices above Scarcroft Square in that building owned by the duke. The room was lit by a high bull's-eye window, though gloomy for all that.

His excellency bade us sit. He went behind his desk and brought out some blown-glass goblets and a brass tankard filled with sauterne, which he offered. As his grace accepted, I did as well, and the Chancellor kindly served us. Then he poured a glass for himself, sat at his desk, and took out a fresh sheet of paper.

"Goodman Quillifer," he said. "I understand that your report was lost when you were captured by Sir Basil of the Heugh. But do you remember the essence of it?"

The report never existed—I was to write it on the journey, with due reference to the Delward translation of the *Rhetorica Forensica*, but Gribbins's insistence on my sleeping in barns and haylofts mitigated against such work. But I knew all the figures, and was able to recite them for the Lord Chancellor. He wrote them down swiftly, the noise of his scratching pen loud in the small room, and when he was finished, he looked up at me from his desk.

"That was singularly comprehensive, young man," he said. "Now, what does your city need? Food?"

"There is plenty of food in the granaries," I said. "The reivers had no way of carrying it off, and so left it alone. What the city needs is money for ransoms and rebuilding, and soldiers for protection."

"Money is all marked for the suppression of rebellion," said the Chancellor. "Food I could possibly have arranged."

"Then sell the food," said I, "and use the money for ransoms."

The Chancellor smiled somewhat as he raised his goblet of sauterne. "Twelve years have I husbanded the resources of the kingdom," he said. "I had hoped that next year, we could at last pay off the remaining loans for the King's last war. And now there will need to be more loans."

I was startled at this, for King Stilwell's last war had ended before I was born, and ended in triumph, with the armies of Duisland occupying whole districts of western Loretto. King Edouardo of that country had been forced to ransom his own cities for a fabulous sum, and then was forced to submit to captivity until the sum was paid. Eventually, he had to return to Loretto to raise the money personally, but his son and heir took his place in the gilded prison in Howel, and after a few years died there.

On account of Prince Antonio's death, and Edouardo's a year later, the ransom was never handed over; but it had not occurred to me that in a score of years a war could not be paid for.

"We may hope for a short war," said the duke.

"So we may hope," said the Chancellor, musing into his cup, "but I dare not wager the future of the state upon a short campaign. The foundations of revenue must be laid brick by brick, to support the weight of the kingdom withal. And, to speak frankly, I may not have the time to do you much service—there are many who would gladly sit in this chair, and hurl crowns and royals to the people in hopes of buying popularity. And these may influence the Queen more than I."

"I will urge her majesty to retain you," said the duke. "The treasury is too vital to be left to some base office-seeker."

"I give you thanks, though I am ever reminded that I am by many considered that selfsame base seeker. Your grace is kind enough to overlook my common birth, but others are not." The Chancellor raised his eyes from his goblet to me. "I hope you do not find these obstacles too discouraging."

"Sir," said I, "over the last months, I am grown used to discouragement." Those crowns and royals whirled in my mind, and I leaned forward as an idea took me. I donned my learnèd-advocate face. "Sir, you must spend money to make a war. Can you not spend some of it in Ethlebight? There is a royal dockyard that could provide small craft to the fleet, pinnaces and tenders and powder-hoys."

The Chancellor gave a small, discreet nod. "Some of these sorts of arrangements are within my scope. Others will require consultation with the Lords Commissioners of the Admiralty."

"The army and fleet will also need victuals—biscuit, cheeses, salt beef, salt mutton. Ethlebight is rich in foodstuffs, and could provide more than its share."

Another small nod. "Indeed."

"And consider our reputation as privateersmen." My enthusiasm grew as I spoke. "Armed with privateering commissions, our captains could haunt Clayborne's shores and sew up his commerce neater than a pin tuck. The prizes would come back to Ethlebight for the benefit of the city."

The Chancellor held up a gloved finger. "There is some danger in this. For in such a broil as a civil war, who is to know whether a ship holds to Clayborne's cause or no? Should one of your privateers take a ship, and the captain say, 'I am a loyal subject of the Queen who found myself in Bonille by chance,' how could we sort these claims?"

"Sir, there are prize courts for the purpose. And the ship's papers would be carefully examined, and if any of the Queen's enemies were found among the owners, the ship and its contents could be rightly—and justly—sold. If one of our captains took a ship owned by anyone known for their loyalty, I'm sure the ship would be released, for no captain would want to prosecute a hopeless cause."

"You prosecute your own cause with some ability," the Chancellor observed. "But this is a matter in which I must approach the Queen."

"Very good, sir."

He sipped his sauterne. "Have you any other notions for enlarging Ethlebight's capital?"

"The foundations of Ethlebight's prosperity are built upon wool," said I. "Surely, the Queen's army needs clothing, as well as tents and blankets and the like. And we also export fine leather, for harness both of horses and war, and for buff coats and cuir-bouilli."

"I shall so note." The Chancellor returned to his pen, made a few scribbles, and looked up. "Your city should rejoice in your embassy," he said. "You are an able advocate."

I put on my attentive-courtier face. "Sir, I am but a loyal servant to the Queen."

He smiled. "As are all of us, to be sure." He then passed to the subject of royal offices in Ethlebight, and who should fill them. I had no confidence in Sir Towsley Cobb as the new Lord Warden, and with feigned reluctance said so. I also remarked that Sir Stanley Mattingly was a great huntsman and a self-proclaimed bold veteran of the late King's wars; but that I knew he had cheated a gentleman in a land purchase, and I didn't know whether her majesty would be justified in confirming Sir Stanley as Lord Lieutenant, not if there were monies involved, and temptations too great.

Having, I hope, successfully scuppered the hopes of the two splenetive swashers, I listened while the Chancellor and the duke, between them, proposed a list of candidates for the offices. I knew that two of them had been taken by the reivers, and said so, and other names were proposed. But for the most part I sipped my excellent sauterne, and gave thought to my schemes for improving Ethlebight, and possibly improving my own fortunes as well.

The Chancellor put his pen aside, and turned again to me. "I understand from his grace that you were taken by bandits on your way to the capital."

I gave his excellency an outline of my time as a guest of Sir Basil, and did not omit that I had witnessed two murders during my few days as a captive.

"He is a bloodthirsty assassin, and probably mad," I said. "If he is not roused out of the Toppings and sent to the hangman, there will be more good people killed."

"I am not responsible for the apprehension of criminals," said the Chancellor. "You should apply to the Attorney General, once her majesty appoints one."

"I will do it."

"How did you escape?"

I had given thought to how I would answer this question, and decided that any mention of nymphs might bring my veracity into question. I gave the Chancellor the answer I had prepared.

"We were counted before we went down into the dungeon for the night. But I took advantage of some confusion, and managed to slip away in the growing twilight."

"Very enterprising," said the Chancellor.

"It was more enterprise than that great following of Stayne showed," I said. "He had a small army with him, all riding off to join his warship in Amberstone, and they surrendered meekly as lambs, and even acted as under-footmen at the bandits' table."

A glimmer of interest shone in the Chancellor's mild eyes. "Army?" said he. "Warship?"

I explained the Marquess of Stayne being captured along with much of his armed force, and the galleon *Irresistible*, its gunports filled with ordnance, that awaited the party's arrival.

"How very unfortunate for his lordship," said the Chancellor, and made a note.

Half an hour later, my cheeks flushed with wine, I bade farewell to the duke and Chancellor, both of whom had other business, and walked down the great stairway to the ground floor. I saw that it was raining quite heavily, and so I re-entered the Great Reception Room. Queen Berlauda sat quite grandly on her throne, and was surrounded by ladies and gentlemen, including the ever-smiling Viscount Broughton of Hart Ness.

Led by the viscount, the dance about her continued, the never-ending quest for office and opportunity. A few pigeons flapped overhead, and let their droppings fall on the grand folk below by way of comment on the proceedings.

Standing in the hall, I observed my hostess, the Duchess of Roundsilver, speaking with some gentlemen, and I walked in her direction. She was splendidly attired in a gown sprinkled with margery-pearls and yellow sapphires, and even in the dim light of the room glittered like a beacon. I put on a broad smile and approached, and took off my hat and bowed.

"I hope you will congratulate me, your grace," I said, "for thanks in part to your husband's efforts, I am to be appointed Groom of the Pudding, with the announcement to come next Wednesday."

She blinked up at me in surprise, and then mischief kindled in her blue eyes. "How splendid!" she said.

"I am sorry, sir," said one of the gentlemen. "I have not made your acquaintance, nor am I familiar with this office."

I put on my superior-prefect face. "I am Quillifer," I said. "And my office is new, for his late majesty was not as fond of puddings as our new Queen. But since her majesty is uncommon fond of fig puddings, and plum puddings, and suet puddings with raisins . . ."

"Blancmange," added her grace. "Cabinet pudding."

"O, her favorite!" I proclaimed. "As well as dock pudding, clafouti, frumenty, toffee pudding, crow's nest . . ."

"Treacle pudding," said the duchess. "Date pudding, groat pudding, pease pudding, flummery."

"Baby pancake and clootie!" said I by way of a grand conclusion, and then turned to the gentlemen. "In fact, her majesty is devoted to all puddings, and she desires a pudding-bearer to be near her at all times."

"Groom of the Pudding!" The duchess was great in her admiration. "You shall be at the Queen's very elbow!"

I bowed. "I shall have that honor," I said. "And rest assured, your grace, that I shall do my utmost to repay your kindness by advancing your interest with her majesty whenever possible."

"I am sorry, sir," said one of the gentlemen. "I failed to quite catch your name."

The duchess and I continued to amuse ourselves with the poor ambitious gentlemen, and as we rhapsodized about my wonderful new office, I could see the news passing among the throng like a burst of hailshot. Not everyone believed the story, but to some it seemed possible, perhaps even likely. After all, the Groom of the Pudding was scarcely more absurd than the keeper of the King's thunder-box, known more formally as the Groom of the King's Close-Stool. This was an ancient, well-established office, originally the lowly servant who, when the monarch was performing his private office, handed the ruler his cleaning-cloths; but which became, on account of the groom's intimate and private contact with the King, a powerful post much sought by the well-born.

I found myself the cynosure of at least a few eyes, and discoursed on puddings in general and the kindness of the Roundsilvers. I confided my hope that I could convert the Queen to the cause of savory puddings, and offered as an example my mother's recipe for a pudding of minced lamb's kidneys. When this line of discourse began to flag, I related my account of the sack of Ethlebight, and again the story of my capture by Sir Basil of the Heugh, along with my subsequent escape in its emended version.

I have mentioned elsewhere the necessity of my demonstrating my gifts to the people, lest they overlook me entirely. And here I found I was not ignored, for I was approached by a young woman wrapped in what looked like an elaborate, ruffled dressing gown of a brilliant satin green, its sleeved puffed and purfled, its hem embroidered with gold thread and cat's-eye chrysoberyls. Pearls wound their way through her tawny hair, and a necklace of emeralds and diamonds held her long throat in a close embrace. A peacock-feather fan hung carelessly from one hand. She blinked at me with long, lazy dark eyes that made her look as if she had just risen from a luxurious sleep.

"You are Lord Quillifer?" she said. "I believe you have news of my husband."

I did not make a guess at the identity of the husband, but at once I swept off my hat and bowed.

"Quillifer," said the duchess, "may I present her ladyship, the Marchioness of Stayne?"

I rose and viewed the silk-swathed woman before me. "When last I saw your husband, he was well," said I. "He was being closely guarded, but he was not shackled or otherwise mistreated." I smiled at her. "You should also know," I said, "that I rescued his signet from the bandit treasure-house, and have it in my possession."

The lazy eyes widened. "Do you have it with you?" she asked.

"I secured it in a strongbox until I found a means of contacting you," I said.

The marchioness smiled with small white, chisel-like teeth. "I shall be at home tomorrow afternoon," she said. "If you bring the signet and more information concerning my lord and his friends, you will find me grateful."

I bowed again. "Your ladyship honors me," I said, and rose to find her sauntering away, her peacock-feather fan dangling by its cord from her wrist. I watched the lazy motion of her hips as she flowed across the floor, and turned to find the little duchess watching me with narrow-eyed surmise.

"Master Quillifer," she said, "I think you have progressed from puddings."

CHAPTER THIRTEEN

gain, sweet, I am compelled to honesty, and to state that four days later, the Marchioness of Stayne and I lay nestled like spoons on my new feather bed, in my apartment off Chancellery Road. A heavy rain drummed on the roof, and a fire glowed in the fireplace.

Her ladyship's fingers toyed with the rim of a chased silver goblet while her long eyes regarded me from over her shoulder. "Your room is but half-furnished," said she, "yet you have taken care to provide yourself with the most needful items."

"A bed, fine sheets, pillows scented with lavender, wine, a fire," I itemized. "The table and chairs, in the other room, I account pure luxury."

She sipped wine from the silver goblet and passed it to me. It was a sweet Varcellan moscatto, reminiscent of another occasion, when I kissed the wine from dark Ella's lips. Inspired by the memory, I kissed her ladyship's mouth.

"Yet what I shall do with the saddle," I said, "I know not."

"You could buy a horse."

The saddle, beautifully tooled black-and-red leather, regarded me reproachfully from the table. The saddle, the set of four silver goblets, the silver hat-pin, the pomander, the rundlet of Varcellan wine, and the gold-plated medallion were among the gifts that had begun arriving at Roundsilver Palace the morning after I proclaimed myself the new Groom of the Pudding. They were frankly intended as bribes, and sent by people who hoped that I would use my influence with the Queen on their behalf.

I had not expected my joke to go so far, and when the gifts began to arrive, had not known what to do. I immediately sought the advice of the duke and duchess. The duke first reproached me for letting the matter get out of hand.

"If word of this reaches the Queen," he said, "it may very well injure our efforts to aid Ethlebight. She is not noted for her love of pranks."

I looked at him in horror. "What should I do?"

He lifted a shoulder in a half shrug. "Write very becoming letters of thanks," he said, "and assure the donors of your gratitude and friendship."

"I should not return the gifts?"

"They were given freely," said the duke. "It would be an insult to return them. But if one of your new friends asks for a gift to be returned, then by all means hand it back."

"Oh, but it was so comical!" said the duchess. And she recounted the whole episode in detail, and in the end the duke was laughing as well as she.

Nor did the incident affect plans for Ethlebight's relief. For, sitting next to the saddle on my table, was the black leather portfolio containing ten privateering commissions, signed with the royal seal and delivered to my care just that morning by the Chancellor. Along with these was my own commission to travel to Ethlebight and be the Chancellor's agent in seeing the licenses well bestowed upon the city's captains.

"A horse?" I said. "I should prefer not to ride a horse in this weather."

Her ladyship turned onto her back, her head and her great mass of fair hair lying warm across my arm. "Ay," she said. "You prefer to gallop indoors."

I kissed her again. "I am more than happy to venture a ride out-of-doors," I said. "But not in such weather as this."

She smiled, revealing those small, chisel-shaped teeth, which against all likelihood I found perfectly enchanting. I rested my hand upon the rounded curve of her abdomen.

The marchioness had been born Lady Amalie Brilliana Trevil, the seventh child and fifth daughter of the Count of Culme. Such was the abundance of daughters in his gloomy northern stronghold that Culme rather haphazardly gave Amalie in marriage to his friend the widowed Marquess of Stayne, for the express purpose of breeding an heir. Married at sixteen, Amalie was now seventeen and had been carrying the heir for five months. The *nausea gravidarum* having passed, and her husband having ridden off with his army on an ill-fated attempt to overthrow the kingdom, Amalie now felt ready for her own adventure.

I had called upon her at her invitation, and found her with a small circle of friends. I presented her with Stayne's signet, and she offered thanks and refreshment. We chatted most pleasantly for an hour—I fought myself looking in those long dark eyes for a sign—and by and by, I found it smoldering there. We first met at my apartment the following afternoon.

For the world she had adopted a style that was slow and languid, and in response I stroked her as if she were a lazy kitten. But when my caresses brought a rosy bloom to her cheeks, and her breath caught in her throat, the languid pose vanished, and she became a tiger-cat in my arms.

Pregnancy had strangely improved her. Her body seemed flushed with warmth and vitality. Her skin was smooth and rich as samite, and her breasts were exquisitely sensitive. The rounding of her abdomen was strangely attractive, and her condition did not yet preclude intimacy.

"It may yet be a long while before my husband returns," she said as she nestled against my arm. "I have applied without success to a number of moneylenders."

"The signet will not serve?"

"Stayne's already in debt to up to his eyes, and he borrowed more in order to outfit his ship and crew. Many of his lands are off in Clayborne's country, and he'll have no rents till the war's over."

"How much is Sir Basil demanding?"

"Four thousand royals."

I whistled. "I would not know where to apply for such a sum."

"I have asked our steward and our man of business, and it seems the respectable bankers already possess an abundance of Stayne's debt. I think in the end I must apply to a usurer—or more than one."

It had occurred to me that Amalie might be better off if her husband did not return—she would be a free widow, mother of the heir, and at liberty to pursue a life of pleasure. Yet I did not care to suggest such a thing—I remembered poor Higgs, the captive whose brother had apparently abandoned him to the bandits, and I should not like to see anyone thrown on the mercy of Sir Basil of the Heugh.

Yet how could Amalie avoid these thoughts entirely? Surely, she understood her own situation. Yet I should be a bit uneasy if I found myself lying next to a woman who I knew had disposed of a husband. How much more lightly could she dispose of a lover?

I decided these thoughts were too morbid, and nestled closer to Amalie on the bed.

"Take us our pleasures while we may," said I.

"And the less we consider tomorrow, the greater our pleasure today."

She turned to me, and our lips met. She still tasted of the moscatto.

"Are you also then a poet?" she said.

224 WALTER JON WILLIAMS

"The verse is mine, such as it is. Though the sentiment is hardly original."

Her arms came around my neck, and for a long time we kissed, till a hammering came on my door. I looked at her.

"You are not looked for?" I said.

"No one knows I'm here."

The hammering continued. I kissed Amalie and rose from the bed. I threw on a cloak and walked into the front room, and there looked for a weapon—for it had not escaped my mind that here I was in adultery with a high-born woman, and that some nosy relative or in-law might be taking an interest in her whereabouts. I found no weapon but the fireplace poker, and so equipped, I approached the door.

"Who is it?"

A clipped voice called from beyond the door. "I come from the Count of Wenlock!"

I had not expected a messenger from Lord Utterback's father, and so I hesitated for a moment before responding while I counted the days. Two days for my letter to reach Blacksykes, where Wenlock was Lord Lieutenant, and two days for his lackey to return.

"What do you want?" I asked.

"I have come for Lord Utterback's ring."

Well, that was simple enough. I looked at Amalie, who was reclining on a pillow laughing and blowing kisses, and turned back to the door.

"I don't have the ring here. Come back tomorrow afternoon."

My answer was a renewed banging on the door. "Open or I'll break it down!"

I looked at Amalie and made my screaming-infant face. She laughed. The door began to jump in its frame.

"Very well!" I said. "I'll let you in!"

I closed the door into the bedroom and then unbarred the door to the stair. Three large men entered, each wearing under rain-spattered cloaks the Wenlock livery of blue and royal gold. I felt a cold hand touch the back of my neck as I saw that each wore a broadsword on a baldric over one shoulder, and a sturdy dagger thrust into their belt in the back.

"Well," I said, rather obviously naked beneath my cloak. "As you see, I wear no ring."

The leader scowled from behind a grizzled beard. "Where is it?"

"Safe in a strongbox," I said.

The leader nodded to one of his men, who walked to the bedroom door and opened it. I heard a gasp from Amalie, and saw that she'd had the sense to turn away from the intruder, pulling the bedclothes up to her chin.

"Naught but a whore," said the lackey. I fancied that even through the bedclothes I could see Amalie's spine stiffen in outrage.

The leader looked at me again. "Where is it?"

"Not here."

He snarled. "Then you'd better take me to it."

I considered my position. "May I put on some clothes? It seems to be raining."

He sneered at me. "No tricks, now," he said. "Or I'll treat you like the bandit that you are."

"Considering that I freely wrote your master and offered to give him the ring," said I, "I consider that word harsh."

"Did you steal it, or didn't you?" One of his fellows snickered, as if this were the epitome of wit.

"I stole it from an outlaw," I said.

"A man in a position to steal from an outlaw is naught but a thief who keeps the company of thieves." Again his fellow guffawed.

I went into the bedroom and put on my clothes. "I'll soon be back," I whispered to Amalie, and squeezed her ankle through the bed-clothes. Then I threw on my cloak, took my hat, and led Wenlock's three lackeys into the rain. They trod close on my heels, as if to assure me of my helplessness.

When it rains, Selford smells like a cesspool. The filth lies in alleys and the street, and rain washes it into view, and down the public lanes. Eventually, it finds its way to the creeks and gullies that take it to the Saelle, but not before its odor rises to the nostrils of the citizens.

The hall of the Worshipfull Societie of Butchers, a refuge from the reek, lay just past the bottom of Chancellery Road, a fine high-vaulted building of the local white stone. Rainwater shot from the mouths of the carved beasts that ornamented the eaves, and lamplight glowed through the stained-glass windows that showed shepherds, stock-men, goatherds, and their charges. I had been a guest in the hall just the night before, as bells were rung and incense burned in honor of my father's Leave-Taking.

That Leave-Taking had been a lovely thing, with a chorus of apprentice boys whose voices echoed from the high beams, and the Dean and Warden each giving an address in which my father's virtues had been enumerated. I had spent the time beneath the stained glass, in a reverie, alternately pierced with sadness at the loss of my family and exalted by the ceremony. The death of my loved ones was a bottomless cavern, but the Leave-Taking had filled the cavern, temporarily at least, with a kind of delight.

Afterward, I had thanked the Dean and the Warden profusely for the ceremony. Now I was returning to the guild hall under somewhat different circumstances.

I walked up under the portico and rang the bell, and while I waited, the lackeys' leader gave me a suspicious look.

"What is this place?"

"The place where your master's ring is secured," said I. The door opened, and an apprentice looked out. I recognized him from the previous night.

"Hello, Roger."

"Sir."

I made a sign with my fingers. "I should like to see the Dean or the Warden, if I may. Or Master Onofrio."

Roger's eyes widened, and he looked over the three big men looming behind me. "Yes," he said, a bit uncertainly. "Please come in and wait."

The door led past a porter's lodge directly into the main hall. Under the supervision of a pair of apprentices, a chine of beef turned on a spit before the hearth, stews bubbled in iron pots hung over the flames, and the air was savory with the odor of cooking. The lamps had been lit on account of the darkened day, and the light glowed on monuments and memorial plaques to dead masters, and glowed as well on pollaxes, knives, and other instruments of the Butcher's trade that were hung on the walls.

Roger went to the apprentices by the hearth, and spoke to them in a low voice. They looked startled and glanced in our direction, and then returned for the moment to their work. Roger went out of the room, and we waited, our cloaks dripping on the flagstone floor.

In a few minutes, the Dean came out, a most civil and respectable old gentleman, dressed for warmth's sake in a long robe of fitch fur, with a fur cap on his bald head. He carried his staff of office in one gloved hand, knobbed on the top like a hand-mace.

"Yes?" he said as he eyed the three lackeys. "You have asked for Master Onofrio?"

"I have," I said.

"He is being sent for." He approached and frowned at me. "May I help you in the meantime?"

"I need to visit my box in the strong-room," I said.

He looked again at my three companions, then nodded. "Very well." He led us toward the back of the hall, reached the door that led to the undercroft, took a lantern from the wall, and turned. "Goodman

Quillifer," he said, "you may come with me. These gentlemen may wait."

The lackeys' leader shouldered his way past me. "We're coming with him."

The Dean stared at them down his long nose. "You are most certainly not. You have not the right to enter the strong-room, and are only allowed into the hall as a guest of a member."

The chief lackey seemed not to have a response to this, and so I followed the Dean through the door, and down a winding stone stair into the undercroft. The light of his lantern glimmered on the pillars and pale low arches that supported the hall above.

"They are robbers?" he asked.

"I know not what they are. The errand that brings them may be legitimate, but they are rude, discourteous, threatening, and armed."

"So I have observed. Do you actually need the strong-room, or was it a pretense to get away from those ruffians?"

"I truly need to get into my box."

He took me to the strong-room and opened the iron-strapped door with a key. He entered with his lantern, and I found my box without delay.

"Do you need me to withdraw?" asked the Dean.

"Nay. This will take but a moment."

I found Utterback's ring at once and put it in my pocket. Then, after a moment's thought, I took two more of the rings I had plundered from Sir Basil's treasure house, and then returned to the hall with the Dean.

During my time in the undercroft, the population of the hall had increased. Three strapping young journeyman had arrived along with their burly master, and stood by the fire speaking casually with the apprentices. Between them I counted three pollaxes, two great carving knives, a cleaver, and a meat axe. As the Dean closed and locked the door to the undercroft, I saw three more enter, a brawny woman and her two journeymen, each with a pollaxe.

I was not surprised. To the apprentice who had answered the door, I had made a secret sign of distress, and my asking for "Master Onofrio" was a signal that called for help. The word for Master Onofrio was even now passing from one butcher shop to the next, and the apprentices mustering under their masters and marching to the hall.

The three henchmen were looking uneasily from the apprentices to one another. While the Dean was re-hanging his lantern, I walked to one of the trestle tables that ran the length of the hall, and I took the three rings from my pocket and placed them on the table. Then— as a pair of masters entered with a train of armed apprentices—I gestured for the lackeys to join me.

They came warily. I saw they had drawn their cloaks back from the hilts of their broadswords.

"You see three rings on the table," said I. "If you can identify the one you want, you may take it with you."

The leader took a moment to study the rings, then pointed to Utterback's signet, which featured a seahorse carved on blue tourmaline. At least he'd proven he was familiar with the item he sought.

"Very well," I said. I swept all three off the table and returned them to the pocket. "Now if you will sign a receipt that I have delivered the ring as promised."

The three looked at each other. Behind them, the door boomed as more armed men entered.

"We can't write our names," the leader said.

"Then you can make your marks, and I will write your names beneath."

And calling for a piece of paper and a pen, I wrote:

We, the undersigned, have by brutal threats of violence, housebreaking, and assault, and with contemptible insult and infamous use of language, procured the signet ring of

Lord Utterback from Quillifer the Younger of Ethlebight,
who we acknowledge rescued it at the risk of his life from
the outlaw Sir Basil of the Heugh. We acknowledge the dis-
grace with which our conduct has disenhanced the reputa-
tion of our virtuous employer, the Count of Wenlock.

I made two copies and presented them to the lackeys, who by now
were surrounded by a half circle of armed men. The leader looked
resentfully at the new arrivals, but in the center of this ring of steel,
any thought of defiance had vanished, and he took the pen from my
hand and made his mark. His two companions followed his example.
I took the papers and the pen.

"Your names?" These being given, I wrote the names beneath
the marks, then offered the pen to the members of the Worshipfull
Companie. "Would anyone care to witness?"

The Dean inscribed his signature, and added his own seal, as did
one of the masters. I then offered a copy of the document to the lackeys' leader.

"You may give that to your master," I said. Then I reached in my
pocket for the rings, picked out that of Lord Utterback, and tossed it
into a far corner of the room. It rang on the stone flags.

"Go snuffle for it, dogs," I said.

The three glared at me, jaws working, hands twitching closer to
the hilts of their swords. Then the leader turned abruptly and began
to move in the direction of the ring. The circle around him parted but
slowly, and when he was free, he walked stiffly toward his object, and
refused to look behind to see whether he was followed.

"They will remember you," murmured the Dean, close by my ear.
"Maybe they will remember you too well."

I shrugged. "Maybe in future they will remember their manners."

The Dean looked down at the document before me on the table.
"Disenhanced?" he asked.

"It's a new word. I made it up."

He smiled. "Will you be joining us for supper?"

"I have a friend waiting, unfortunately."

He smiled. "Are you sure you didn't mean 'disfortunately'?"

The three lackeys had found the ring, and now marched for the front door—though they had to wait, because a gang of armed journeymen were filing into the hall. At last the doorway was free, and the three made their way out.

I rose, and turned to address the crowd of Butchers who had come to my aid. I thanked them for their arrival, told them the reasons they had been summoned, and expressed a willingness, should the occasion ever arise, to aid them in return. I spoke warmly of our brotherhood, and the bonds that united us; I praised their courage, and otherwise flattered them as shamelessly as I could.

"I think I will have a few of our brethren escort you home," said the Dean.

"I should visit my box first."

I put the document into the box, along with the two rings I'd taken, and was then accompanied home by three journeymen carrying pollaxes. I had taken a pollaxe from its display in the hall, and we four made a brave sight, soldiering on in the rain like veterans of the wars. I thanked my escort at the door, and carrying my weapon made my way up the stair to where the marchioness awaited.

She broke into a smile as I came through the door, and I was favored with the sight of those little white teeth. She had dressed while I was gone, in the style she favored in her pregnancy. Rather than wear conventional gowns with their farthingales and tight lacings, she had adopted instead an elaborate sort of dressing gown, frogged across the front with heavy braid that held the creation together. These silk and satin fantasies were just as extravagantly ornamented as court gowns, with gems and pearls and paint, but they were much more comfortable for someone in Amalie's condition. A fact that I found more to my taste was that they didn't require a ladies' maid to lace her into the outfit, or unlace her afterward.

These gowns were entirely Amalie's own style, and had created a sensation at court when she had first displayed them. It was thought that the Queen disapproved, though Berlauda had been perfectly civil to Amalie when they'd spoken, so it was hard to say where this rumor of disapproval originated. As was the case with most court rumors, alas.

She brightened when I came in. I put my weapon aside, barred the door, and took Amalie in my arms.

"No ill effects?" she said. "No violence?"

"None. They got what they came for, and a little more besides."

She rested her head on my shoulder. "I was worried. I was going to wait another hour, and then go to Roundsilver's and say that I'd seen you marched away by an armed gang in Wenlock livery."

I reached for the front of her gown and began to loosen the braided froggings from their silver buttons. "Your concern is commendable. I shall reward you directly."

I opened her gown and took her in my arms, the sunny warmth of her flesh a welcome contrast to the chill, wet day. A low laugh came from Amalie's throat.

"You are cold, sir. Let me remove those wet clothes, and put you in your warm bed."

"A delightful prospect. You are a fine nurse." My lips grazed the flesh of her naked shoulder, and she shivered.

Overhead, the sky rumbled, and promised another bout of rain.

CHAPTER FOURTEEN

T he next morning, I made my way downriver to Innismore, the capital city's principal port, on a large island
on the left bank of the Saelle. The wharves were dark
with men and cargo, and the masts and rigging of galleons and round ships laced the slate-gray sky. The Royal Dockyard
was boiling with activity, as shipwrights worked to ready the Queen's
Navy for the war. Almost all the warships had been laid up in ordinary, their upper masts taken down and sheds built over the decks to
guard against the weather. The great guns, the rigging, anchors, and
sails had been stored ashore, and left to rot or rust in warehouses, and
so now there was great bustle to make all ready to repel any assault
by the rebel Clayborne.

I paid little attention to the royal ships, for I was looking for a private ship that could take me as a passenger to Ethlebight, or at least
as near as Amberstone. I had no intention of riding home overland,
not over any path that might take me again within range of Sir Basil,
or for that matter Orlanda.

I had spoken to several captains and mates, and so far found no
vessel bound for the southwest, but still as I walked along the wharfs,

I found my spirits lifting. Walking through the port, I felt the pull of home, and delighted in the fresh breeze that carried the scent of the sea to mix with the odors of tar and salt marsh, and the rich perfume of the tide that foamed against the pilings and tugged at the ships until their hawsers stretched taut as bowstrings.

I walked around the sterncastle of a great high-charged galleon, and saw the smaller vessel moored behind. The sight of the yellow ochre strakes touched my memory, and then with a start I recognized the *Meteor*, the small galleon I had last seen in Amberstone. *Meteor*, which was owned whole or in part by Kevin Spellman's family. *Meteor*, moored fast to the wharf and discharging tuns of wine.

I dodged around a stack of stiff, untanned hides just offloaded from a barge, and trotted up to *Meteor*'s gangplank. Tackles fixed to the mainyard creaked overhead as they took the strain of a cargo net filled with wine casks, and I blinked up at the sterncastle to see if I could identify the ship's master. Instead, I saw Kevin, still wearing his tall stiff hat with the brim pinned up on the side. "Hoy!" I called. "Master Spellman!"

He looked in puzzlement, then surprise, then joy. I ran up the gangway as he bounded down the poop companion, and we met on the quarterdeck and embraced. We each burst out with questions, which neither of us answered because each kept blurting out questions without waiting for an answer. Finally, we paused for breath, and I got the first question in after the interval.

"Why are you here?"

Kevin gasped for breath and grinned. "It's your fault. You sent me the letter telling me that *Meteor* was in, so I rode to Amberstone to see to the ship personally. The wine was to be delivered to Selford anyway, and I came along both to ensure payment and to see if I could manage a loan to build new ships."

"The reivers are gone?"

"They made off a day or two after you left Amberstone." His face darkened. "Left nearly three hundred corpses on Cow Island, folk they decided were worthless as slaves, and who wouldn't fetch a ransom."

I felt a shard of ice touch my heart. "Anyone we know?"

"I don't have all the names, but one was Mrs. Vayne."

A wave of sadness washed through me. "I bought three baskets of her pearmains the day before the attack."

"And Master Crook."

My sadness deepened. "He had no family. I suppose therefore we may keep his library."

Kevin spread his hands helplessly. "It is a long tragedy, and we have seen only the first two acts. Even if we raise all the necessary ransoms, still our people will be in captivity for months, more likely years, and in all that time no one knows what horrors they will endure."

We both paused to contemplate this grim and unenviable truth, and then Kevin looked at me. "What of the Embassy Royal? Have you managed to bring us aid?"

My laughter was bitter. "I *am* the Embassy now! And I have spoken to the Chancellor, and briefly to her majesty, and have managed to pry a few favors from the court—and indeed, brother"—putting a hand on his shoulder—"I have a set of commissions on which I must have your counsel, both for our profit and that of our city."

His eyes grew puzzled. "You are the only ambassador? What has become of Gribbins and Utterback?"

"That is a long tale. But first, let me ask—have you received a letter asking ransom for me?"

"Ransom?" Kevin was taken aback. "Nay, I've received nothing like that."

"It won't have caught up with you, not if you left Ethlebight just after I was in Amberstone. The letter will be in my hand, but you may safely ignore it. And as for the tonsured swine who delivers it, you may knock him on the head with my compliments, or deliver him bound to the sheriff."

His eyes widened. "I can see there is an adventure here."

"I have writ you a letter about all that, and I wished to find a captain to deliver it, but then decided to find a captain who would deliver my self instead." I took him by the arm. "Come, let us go ashore and find a tavern, and I will tell you what has become of the Embassy."

Kevin gave a regretful shake of his head. "Nay, I have too much business today. I have to see mercers, bankers, warehousemen. . . ."

"I can come tomorrow morning."

"I will be at the Mercers' Lodge here in Innismore. Come early, and I will give you breakfast."

"One final question, then. Will you be returning to Ethlebight from here?"

"*Meteor* draws too much water for Ethlebight. But if I can raise money and a cargo, we'll sail for Amberstone, and from there I can ride to Ethlebight, or take a smaller craft."

"Good. For I think you will want to make that journey as soon as you can."

"Ay?" He looked as if he were about to throw another half dozen questions my way, and then he stopped himself, and shrugged. "Well, you will tell me tomorrow."

"Yes. And buy a stock of good gunpowder, for it will come in handy."

And there I left him to his business, puzzled yet eager for our next meeting.

I was still on the left bank, in the town of Mossthorpe across the river from Selford, when the skies opened with a great crash, the freezing rain poured down, and I sought shelter beneath the gate of an inn. Somewhat to my surprise, I found that the inn's courtyard featured a wooden stage, complete with a kind of tower and a balcony, and that the stage had been roofed with thatch to keep the rain off the players. They were involved with a rehearsal, none of which I could hear because of the pouring rain. On the stage I recognized the lean form of Blackwell, the actor I had met at the Roundsilver Palace, and so I sidled around the court until I found shelter by a corner of the stage, and watched the rehearsal. I had not been there long before I realized that I was watching *The Red Horse, or the History of King Emelin*, which Blackwell had written and which would shortly be performed for the Queen.

There was a great deal of declamation and striding about—it seemed more a pageant than a play—but the long, thundering speeches were at least relieved now and again by the nonsense of the clowns. It required an effort of the imagination to view as female the boys who played the women's parts, especially as this was a rehearsal and they were not dressed or painted as women. By the end of the play, King Emelin of Fornland had conquered the two warring royal cousins of Bonille, along with a late-arriving pretender from Loretto, and united the realm of Duisland to bring about a generation of peace. Which union had been preserved for the last four hundred years, at least until now, when the bastard Clayborne had succeeded in uniting most of Bonille against the Queen.

The unification of the realm, I saw, was a most pertinent topic for a play at this present unsettled time. I mentally congratulated Blackwell for his political acuity.

Blackwell played Prince Alain, one of Emelin's two Bonillean rivals, posing and declaiming with the rest. The author had awarded himself a graceful speech upon his surrender to Emelin, after which the historical Alain was marched off to a dungeon to be quietly murdered, though the patriotic play tactfully passed over this last.

By the time the rehearsal was over, the rain had ceased to fall, and a golden sun warmed Emelin's final speech about peace, amity, just rule, and the glory that is Duisland. But I paid little attention to the words, because watching an earlier scene had made me consider how this drama might be made more amusing.

After the last speech, the actors fell out of character, shambled about, and awaited the corrections of the director—which, when they came, were brief and to the point. After which I mounted the stage and greeted Blackwell.

"Normally, we charge a penny to see a play," the actor said.

I reached into my purse and dropped a penny into his palm. "Well worth the expense," I said. "Though if I am paying, I should also be entitled to offer my opinion of the work."

He spread his hands gracefully. "I willingly accept all praise."

"Might it still be possible to expand a little the parts of the clowns?"

He smiled. "I know not if more japes will please the Queen, but they will certainly please the clowns."

"While I was watching, I thought of some dozen or sixteen lines which might improve their comedy."

Blackwell looked over his shoulders at the lead clown, who was slouching about the stage in a false belly and a frizzled wig. "Improving the comedy is not so very hard," he said. "But I wish not to give them license, for then they go straight to gigues and bawdy, and this is not a vulgar play. No vulgarities before the Queen, not in a play about her royal ancestor."

"I can write the lines down. You can keep your clowns on the book, can you not?"

"I can try. But Quillifer." His deep blue eyes turned inward, as he considered his most tactful response. "If you intend to turn playwright, I think it only fair that you contribute in other ways to the welfare of the company."

I laughed. "My silver is at your service! But see the lines first, and if they improve the play, you will use them to your greater glory, and I should not pay. But if my lines do naught but mar your production, then I will open my purse, and pay you for your trouble."

"That is just," he allowed.

"Can you give me some ink and sheets of paper? I'll have my dinner at the inn, and show you my work this afternoon."

He agreed, and I went into the inn and ordered a glass of beer and a bacon pie, which arrived pleasantly flavored with cinnamon, cloves, and thyme. With this inspiration I set out to improve the tale of Lord Antonius Bellicosus.

As written by Blackwell, Bellicosus was a braggart soldier who, with his henchmen Sir Slope and Lord Craven, followed the Bonillean King Rolf about, bragged about their great deeds, made rude jokes, and fled the scene as soon as the heroic King Emelin's banners appeared on the horizon. At the end, Emelin forgave them and sent them home much cowed.

I improved this by giving Bellicosus a plot of his own, what Blackwell would call a sub-story. I had Bellicosus raise a company and march off to join King Rolf, intending to win such glory on the field that he would be offered the crown himself, of Fornland if not of Bonille. But he dawdled too long and found Rolf dead and Emelin already in triumph. So, he turned around and marched off to join Prince Alain, formerly his enemy, but on the route was subjected to a bandit attack, fled, and was captured by the bandits along with his little army. Having ruined himself by paying his ransom, he turned up in time for the final scene, where he joined in the general acclamation for King Emelin, and wanly expressed futile hopes of obtaining office.

I gave Bellicosus speeches that were prose burlesques of the poetical speeches given by the other players, and made his open greed and hunger for power a comment on the ambitions of the rival kings. Once I had begun, I found I had a lot to say, and ended up by filling four pages of crown paper. By this time, I was finished with dinner and well into my second glass of beer.

I returned to the stage, where the actors were blocking the final combat between Alain and Emelin, and during a break in the action I showed the sheets to Blackwell. He read them quickly, his face set in a frown, and then looked up.

"This will do very well. So pressed for time was I to produce this play that I had not the time to perfect the clowns' parts, and this I think will please both the clowns and the audience."

"So, need I open my purse?" asked I.

Blackwell feigned disappointment. "Alas, you do not."

"May I offer another suggestion, as long as you are in a receptive frame of mind?"

The actor raised a hand in a gesture of blessing. "You may."

"I notice that one of Bellicosus's henchmen is called Slope. Perhaps he should be seen by the audience to visibly slope—his shoulders, for example."

Blackwell nodded. "Plausible," he said.

"And the other fellow, Lord Craven—could he perhaps wear a forked beard?"

The actor was puzzled. "Why should he?"

"For two reasons. First, forked beards are comical. Second, it will distinguish his character for the audience."

Blackwell absorbed this idea with an inward expression. "Interesting," he said. "I will consider the suggestion."

"Have you also reviewed my suggestion regarding the purple-haired lady?"

He laughed. "She remains under consideration."

I left the inn very pleased with my hour's labors. I didn't know if Blackwell knew enough of the court and its politics to understand the significance of my additions; but when the play was performed before the Queen and her court, many would recognize in Bellicosus the Marquess of Stayne, not to mention his minions Fork-Beard and Slope-Shoulder. The bold cavalier and his friends who meant to overthrow a kingdom, but who were routed and taken prisoner by a bandit—and who now would be the subject of mockery by the entire court, and shunned by the Queen as an unproven rebel.

And whose wife I would be quietly enjoying, in my little apartment above Chancellery Road.

I returned to my rooms and found a messenger from Amalie saying that Mistress Freeman could come that afternoon. She was always careful with her messengers, and used no-one from her husband's household, and never used her own name. Instead, she would venture in the morning to court or to visit a friend, and from there choose a messenger from the various hangers-on always to be found in the street. Then she would hire a litter to carry her to my apartment, and when it was time for her to leave, I would find another litter to take her home.

I gave a crown to the messenger and readied myself for Amalie's visit, building a fire, bringing out two of my silver cups, and filling them with moscatto. She arrived after half an hour, having come straight from court. When I helped her free of the cloak and hood she had worn to remain unrecognized, I saw that her court gown was scarlet satin, frogged across the front in her personal style, and she wore a collar of rubies about her throat and strands of pearls in her tawny hair. I kissed her just below the ear, and she smiled with her little white teeth.

"Much ado at court this morning," she said. "It was announced that the new Master of the Hunt would arrange a great hunting party for the first week in November, at the Queen's lodge in Kingsmere."

I dropped the bar on my door, and checked that the pollaxe was where I had left it—I had no intention of my afternoon being interrupted again. Then I hung Amalie's cloak from a hook.

"Will you go to this party?" I asked.

"I shall *now*. For no sooner had the announcement been made, and the Queen publicly congratulated Viscount Broughton on his arrangements, than Broughton's wife appeared along with her father. She'd been kept out of the way at Hart Ness, but her father must have ridden there to let her know of the Queen's interest in her husband, for she came fully armed to the battle in a gown painted with serpents. She walked to where her husband stood by the throne, and kissed him full on the lips before turning to acknowledge the Queen."

"Did the Queen send her to a dungeon, or hack off her head?"

A smile tugged at the corners of Amalie's languid long eyes. "No, she did not."

"We have a civilized monarch, to be sure. What did her majesty do?"

"Sat in that cold way of hers, nodded to the viscountess and her father, and then turned away to speak with her mother."

"Who was laughing and cackling in obscene triumph?" For Leonora hated Broughton and was thought to favor the Loretto alliance, or so Amalie had told me.

"She managed," Amalie said, "to screw her face into something like an attitude of sympathy."

"That must have taken great strength of will." I picked up the wine-cups and sighed. "Yet I want the lovers to find happiness—want *all* lovers to find happiness." I kissed Amalie and offered her a cup. She took it.

"All lovers may find *some* happiness," she said. Her hand played with the laces of my doublet. "But we must know the proper moment to take it."

At times, she seemed much older than seventeen. Perhaps carrying a child did that, or it was simply her upbringing, brought up in a house full of servants and treasures and the political schemes of her family.

Or so it seemed an hour later, reclining on a pillow with Amalie's head on my shoulder, and my senses aswim with the scent of her hair and the wine and our coupling. The pearls she wore in her hair had come partly undone, and lay across my arm. She was telling me her latest efforts to raise Stayne's ransom.

"Do you truly want him back?" I asked.

She gave a serious frown. "I must do some things, and be seen to do them," she said.

"You do not speak of him with any great affection."

Again she frowned. "I've known him all my life. I do not despise him." Her long, lazy-lidded eyes gazed up at the beams of the ceiling. "My expectations of marriage were never sanguine. My mother told me that in service to my family, I would be expected to lie with a man I did not like, and have children by that man, and that I would love the children if not the man, and provided there were children, I could then do what I liked." She kissed my cheek. "So, I will have a child, and in the meantime I am doing what I like."

For the first time, I felt sadness for the glittering noblewomen who paraded through the court in their glittering satins. Sadness for Amalie, sadness for the Queen and the viscountess, victims alike to the ambitions of one pretty man.

Butchers' daughters, I believe, are permitted to marry for love, if only because there is so very little at stake; but for the daughters of the wealthy, there is too much money and influence in the business for affection to overrule calculation.

"I fear what might happen if you are discovered here," I said.

Again amusement creased her long eyes. "Very little will happen to *me*, I think. I am concerned more for you—your birth does not give you the kind of immunity my own confers upon me."

I tried to shift the conversation away from the implications of this. Her husband, I remembered, had raised half a troop from among his friends, well-armed and well-disposed to violence. I wondered how vengeful he might be.

"Your husband will not lock you in a tower?"

"He is notoriously careless with his possessions—I don't think he cares enough for me to do such a thing. After all, he rode off to war and rebellion and stranded me here among his enemies."

I picked up the pearls that draped my arm, dandled them from my fingers. "I have wondered about King Stilwell's death, coming at a moment that seemed so propitious for his bastard son."

"You imagine a plot?" She gave a little shake of her head. "Were there a scheme to do away with the King and put Clayborne on the throne, my husband and father would have been neck-deep in it. Yet they were as surprised as everyone else when the King died, and were away from court when it happened, with the salt sea between them and Clayborne. I think the plot was hatched when Stilwell fell ill, and thrown together in great haste with as many conspirators as were already at hand."

Amalie took the strand of pearls from my hand, and twirled it lazily in the air.

"The light gives the pearls a rosy cast," I observed. "As if they were blushing."

She was amused by that. "Let them blush for me, then," she said. "For I do not blush."

"I have seen the color rise in your cheeks," I said, and caressed her cheek with the backs of my fingers. She ran her jaw along my fingers, like a cat. My hand sought her breast. "And I have seen you blush elsewhere," I said.

Amalie turned to me, her body warm and languorous in my arms. She draped the pearls carelessly across her throat, an act that made her throat more desirable than ever it had been.

"I do not believe that I blush," she said. "And I do not believe that you can make me."

I felt myself smile. "Hardly a challenge I can resist."

She gave me her lazy smile and stretched her arms above her head, as might an athlete readying herself for a contest.

"Sir," she said, "you have my leave to try."

CHAPTER FIFTEEN

I met in the morning with Kevin Spellman, and brought with me my folder containing the privateering commissions, plus a legal document I had drawn up after Amalie had left late in the afternoon. In it, Kevin and I became partners in a nautical venture, from which the income was to be divided equally. I signed one of the commissions over to Kevin, so that his ship, *Meteor*, could act henceforth as a privateer, half the prize money coming to me after the taxes and crew's share were taken out. The remaining nine commissions would be taken by Kevin to Ethlebight, who would award them to likely candidates at the price of one-third of moneys received from all prizes.

Thus we stood to win a share of the profits from those nine commissions, and without risk or expense to ourselves. Ethlebight's smaller ships, the pinnaces and so forth, were ideal privateers, since what was required to capture merchant ships was speed and aggression, not large broadsides of great guns.

We would be making money for ourselves, but would also serve the Chancellor's larger objective, which was to bring wealth to Ethlebight. I would use my profits to rebuild my family home, and Kevin would ransom his family, build ships, and expand the Spellman business.

Since Kevin met me at the Mercers' Lodge, where men of business met daily, it was easy enough to find a notary to review our agreement, and others to witness our signatures. Then Kevin left to prepare *Meteor* for the outward journey, including the purchase of the fine corned gunpowder that I had suggested the day before, and I made my way back to Selford very pleased with my morning.

No messenger awaited from Amalie, so I put on my apprentice cap and went up Chancellery Road to the various Moots, in hopes of obtaining my certification as a lawyer. None were willing to take my word that I was ready to practice, which was nothing less but what I had expected. I hoped to be able to enroll as an apprentice, but as I did not come recommended by any lawyer of their acquaintance, this ambition was also dashed. Carefully I explained that my master had been taken by pirates, and that my letter of recommendation from Judge Travers had been captured by bandits, but this obtained me no leniency.

"You seem a careless person to have so misplaced your master and your recommendations," said one little clerk. "We desire no careless lawyers in the Yeomanry Moot. Good afternoon."

I was now at a loss. I had come to Selford to make my reputation as a lawyer, but that was now impossible. I had no hope of office, no prospects for employment. My only occupation, if you could call it that, was to be the covert companion to the Marchioness of Stayne— which, viewed as employment, was hardly flattering.

I wondered what my father would have said if he could have viewed me now. Nothing good, I thought, and in a downhearted spirit I left the Yeomanry Moot.

Yet, I thought, I had friends, some high-placed. My privateering prospects were good. Perhaps I should become a man of business, like my friend Kevin.

I walked down Chancellery Road to the sound of bells ringing, and guns being fired from the Castle. I asked someone on the street what had caused the celebration, and was told that "Old de Berardinis hath held Longfirth for the Queen." I knew not who Old de Berardinis might be, but I knew that Longfirth was a large port city on Bonille, just across the sea from Selford, and that its declaring for the Queen meant that the war would begin there, either as Clayborne sieged the place or as the city was used as a springboard for the Queen's invasion of Bonille.

I later learned that Sir Andrew de Berardinis was the Lord Warden of the city's royal garrison, and that after some days of confusion he had seized the city by main force, cutting off the heads of the mayor and the Lord Lieutenant of the county, both of whom favored Clayborne. Selford's Trained Bands, the militia based in the capital, were now to be mustered in great haste by the Queen and sent to reinforce Sir Andrew by whatever ships could be found in the port—fortunately, *Meteor*, with its privateer's commission, was exempt, being already in the Queen's service.

I had not been to court since my debut as Groom of the Pudding, and did not care to return so long as I kept the bribes I had received in that character. I did not wish to reject the gifts, which might offend, and yet I did not wish to remain in the debt of these gullible strangers; so I decided to send gifts of equivalent value to my benefactors, along with expressions of eternal goodwill and friendship. Accordingly I despatched rock-crystal goblets, a gold-plated salt cellar, pearl studs, biliments, girdles, and other small treasures to my new friends, who now at least were no poorer than before.

And while I was visiting the jewelers, I found something for Amalie that I thought would suit her very well.

At a pawnshop I found a black lawyer's robe trimmed with marten fur, hardly worn at all, and thereafter I went to court whenever I pleased. The Yeoman Archers, in their red caps and black leather costumes, would turn away anyone who obviously did not belong; but in my robe and apprentice cap I looked respectable enough, hardly a great lord but plausibly someone who had business in the castle. I took Kevin with me on one of these occasions, and was able to introduce him to Their Graces of Roundsilver. Roundsilver knew his father, of course, and was pleased to know that Kevin would be advising me in the matter of awarding the privateering commissions.

The night before Kevin and *Meteor* planned to set out for Amberstone, I joined Kevin at the Castle for the command performance of Blackwell's history of King Emelin. A stage had been constructed in the vast chill space of the Great Reception Room. The Queen, wearing a gold circlet on her pale hair, faced the stage on her throne. Before and about her the nobles had chairs, and the rest of us sat on benches or on the flagstone floor. I had come early and tipped a porter to give us benches close to the stage—though we were forced to sit on the side, so as to give the nobles a better view. Knowing how difficult it was to warm the enormous room, I had brought cushions so we would be comfortable, and rugs so that we would stay warm.

Near the Queen's lady mother sat the Marchioness of Stayne, a vision of beguiling languor wrapped to the throat in shadow fox fur. She looked at me only once, from the corners of her long eyes, and lifted one eyebrow, which by itself was enough to send a surge of blood to my limbs.

A trumpet call echoed from the ancient roof beams. Blackwell opened the program with a pair of poems, the first on the virtues of the Queen, and the second an epithalamium—some months late—for the nuptials of his patrons, the Duke and Duchess of Roundsilver.

> *What Joy, or honors can compare*
> *With holy Nuptials, when they are*
> *Made out of equal parts*
> *Of years, of states, of hands, of hearts?*
> *When, in the happy choice,*
> *The Spouse, and Spoused have the foremost voice!*

The sentiments were lovely and the verses fine, but both poems invoked a multitude of goddesses (those of Virtue, Victory, Fertility, the Marriage Bed, etc.) to bless their subjects, or to serve as a flattering comparison. I found myself wondering if Orlanda would answer the summons and appear, either to bless the Queen or skin me alive.

No actual goddesses appeared, so far as I knew.

After applause, Blackwell withdrew and Lord Bellicosus and his minions entered, and I enjoyed hearing one of the ranting speeches I'd written for him. Blackwell had added exposition explaining the civil conflict in Bonille in which King Emelin intended to interfere, and the clowns had added enough comic business that I felt a little offended that they were not paying more attention to my lines.

After Bellicosus marched off, King Emelin came on, with a speech about the dangers of civil rancor and foreign intervention, and the necessity of reuniting the broken halves of the ancient kingdom of Duisland, which had come apart some hundreds of years earlier under the assaults of the Osby Lords. Situated as I was to the side of the stage, I kept one eye on Queen Berlauda, and saw that she seemed quite enraptured by her ancestor's words.

Nor was she alone. Emelin exited to such enthusiastic applause that King Rolf's entrance was delayed.

The play, as I have said, was more of a pageant than a drama, and it wound its stately way through the evening. It was the first play I had seen indoors, and the first at night, which admitted tricks of lighting and shadow that wouldn't have been possible outdoors. I was particularly impressed by a glowing crepuscular red light meant to impersonate a burning city.

I was also amused that Blackwell, in person so remarkably lean, had to wear padding to enact a stout respectable warrior-prince. Without the simulated muscle, Prince Alain would have been blown away by his own trumpets.

There were long delays between acts, because the room's

chandeliers had to be lowered and the candles replaced as they burned down. During the intermissions, the Queen and her friends went to her apartments for refreshment, and for the rest of us there was food and drink available out-of-doors in the Inner Ward, where Lord Roundsilver's minstrels played a series of high-spirited tunes. There I saw the Queen's favorite, the pretty, young Viscount Broughton, who dined not with her majesty, but rather walked in the ward with his wife, a tall dark woman, a little older than he and very handsome, attached like a remora to one arm. It was both amusing and touching to see the two unhappy people so united in their misery.

Kevin and I bought some mulled wine and a packet of roasted chestnuts, and then strolled through the Inner Ward. As usual, Kevin was more splendidly dressed than I, still a walking advertisement for his family business, and people probably thought him a provincial noble. I walked in his shadow, enjoying the night and the cool night air until a familiar voice spoke in my ear.

"Well, Master Secretary, how fares the Embassy?"

I gave a start, then turned to see Lord Utterback in a fur coat, its broad collar turned up against the night. Dancing torchlight reflected the saturnine amusement in his eyes. Surprise stilled my tongue for a moment as I stared. I bowed, then managed to overcome my surprise and somehow to compose my thoughts enough to answer his question.

"My lord, I have managed to do some good, and more good may be done now you are here. Lord Utterback, do you know my friend Kevin Spellman, Mercer of Ethlebight?"

He turned to Kevin. "I know your father, of course. Have you heard from your family?"

"Not yet. I am trying to bring our scattered affairs into order."

"May you all be reunited."

"My lord," said I, "how long have you been free?"

"Some five days," said Utterback. "I arrived in the city yesterday. My father paid our ransoms promptly." He smiled. "Though *you* did not await his generosity."

I was taken aback. "Your father paid my ransom?"

"I arranged a price to liberate our entire party, save for poor Master Gribbins, who Sir Basil was determined to squeeze separately."

I laughed. "Sir Basil arranged for a separate ransom for the rest of us! That's why he put you in your little house, so we wouldn't find out you'd already paid for our release!"

Dark amusement twisted at Lord Utterback's smile. "Who'd ha' thought a criminal would be so dishonest?"

"I will repay the money," said I. "Or your father, I suppose. How much did Sir Basil demand for me?"

"Ten royals."

"So much? He asked only five of me."

Utterback seemed skeptical. "You can afford even five?"

"I can afford ten. I helped myself to Sir Basil's treasury as I fled."

Again Utterback laughed. "That explains his frenzy! When Sir Basil learned you were missing, he searched the whole camp—he even searched the Oak House I was sharing with Stayne, on the chance you might be found hiding beneath the supper-table. He sent horsemen tearing off in all directions, and even sent a party to search some old mines in the hill behind the camp."

I smiled at the thought of the outlaw's fury. "Would that I had seen it!"

"He was practically barking in his rage, and beat several of the captives, thinking that they'd helped you. And then for some reason he beat his wyverns, and one of them blew out a breath that singed his beard, and after that he was absolutely frothing." Utterback shook his head. "For once, I was glad to be locked in the Oak House, while he inflicted his anger on the helpless folk outside."

I told Lord Utterback that I had rescued his signet ring from the treasure house, and also that of Lord Stayne, which I had given to his lady.

I felt a certain unease, like cold fingers wrapping about my throat. "Is Lord Stayne free also?" I asked.

"Nay, his ransom has not yet come. And I don't know how it will find him, for Sir Basil, fearing you would lead a force of militia to his camp, marched everyone away to another of his hiding places."

"He uses monks as his treasure-bearers, and monasteries as his banks. I'm sure he will find his money when he needs it, being prayed over by as devout a crew as he could wish."

Lord Utterback was delighted by this revelation. "Bandit-banks! Truly we live in an age of wonders!"

A member of the acting company came out ringing a handbell to let us know that the next act of the play was to begin. I leaned close to Lord Utterback as we made our way back to the Great Reception Room. "Regarding your signet," I said, "there is something I should share with you."

I told him the story of the three men his father had sent to my lodgings, apparently under the impression I was some kind of thief; and of the sequel at the Butcher's fraternity, and the admission I had compelled them to sign.

"I believe I know the men," he said. "They are not at Wenlock House at present, so they must have taken my ring back to my father at Blacksykes."

"Are they inclined to vengeance, do you think? Or," I added, "your father?"

He laughed. "Tell me, how have you survived on this earth so long as eighteen years?" he asked. "Is it not enough to have escaped pirates and to have the greatest bandit of the age lusting for your death?" He patted my arm. "I will write to my father and explain that you are a respectable citizen. I will vouch for you, and urge him to restrain his retainers."

I thanked him, and I returned with Kevin to our bench. "You've been living a more interesting life than you've given me to understand," he said.

"We've been so occupied with matters of business that I haven't had time to acquaint you with everything."

He stretched out his legs before him and crossed his arms. "We have all the time between now and tomorrow's tide."

"Then in that time I will tell you everything I can."

A sennet was played, and Lord Bellicosus appeared onstage to recite more of my lines. Laughter was general within the company, and I felt no small gratification. I glanced at the Queen and saw no amusement on her face, though I could not tell whether she disapproved of the clowns or of the appearance of the Viscountess Broughton.

Acts followed in succession, declamatory speeches, rather too much alike, alternating with brisk comedy. I kept one eye on the Queen to see whether she enjoyed the play. At one point, during one of Bellicosus's declamations, I saw the Queen's lady mother lean over to whisper in her ear, and at last I saw her majesty smile. Perhaps Leonora had detected the target of my satire.

I looked over at Amalie, and saw that she gazed at the stage with narrowed eyes, a frown plucking at her lips. Quite suddenly, I realized that I had left her out of my calculations. My contribution to the play had been intended as an exercise in cleverness, and the mocking of a person who was worth mocking, but I had not considered the effect of my cleverness on my victim's wife. I had certainly never intended to humiliate my lover, and now I feared that I had.

The play ended to general applause, and the clowns came out to dance a gigue. Their usual bawdy humor, and the gigue itself, were curtailed somewhat in the royal presence, and the revels ended. The Queen and her party retired to a late supper, and I stayed only to congratulate Blackwell upon his success.

"It went well enough," he sighed. "Her majesty seemed to like her ancestor's speeches, at least."

"She has a great many ancestors," I pointed out. "You can write speeches for all of them."

"Perhaps I will. But first I am writing the story you provided me."

I felt a warning hand caress my neck. "Which one?"

"The tale of the burgess and his water nymph."

Plainly, I possessed no means to dissuade him from employing this theme, and so I forced a smile. "Comedy or tragedy?"

"Comedy," he said, somewhat to my relief.

I looked at him. "May it be worthy of the goddess, then."

"It needs not that, but rather to be worthy of the Queen, since it will be performed for her during the hunting party at Kingsmere."

I considered the gloom that this hunting party had already cast about the court, and tried to imagine the dismal, cheerless prospect of Broughton, Broughton's wife, and the Queen lodging in the same country house for a week, and wondered if that could be managed without the house bursting into flames, or without any of the company losing their heads.

"You set yourself a formidable task," said I, "to create a comedy in such a setting."

Blackwell raised an eyebrow. "The Master of the Revels requested it," he said. "And a masque on the theme of royal virtue."

I could only imagine what jolly fun this last would be. But then I reflected that the mood at the party might be so black that the play would be a failure, and never performed again, and I grew more cheerful.

Kevin and I picked up our rugs and cushions and walked down Chancellery Road to my lodgings, where I built up the fire, poured moscatto into my gift cups, and spent the long night telling Kevin of my adventures. Flushed with both wine and friendship, toward dawn I even let slip the story of Orlanda, which caused his eyes to widen.

"I would not have believed this," he said, "did it not come from you. But yet, did you not but recently urge me to spin a tale of tritons? Is this nymph but an element of some triton-tale?"

I looked at him. "Nay, it happened. I will swear on anything you like that I speak the truth. You are the only person I have told, and you may not tell anyone else."

He looked at me in wonder. "Who else would I tell? Who else would believe? I don't know if I believe it myself."

"Even to me, it begins to seem like a dream," said I. "But when I view my box in the strong-room of the Societie of Butchers, and see the gold lying there, then the truth of it comes home to me."

We talked till dawn, and then I walked with him across the bridge to Mossthorpe. As we said good-bye, I gave him a purse of silver worth thirty-five royals, ten to be employed at building a tomb for my family, and the rest to be employed in ransoming Ethlebight's citizens, and then Kevin hired a boat to take him down the river to Innismore and the *Meteor*. My head still aswim with moscatto, I returned to my lodgings, ate the breakfast porridge my landlady had prepared, and slept till early afternoon, when Amalie's messenger knocked on the door to tell me she would come.

"The whole court saw Stayne in that character," Amalie said later, as we lay in repose beneath my quilt. "Stayne and two of his friends. And now the whole court laughs and titters behind their hands, and make remarks I am meant only to half-hear. Even the Queen looks at me in a knowing way."

I reflected that if I were an honorable man, I would confess my part and beg forgiveness. Instead I kissed her and told her that the play was no reflection on *her*, that the satire was intended for her husband only.

"Then let them play it before my husband!" she said. "Nay, it was intended only to humiliate me."

"Are you humiliated?" I asked.

"Nay. I am *angry*."

"Well, then, if you are not humiliated, their attempts have missed the mark. You are not the fool they think you. Instead, you are angry at their presumption. They think to judge you, and they have neither the right nor the wit."

Amalie set her jaw. "That is exactly the case."

"Bide your time, then. Their own humiliations will come, and then you may have your revenge. But in the meantime, you must show everyone that the play had nothing to do with you." I considered her indolent, prowling walk, her attitude of sublime languor. It was difficult to picture someone who presented herself in such a way cowering before the laughter of others. "Laugh with them, if you can," said I. "But not because you thought the satire struck its target, but because the satire missed completely. Such an attitude should be easy for you. Or you can laugh privately to yourself, as if you knew something they didn't."

She looked at me sidelong. "And what would that be?"

"That those who believed in the existence of a Groom of the Pudding have no right to feel superior to anyone."

She laughed. "Well," said she. "That is a point in my favor. I never believed in the existence of the Groom of the Pudding."

I gave her a look. "I can demonstrate that person's existence, an it please you."

"Well," she said, looking at me under her lashes. "I think I am willing to let you make that demonstration, if you will but first refill my glass."

I refilled her glass, and then brought out my gift, a girdle of gold links to encircle her waist, and two pendants, one the mirror of the other. Each was of gold, and had at its center a baroque pearl, circled by a design of leaping dolphins. From this central boss shone rays of pearls, in the one case, and polished jet cabochons in the other.

"You may choose whichever of these you like," I told her, "and I will wear the other. It can be a secret sign of our affection."

She loved pearls above all other gems, and so I was not surprised when she chose the pearl pendant. "I will take the other," said I, "and remain the dark shadow behind your brightness."

And like a shadow, I thought, *I will follow you until the light about you grows too bright, until it is impossible to hide any longer, and then I will fade away.*

Meteor sailed away, carrying my and Kevin's combined fortunes. I attended court but found it supremely dull, everyone standing and chatting and waiting for the Queen to do or say something so that they could praise it, so I gave up attending unless the Master of Revels had devised some entertainment. I called upon Lord Utterback and repaid the ten royals for my ransom, and called also on Their Graces of Roundsilver, who were never less than exquisitely kind. I resolved to make use of the saddle I had been given and engaged a master for riding lessons, in hopes of resolving the conflict between myself and horse-kind. Perhaps I made a little progress in that regard.

Amalie came when she could, bearing court gossip to which I otherwise had no access.

I came to Roundsilver Palace one day bearing a gift to thank them for their kindnesses to me. It was a salt cellar of gold and enamel featuring the naked figure of some Eastern sea-god stretched out between vessels for salt and pepper, each wrought in the form of a sea shell. It was the first object I had seen at the jeweler's that I thought reflected the duke's taste, and I bought it even though I was a little shocked by the cost.

The duke was very taken by the piece, and thought he could name the artisan who had made it, or at least his school in far-off Tabarzam. He brought it to the duchess to admire, and asked me at once to dinner in the Great Hall. Blackwell was also a guest, along with a singer from Loretto named Castinatto.

Both they and their hosts were to journey to Kingsmere for the royal hunt, their graces as guests, and the others as performers. In an offhand way the duke asked if I would consent to be one of their party. I was flattered and accepted.

"Though I am not as skilled an entertainer as these gentlemen," said I, nodding to the actor and the singer, "yet I will endeavor to provide some amusement."

The duke nodded his fine golden head. "Try not too hard," he said. "It is, after all, meant to be a holiday."

CHAPTER SIXTEEN

The royal lodge at Kingsmere is a mere twelve leagues north and west from Selford, but it took the court two days to reach it, for the Queen was accompanied by her mother, Leonora, her half sister Floria, her particular friend the Countess of Coldwater, as well as three dukes, four marquesses, nine counts, eighteen knights, and the two hundred servants of her household deemed most essential to the maintenance of her majesty. To these were added the wives and servants of the male guests, detachments of the Yeoman Archers, Roundsilver's Company of Players, a band of monks, a boys' choir, and assorted acrobats, minstrels, dancers, and the carters whose task it was to move the entire assembly from one place to another in more than two hundred carriages and carts.

The Marchioness of Stayne, regally with child, rode in her own carriage and disdained other company, thus proving, at least in her own mind, her superiority to the court at large.

Showing my fine saddle and indifferent horsemanship, I had rented a courser and was assigned a place in the column, behind the carriages of the guests and before the servants' carts. I found myself amid a group of lawyers from the Chancellery, and they were pleasant enough company, though none were in a position to offer me employment.

The bridge to Mossthorpe was closed to other traffic while the great convoy rolled over it, which took almost half a day. After a night at the royal castle of Shornside, where I slept in an attic with the lawyers, we continued to the town of Gilmorton Royal, where the inhabitants turned out to cheer the Queen as she passed. Most of them, I am sure, were employed at Kingsmere for at least part of the year.

At the limit of the village we turned onto the manor grounds, and after passing through forests of quickbeam, oak, and ash, came to open grazing land, where we were greeted by a pair of giants—figures six or eight yards tall, one of which beat kettledrums while the other raised a great glittering trumpet to its lips and blew a call to welcome the Queen. (I think there were actual trumpeters hidden in its wickerwork breast.) These great puppets, worked by hidden cables and pulleys, wore tabards that showed the Red Horse, and bowed their leafy heads as Berlauda passed.

Here Viscount Broughton and his lady wife stood by the road to greet her majesty, along with the steward of the house, the gamekeepers, and the foresters. The lover and the wife and the Queen must all have been civil, for I heard no shots fired.

Over the course of the late afternoon the traveling fair that was the court disposed itself about Kingsmere. The old hunting lodge, bought by the Queen's grandfather, had been enlarged and improved, and was now in the form of a long central building of golden sandstone, graced by a pair of long wings stretching forward and back on either side, the whole in the shape of an *H*. The central part was for the Queen and her noble guests, one of the large wings for their friends and servants, and the other wing was shared by the staff of the lodge and by a large stable block for the party's hunting coursers. Lesser beasts were put up in barns, stables, and paddocks.

The lawn before the house sloped down to the lake, both lawn and lake rippled by the breeze. The low sun outlined the ripples with gold. At the pier was a boat that Broughton had constructed for her majesty, built in the shape of a swan and covered with real swan feathers.

After seeing to my horse, I was given a generous supper at a table set up in an outdoor garden—the Queen and her particular guests dined in the Great Hall inside—and then I slept on a rag-stuffed mattress, smelling of mildew, in a room reserved for the duke's retinue, which in this case meant about half a dozen of the actors, none of whom I knew, but most of whom were already blind drunk, and had been for most of the day. There was little choice but to drink along with them, some sort of foul liquor which I hope never to encounter again.

Next morning, as morning bells tolled painfully in my skull, I joined the Roundsilvers for a day of shooting. We hunters were arrayed in a line, while a legion of beaters, recruited from the village, drove past us great flocks of pheasant, quail, and black grouse. The duke and duchess, firing a pair of matched silver-chased calivers, brought down their targets again and again. I had been loaned a caliver myself, a wheellock venerable but well maintained, but I barely knew how to load it, let alone shoot. I struck down none of the flying targets, but I enjoyed myself, standing with the others on a fine autumn day with the bracing scent of gunpowder on the wind. Nearly three thousand birds were killed during the course of the morning, and we would dine on the fowl, off and on, for the rest of the week.

That afternoon, the weather was suitable for a day on the lake, and so her majesty went out on Kingsmere in her swan-boat, this time with Broughton, whose wife disliked boats and would not go on the water. But her majesty was not entirely alone with him, for there were many other boats on the water filled with members of the court, and one barge with filled with minstrels, and Castinatto in the bow singing.

Still, I could see their heads together as they sat beneath the canopy in the stern, as in full view of the court as they were being rowed about by six men in Broughton livery.

Throughout the day I remained aware of Amalie, who had participated in the bird hunt, and who now lounged beneath an umbrella while being rowed about the lake by a servant. I'd had no opportunity to speak with her, let alone speak privately. Yet I was constantly aware of her presence, a kind of tremor in the atmosphere of which I was subtly aware, as if she were radiating some sort of invisible beams that prickled over my skin. She was always present, yet always unavailable. I was impatient and filled to the eyebrows with frustration, and it was in this mood that in the evening I viewed *The Triumph of Virtue*, the masque that Blackwell had been employed to write.

Few of the company's actors were involved, for most of the parts in the masque that did not involve singing were taken by members of the court, all dressed in extravagant costumes that no acting company could possibly afford. There was a good deal of dancing, and I saw Their Graces of Roundsilver in the ballet company, masked and enjoying themselves.

The story was an allegory—which made it tedious—and involved the singer Castinatto as the demon Iniquity, who was rejoicing in the fact that he'd succeeded in capturing and imprisoning Virtue and her friends Honor, Purity, and Piety.

Whatever dungeon he'd put them in, it was a place with a lot of music and dancing.

Queen Berlauda played no part in the production other than watching it from her throne and nodding approvingly at the masque's moral sentiments. The part of Virtue, however, was played by the little princess Floria, who to my surprise sang in a perfectly respectable contralto. Her acting I thought more mannered, for she delivered her moralizing speeches with a serene expression that seemed to combine complacency with self-satisfaction—and then, with a shock, I realized that Floria was doing a perfect imitation of her half sister's vacant dignity, and doing it right in front of Berlauda and the whole court. At once my gaze snapped to Berlauda, whose expression mirrored that exact lofty self-satisfaction. She seemed perfectly unaware that she was being mocked.

I turned to the rest of the audience, and their expressions were approving when they weren't completely bored. It seemed the princess and I were sharing a secret.

The masque had turned interesting. I watched till the end, when Virtue and her comrades broke free of the prison and celebrated with a galliard, and I joyously applauded Floria as she took her bow at the end.

Next day opened with a deer hunt on horseback, with hounds. My limited horsemanship kept me from participating fully—I was always at the rear of the hunt, and quite happy to be there, since the front bristled with reckless spirits and sharp weapons. I avoided the jumps when I could, and when a jump was unavoidable, it was my courser who took me over the jumps rather than the other way around.

The deer hunt was for the most part a masculine pursuit, and most of the ladies remained at the lodge or followed the hunt in carriages. Yet there were women in the hunt, some unknown to me, and another known by sight—the princess Floria, who bent so low over her horse's neck that her flying dark hair seemed an extension of the animal's mane. She was so small and light that her steed carried her well to the front, and it was all her two grooms could do to keep up with her.

Nor could they keep her from falling as her courser failed to jump a little creek—Floria's little form, tucked protectively into a ball, was hurled like a roundshot into a dogwood and produced an explosion of leaves and bright red fruit. My heart gave a leap, and I spurred my horse toward the overthrow. I pulled up at the creek, dismounted, vaulted the obstacle rather better than had Floria's horse, and found the princess upside down in the bush, her arms flapping as she tried to keep the burly grooms from picking her up and setting her upright.

"Is your highness injured?"

She did not answer but fixed at me with hazel eyes. "Pray leave me alone," she said. Her words were enunciated with formal clarity. "I'll get myself out of this."

Anxiety plucked at my nerves as I watched the princess carefully extricate herself from amid the dogwood's daggerlike branches. At last she rose teetering on her high-heeled riding boots and plucked twigs and scarlet dogberries from her riding costume. Her tough cheviot skirt had been torn by one of the dogwood's lances, but her long-sleeved riding jerkin of red leather had protected her from further harm.

She took several breaths before speaking. "Morris," she said to one of the grooms, "please fetch me my horse."

"Your highness will continue the hunt?" I asked. She fixed me with a birdlike glance from her hazel eyes.

"It is either that or eat pudding, Master Groom," she said, "and you have failed to bring the pudding!"

It took me a moment for my mind to shift from that of a reluctant huntsman to Groom of the Pudding, during which time I stood flat-footed as a bumpkin.

"I apologize, your highness," I managed at last. "The cook has been damnably lax. What sort of pudding does your highness desire?"

"Frumenty!" She snarled the word as the groom arrived with her courser. The second groom bent to catch her foot in his cupped hands, and hurled her up into the seat. As the princess was arranging herself on the side-saddle—petticoats billowed from the slash in her skirt—an open-topped carriage full of ladies drew up. I saw that one of those in the carriage was Floria's mother, the divorced Queen Natalie, and I bowed.

"Floria, my dear, please be careful!" called Natalie.

"Why?" The princess gathered the reins and answered from over her shoulder. "Berlauda won't mourn if I break my neck!"

I pondered this truth as Floria rode off, then bowed again to the former Queen and returned to my own horse.

I was well behind the pack, and by the time I caught up, the deer had all been driven into a great pen made of fences, hedges, and nets, all too high for the prey to leap. There were both red deer and fallow deer in the enclosure, and as the stags were all in rut, the air filled with the sound of clashing antlers as they fought each other for possession of the does.

In vain, however, for grooms rode into the pen and carefully separated the females from the males. The does were driven through a gate, down a lane surrounded by high hedges, and into another enclosure, where they would be shot, for the most part by the ladies. The stags, on the other hand, would be despatched by the men with lance and sword.

The does came first, and the Queen fired the first shot standing in her carriage, and dropped a fallow doe to applause and cries of "Well done!" I saw that Broughton was with her in the carriage, and that there was no sign of his viscountess.

There followed a massacre conducted in strict order of precedence, the second shot being taken by Berlauda's mother, the next by Floria firing her caliver from horseback, and so on. Such women as chose to fire seemed all to be practiced shots. The bracing scent of gunpowder floated free in the air.

I was not bothered by the bloodshed or the butchery, as I had grown up with animals being killed and cut up as a matter of course, and the difference between this and my father's occupation was one of degree, not intention. Yet in this ritual display that brought all these glittering people to the killing ground, I felt there was more than assuring a supply of meat for the night's supper. I reflected on how these noble families had gained power, and for the most part it was war, as with Emelin who had slain other kings, or at least some form of combat, as with Roundsilver's ancestor who slew the dragon. The nobles had achieved preëminence through combat, and this ritual bloodletting wasn't sport only, but practice for war.

I saw that the Duchess of Roundsilver was readying herself to fire, and I rode to join her indulgent husband, who sat behind her on his horse, which still trembled and sweated from the chase. The duchess fired from on foot, bent over and bracing her silver-chased caliver against the fence, and killed a red doe with a single shot.

"Splendid!" said the duke as he applauded, and turned to me with an expression of blissful happiness. "Is my darling not perfect?" he said. "Hair of gold, skin like cream, the eye of an eagle, and hips just like a boy!"

"It would be improper for me to notice her grace's hips," said I, "but your other remarks are more than just."

When the slaughter was over, an army of Butchers ran into the enclosure to clean the deer and prepare them for the night's grand supper. The dogs were wild with the excitement of being left the offal. The rest of us went to the other enclosure to view the deaths of the stags.

This was done with less protocol than the shooting—there was no standing on order of precedence, but any gentleman who desired to enter the enclosure and fight a stag was permitted to do so. Most came in on horseback and ran at the stags with a lance, and some with swords; but only a few entered on foot to fight a rutting stag as if in a duel.

Even on horseback, this sport was dangerous. Some of the red deer were larger than ponies, and were far more aggressive, charging and then slashing with their antlers. The blood on the ground did not belong only to the stags. At least twice, horses were bowled over by a charging buck, and their riders extricated only with difficulty by the grooms. One horse was disemboweled and had to be killed. Those who entered on foot with their broadswords fought only the smaller fallow deer, and even so a number of them retired badly cut, either from the antlers or from slashing forefeet. One unlucky baronet was hurled down by a charging deer, knocked unconscious, and trampled. He was dragged from the ring feet-first, and left a red trail on the green grass.

Broughton and the Queen watched from her carriage, their heads together, their words meant only for each other. Across the arena, Floria watched her sister from horseback. I was with the Roundsilvers, and our conversation glided from topic to topic, the hunt and the entertainments and the poems of Rudland.

Again I thought of war, and how this hunt was as close to personal combat as civilized custom would allow. But this hunt was not merely the enacting of a near-martial ritual—it was a rehearsal. For the nation was now at war, and in a matter of months many of these gentlemen would be facing an enemy on the field, an enemy far more dangerous than a fallow deer. Better to learn here to face a foe in the field than to learn it against an enemy host armed for battle.

I watched the fighters with interest. Most provoked the buck into a charge, then leapt to the side and tried a cut to the neck to break the spine. Sometimes this worked, but usually it had to be tried more than once.

Another technique involved diving between the antlers to thrust the sword down between the shoulder blades and thereby reach the heart, or perhaps one of the major arteries. Several tried this, but only one man succeeded, the buck dropping at his feet. All others who tried the technique were hurled to the ground.

The man who triumphed was roundly applauded, and he raised his dripping sword on high in acknowledgement. When he left the enclosure, he ended in my vicinity. He was a tall, burly man only a little older than me. His black riding leathers had fringes, and he wore his long dark hair braided with red grosgrain ribbon. As he cleaned his sword with a cloth, he looked up at me from beneath the brim of his leather hat.

"You are the Pudding-Man, are you not?" said he.

My nerves sang a warning at a glimpse of the predator gazing from his eyes. "My name is Quillifer," I said.

"Yes. Quillifer the Pudding-Man." His lip curled beneath his dark clipped beard. He nodded at the enclosure. "Will you take a turn in the ring, and slice something more challenging than syllabub?"

I looked down at him from my horse and considered how best to deal with this rude monster.

"I do not know who I am addressing," said I.

"I am the Lord of Mablethorpe Cross." He threw his bloody rag down with an air of contempt, then was handed a sheepskin by a groom, and began polishing his blade with the fleece. His cunning eyes glimmered up at me from beneath the brim of his hat. "What say you, Pudding-Man?" he said. "Will you take a sword into the ring and show that your heart and stomach are not made of blancmange?"

Out of the slant of my eye I could see the duchess looking at me in horror. She gave a little shake of her head, and I responded with a minute twitch of an eyelid to show that I understood, and had no intention of risking myself.

"I am no great hand with a sword," said I to the lordling—and then, in hopes that I could flatter my way out of this difficulty, I added, "Not like you, with that diving lunge of yours."

"Ah." His sheepskin glided along the bright steel. "That's right, you are a Butcher's son, are you not? Would you rather do the business with a meat axe?"

Apparently, I had been more discussed at court than I thought, for so much to have reached the ears of some bravo from Mablethorpe Cross, which judging from its lord's dialect was in the far northwest of the country. I mentally considered a meat axe, and what it would do to the lordling's skull.

I tried to keep my voice offhand, though my blood was pounding hot in my ears. "You say 'Butcher's son,'" I said, "as if it were something of which I should be ashamed."

"Were I a Butcher's son," he said, "I would wonder what I was doing here among my betters, and perhaps live ashamed that I had not the proper breeding to grace the court."

"Perhaps my breeding is insufficient for noble society in Mablethorpe Cross, wherever that might be," said I, "but I have been welcomed here, by kind friends." And with that I looked at Their Graces of Roundsilver, both of whom were paying close attention, the duchess pale with concern, and duke looking down, with pursed lips, as if trying to decide how to intervene and when.

"But Butchers," I continued as I turned to the lordling, "do not ply their trade without payment. You want a stag brought down—very well. What am I offered for this piece of work?"

He looked up at me sharply, his mouth slightly open as if reaching into the air for a word that was not there. Finally he spluttered, "You want to be *paid*?"

"For my work," said I. "I am a tradesman, as you insist on pointing out, so therefore let us trade. If you want me to kill an animal for you, you should expect to pay my fee, which will be higher than normal because the work puts me in some danger. So, if you are unwilling to pay the twenty royals . . ."

The lordling turned crimson. "Twenty *royals*! To a *Butcher*!"

"You think I would risk my life for white money?" I asked. "Besides, if you find my fees high, you are at liberty to negotiate a lower fee with another."

"Ridiculous!" he said, and spun on his heel. He went to his horse, mounted, and spurred away, savagely digging silver rowels into the poor beast's sides. I watched him depart, then turned to the duchess.

"Thank you for your concern and good advice," I said.

Her lips were narrow and tight. "I'm glad you escaped hazard. I wonder if that man is mad."

"I would not have fought a buck hand-to-hand," I said. "There was no danger of that—and as for the insults, I should probably grow used to them."

We continued watching the combats, and I was very surprised, ten minutes later, to see the Lord of Mablethorpe Cross gallop to my side, draw rein, and hold out a purse.

"Here's twenty royals for you, Pudding-Man! Let's see you kill a stag for me!"

I took the purse while I considered a response, and saw in the bag enough silver crowns and half-royals to make up the fee I'd quoted. I held the heavy purse in my palm, and it felt as heavy as a tombstone.

"D'you lack a sword, Pudding-Man?" asked the lordling. "I brought a spare."

I turned and handed the purse to the duchess. "Her grace can hold my money," I said.

"Quillifer," said her grace. Her blue eyes were wide. "*You may not do this.*"

I gave her what I hoped was a confident, confiding smile. "Fear not, your grace. I am not unskilled."

I turned back to the lordling and saw him offering a sword. "I'll take one of those spears instead," said I.

My heart was racing in my chest as I slipped from my saddle and went to the group of gentlemen clustering about the gate. They had all taken at least one run against the deer, and I was able to borrow one of their lances. I chose the shortest one I could find, eight feet or so of straight ash, with a stout triangular blade that would not easily snap. I would have preferred a haft shorter still, about my height, which was the length of the pollaxe to which I had become accustomed.

I hadn't been lying when I assured the duchess of my skills. During the course of my apprenticeship with my father, I had killed hundreds of cattle with the pollaxe.

A pollaxe has a spike on either end, as well as an axe-blade backed either with a hammer or with another spike. The axe-blade can be used from the flank to cut the animal's spine, or to cut its throat from below if you do not mind wasting the blood. But by far the best way to kill a cow is from the front, by using the weapon like a spear and driving the spike through the animal's forehead and into the brain. The animal drops in its tracks and does not suffer, and the animal's heart will continue to beat for a while so the blood may be recovered and used in cooking.

While I had never killed a stag this way, hunters had brought deer into my father's shop, and there I had butchered them enough to understand their anatomy. The brain was more or less where I would have expected it to be, and the skull was if anything more delicate than that of a cow.

There were some other gentlemen ahead of me, so I waited for them to take their turn while I studied their encounters, and particularly the way that the stags attacked and the best way to avoid their charge. Thus it was that I failed to notice that the Lord of Mablethorpe Cross had entered the ring ahead of me, and had some speech with the grooms who organized the fights, and very likely bribed them.

For when I entered the enclosure, grinning grooms on horseback cut out from the mass not a fallow deer, but a red buck—and not just any red buck, but the largest of all, what is called a "hart of ten," with a great complicated thicket of antler dripping with torn velvet, like old trees laden with moss. All ten daggerlike points were brandished toward me, and bore a reddish color, like old blood. A thick dark mane wrapped the animal's neck, and its eyes rolled with mixed terror and aggression. A guttural roaring was already sounding from its throat.

This beast came trotting toward me, and it seemed as big as a horse. My heart leaped into my throat while my hands tightened on the spear. I held the weapon over my right shoulder, as if intending to throw it, with the point dropping slightly toward the target, the same posture adopted when killing cattle with the pollaxe.

It occurred to me, far too late, that when I killed a cow in this way, there were generally a couple burly journeymen holding the animal still.

"That's the way, Pudding-Man!" called the lordling. "Earn your fee, now!" His voice was full of self-approval, and caused a stir of laughter in his audience.

The enclosure reeked of blood and the rut of the stags. Somehow, I managed to make my feet move, and I moved toward the hart in a shuffling glide without my feet ever quite leaving the ground. I was having a hard time catching my breath, and was almost panting for air. My head swam. I tried to measure the distance between the spear point and the animal's forehead.

When the stag charged, it caught me by surprise, for it didn't attack with head lowered, but rather reared up on its hind legs, hopping forward while slashing with its forefeet. I was so startled by this assault that I failed to realize that I could thrust for the animal's throat, and by the time the thought occurred to me it was too late, for the flying hooves had batted the spear out of the way. I bolted and ran madly to the side, dragging the spear along the ground, to the laughter both of the lordling and his claque.

I gathered myself again and readied my spear. My heart was leaping wildly against my ribs, and I clenched my fists on the ash spear to keep them from trembling. The animal's eyes had followed me, but on its hind legs, the hart couldn't turn fast enough to spin and charge, and so it dropped to all fours again and turned to face me, bellowing. Behind the hart I could see the faces of onlookers, the Queen as impassive as ever, Floria with keen-eyed interest, and the duchess pale with fright.

The stag's war cry came to an end, dying as an echo among the trees. We regarded each other for a brief moment at a distance of about five yards, and then the great hart lowered its head and charged. I marked my target and lunged forward, putting as much of my weight into the spear as I could.

The impact knocked me back six or ten feet. My teeth clacked together and my eyes lost all focus, but I managed to retain my feet and my spear, and it took me a second or two to recover and realize that the spear dripped blood and that the great hart had fallen to the turf with a three-sided hole in its forehead.

Shouts and cheers went up. My knees felt suddenly weak, and I lowered the butt of the spear to the ground and leaned on it for a moment while I caught my breath. Then a surge of triumph went through me, and I raised a hand to acknowledge the cheers of the crowd.

I returned the spear to its owner and accepted congratulations from the gentlemen clustered around the gate. None had ever seen a stag despatched in that way, and they thought it a novelty. "What call you that strike?" asked one.

"I don't know that it has a name," I said.

"The *coup de Quillifer*," one admirer suggested, and I graciously allowed that this name might serve.

By and by, I rejoined my horse, which had been held for me by one of the Roundsilver grooms. Her grace had been joined by her husband, who gave me a speculative look. I believe I had succeeded in surprising him. I reclaimed my purse of twenty royals.

"I feel as if I've earned it," I said, and grinned, and then my grin broadened as I saw their graces looking at me with identical expressions, brows furrowed, lips pursed in concern.

"Quillifer," said the duchess, "you must promise me you will never do such a thing ever again."

I laughed. "It is an easy promise to make."

Her look was unsmiling, her blue eyes shards of ice. "Make me that promise, then."

Her stern tone caught me by surprise. She had been so gracious and kind to me that I had never seen her in her more formal style as a high noble and relative of the Queen, born a member of a conquering dynasty bred to command. That I towered over her, or that we were of an age, now scarcely seemed to matter. At her tone I found myself straightening in the saddle, as if in response to an order. Yet despite her severity I found myself flooded with warmth at the realization that she—and the duke, I hoped—cared whether I prospered or failed, lived or died. Cared enough to extract this promise from me.

I took off my cap and held it over my heart. "I shall obey, madame," I said. "I promise never to fight another stag, on foot or on horse, without your grace's express permission."

"Which I shall not give," said the duchess.

"That's as your grace pleases."

Her look softened. "You have work to do here and in Ethlebight," she said. "You must not throw your life away."

I put on my cap. "Your grace places a higher value on my life than I, and therefore I shall strive to live up to your expectations, and not my own."

I turned at a gasp from the crowd. One of the hunters had attempted the *coup de Quillifer* with a lance against a fallow deer, and been knocked sprawling for his pains.

I watched for a while longer, and accepted a congratulation or two from a well-wisher, and then I had an idea how best to end the morning. I excused myself, rode to the stables, and groomed my horse after its adventures. After which I went to the kitchens.

For the most part the cooking was done out-of-doors, the spits turning over great fire pits built on one side of the old lodge while a hundred servants labored over the preparations. I found the appropriate cook, a tall Aekoi who spoke in the accent of Loretto, and managed to bribe her to produce a pair of frumenty puddings.

Frumenty is traditional with venison, of course, but the venison would not be roasted till supper, where it was planned for frumenty to be served as a pottage alongside the meat. Yet all the ingredients were there, the cracked wheat and so on, and while my dishes were being prepared, I went to my room, changed out of my riding leathers, and washed as much as a pitcher of water permitted. I donned my sober brown suit and went looking for some footmen to bribe.

Two hours later, and the day being fine, the entire company had sat down to a banquet out-of-doors, on the lawn between the lodge and the lake. Tables were set up in a *U* shape with the Queen and high nobles gracing a raised platform on the end. Berlauda presided from one of her thrones, and a boys' choir from one of capital's monasteries sang morally improving songs in a complex polyphony. I claimed a seat among the actors and musicians, drank half a cup of excellent wine, then rose and brought in the footmen I'd paid to undertake a special task.

I donned my pompous-magistrate face and we marched up the sward to the platform where the royal family sat, Berlauda and her throne at the center. I was aware of the Marchioness of Stayne, near the head of the company, watching me with her long eyes and a frown on her lips. I knelt to the Queen, or perhaps more properly to her throne of majesty, and then rose and brought a groom forward with a covered dish, which he presented to the princess Floria. With a flourish I removed the chased silver cover, and revealed there a frumenty that formed a perfect hemisphere, made with eggs, sugar, and saffron, dotted with almonds, and scented with orange water.

"Your pudding, highness," I said. "May I give you some?"

Floria seemed too surprised to reply, so I took a spoon and put a generous sample of the pudding into a dish. I laid the dish before the princess, and found her studying me with her sparrow's eyes.

"You're lucky I didn't ask you for a mess of larks' tongues," she said.

"Surely, there are tongues enough buzzing about the court," said I.

"Pity they're not all in aspic," said Floria.

The Queen turned her bland countenance upon me. "Lord Quillifer," said she, "what is this business with the frumenty? We thought the frumenty was to be served tonight."

It occurred to me that perhaps I had committed an error of protocol by failing to serve the Queen first. I turned to her at once and bowed.

"The frumenty will be served with the venison tonight," I said. "But this morning, during the hunt, her highness asked me for a frumenty. While I thought she most likely spoke in jest, I did not wish to cause any offense by failing to act upon her wishes, and so I have procured the dish." I offered the dish to the Queen. "Does your majesty desire me to serve you?"

"Thank you," said she. "We do."

But then her mother, who sat beside her, put a hand on her arm and said in an urgent whisper, "Remember the Yeoman Pregustator!" Who was the unfortunate man assigned to taste the royal dishes, and therefore the first to be blasted by any poison.

On hearing this advice Berlauda reconsidered, and shook her head. "We think we shall not have the frumenty after all."

"As your majesty wishes," said I.

She raised a hand to dismiss me, then lowered it. "We saw you strike down the hart this morning," she said. "Your blow was most original. We wondered if it has a name."

"I have no name for it," said I, "but I heard others refer to the *coup de Quillifer.*"

A faint smile drifted across the Queen's face. "That is appropriate," she said. "We approve."

Again her mother touched her on the arm, and whispered something in her ear. Berlauda's faint smile turned to a faint frown.

"I am told that we have addressed you incorrectly," she said. "That you are not entitled to the appellation of 'lord.'"

"I did not wish to correct your majesty," said I, "on such a trivial matter."

The Queen's expression suggested that whether a man was noble or not was not a trivial matter to *her*, but she said nothing more and dismissed me. I knelt again, and then I and the footmen retired to collect my second pudding. This I delivered to my Lord of Mablethorpe Cross, who sat at a bench with some of his cronies.

"Compliments of the Pudding-Man," said I. "I urge you to eat it all, for you have assuredly paid greatly for it."

He glared at me, but his friends thought this a capital jest, and were repeating it loudly as I retired.

I resumed my seat, and ate my dinner with great pleasure.

CHAPTER SEVENTEEN

The afternoon featured another excursion on the lake, with music and a barge on which cavorted a group of girl-children dressed as water nymphs. I did not want to think about water nymphs and did not go onto the water, but again I saw Berlauda and Broughton together in the swan-boat, and I remarked that Broughton's wife and father-in-law were not in evidence. Perhaps, I thought, they had surrendered to the inevitable, and were making plans to extort as much from the Throne as possible in order to permit a divorce.

While I was contemplating these complexities of love, I saw Amalie walking past the hedges into one of the gardens, and I followed, pretending not to know she was there. The garden was formally laid out, in its center the worn statue of an old man or venerable god, so eroded that he seemed all gaping black eyes and hollowed-out beard. The flowers were brown and dead, and the avenues lined with fallen leaves that crackled beneath my boots. I affected to be surprised by the presence of a marchioness in this place, all in a gown of pure black with a tall collar that rose to her chin, and I took off my cap and "louted low," as the saying is. A cool breeze floated past, and autumn leaves rained down from the trees and skittered along the gravel walks.

"Goodman Quillifer," she said, "you are much discussed."

"Pleasantly, I hope." I straightened and put on my cap.

She frowned. "I thought the business of the pudding was overdone. That joke has grown stale."

"I'll forgo any more jokes about puddings."

"Be advised that you should." She stepped near, and I restrained my desire to put my arms around her. I saw that she wore the pearl pendant I had given her on the gold link girdle, as I wore its dark twin. She touched her chin with the tip of her closed fan.

"Yet it is said that you distinguished yourself in the hunt."

"I did well enough." I looked at her. "Yet I hope some other manner of hunting will prove more lucky for me."

She looked at me from her long eyes. "What manner is that?"

"I hope to track you to your den, my lady."

She flashed her little white teeth. "I would bite you if you did." She let fall her fan. "But your hunt would fail. The guest rooms are crowded, and I share a room with my two maids. We would not be alone."

I fell into step with her. "A few days ago, we speculated on the possibility of taking a ride out-of-doors," I said. "It is a fine day, and perhaps we might find a mossy nook in the forest."

"Too many eyes," she said.

"Tonight, then, after the play?" I paused by the corroded old statue, and turned to face her. "We could meet here. I could bring blankets and a flask with a warming beverage."

She smiled and touched my arm with her fan. "I will not say no, but I can make no promises."

Other people came into the garden then, and Amalie and I parted. I procured blankets and a flask of brandy, which I rolled up and hid beneath a bench in a shadowed part of the garden.

That night we again ate out-of-doors, this time by torchlight, a great venison feast that had been cooking all afternoon. But before the food was served, a harp was struck, while a flute played low, muttering tones, and as that music played, into the *U* of the tables came the wood-woses, the wild men of the forest, who presented the heads of the stags slain that morning. The wild men were covered all in hair, with great thickets of beard, and spun into sight in a slow circular dance, carrying the heads on wooden platters. In their midst was their master, a Green Man whose foliage and viridian paint did not quite conceal the tall, angular form of the actor Blackwell.

The greatest head was dubbed the Stag Royal, the antlers were twined with tinsel of gold leaf, and a gold crown was placed upon its head. The head was so large that it was borne by two of the wild men, who first came to me, where I was seated with the Chancellery's lawyers, and bowed to show me the head—one that I recognized even without viewing the triangular wound in its forehead. Then the woses carried the Stag Royal to the Queen, knelt, and then placed the head as a centerpiece at the high table. After which the wild men, still accompanied by the harp, did their slow revolving dance until they vanished from sight. I saw Blackwell's intelligent eyes looking at me from behind his curtain of leaves, and he gave me little wink and nod in acknowledgment of my triumph.

Pride blazed up in me like a firework, and I received toasts and congratulations from many in that large, splendid company.

Servants came in, bearing platters of food. There were dishes of roast venison, venison stewed with vegetables and herbs, venison breaded and fried, venison backstrap wrapped in bacon and broiled. There were sweet sauces composed of cherry and apricot, plum and raspberry. Venison pie was presented, at the high table with pastry sculptures of harts and does. Several varieties were presented each of venison soup, venison patties, and venison sausage. There were kidneys seared, or deviled along with the liver, or fried and doused with sherry and mustard. The deer hearts were cut up, marinated in sweet vinegar, fried, and served on greens. The liver was fried with butter, bacon, parsley, onions, and rosemary, or mixed with venison to make the large meatballs called "faggots." The tongue was roasted and served sliced thin on salad or braised and served on simnel bread with gravy.

With the venison was served the traditional frumenty, done in a dozen different ways, both sweet and savory.

I supped vastly, as I felt I deserved, and then we watched Blackwell's new play premiered on the outdoor stage. A chill wind was rising, and the autumn air was cool enough that I wished that I'd worn the blankets instead of hiding them in the garden.

Again Blackwell opened the program with a poem in praise of the Queen, neither better nor worse nor less flattering than the last. And then the troop of wild men, shorn of their hairy suits and beards and transformed into mere actors, came onto the stage.

The Nymph was a success. Blackwell had taken the small incidents of my story and stretched them along for two hours, adding pairs of young lovers and sub-stories and clowns and japes and song. The appearances of the nymph were accompanied by an otherworldly duet of harp and lute, and by some manner of lighting effect that seemed to cause the very air to shimmer, a sign that the action had entered a magical realm. I almost forgot that the nymph was a young boy, and I almost forgot that I had known that nymph, and gazed into those leaf-green eyes, and myself stood on the brink of that preternatural domaine. Afterward came the abbreviated gigue with its bawdy jokes restrained in the royal presence.

I applauded with the rest and then hastened through the cold wind to my lodgings for my old tweed overcoat, which I brought with me to the garden, where I retrieved my bundle and waited for Amalie. I stood in the lee of the wind by the old statue and watched high clouds scud across the stars, and when the wind blew cold up my neck, I reached for the bottle of brandy and took a swallow of its fire.

"Your whore will not come," said Orlanda. "Did you think she would venture into the freezing cold merely to couple with the likes of you?"

I turned and gazed with rising terror into the blazing emerald eyes of the goddess. Her gown was green and glittered with gemstones, rubies and garnets nestled in her hair, a carcanet of gold and girasol wrapped her throat, and fury was plain on her face. She glowed in the night with an otherworldly luminescence that put to shame the stage lights that had shimmered over the play's occult realm.

"I had not thought you so low as to have me mocked in this way," said she, "played by some squeaking Orlanda-boy in the posture of a comic flirt and jade."

Though fear rooted me to the spot, I managed to free my tongue from paralysis. "Lady," I said, "I did not make the play."

"Nay, but you inspired it. You spoke with that yew-stave of a play-wright."

"If you know that," said I, "you also know that I told him not to write that story."

"What I know," said Orlanda, "is that your words are sundered from the desires of your inward self. I know that you are false, that your heart is filled with mockery, and that this production was nothing but a sneaking *coup de Quillifer* at my expense."

"I have never mocked you," I said. "I have never spoken of you with disrespect. I posed merely a hypothetical question to an old man who claimed knowledge of worlds not his own. The playwright overheard, and his imagination did the rest."

"And yet," said Orlanda, "I see myself portrayed on stage as a giddy, thoughtless, lovesick object of scorn, and when I ask to myself the question, *Who is responsible for this outrage?*, there is but one name that rises to my thoughts." She took a step closer and surveyed me from a distance of only a few inches. I could breathe in the loamy scent of her hair, taste the rosemary savor of her breath, feel her angry warmth prickling my skin.

"Is this the life for which you rejected my love?" she demanded. "Failing to find office or favor? Amusing your betters by playing the clownish Pudding-Man at court? Abusing the Queen's commissions by selling them? Becoming the toy of some indolent, slinking, sloe-eyed bitch who loves you not, and who carries another man's child?" She snarled. "Is this your triumph, Quillifer?"

"I have been here but a few weeks," I pointed out, feebly perhaps. My mind had begun to thrash its way out of the clutches of surprise and terror, and I frowned at her. "You seem to know a great deal about my life. Have you been spying on me?"

"I do not *spy*," she said, and in her anger she hissed the word. "But I am *aware* of you. To have you thus in my mind is not something I chose, and I assure you it is a condition far less pleasant for me than for you."

I straightened. "Since I last saw you, I have accomplished most of the tasks that carried me away from you—"

She laughed. "Your vast and important worldly errands are complete, and now you beg me to take you? I tell you that I do not make such offers a second time!"

"I don't ask you to repeat your offer," said I. "But I will repeat mine. I ask you to join me *here*. In the capital, or anywhere else in the wide world, so it *be* in the world. I owe you my freedom, and I owe you my fortune, and I would share these both with you."

That offer struck her to silence, and so I continued. "You say that you are aware of me, and of my actions here—and if you are so aware, you may as well be here in your person. We can live here in the world, and in the embrace of enchantment both." I reached out to take her hands. "Will you not stay here with me?"

She snatched her hands away. "I will not aid you in your futile ambitions!" she said. "I will not join you in the stink and mire and folly of the court! I am not one of your foolish females to be so charmed and cozened!"

"How else then may I serve you?" I asked. "I have said there is one thing I will not do, but I will do aught else."

The green eyes narrowed. "I am *aware* of you," she said. "Perhaps it is time you become *aware* of *me*."

And then she disappeared into the shadows, as if she had stepped from one world into the next, and left me alone in the garden, my teeth chattering with fear and with the cold. Her disappearance, silent and sinister, was more ominous than if she had vanished in a clap of thunder.

Become aware of me. It was a promise that was enough to strike the heart. I took another mouthful of the brandy as a gust swirled falling leaves around me, and sent them skittering along the gravel walks.

Amalie would not come, not in this cold. I did not doubt Orlanda's word on that matter. I picked up my bundle and carried it toward the lodge, expecting at any moment for Orlanda or some other wight to lunge at me from out of the hedges. But nothing moved, nothing but a torrent of leaves, and as I neared the lodge I saw the lights blazing, and merriment and music sounding from within.

I paused before the door that led to the guests' wing, where I had my lodging with the actors, and as if on the wind, I heard Orlanda's voice.

"There will be knives."

CHAPTER EIGHTEEN

There will be knives.

Orlanda's words pealed like bells in my head all that long evening, even as the court continued their joyous holiday, as strangers offered their admiration for my killing of the Stag Royal, and as actors rolled from room to room as drunk as kings. Amalie I found comfortably seated in a parlor, with her slippered feet on a hassock, and in the company of some women, with whom apparently she was now friends. She sipped from a glass of wine and pretended not to see me, so I pretended not to see her.

Indolent, slinking, sloe-eyed bitch who loves you not. I found myself thinking of Amalie in light of those words, the words like poison to my soul, and in a fury of resentment I decided that even if it were true, it was hardly Orlanda's business.

As I walked through the crowded, noisy rooms I found myself alert for signs of conspiracy, for assassins, for armed henchmen loitering in the corners. I searched the faces of those who entered the room in order to recognize a possible attacker: the Lord of Mablethorpe Cross, those lackeys of the Count of Wenlock who had so rudely entered my chambers, even Sir Basil of the Heugh come for his lost money. No one looked at me with less than a friendly countenance.

I thought that perhaps I should arm myself with something more deadly than the small knife I carried to cut both my meat and the quills I used for writing. All sorts of weaponry were displayed on the walls, but a half-pike or a boar spear would have been too absurd.

In the end, I went to my room, already filled with rioting actors, and did my best to sleep as the actors sang and joked, and the rising wind howled and hunted among the chimneys.

By morning, the wind had strengthened and freezing rain was slashing down. The lake was so turned to froth that it looked like milk, and the Queen's swan-boat pitched at its mooring while the wind tore its feathers free. The lodge was filled with hunters unable to hunt, and their mood was sour and irritable. Some played at cards for more money than I could afford, and others played chess.

The Queen was not in view, for she was closeted with her spiritual advisors for a round of chants and prayers. Her favorite, Broughton, must have been praying alongside of her, for he was not present either.

I watched a few games of chess, but I found myself frustrated in the same way that I had been when I'd first learned the game. The board presented a rigid field of sixty-four squares, and the pieces maneuvered in ways that were inflexible. A knight had to move a certain way, and the abbot another, and the king a third. Yet I had never understood why any of this was necessary: why should not a queen move like a knight, or a cunning abbot dissolve the boundaries between its white square and the black square adjacent, and so occupy it? Wherefore should not a mighty king move with the same range and power as the queen—and for that matter, why should only one piece move at a time? A proper King should be able to marshal his forces and move his whole army at once, to the thunder of drums and the clangor of trumpets.

It seemed to me that chess did not represent the world as I

understood it, or at any rate as I wished it to be. Were I a pawn on that board, I would have slipped away from that confining arrangement of sixty-four squares, taken advantage of cover available on the tabletop—a cup here, a candlestick there—to march unobserved behind the enemy, and from there launch a surprise attack to capture a castle or stab the enemy king. But alas, the pieces are confined to their roles, and pawns may not leave the board unless captured, and once captured they may not escape. I could not help but feel that all the pieces lacked proper imagination.

Chess is a game I could much improve upon if only given the opportunity.

While the chess games went on the wind died down, and the rain decreased to a misty drizzle. Some of the guests began to talk hopefully of going out to shoot some rabbits. I grew tired of watching lords play chess badly, and walked through a series of drawing rooms toward another room where I had seen a table of skittles. So involved were my musings on chess that I had forgotten Orlanda's words, and I was taken completely by surprise when, behind me, I heard the shrieks of women.

I spun toward the sound, and a door banged open right in front of me. A tall cavalier, hat and long coat starry with rain, burst out of the door and ran into me as he dashed through the room. I felt a savage impact on my shoulder and the breath went out of me in a great rush. I had just turned about and was unbalanced even before the stranger struck me, and the blow knocked me sprawling. The shrieks continued, accompanied now by the clank of the cavalier's rowelled spurs, and the noises scraped my nerves as I strove to still my whirling mind. I got my feet under me and stood, and only then remembered Orlanda's warning—and as I staggered toward the screams, I was groping at myself to find if the stranger had stabbed me.

I reeled through the open door and found myself in a withdrawing room full of ladies. The Viscountess Broughton sat on the carpet clutching at her abdomen with both hands, and everyone else was frozen in postures of surprise and horror.

Only a few seconds had passed since I first heard the screams.

I knelt by the stricken noblewoman and touched her cold, pale hands. "Are you all right, my lady?"

She looked at me with wide eyes. "He stabbed me!" she said.

I gently parted her hands. I saw no blood, no deadly gash in the daffodil-yellow silk of her gown. I looked then at her lap, and saw the blackened steel of a dagger blade lying in the folds of her skirt. I plucked it forth, and saw that it had broken near the hilt.

"I think you may be unwounded, madame," I said.

She gasped and searched her gown, finding only a small tear over her abdomen. Tears spilled from her eyes. "My busk!" she said. "I'm wearing a steel busk!"

"There will be knives." Orlanda's words echoed in my senses. For a wild moment, I wondered if Orlanda's chosen instrument had missed completely and stabbed Lady Broughton instead of me.

But at this point other men arrived demanding to know what had happened, and more kept arriving over the next few minutes, and everything kept having to be explained all over again. They were all members of the nobility, and all wanted to be in charge. One of them snatched the knife-blade away, and I never got it back.

Then someone called out "Hue and cry!," and half the gentlemen ran from the room. The words "hue and cry" were then shouted out all over the lodge, pointlessly because a hue and cry was supposed to be raised when the criminal was in sight, to keep him from escaping, and the cavalier had not been in sight since he vanished from the room with spurs clanking, and not one of the pursuers knew what he looked like.

Then more cries rose—"Guard the Queen!"—and more men ran off to form a wall around the monarch. Lady Broughton ignored all the questions hurled at her and continued to weep, slow tears dropping steadily from her eyes. The floral aroma of a cordial floated through the air, and I looked to see the Duchess of Roundsilver holding out a delicate crystal cup. I had not noticed her in the room till that moment. "I think perhaps Lady Broughton needs a restorative," she said.

I passed the glass to Lady Broughton, and she drank. This action seemed to bring her a little more into an awareness of her situation, and she looked around at the circle of ladies. "Who was he? Does anyone know him?"

No one seemed to have recognized him, and they all began to discourse at length concerning how little they knew. "Perhaps we could shift Lady Broughton to a couch?" suggested the duchess, and they all agreed. The ladies clustered around the stricken woman—neither I nor any other man was permitted to assist—and they helped her to rise and placed her on a couch, where they arranged satin cushions beneath her back.

Being useless, I let my attention wander over the scene, and I saw the hilt of the dagger lying on the floor near the door. I bent to retrieve it. It was what is called a sword-hilt dagger, as the hilt resembles the cross-hilt of a sword, with a disk-shaped pommel. The blade had snapped off about an inch below the hilt, leaving the smith's hallmark visible where it was stamped on the blade, a triangular shield holding an imperial crown. The pommel was made of red jasper, and was carved in a strange design: an arm with a wing where the shoulder should be, and carrying a mace with a tip that resembled a crown. I tried to read it as a rebus: wing-arm-mace-crown. Mace-crown-arm-feathers. Flying-arm-club. Clearly, I was misreading the message, whatever it was.

I was still puzzling over this when a compact yellow-haired man arrived wearing that very design embroidered into his doublet: Viscount Broughton of Hart Ness, the husband of the victim, and the Queen's favorite. As soon as he came into the room, all conversation ceased. He approached his wife, hesitated a moment, and then took her hand. If there were affection or concern in his heart, it did not show on his face. Instead, he was very pale, and was no doubt considering what this would mean regarding his relationship with the Queen.

His wife's life had been spared because she was wearing her corset, as did all well-bred ladies of fashion. The busk, usually a piece of wood or bone, was a wedge-shaped stiffener worn at the front of the corset, and intended to flatten the bosom to conform to the dictates of current fashion. I do not know why fashion insisted that women alter their natural shapes in order to display chests as flat as those of young boys, but fashion saved Lady Broughton's life that morning, as did the fact that she could afford a high-quality steel busk, which being more flexible than wood was more comfortable.

We were all pretending not to watch Lord and Lady Broughton when a sergeant of the Yeoman Archers arrived, carrying a half-pike so as to skewer any available traitors. He demanded information, which was given by all the ladies at once. No sooner had he sorted all this out than his lieutenant appeared, his hand on the hilt of his sword, and he had to sort through the clamor all over again. The lieutenant was just beginning to make sense of this when his captain arrived, and it all had to be gone through once more.

"Her majesty is safe." The captain wanted to reassure everyone on that point. "The house is being searched, and the ruffian will be found."

"He came in from out-of-doors," I said. "His hat and coat were wet from the rain." I pointed. "He ran that way, probably to flee the lodge."

The captain looked at the lieutenant, who looked at the sergeant. "That next room leads outside, ay," he said. "We make sure the door is locked on our nightly patrols."

I handed the captain the hilt of the broken dagger. "This is the knife that broke," I said. "I know not where the blade has gone—someone took it."

The captain examined the dagger, saw the device on the red jasper pommel, and looked up at Broughton in cold surmise. He seemed about to say something, then decided against it. He turned and left the room, followed by the other Yeoman Archers, and he followed the assassin into the room with skittle tables. I followed the gang of Archers along with some of the remaining gentlemen. It seemed the excitement in Lady Broughton's room was over.

From the skittle room, we passed through a sturdy oaken door to the outside. The rain had died down to a soft mist that touched my face with cool fingers. The air smelled of broken, beaten vegetation.

A wide gravel drive circled around the house, and on the far side was a garden. A stooped gardener, in big boots, cloak, and hat, was attempting to repair storm damage to the garden.

"You, there!" called the captain. "Did you see anyone leave by this door?"

Raindrops slid from the sagging brim of his hat as the gardener straightened. He was an old man with a long beard that stretched out over his chest in wet serpentine fingers.

"Ay, sir!" he said. "He asked me to hold his horse."

The captain quickly ascertained that the man had ridden up, paid the gardener a crown to hold his horse, and then gone into the lodge. A few minutes later he'd come out, mounted his horse, and trotted away, in the direction of the gate.

"We must pursue him, sir!" said the lieutenant, stoutly.

"Hue and cry!" said one of the gentlemen.

"Not just yet." The captain turned to the gardener. "What kind of horse did the fellow ride?"

"A chestnut, sir."

The captain turned to his lieutenant. "Choose a party to ride in pursuit. Good riders, good horses. We should only need a half dozen or so. I will report to her majesty."

"Hue and cry!" shouted the gentleman again, and they all rushed off. I looked down the gravel drive in the direction the cavalier had fled. The pursuers would ride two leagues through the forest to the main gate, and then have to decide whether the cavalier had turned right, to Selford, or to the left, for Blacksykes and the north.

That was assuming the cavalier took the road at all, instead of riding off through the woods to some hidden destination of his own.

I approached the gardener. "Father," said I. "You say the horse was a chestnut?"

"Yes, sir." He leaned on his rake. "What they call a liver chestnut, very dark, more brown than red."

"Did you get a good look at him?"

"Nay, sir. His collar was up, and he wore his hat pulled low over his face. I think he may have had a beard, sir."

A beard he shared with most of the men in the kingdom. "Did you mark his voice, father? Where he might have come from?"

"He talked somewhat like they of Bonille," said the gardener. "Like most of them at the big house."

Indeed, most of those at court tended to soften their consonants in the style of Bonille, whether they were born there or not.

"And the tack?"

"Finely made, sir. A saddle such as they use here for the chase, brown leather. There were steel roundels on the breast collar. Medallions like, for decoration."

"Of any particular pattern?"

"They had like rays on them, sir."

"Any other ornaments on the saddle?"

"Nay, I can think of none."

"The leather was not tooled or ornamented?"

"Nay. It was plain, but well made, and nearly new. Brown leather, as I said."

"The bridle likewise?"

"Ay."

I supposed I could continue to ask about the girth and the stirrups and the bit, but I was already feeling this line of inquiry was hopeless. And then I remembered the crown-and-shield hallmark on the broken dagger, and I felt a flush of icy water flood my veins and shock me into sudden alertness.

"Was there a mark on the saddle? A hallmark, stamped on the saddle by a maker?"

The old man's eyes brightened. "Ay, sir! There was the figure of a bird stamped on the flap, near the rider's left knee. I noticed it when I helped his foot into the stirrup."

"A hawk? Eagle?"

"Nay, sir. A small bird. A sparrow, may be, or warbler or some such."

I gave the gardener a silver crown. "Thank you, father. That is very useful."

He touched the brim of his hat. "I'm very grateful, sir. It's a proper gentleman you are."

I grinned at him. "I'm no gentleman at all!" I returned to the lodge.

A pair of Yeoman Archers stood guard outside the withdrawing room where Lady Broughton was undergoing an examination by the royal physician. Broughton leaned on the wall of the next room, pensive eyes fixed on the floorboards, his heel kicking idly at the wainscoting.

I returned to the parlor, where cards were scattered on the tables, and chessmen stood abandoned in their ranks and files. Events had overleaped the boundaries of the game, and only a piece that had already left the board could possibly be of use. Small groups of people clustered together and spoke in low voices. I saw the Roundsilvers with some of their friends by the fireplace, and I walked to join them, standing politely and waiting my turn to speak.

Two gentlemen dashed into the room, booted, cloaked, and spurred, on the way to the stables. They paused long enough for a cup of wine apiece, then continued on their way. One of the duke's friends looked at me.

"You are not joining the pursuit?"

"My horse is a stout animal," said I, "but not a racer." Which referred not so much to the horse but to myself. I turned to the duchess. "Lady Broughton is no worse?"

"It was a dreadful shock," said she. "I cannot speak to the state of her mind, but I think her body is unharmed."

"I do not understand how Broughton can survive this," said the duke. Somehow, he made his absurd lisp sound both grave and prophetic. "He will be accused of trying to make away with his wife in order to marry the Queen."

"The attempt failed," said one of the gentlemen.

"That does not matter," said the duke. "What matters is that he will be accused."

"He will be accused," said I. "But he may not be guilty."

The duke's eyes flickered over the company, and apparently decided those within hearing were safe for this line of conversation. "There are easier ways of making away with one's wife," he said, "than having it done in front of half a dozen witnesses."

"And a better way of arranging it," said I, "than to leave behind a dagger that will point straight to you."

The others had not heard of this development. While I was explaining about the carved jasper pommel, the sounds of the chase came from the front of the building, yips and shouts, as a pack of gentlemen raced off in pursuit of the assassin. They had come for the hunt, had been confined indoors to their frustration, and now launched themselves on this new hunt with all the joy and vigor they would have applied to the pursuit of a stag.

While those around the fireplace discussed Broughton's future, I considered my own. Orlanda's threat loomed in my thoughts, sharp as the promised knives, and I tried to work out how this failed assassination could possibly be a part of her plan. I was not involved in any way, save as a witness. I was neither a victim nor an actor. Perhaps this had nothing to do with Orlanda, and her own strike had yet to come.

Yet my being revolted against the idea of simply waiting for my doom to manifest itself. I would have protested were there any forum for protest, but there was no court competent to judge my situation, and no advocate to take my case. Therefore, I decided, I would act on my own.

An equerry arrived from the Queen asking Roundsilver and other members of the Great Council to attend her majesty, and the duke left the company while the party around the fireplace dispersed. I found myself with the duchess.

"I would like to thank you and his grace for allowing me to join you here," said I.

She looked up at me. "People will be talking about this sad event for a long time," she said. "But you sound as if you are preparing to leave. Are you going to pursue the assassin after all?"

"In my fashion," said I. "I think I may be able to identify him if I ride to Selford."

She looked off through the diamond-pane windows at the Yeoman Archers on the lawn, preparing to depart. She frowned.

"I wonder if that knowledge would be to anyone's benefit?" she wondered.

I was surprised. "If your grace thinks I should not go," I said, "I will remain here."

"I cannot say whether your errand is for good or ill," she said. "And I hardly think the Queen's party will remain at the lodge, in any case. I'm sure the Council will recommend a return to Selford, but it will take the rest of the day to organize it, and her majesty will not leave till tomorrow."

"Then if I may have your leave?"

She looked at me with some slight surprise, as if she were startled I asked her permission. "Of course. Try not to be captured by brigands or pirates on your journey."

I smiled. "I will happily comply."

"And, should you find the villain, think carefully what you do."

This seemed curious advice, so I merely said that I would, bowed, and went to my room. I changed into boots, leather jerkin and trousers, and stuffed everything else in my saddlebags. I donned the overcoat I had carried since I left Ethlebight, and also brought a hooded cloak against rain.

I stopped by the kitchens and begged a pair of venison pies, which I put in my coat pockets. I filled my leather bottle with small beer, then I made my way to the stables, where the captain of the Yeoman Archers was just departing with his party of pursuers, all armed with swords and pistols.

Though I had no hopes of riding down the assassin, I intended to set a brisk pace, for I had twelve leagues to cover before nightfall, when the city gates would be closed against me. I knew not whether I could bribe my way past the guards, and I preferred not to have to test their honesty one way or another.

The Yeoman Archers spurred away. Perhaps I should remark that I never saw a man of the Yeoman Archers carrying a bow, as the corps was armed entirely with pikes, swords, and firelocks. Modern warfare may have made the bow obsolete, but so devoted to tradition was the palace that its guards remained Archers in name, and probably would remain Archers so long as the palace continued to stand.

As I was saddling my mount, Amalie appeared, with her maids, coachman, footmen, and baggage. She looked at me in surprise.

"Quillifer!" said she. "Are you also abandoning this 'sad cockpit of ruined ambition'?"

"I am. And that is a quote from Bello, is it not?"

"I know not and I care not," said she. "You may join me, if you can keep up."

I debated with myself whether or not to accept her offer—I truly wanted to get to the city as soon as I could, and though a ride with

Amalie would be diverting, there would almost certainly be delays.

Yet, I thought, if the assassin was in Selford tonight, he would probably still be there tomorrow.

Amalie ordered the carriage's top lowered, so we might converse, which meant that she and her servants had to wrap warmly in furs against the cold day. Her four horses were matched and of the type called cremello, white with rose-pink noses and brilliant blue eyes. Not only were they a striking and beautiful quartet, they set a rattling pace, and my fears of being delayed soon faded. Indeed, my borrowed beast was hard put to keep up.

We wound our way through the Queen's forest, splashed through puddles, and detoured around fallen limbs. Along the way, we passed the ruins of Broughton's giants, the two great puppets brought low by the storm, a pointed symbol of Broughton's aspirations.

It was not long before we encountered the first of the pursuers returning. They had galloped after their quarry as though he were a stag. Soon enough their horses were blown, and they were forced to return. You would think that this likelihood might have occurred, even to the nobility, well before they spurred off. Those who actually cared about their animals led them home on foot, and the rest rode lathered, staggering, pitiful beasts.

Once we were on the main road, I rode alongside the carriage in order to better talk with Amalie, but the wheels kept throwing up mud and debris, and I spurred ahead. Eventually Amalie had a groom call me back, and I joined her and her maidservants in the carriage, while my horse followed on a lead. Amalie had a bottle of wine opened, and I shared my meat pies. Our conversation was lively, for the maids remained excited by the morning's developments, and during their tenure in the servants' quarters had managed to absorb quite a number of rumors, for instance that the would-be assassin had been hired by the usurper Clayborne, the ambassador from Loretto, by Broughton, or by the Queen herself.

"Why would Clayborne want to kill the Viscountess?" Amalie scorned. Though she did put some effort into an examination of the theory that the ambassador was behind it, in order to secure the Queen for his prince.

While this speculation was taking place, I was able to take Amalie's hand beneath the fur that we shared, and now and again stroked her thigh, causing her to take a little intake of breath. But I dared not risk that intake of breath too often, not under the sharp eyes of the two gossips, nor take any other liberties.

Howsoever, judging by the gleam in her eye, I believe that at least one of the maids became very fond of me during that ride, though I did not put this surmise to the test.

As we rode we encountered more and more of the pursuers, all returning to the lodge. Though none of these had blown their horses in an over-hasty pursuit, they had all concluded they stood no chance of catching the assassin, and turned around in time to enjoy supper at the lodge. One of these was the Lord of Mablethorpe Cross, who gave me a baleful look as he saw me enjoying my wine in the company of the marchioness.

Last of all was the dispirited troop of Yeoman Archers, who had pursued longer than the others. The lieutenant had been sent on to warn the capital's gate guards, just in case the fugitive had spent part of the day hiding and rode in after nightfall, but the rest were riding their weary way back to the lodge, to report their failure to Queen Berlauda.

Even though the carriage maintained a good pace when the road was clear, still we followed the storm, and the road was full of mud and muck and fallen limbs, some of which were so heavy that the footmen and I could barely shift them. This meant delays, and shadows were growing long by the time we passed Shornside's royal castle.

"We will probably not make Selford before nightfall," I said. "Your ladyship might want to look for an inn."

"Oh! That will not be necessary." She gave me a look from out of those long eyes. "We have a country house not far from here, and I've sent word ahead, and will sleep and sup there. The steward will find a bed for you somewhere, if you are not bent on galloping for the capital tonight." And, as her hand grazed along my thigh as she spoke her invitation, I overcame feigned reluctance and accepted.

The fugitive would still be there tomorrow, I decided. Assuming he was there at all.

The promised bed was on the same floor as Amalie's chambers, and was very comfortable, not that I spent a lot of time in it. For as soon as the house grew quiet, I stole down the hall to quietly knock on Amalie's door, and the two of us spent a delightful night galloping beneath the grand canopy of her bed, though I confess myself distracted by the thought that Orlanda might appear shrieking, a knife in either hand to stab us to death.

But no goddess appeared, unless it was one of pleasure and laughter. When I finally fell asleep, I slept so well that, in the morning, I was hard put to scramble back to my room before the servant came up to bring me my shaving water.

CHAPTER NINETEEN

fter breakfast, I put on my grateful-suppliant face, kissed Amalie's hand, and rode off to the capital, where I arrived before midmorning. Low clouds hung over the day, and the wind was brisk. I returned my horse to the livery stable in Mossthorpe and walked across the bridge to Selford with my saddle-bags on my shoulder, then to my lodgings on Chancellery Road. I emptied my saddlebags, then without changing out of my riding leathers walked to Clattering Lane, where all the knife- and swordmakers clustered, and viewed the signs overhanging the street. With the ringing sound of hammers on anvils echoing on either hand, I found the sign shaped like a shield, with a crown in its center, and entered the shop of Roweson Crowninshield—whose name, as I discovered when I asked for the master, was pronounced something like "Grunsel."

I asked Master Crowninshield about the sword-hilted dagger with the Broughton badge, and he remembered it quite well. He had made the dagger himself, and it had been on display in his shop. A customer had walked in from the street and bought it on condition that the plain steel pommel be replaced by one with the Broughton blazon. Crowninshield customarily worked with a cameo-carver on such commissions, and both were paid extra for carving and mounting the jasper swiftly.

Crowninshield was told that dagger was a gift for Broughton's son. He was hardly to be blamed for not knowing that no such son existed.

"Who commissioned the dagger?" I asked, and was surprised to hear that it was a lady. I asked for a description.

Crowninshield's lengthy description, given with many digressions over four or five minutes, amounted to the lady being generally lady-shaped, and having a face similar in large degree to that of a lady. Her accent was either that of Bonille, or of south Fornland, neither of which resembled one another. I made a note to myself that, should I ever be qualified as a lawyer, never to call Crowninshield as a witness.

"Not a grand lady, mind," he added. "But respectable. May be a servant, but a superior sort of servant. A housekeeper, or a governess."

In order to protect myself from any housekeepers and governesses and their murder plots, I bought a sword-hilted dagger of my very own, and thrust it into my belt behind, under my cloak, where I could draw it easily with the right hand. I then thanked Master Crowinshield and made my way to Saddlers Row, where I failed to find any shop signs displaying a sparrow, warbler, or any small bird. This sent me farther up the row to the Honorable Companie of Loriners and Saddlers, where a helpful apprentice showed me the book of marks used by members of the guild, and found the bird mark straightaway.

"That would be the shop of Dagobert Finch, sir," he said.

"Where would I find it?"

"Across the river, in Mossthorpe."

So I retraced my steps across the great bridge to the House of Finch in Mossthorpe. It was near enough to Blackwell's theater that I must have passed beneath the sign more than once, but I hadn't noted it at the time.

The shop was rich with the scent of leather and prime neatsfoot oil, and saddles hung beneath the roof beams like carcases at my father's butchery. Master Saddler Finch was a short, peppery man with a bristly mustache. "I sell a great many saddles, younker," said he.

"This would have been sold to a gentleman about my height," I said. "Wore a beard when I met him yesterday. He rides a liver chestnut."

I saw from a sudden gleam in Finch's eye that he recognized my description, but then his look grew cautious. "Why do you want to know?"

"I owe him money," said I. "We were both at the hunt at Kingsmere two days ago, and we wagered on one of the gentlemen fighting a stag with a sword, and I lost. Yet in the excitement of the betting, I failed to get the gentleman's name."

"Yet it is unusual for a man to pursue another, and all to willingly give money away."

"I can afford it," I said. "I won my other bets." And, to demonstrate my prosperity, I passed a couple of crowns across the table.

"Sir Hector Burgoyne," said Finch. "A military gentleman, yes? He will be glad of your money. He commissioned the saddle over a year ago, but I only gave it to him last month when he finally paid the balance on his account."

"Know you where he lives?"

"Nay, younker. But he keeps his courser at Mundy's on the main road, and they will probably know."

So off I went to Mundy's livery stable, and one of the grooms, once I had given him his vail, was able to direct me to Burgoyne's garret in Selford, in the stew called Ramscallion Lane. Wearing my hood over my head as a disguise, I found the building without trouble, a half-timbered structure sagging over the street, with ancient thatch hanging over the eaves like untidy bangs. It hardly seemed the sort of place for a knight to lodge unless he was desperate for money— desperate enough to commit murder, I supposed.

A fetid, rank odor hung about the lane, both from the rubbish thrown in the streets and the ditch that ran behind the neighborhood, a ditch full of the sewage of the district as well as that which had run down the hill. From the high-water marks on some of the buildings, I judged that the river sometimes flooded this district, though not so deep that houses were wrecked or swept away. I kept my hand on my purse the entire visit, to avoid being robbed by the thieves, custrels, apple-squires, and trulls that infested the district. I could see my silver reflected in their pouched, greedy eyes.

I now had a number of choices. I could apprehend Burgoyne myself, but I cared little for the idea of nabbing a desperate villain in a rathole like Ramscallion Lane. I could hire some professional thief-takers, but that would cost money—and besides, in the course of my legal apprenticeship, I had met the thief-takers of Ethlebight, who I suspect did their own share of thieving, then "recovered" the stolen items to sell back to their owners.

I could disdain the thief-takers and go to a magistrate, who would give me a warrant, but then I would still have to find someone to serve the warrant, and be scarcely any better than I had before.

I might go to the sheriff, if he was in the city and not elsewhere in the county. But then he would bring his own thief-takers, and would probably claim credit for the arrest.

I could not go to the Attorney General, for the simple reason that Queen Berlauda had not yet appointed one.

The one place I absolutely could not go was the barracks of the Yeoman Archers. The City of Selford rejoiced in its traditional liberties, which included freedom from interference by the Queen's Army. The army was forbidden to apprehend lawbreakers, or otherwise disturb the orderly business of criminality, unless there was hue and cry (in which case soldiers could apprehend a felon while acting in the character of private individuals, rather than members of a military company), or if there was a riot or insurrection and a magistrate certified that the Act to Prevent Tumult applied, in which case the army was allowed to massacre at will.

304 † WALTER JON WILLIAMS

Should the pursuing Archers have caught the assassin, I thought, it would have raised an interesting point. Could Sir Hector Burgoyne claim at his trial that his arrest was illegal, as the army had no right to apprehend him?

Of course, the prosecution could claim that a hue and cry had been raised, but the defense could counter that a hue and cry only applied when the quarry was actually in sight.

I would have enjoyed arguing it either way.

But in order to apprehend Burgoyne, I might go to a member of the Watch. But the Watch were mostly elderly pensioners who wandered the city at night, calling that all was well while ringing a bell. (The point of the bell was to let everyone know they weren't sleeping on duty.) If a watchman discovered a fire or a crime in progress, he did not intervene, but rang the bell continuously and called for help.

The decrepit, underpaid members of the Watch were unlikely to provide enough brawn to apprehend a vigorous, unscrupulous man in Ramscallion Lane, so I thought instead of those who pay the Watch, which is to say the guilds. It is the guilds who maintain and pay the Watch—and pay them as little as possible, which accounts for the infirm condition of the watchmen—but the guilds themselves are filled with strapping young journeymen who might well enjoy a brawl in a place like the Ramscallions. They had come to my aid most admirably when I was oppressed by Count Wenlock's henchmen, and I thought that with small encouragement I could bring a considerable force to the stews and apprehend my man without trouble.

But then I decided against it. Were I to show up in Ramscallion Lane with an army of pollaxe-wielding journeymen, there would not be an arrest but a battle. The entire lawless district would rise in arms against the invaders, and while violence raged in the streets, Burgoyne would escape.

Selford and the law provided any number of ways to take up a criminal, and none of them were of any use to me.

So, it must be the thief-takers after all. I went up Chancellery Road to the courts, where such people made themselves available for hire, and acquired for three crowns each, and a share in any reward, the services of two very large men named Merton and Toland. From their broken noses, missing teeth, and the scars on their pates, I marked them as former prizefighters, which meant they had practical experience in the ring against opponents carrying broadswords, halberds, and flails. Toland, indeed, looked as if his entire face had been flattened in a collision with a buckler.

I explained that Burgoyne was wanted for attempted murder, and warned that he was a former military man and probably dangerous.

"Should I not hire some more men?" asked I.

"Nay, sir." Merton spoke in a plausible, peaceful voice that belied his formidable appearance. "We two are used to taking felons quietly, and if we bring a large group into the Ramscallions, we're asking for trouble. Let's keep the reward between the three of us." Merton nodded sagely. "And I will need another couple of crowns."

"For what purpose?"

"For the landlady, so she won't make a fuss."

This was sensible, and I passed over the silver. I was a little surprised when, even after my warnings, the thief-takers armed themselves only with wooden cudgels, which they hid beneath their cloaks.

"Are you sure those clubs will do the job?" I asked.

Merton seemed offended. "Sir, they haven't failed yet—these veteran crown-knockers must have tamed an hundred villains, and turned them docile as little fluff-cats."

We made our way down the hill to Ramscallion Lane, and while the stench clawed at the back of my throat, I pointed out Burgoyne's building. Merton and Toland gave it a professional survey, and then Merton disappeared inside. I followed, and in the deep interior darkness of the hall saw one of my crowns make an appearance and vanish into the grimy hands of a beak-nosed slattern on the ground floor.

"Sir Hector?" Merton inquired.

"Top of the stair. Uphill side."

Merton wasted no time with thanks, but stuck his head out the door and gestured to his partner.

"Master Toland will stay outside the house," he explained, "to make certain that Sir Hector does not escape by his window. You should stand with him, if you please, and I'll howster out this villain."

"I'll go with you," said I.

Merton made no reply, and went to the stair—I doubt he cared whether I lived or died, but he had done his duty in trying to keep me away from any violence. There was no light on the stair, and its upper reaches were black as midnight. The steps creaked and shuddered under Merton's weight. My hand reached for the hilt of my new dagger. Then there was a flash and a shot louder than thunder, and Merton pitched backward into my arms.

I struggled with the weight of the body as I gaped in astonishment up the stair, and there in the gloom I saw Burgoyne looking more or less as I'd last seen him, in a hat and a long coat, but this time with a big horse-pistol in his fist. He looked down at me in a searching, contemplative way, as if he were trying to work out where he'd seen me before, and then he turned and vanished into the murk. My ears, ringing from the shot, could still mark the clank of his rowelled spurs as he retreated.

I laid Merton down on the steep stair, and one look told me that he was dead, having been shot with a heavy ball right in the middle of his forehead. I was staring down at the man's face, my heart beating high in my throat, when Toland came running in and staggered to a halt at the sight of his partner.

Anger and excitement blazed up in me like sparks in a forge. "Burgoyne shot him!" I said. *"Let's take him!"*

I drew my dagger and hurled myself up the stair, stumbling over the body as I went. The top of the stair reeked of powder, but that scent was fresh and wholesome compared to the other smells of the place. I got to the top and saw gray light at the end of the passage, and I lurched toward it, stumbling over rubbish that people had left in the corridor.

I burst through the low doorway at the end of the hall, and found myself outside, at the top of another steep stair, made of weathered planks, that dropped onto the narrow path that ran alongside the sewer-ditch behind the Ramscallions. A dark, sinister muck thicker than treacle oozed down the ditch. Dead dogs floated belly-up in the mire, and the place stank worse than a charnel house, worse than the slop tub in Sir Basil's dungeon when I upended that slope-shouldered knight.

Burgoyne was fifty feet down the path, loping comfortably along as he looked over his shoulder at me. Even at this distance I could see that he retained that thoughtful expression with which he had viewed me from the top of the stair. If my blood hadn't been burning hot in my veins, if I hadn't been half mad with the frenzy of pursuit, I would have understood that look for what it was, the calculating glance of a professional as he evaluated his foe.

Burgoyne had taken out the lever used to rewind his pistol, and he was cranking the wheellock as he hastened down the path. Even in my state of excitement, I calculated that he couldn't possibly have had time to pour powder and ball down the barrel, or prime the pistol to fire, and I knew that I had to catch him before he could reload.

I dived down the steep, rickety stair three steps at a time and charged after him. Apparently, he realized the futility of reloading, and he turned away and began to run faster. "Stop!" I shouted. "Stop!" The words "hue and cry" flashed through my mind, and I realized that "Stop!" and "Stop, thief!" were probably heard twenty times a day in the Ramscallions, only to raise laughter and derision on the part of the inhabitants.

"Stop, murderer!" I shouted. *"Reward for the murderer!"*

I guessed that the promise of reward might well bring more aid than a plea for help, and indeed as we ran along, I saw windows opening, and faces peering past shutters.

"*Reward!*" I cried. "*Reward for the murderer!*" At the words Burgoyne cast a choleric look over his shoulder, but kept running.

The path was slippery and choked with rubbish and a truly astounding array of dead animals, and we both had trouble keeping our feet under us. Still I closed the distance. Looking ahead, I could see a broad gray expanse of water, the Saelle swollen at high tide and backing the water up into the ditch, and I realized that Burgoyne was going to have to turn left, to run along the river's bank, or else wade across the horrid ditch, which I could not imagine him doing if he had a choice.

And indeed, he went neither left nor right. At the end of the path he turned, drew his rapier, and directed its point at my breast.

My blood went from scalding hot to frigid cold in an instant. I stopped in mid-career, my feet sliding in the mud fifteen feet away. I stared at the weapon, which seemed long as a lance. My dagger now seemed preposterously inadequate as a weapon.

"Thus, boy," said Burgoyne, "your chase is brought to an end." His accent was that of northern Bonille.

I gasped, my heart thrashing in its cage, then drew in a breath and called out. "*Reward for the murderer!*"

He snarled at me, his teeth flashing yellow in his beard. "Pursue me further and I'll murder you in truth."

I saw an old bottle lying by the path, and I bent and flung it at him. He dodged it with an easy, contemptuous shift of his hips. Next to me was a tumbled-down stone wall, once a part of a shed, and I bent to pick up a stone. Burgoyne turned and vanished down the Saelle embankment.

For an instant, I readied myself to chase again, and then I thought that he might lurk just around the corner of the last building before the embankment, waiting for me to run into range of his rapier. I looked at the old shed on my left, with its broken wall and half-fallen roofbeams. I put my dagger in my teeth—an expedient I would have found ridiculous had I seen it in one of Blackwell's plays—and I jumped atop the half-fallen wall, and hoisted myself from thence to the roofbeams. I jumped along the beams, the shed shaking under my weight, and then leaped from there to the moldy old thatch of an ancient, decrepit house. My footfalls nearly silent on the straw, I rustled across the roof's ridge, then down the other side.

I saw that my shouts and the promise of reward had brought out some of the more enterprising inhabitants of the district, men rough and dubious, and some of these stood at the end of Ramscallion Lane, looking along the side of the building on which I stood. It was no great deduction on my part to conclude that their neighbor Burgoyne stood there.

I ventured to peer over the edge of the roof, and I saw from above Burgoyne's broad hat at the corner of the building. He was, as I suspected, at the corner, waiting for me to come dashing around to be skewered like a capon. I disappointed him, apparently, because the hat bent as he peered around the corner and failed to see me. Then he turned and appeared in plain sight, walking toward Ramscallion Lane with his rapier still in his hand.

He called to his neighbors. "D'ye see that troublesome urchin anywhere?" Some of them looked up at me on the thatch, and I knew he'd follow their glance and realize I was above him; and so I snatched the dagger out of my teeth and leaped.

I landed behind and to his left side, near enough that I fell into him and knocked him toward the river, but more importantly, I'd brought the pommel of the dagger down on top of his head as I came down. His hat protected his crown somewhat, but he was dazed, and when I rose from the crouch into which the fall had sent me, I was on him, my left hand clutched around his coat collar while my right struck again with the hilt of the dagger. As long as I stayed close, he couldn't use the rapier.

I did not want to stab him. It was clear Burgoyne was a hireling merely, and I wanted to haul him before a magistrate for interrogation, and have him reveal the source of the conspiracy.

As I pummeled my quarry, I could hear shouts of joy from the Ramscallions in the lane. I'm sure they loved nothing so much as a fight.

Burgoyne managed to fend off most of my blows as I wrenched him around by his collar, shaking him as a terrier shakes a rat. He tried to strike with the hilt of the rapier, but I parried with my own weapon, and cut a gash in his overcoat sleeve. I smashed at his head again and was warded off. I know not what happened next, but somehow he twisted under me, I felt a hand grasp my left wrist, and suddenly I was tumbling through the air.

I landed on my back with some force, but panic picked me from the ground and rolled me forward to my feet. Plain murder gleamed pale in his eyes. My heart sank as I realized that he could now use his rapier, and I leaped back and parried with the knife as the narrow blade sprang for my vitals. He charged on and I skipped away, out into Ramscallion Lane, with our audience scattering as the blades gleamed in the day's dull light.

Burgoyne paused in his pursuit as he gasped for breath. I pointed at him.

"Reward!" I cried. "Reward for the murderer!"

Burgoyne snarled and lunged at me again, and I danced away. We were in a growing half circle of observers, men and women and laughing children. Anticipation, cruelty, and greed shone in their eyes, as if we were dogs fighting in a pit for their entertainment. I pointed again.

"Knock him down!" said I. "Throw rocks! Throw bottles! Trip him up! There's a reward!"

"How much?" asked some pragmatist. A young man hurled a bottle, and it whistled past Burgoyne's head. He glared at his neighbor and mouthed a curse.

More bottles followed, and pans, and stones. A slop pot, hurled from an upper storey, landed at his feet and spattered him with its contents. I had turned the neighborhood into my accomplices. Burgoyne fended off most of the missiles, but they slowed him down, and then one caught him on the forehead. After that, blood poured into his eyes, and he had to keep wiping them.

I could see the resolve building in him, and so I was ready when he made another attempt to kill me, running at me with the sword thrusting for my heart—and I would have got away if the growing crowd hadn't hampered me. Suddenly, I was within range of the blade, and I frantically twisted away from it as it plucked at the buttons of my leather riding jerkin. I stabbed at him with my knife, and felt the blade enter the right shoulder. And then one of the crowd failed to get out of the way in time, and I tripped over him and fell. . . . And there I was, helpless as the killer stood over me with growing triumph in his eyes. His arm came back for the final thrust.

At which point the thief-taker Toland, who had come up through the crowd, swung his cudgel, and caught Burgoyne behind the ear, and so laid out the murderer atop me.

CHAPTER TWENTY

T he high-ribbed timber ceiling, which resembled nothing so much as a ship inverted, echoed to the chanting
of monks. Smoke dulled the fitful light. The air was
scented with burning charcoal and the searing stench
of white-hot metal.

"It sorrows me to say this," said His Grace of Roundsilver. "But I
think it best if you stayed away from court for the present."

I felt defiance straighten my spine. "I have done nothing wrong,"
said I. "I have in fact done the Queen a service. Why should I hide?"

"The whole world knows of the Queen's distaste for your presence,"
said Roundsilver. "Should you appear at court, any who hope for royal
favor will be obliged to shun you. It will be humiliating, and will do
your cause no good."

I thought for a long moment. Anger boomed dully in my veins. "I
understand," said I.

"Other matters will soon occupy the court's attention. After that,
you may return."

The duchess looked up at me, her blue eyes deep with compassion.
"I warned you, did I not, that you should think before you acted?"

"A court conspiracy," said the duke, "is sometimes better left unmasked. If you meant to help Broughton, you failed. If you meant to uncover the guilty, you succeeded all too well. The Queen was forced to take action, and well does she resent you for making her take notice of the intrigue at her court."

After capturing Burgoyne, Toland and I had taken the renegade knight to a magistrate, accompanied by a pack of the inhabitants of Ramscallion Lane. The sheriff's men turned out, not because of the prisoner, but because they thought a riot was about to begin.

While Burgoyne was marched to jail, I led the mob to one of the countinghouses where I kept my funds. At the sight of this pack of unruly stew-dwellers, the good bankers began locking doors and slamming shutters, certain they were about to be stormed by an angry rabble. It took a bit of negotiation, but eventually I was allowed inside to collect some of my silver, after which I paid the mob to go away.

That same morning, before leaving Kingsmere for the capital, the Queen had appointed Lord Slaithstowe to be the new Attorney General, and put the investigation into his hands. Slaithstowe rode ahead of the Queen's party and arrived late in the afternoon to find Burgoyne already in custody.

The Queen in the interim announced a reward of three hundred royals to the person capturing the fugitive, again without knowing that Burgoyne had been taken.

The next day Slaithstowe spent in putting the assassin to the question before the Court of the Siege Royal and coercing him to name his accomplices. What Slaithstowe heard probably had him tearing his beard out by the roots, but he did his duty, copied the transcript of the interrogation in his own hand—not trusting anyone else—and reported to the Queen first thing the next morning.

For Burgoyne admitted that he was in the pay of both Leonora, the Queen's own mother, and her best friend, the Countess of Coldwater.

Each rejoiced in her nearness to the Queen, and both feared losing the Queen's love to the interloper Broughton—and in addition Leonora, for reasons of policy, favored Berlauda's marriage to Loretto's prince and heir, rather than to a minor viscount with a pretty face.

The countess's father, old Coldwater, had been Burgoyne's liege-lord. Burgoyne's service in foreign wars had allowed him to return to Duisland with a competence but, being a rake and gambler, he had lost it all. The Countess gave him a few crowns now and again and kept him in reserve, in case she needed someone to intercept a messenger or cut a throat. And then came the inspiration to kill Broughton's wife and blame the husband for the deed. It was one of the Countess's ladies who commissioned the dagger with the Broughton badge.

Queen Berlauda must have been appalled and devastated by the news, but she lacked neither courage nor resolution. Burgoyne was sent to the gallows that very day. The Countess of Coldwater was ordered to Coldwater House on the northeast coast, there to await the Queen's pleasure; and Queen Leonora was sent to the royal residence and fort at West Moss, beyond the Minnith Peaks, and as far from the capital as it is possible to travel without actually wading out into the ocean.

As for Broughton, the scandal was too great for a man without powerful friends to survive. Though he was innocent of anything but ambition, he was obliged to resign his post as Master of the Hunt, given the new office of Inspector General of Fortifications, and sent off to view and report on the state of every fort, castle, and city wall in the kingdom. And, as he had borrowed heavily to outfit himself as a great man at court, and to provide the entertainments at Kingsmere, he would be pursued on this pilgrimage by his creditors, or their representatives.

Whether Lady Broughton rejoiced in the return of her husband, I do not know.

An official announcement was made that Burgoyne had been hanged after an attempt to assassinate the Queen. No mention was made of the Countess or Queen Leonora, though everyone at court knew the story within hours. Presumably the bastard Clayborne, when he read the despatches of his spies, was greatly entertained by the affair.

Those responsible for the violence were punished, but the punishment did not stop there, for Berlauda deeply resented losing everyone she loved and trusted, and viewed without charity those who had brought her this intelligence. She could not abide the sight of Lord Slaithstowe, and found the pain of his presence too much to bear. He kept his office less than a week, which must have been a great blow, as he had performed his duty as well as it could be done—and he lost also the sweeteners he would have been paid by anyone whose business brought them before the Attorney General, a sum that would over time have been a great fortune. Instead, he was appointed Commissioner of the Royal Dockyard in Amberstone, where the opportunities for enrichment were small by comparison.

And as for me—I, who had been the subject of praise and the object of envy after my capture of Burgoyne—I was told merely that the sight of me was disagreeable to her majesty, and that I should avoid her royal presence. Unlike Slaithstowe, I was not offered a job, lest the offer be construed as a reward rather than a punishment.

I wondered if Virtue had triumphed over Iniquity, as in Blackwell's masque. Berlauda's court had been cleansed of one conspirator and one adulterous nobleman, but no doubt there were many of that sort who remained. The court was also rid of one half-lawyer who trusted too much to his own luck, and had suffered the consequence of that trust. I could almost hear the laughter as it echoed from the great roof beams of the foundry.

Was it Virtue who laughed in her chaste home, or was the laughter that of her demicolleague, Iniquity?

I still waited for the three hundred royals promised for Burgoyne. If I ever received it, I would divide it evenly between Toland, Merton's family, and Ethlebight's fund for redeeming prisoners.

At least the Roundsilvers did not shun my company—they moved in a circle so grand that the whims of the monarch barely mattered. I had been invited to the foundry at Innismore where the duke intended to cast his two great siege cannons, and if I had not been so angry at Berlauda and her court, I might have found it interesting. Instead, I found the business intolerable.

The twenty-four monks, who sat in a gallery built specially for them, sat with their backs to us, so the purity of their hearts and prayers would not be distracted by the activities of the profane. Their droning was maddening, like that of an audience bored with the play, and I felt like an actor on the stage before that audience. So frustrated and miserable was I that I wondered if my mere presence would negate weeks of chanting.

Nearer at hand, the engineer Ransome and the Abbot Ambrosius, who I had met at that dinner at the Roundsilver Palace, competed with one another in smug self-satisfaction. Rather than listen to them, I kept my mind on the details of the casting.

The cannons had been first created in wax, tons of the stuff molded into vast effigies that modeled the great guns in every detail, from the cascabel to the chase. Also modeled were the many ornaments, from the royal arms, the royal cypher BR, the handles in the shape of leaping dolphins, the laurels of victory that gracefully twined the breech, the images of old gods hurling thunderbolts, and goddesses puffing out their cheeks to blow the cannonball toward its enemy, the inscription and date ascribing the casting of the cannon to the duke, and sorcerous formulae that promised strength and destructive power. The duke had not abandoned his worship of Beauty, even in so deadly an instrument as a cannon.

The effigies had been packed in clay and then heated, so that the wax melted and ran out, leaving a hardened clay mold behind. The molds were set upright in a pit, near the great crucibles that held the molten bronze.

Ransome urged us to withdraw so that we would not be spattered with hot metal when the pour began. He had been bustling over the last hour, supervising the melting metal, sprinkling his alchemical powders into the crucible. I drew back and found myself standing next to a white-haired man in a worn leather jerkin and a cloth bonnet that bagged out about his ears, and failed to entirely conceal his baldness.

"If yon fellow scurries much faster," he said as he nodded at Ransome, "he may accidentally leave behind his conceit."

"Or the cannon may crack. That will dent his vanity."

He shook his pointed white beard. "If the cannon cracks, he will blame the monks. One of them may have harbored an impure thought or two during in the last twenty-odd days, sure, and spoiled the spell."

The man had the accent of the northwest, with its lilt and lolling r's. I looked at him.

"Do you work here at the foundry?" asked I.

"Nay. I am a master cannoneer. I represent the guild, which requires that one of its masters be present at the creation of every gun destined for the royal armory."

In my rambles about the city, I had passed by the hall of the Loyall and Worshipfull Companie of Cannoneers, and marked the sheer aggression of its facade, with genuine if venerable pieces of artillery mounted on the roof parapets, and aimed casually down the street, or at neighboring houses.

"I have seen your guild hall," said I. "I know of no other hall that so successfully threatens an entire neighborhood."

He grinned at me with crooked, yellow teeth. "We are a formidable crew, to be sure. No element of a contract goes unenforced."

"I shall examine your contract carefully, then, should I ever require some artillery."

"Ah! Look! Something is afoot."

Abbot Ambrosius walked purposefully to the monks, sat in front of them—facing both the monks and the rest of the building—and in silence signaled for a change in the chant. The monks began a new incantation, raising their voices to echo more forcefully off the great wooden beams of the ceiling.

The alchemist Ransome hardly waited for the new chant before he waved an arm to begin the pour. The foundry's journeymen tipped the great crucible, and ninety hundredweight of brilliant, white-hot bronze poured into a channel that led straight to the cannon's mouth. Smoke, steam, and sparks shot upward, and there was a growling dragon's roar as superheated air began to hiss from the channels of the clay mold. I held out a hand to shield my eyes from the glare.

Bronze filled the matrix and began to overspill from the funnel-shaped depression on the end of the mold. Sparks danced on the foundry floor. Ransome gave a shout and a wave, and the journeymen returned the crucible to its upright position and began throwing into it ingots of copper, tin, and zinc, all in proportions to Ransome's alchemical formula. Other apprentices readied themselves to shift the channels so that the next pour would be directed into the matrix of the second gun.

The monks lowered their voices and began a less strident chant. It would be hours before the cannon cooled, and some time before the metal intended for the second gun was ready, and so I congratulated the duke and duchess on their new destructive power, and left the foundry's blazing heat for the crisp November day outside.

The wan winter sun hung over the yardarms of the ships clustered at Innismore's wharves. The air was filled with the scents of tar, smoke, and the abundant richness of the flowing tide. From somewhere, over the cry of gulls, I could hear the clack of capstan pawls along with the song and stamp of a chantey and the cheerful song of a pennywhistle.

At the sights and sounds of the harbor I felt the onset of a great homesickness, and suddenly I yearned to be in Ethlebight. I had done what I could for my city during my stay in the capital, and could do no more. I could not advance here, and I might as well be home.

But I knew that I longed not for the blackened, looted Ethlebight as it was now, but the safe, homely Ethlebight of my boyhood, which was gone forever. My yearning was useless. I could not go home even if I tried.

"Like you my work?" said Orlanda.

I had half expected to see her ever since I'd received word of my banishment from court, and so I managed not to leap out of my skin, though my heart still thrashed in my breast like a wild animal. I turned to face her, and tried to master my whirling mind.

Orlanda was dressed in the blue velvet skirt and dark scarf in which I'd first seen her, and didn't look out of place on the waterfront. Her deep green eyes glimmered in triumph.

"I knew of the conspiracy against Broughton," said she. "I knew that bland bitch Berlauda would not welcome the news that her mother was in league with her closest friend and a hired murderer." A cruel spirit tugged at her lips. "And I knew *you*, Quillifer. I knew that you could not refrain from trying to get to the bottom of the affair. You would never hold back, not when there was a chance of flaunting your superiority in front of the whole court." She stepped close. "I know you well, Quillifer. I know that there is one thing that you simply cannot do, and that is to do nothing."

"In that case," said I, "you yourself did nothing. You simply let events take their course."

"No. I confronted you the previous night, and told you that I would be concerning myself with you. I knew that would spur you into action. I knew that you would leap into this business in order to prove to yourself that you were your own master, and not my pawn." Her cruel smile returned. "It was a fine piece of handiwork, think you not?"

"It called for fine judgment," said I. "Though the same events may have occurred in any case, without your lifting a finger."

"But then how could I rejoice in my victory?" She smiled. "Rejoice in the knowledge that it was I who brought you to this pass, and not mere chance?"

I regarded her smile, and nodded. "You may rejoice, as well, that you have taught me a valuable lesson. That my successes, whatever they may be, will be mine. My failures will be your doing, and will reflect not on me."

Her smile faded.

"For you see," I continued, "people are often troubled by their failures, and spend many long, anxious hours scrutinizing their errors, and examining their consciences, and wondering how they might have prevented unhappiness. You have spared me all that—I need concentrate all my efforts only on achieving success."

"Perhaps I will raise you up," she said, "so that your fall will be all the greater."

"You may sport with me, sure," said I, "as a wanton boy with a fly, but it hardly seems worthy of you."

Her eyes narrowed. "What do you know of *worthy*?" she demanded. "Was your conduct toward me *worthy*?"

"Ay," said I, "take me for your teacher, then, and behave as badly as I. Worse, if you like."

"Faithless!" she hissed. Though to my ear the word seemed to lack somewhat of its former conviction.

"I have had time to consider my situation in the last weeks," said I. "And your own as well. And I would like to know, *Where are the rest of you?*" I reached out an arm to encompass the island, the sailors, the ships, the hawkers trundling by with their carts. "According to the old epics, the world was full of nymphs, and naiads, and dryads, and mighty gods, all interfering in the business of mortals. Where did they all go? Are they off on the Comet Periodical, as the follower of the Pilgrim allege?"

"I know nothing of this comet," said Orlanda. "And that Pilgrim, he was naught but a gaunt, bitter cenobite full of slanders."

I looked at her. "Are you the only one left? No wonder you take rejection so to heart."

She laughed. "Perhaps we grew tired of mortals so persistent in their foolishness."

"But yet you are not tired of me, and I am foolish as the rest."

Green fire blazed in her eyes. *You woke me!* she said. "I was content till you came."

"Has bedeviling me then made you more content?" I asked. "Are you more content now than you were a week ago?"

"Are *you?*" Orlanda responded. "That is more to the point." Her lips parted in a thin, angry smile. "I have centuries to find contentment. Have you?"

I blinked, and she was gone, and where I stared was a waterfront lane full of busy chandlers and tipsy sailors going about their day. Perhaps she had made her point; perhaps she was finding a dispute with me harder work than she supposed.

As I pondered this matter, I joined the Roundsilvers in one of the foundry's buildings, where wine and dinner had been provided, and some dull entertainment in the form of Ransome discoursing on his alchemical experiments. He was very much involved, he said, in removing superfluity from his Stone through Calcining, Loosening, Distillation, and Congealing. I asked him what Stone was to be so congealed.

"Any Stone you wisheth," said he. "The process of purification is the same. For look you—" He lifted a piece of honey-cake. "When I eat of this cake, it goeth to my stomach, where my stomach's great heat concocts it, just as it might be concocted in my study by an alembic. The cake is then transformed into chyle, which then passeth to the liver, where it is concocted a second time to become blood. From the liver the blood goeth to the right-hand chamber of the heart, where it receiveth an admixture of vital spirits, and only is then fit to be taken up by the body as nourishment.

"So it is with the Stone. For a Stone must pass through stages until it reacheth perfection, and of course the most useful element for refining is known as the Ravenous Gray Wolf."

I had just had a disturbing interview with a divine being, and that made Ransome's pronouncements about his Stone, and his guts, all the more fatuous. I wished the actor Blackwell present, that I might enjoy his sardonic observations on Ransome and his art, but it appeared that I would have to provide any such entertainment for myself.

"What is this Wolf?" asked I. "Has it another name, or must I believe that purification can only be achieved through the employ- ment of a wild beast?"

Ransome feigned amusement, but he ate his honey-cake before he answered. "We who are adepts in the Art can translate these names esoterical. The Ravenous Gray Wolf, depending on its usage and the occult school to which the philosopher belongs, is known also as the Green Dragon, or—begging your pardon, your grace—the Menstrual Blood of the Whore."

The duchess showed more fascination than embarrassment, so I felt free to continue.

"I fear that I am only more confused," said I, "for I see nothing to connect public women with dragons, or with ravenous wolves, except perhaps the fanciful mind of a dreamer. Perhaps the element has also an exoteric name?"

"Those whose knowledge of the Art is imperfect—an apothecary, perhaps—do call it antimony."

"Terrible stuff," said the gunner Lipton. "A doctor prescribed an antimony purge for me once, and it cleaned me both up and down. I barely survived."

I looked at him. "Did you feel more perfect afterward?"

He cackled. "Nay. But I had lost my superfluity, sure."

I turned back to Ransome. "Why do you need these esoteric names at all? Why not print up your recipes in plain language, like my mother and her recipe for red hippocras?" I turned to the duchess. "Which, by the way, I recommend, for she uses spikenard and ginger, which in winter produce a pleasing warmth in the blood." I looked at Ransome. "Or perhaps in chyle, I forget which it might be."

Ransome's answer was a little short, which indicated perhaps that his patience was growing thin. "With all due honor to your mother," he said, "Practitioners of the Noble Art can scarcely be compared to hostesses and brewsters. Many years of study and experimentation are necessary to perfect our understanding."

"The years would be less if you hadn't had to sort out your Purple of Cassius from your Powder of Algaroth, your Orpiment from your Phlogisticated Air. Why, if you merely wrote the recipes down in plain language, everyone could perfect their own Stones." Lipton gave another cackle. I affected sudden illumination. "Well," said I, "if that were the case, they would not need to pay alchemists, would they?"

"Your examples sort not together," said Ransome, "which demonstrates to the illuminated mind the dangers of an untutored experimenter. For much of what we do is dangerous, and if we hide our Art behind metaphor, it is as much to protect the public as to shield our mysteries." At which point he excused himself, to drop more of his powders into the crucible.

After some hours, the time came for the second pour, which progressed much as the first, with the sparks flying and the pure-hearted monks praying till the roof-beams rang. I joined the Roundsilver party in their galley for the return to the capital, and there returned to my room, empty and cold, and where no message from Amalie waited. I had nothing to do but contemplate my failures, and my longings, and my losses, and wish my mother present with the rest of our family, and hippocras warming on the hearth.

For lack of any other occupation, I returned to the foundry next morning, to see the clay molds knocked off the guns. Revealed were shining red-gold pillars brilliant as a blazing fire, all wreathed with ornament perfectly cast and gleaming in the light. The tubes were marred somewhat by the bronze that had filled the sprues and channels that allowed air to escape the mold, and the metal to reach every part of the matrix. These would be sawn off, and the remainder polished.

Also, the cannon had been cast as solid metal pillars, and the great bores would have to be drilled out. The guns would remain upright for this procedure, lashed on platforms like huge capstans, and rotated by teams of oxen. The drill would be suspended pointdown from the ceiling, and carve out the cannon over the course of many hours.

Now that the cannon had been cast, and the metal cooled, the monks had returned to their home. Apparently, it was not necessary to bless the oxen, or the drill.

Ransome bustled from one task to the next, perfectly satisfied in his own genius.

"He hopes for an appointment as the Queen's Gunfounder," said the gunner Lipton. "The office is vacant."

"He seems at least to have done a good job," I commented.

"We'll see. I'll have to test the guns before her majesty's government can accept them. Put forty pounds of powder in the breech, and fire a sixty-eight-pound solid shot to discover if the gun shatters." He nodded at the guns. "We'll see if Ransome knows his business or not."

Lipton invited me to dinner at the Companie of Cannoneers the next day, and I was pleased to accept.

No message from Amalie waited at home. I began to wonder if the finger of Orlanda was again stirring my affairs.

The dinner with the Cannoneers was pleasant, though there was no talk of artillery. All anyone wanted to do was talk about the court, and about the conspiracy against Broughton, and my own part in uncovering it. The gossip had tumbled down from the castle and spread itself over the town. At least I did not lack for an audience when I told my story.

I did not see Amalie for another few days, when she arrived early, while I was still digesting my breakfast. Her father had been visiting, she told me, and it was impossible to get away. He had agreed to loan the money to ransom Stayne, so provided that Sir Basil remained honest in the matter of ransoms, her husband would soon be free.

I was not entirely delighted to hear this, but tried to be as pragmatic as she in regard to her marriage and its necessities. "We should enjoy your freedom while we may," I said, and she agreed, though only after a cup of wine.

As I was an exile from court, my chief source of news became Amalie, who provided a pleasingly satiric view of life at the Castle. Broughton's departure had cleared the field for every lord in the kingdom to dandle his son before the Queen, and the unending parade of ephebes, imbeciles, rakes, middle-aged widowers, down-at-heels gamblers, jack-a-dandies, and mere schoolboys was described by Amalie with wicked relish. What the Queen thought about them all could hardly be imagined. If Berlauda intended to choose a new favorite, she was keeping her choice to herself.

Indeed, her majesty was proving very adept at not making up her mind. Half the offices in the land remained unfilled, which kept hopeful situation-seekers thronging the court, gossiping, conspiring, and trying to somehow attract the Queen's attention.

And soon there would be more of them, for Berlauda had called the Estates to raise the money in order to prosecute her war with

Clayborne. The Estates normally met over the wintertide, in the winter capital of Howel; but Clayborne was presiding there over his own assembly, and so quarters had to be found in Selford for a new wave of arrivals. The House of Peers would meet in the Great Reception Room of the palace, while the Burgesses would use the prayer hall at the Monastery of the Pilgrim's Treasure. In the meantime, the arguments over taxation had begun, and there was much talk of socage, scutage, tallage, carucage, ship-money, the salt-tax, and escheats. All wanted relief for themselves, and for the taxes to fall more heavily upon others. It was hoped that Chancellor Hulme would keep the Burgesses, at least, in order, though nothing could discipline the nobility, unless it were the monarch herself.

Another pressing issue was the matter of who would command the army. The Knight Marshal was an old veteran of the late King's wars, but perhaps superannuated; and the other candidate was the Count of the Stable, known less formally as the Constable. He was a hale, vital man, martial and gallant, but unfortunately his son and heir, Lord Rufus Glanford, had not only joined the rebels, but taken with him his regiment, the Gendarmes, which were based in Howel, and who with the Yeoman Archers formed the monarch's bodyguard. On account of the son's considerable sins, Berlauda therefore was not inclined to trust the father.

Many of the great nobles also felt themselves qualified to be the Queen's Captain General, and were cultivating a martial appearance, and loudly discussing ravelins, sallies, culverins, and defilades whenever her majesty was within earshot.

"I think the Queen should have a tournament and make them joust," said I. "At least we could see which of the candidates can sit a horse."

Amalie smiled sadly. "Berlauda would never do anything as amusing as that."

I considered the Queen and her throngs of courtiers. "I begin to see a method in Berlauda's decisions," said I, "or rather the lack thereof. As long as so many offices remain unfilled, the candidates will remain in hope, and will strive to please her. Whereas if she fills all the offices before the Estates can meet, they will not only have no reason to please her, but some may be active in thwarting her."

Amalie cocked an eyebrow. "Do you think Berlauda's so ingenious as that?"

"Perhaps not. But the Chancellor is."

"You could ask your exquisite little friend, the duke. He sits on the Great Council."

"He is discreet where those meetings are concerned."

"Offer him your theory. Then see what he says—or admits."

I did so. His grace smiled and said, "Please don't mention this to the office-seekers. They are petulant enough already."

It was some time before I could report this to Amalie, for her husband had returned, though he didn't stay. Berlauda had not forgotten Stayne's presumed treason and snubbed him at court, which convinced him that there was no point in remaining for the meetings of the Estates. Stayne remained in the capital less than a week before riding off south to raise a militia and beat the Toppings for Sir Basil and his gang. I very much doubted whether Stayne would find his quarry, and wondered rather if Sir Basil would capture him a second time.

Amalie once more began to visit my rooms, but we both began to discern that our liaison was undergoing a period of fatigue.

Certainly, our horizons were limited. For fear of discovery by the servants, I could not visit her at her own home, and so we met at my lodgings. Amalie was too well-known among her set to walk with me in the street, or meet me at the theater—she was far too grand to be seen with me, at least without suspicion. Nor could she pass for anyone of my class—her languorous manner, her accent, and her clothing all marked her as a member of the aristocracy, and though the clothing could be changed, the rest could not. Plus, she was carrying a child, which could not be concealed.

And so, we were confined to my two small rooms, which seemed to grow smaller, darker, and colder as wintertide progressed. She came less often, and the visits were not prolonged. When she was not there, I found the rooms filling with memories of her scent, her long, lazy eyes, the satin touch of her skin, even her little white teeth. . . . But I could feel the memories wither, even when she was with me.

I wondered if Orlanda had a hand in the fading of the affair, but I was inclined to doubt it, and instead found myself absorbed in the same sort of self-examination that I had told Orlanda would no longer be a part of my life, and I reviewed my past conduct to see if there was aught I could have done to produce a more hopeful result.

But no, the girl was married, and carrying the child of another man, and our end was foredoomed.

Our doom fell shortly after the new year, when the Marquess of Stayne returned from his punitive expedition to the Toppings, having failed to capture a single outlaw, let alone retrieve his ransom. I didn't hear the news for a week, until the Duchess of Roundsilver informed me at one of her dinners. She looked at me with care as she told me, to see if I was badly affected; but I had been anticipating the news, and merely asked if he'd encountered any bandits, and for the next weeks concentrated on my business.

For, as Orlanda had remarked, I could not do nothing. I had decided to put my fortune, such as it was, out into the world, and earn my living as a speculator. My father had done well in business, and I hoped to emulate his success. But my father had also made most of his income from loans, and I decided against that course, for he had loaned to people from Ethlebight who he'd known all his life; and I knew no one in Selford, and most especially no one I knew to be trustworthy.

I consulted acquaintances at the Butchers' Guild, at that of the cannoneers, where I was now welcome as an amusing friend, and with Blackwell and the Roundsilvers. The duke suggested I invest in property and become a landlord, and Blackwell that I buy an interest in his new play.

I laughed at Blackwell's suggestion, and he, having made the offer facetiously, laughed with me. I decided against buying property because I knew not where I wanted to live, whether I would continue my bleak life in the capital, return to Ethlebight, or travel abroad. So, I returned to the business I knew best, and bought cattle and swine. There was war in Duisland, for all there had yet been no fighting, and I knew that soldiers and officers and sailors must eat. My animals were intended for the camps that would soon be forming around the capital, or to be salted and put up in casks for the navy. This put me in touch with people who contracted to supply the military, and one of them told me of a venture that had fallen short of money. A friend of his had bought a ship with the intent of leasing it to the state to convey soldiers and troops to the war in Bonille. But the ship proved to be in a poorer state than he was led to believe, and required repairs before it could leave port. He had put his entire fortune into the *Sea-Holly*, and was desperate; and so I rescued him, paid for the repairs, and now enjoyed a half-interest in his emprise.

I was a little disturbed to discover that the government paid my new partner not in silver but in bills drawn on the treasury, which would be honored only at the government's convenience. I reflected that I was probably safe enough, as I knew the Chancellor personally, and could apply to him for payment if I so needed. Still, there was a large secondary market in these notes, and I purchased a few of them at a discount, some from my own partner. I could afford to wait to redeem them, as I still had enough to live on and, though running low on coin, had not yet begun to sell the jewelry I had got from Sir Basil's treasury.

The Estates began meeting after the new year, and the new taxes were going into place under the direction of the Chancellor. I owned nothing that could be taxed besides a burned-out house in Ethlebight, and so far the government was not taxing land without whole structures on it.

Master Lipton, the cannoneer, invited me to the tests of the duke's great cannon, and so I paraded out of Innismore along with the glittering guns, each drawn by forty horses, lumbering along with great caissons containing the necessary powder and the round stone cannonballs, the whole array under the command of members of the Guild of Carters and Haulers. Gun crews had been drawn from the Loyall and Worshipfull Companie of Cannoneers, who, once we had arrived at the gun range, took charge of the guns, and also began clearing nearby trenches and earthworks of debris.

The duke himself did not come, as he was involved with the Great Council and the House of Peers, and the duchess was acting as his hostess for a series of dinners and salons in which many of the issues plaguing the Estates would be settled.

The guns were set up on the north bank of the Saelle, and their fire was to be directed at an uninhabited island about three hundred yards away. It took half an hour to load the first gun, what with forty pounds of gunpowder being ladled down the long barrel, and the giant cannonball hoisted up on a special sling. I, along with the Carters and Haulers and most of the cannoneers, watched from an earthwork two hundred yards away as an apprentice put a portfire in the touch hole and lit it. He scampered for safety in a trench, and the huge gun went off with a roar that stunned into silence the gulls and bitterns that had been calling from the mud flats. I could actually see the huge ball fly through the air and plow its way through the reeds on the island bank.

Flame continued to lick from the gun's muzzle even after the stone ball had crashed to a halt in a shower of mud. A vast cloud of white smoke rolled over the scene, and I could taste the sharp taste of brimstone on the air.

Lipton, standing next to me, gave a nod. "That flew well. Maybe there is something in that monkish nonsense chanting after all."

The guns were each fired five times, which took up most of the day, after which Master Cannoneer Lipton agreed to sign the papers certifying that the guns would make a suitable addition to the royal armory. But by that point, I had lost interest in the proceedings, for I recognized a small galleon drifting up the river along with the tide.

Meteor, the privateer's commission of which was shared by myself and Kevin Spellman. And which was coming up the river with flags flying, for behind it came a capture, a galleon even larger than the privateer, and flying the white flag of submission.

CHAPTER TWENTY-ONE

"The prize is owned by the Duke of Andrian," said Kevin. "*Lady Tern* had been gone for a twelvemonth, and her master had no idea there was a war and put up no resistance. And it's loaded with cloves, cinnamon, cardamom, and nutmeg from the Candara Coast, spices so valuable they might as well be bars of silver."

Delight rose in me like bubbles in a mineral spring. "I hardly think the courts will resist depriving Clayborne's stepfather of such a fortune. Not when the Crown gets twenty percent. But," I added cautiously, "perhaps my name should be kept out of the records insofar as that is possible."

Kevin raised his eyebrows. "Your name? Your reputation has been damaged in some way?"

"A mere prejudice on the part of the monarch," said I. "But I am trying to remain out of her sight for the present."

Kevin's look turned cautious. "And . . . the other lady?"

"It is a related story, but for another time."

I hardly wanted to discuss Orlanda at this moment. We were in *Meteor*'s great cabin, or rather the half of it used by Kevin. We ate steak-and-kidney pies I'd bought on shore, and were well into our second bottle of ruby-red Loretto wine.

Kevin had told me all the news from Ethlebight. A well-spoken messenger had arrived bearing a list of the corsairs' captives, along with the sums named for ransom. The Aekoi knew better than to send one of their own on such a mission, and tended to use men from Varcellos for this task, as Varcellos was a nautical nation between Duisland and the Empire, and so this gentleman was a Varcellan.

"I have seen the list of captives," said Kevin. "And I should tell you, your Master Dacket is not on it."

I looked at him in sudden sorrow, both for my master and for my hopes, for he it was who could certify me a lawyer without my having to apply to one of the Moots. That meant another one of my hopes had been pinned to the floor and trampled.

"I saw him taken, he and his sons," I said. "Are the sons on the list?"

Kevin shook his head. "They are not mentioned."

"They might have died in the way to the Empire."

"Or it may be a bookkeeper's error." He put a hand on my arm. "Fear not, it may be sorted."

"I fear he is lost."

"We may be thankful that my family is coming home," he said. "Thanks to our sale of the privateering commissions, I was able to raise the money and pay their ransoms. And a squadron of fast cruisers is now outfitting in Ethlebight, or have already gone to sea in search of prizes."

I told Kevin some of the news from Berlauda's court, and let him know of my various commercial ventures.

"Should I now sponsor you for membership in the Mercers?" asked he.

"I hardly think I'm rich enough."

He looked rueful. "Nor am I now."

I laughed. "After you've taken *Lady Tern*?" said I. "A fortune's just fallen into your lap!"

"There will be no money from *Lady Tern* till the ship is condemned by a prize court, and in the meantime, I must pay the lawyers who argue our case. The ransoms took almost all my silver. I have precious little cash."

"Well." I shrugged. "If you need a loan . . ."

"To provision *Meteor* for another cruise will take more money than you possess, I fear. I'll have to resort to a moneylender."

"With *Lady Tern* as your security, you should have no trouble raising a loan. In fact, I can introduce you to some reliable bankers."

"My family has a banker here." Kevin poured claret into his goblet and gazed at it reflectively. "I think the wine is making me maudlin. We have been luckier than we have any right to be, given the war and all that happened to Ethlebight. And yet I feel sad that I had to pay ransoms, and think not to praise my good fortune that I could afford to pay without pawning my shirt."

"It is hardly a night for sorrow," said I. "Perhaps we should sing a song."

He laughed. "Perhaps we should."

"Yet before we break into 'Saucy Sailor,'" I said, "my *Sea-Holly* sails for Longfirth in a few days with a cargo of soldiers and supplies for the garrison. Perhaps *Meteor* could convoy her to Bonille, and save me the cost of insurance. And then we two could go privateering, and leave Selford in its misery behind."

Kevin had drunk enough wine to think this a perfect idea. While a winter storm roared and rattled through the city, we arranged to leave *Lady Tern* and its precious cargo in the hands of the lawyers, I paid my landlady three months' rent in advance, new supplies were brought aboard, and the soldiers marched up *Sea-Holly*'s gangboard. The storm having passed, and the ships now busked and boun, we dropped down the Saelle on an ebb tide and set off across the Sea of

Duisland to Longfirth, the Queen's fortress-city in Clayborne's rebellious domain.

The last of the storm wind came strong from the southwest, a near gale, and *Sea-Holly* had to reef its topsails, but *Meteor* lived up to its name, and plunged into each wave like an exuberant spaniel, the foam rising in white sheets from its stem. The backstays were taut as harp strings, and the timoneers fought with the whipstaff as the following sea crashed repeatedly into the rudder. The ship had come alive, the wind singing through the rigging, the timbers groaning as they worked, and flags snapping overhead. The ship's master, Captain Oakeshott, kept a keen and practiced eye on the ship and its crew, so that nothing broke or was carried away.

I looked to windward, and saw a line of soldiers on *Sea-Holly*'s lee rail, every one of them seasick and jettisoning their cargo of breakfast into the ocean. There were five hundred such soldiers aboard, and I could only imagine the reeking mess belowdecks.

I was fortunate in not being subject to seasickness, and so I vastly enjoyed my day on the plunging ship, every moment taking me away from Selford, and—I hoped—from Orlanda. I hoped that, as is alleged for some spirits, she could not cross water, but then I reflected that she was a water nymph, and could hardly be brought to a halt by her native element. And then I began to worry what mischief she might be up to, were she aware of my voyage and of *Lady Tern*'s capture. Could Orlanda arrange for the prize court to refuse our suit? Or use her arts to persuade the Queen to confiscate the ship and all its cargo?

Darker suppositions entered my mind. She could set fire to the ship, create a total loss, and leave Kevin in debt. Or exert her power to start a plank on the *Meteor*, so that the ship filled and sank and drowned us all.

I tried to drive these worries from my mind, because if Orlanda were in some way overhearing my thoughts, I wanted not to offer her ideas that might surpass her own. And so I sang to myself "Saucy Sailor" and "The Female Smuggler" and other songs appropriate to the great ocean sea, and by and by my heart lifted, and delight began to fill me, for despite my troubles, I was young and at sea and on a great adventure.

During the brief voyage, I set myself to discover everything I could about the ship and its handling. I wished to be a good privateersman, and sent myself to school to become one.

Captain Oakeshott was a stern man, only two-and-thirty, though the wind, weather, and sun had left their marks on his face, and he looked older. His face had burnt to mahogany, and his long hair and full beard were black. He wore a gold ring in one ear, and looked most piratical.

The captain kept *Meteor* zigzagging in hopes of sighting a prize, but the storm seemed to have driven all ships off the ocean, and when night fell, we shortened sail and kept *Sea-Holly* close company. The screens that divided the great cabin were broken down, and Captain Oakeshott supped with us, and over fiery brandy told us a hundred stories of his life at sea, some of which were doubtless true. Then the screens went up again, and the captain retired to his half of the cabin, and Kevin to his own. I slung a hammock in Kevin's cabin, and with the sea rocking me to slumber, I probably slept better than Kevin in his deep, coffin-like bed.

The weather moderated the next day, and *Sea-Holly* shook the reefs out of its sails, and we continued in company until the long, low, watery country around Longfirth came into sight, with its two lights aglow even in daylight. There we hove to, and raised a flag to summon a pilot.

The pilot was necessary, because the entrance to the River Brood was guarded by sandbanks, and these would likely have shifted in the late storm. The pilots took our two ships through the sandbanks, past the wooden lighthouses, and then guided us up the eight leagues of water that separated Longfirth from the ocean.

The wind was still favorable, and we arrived in the city just before sunset. *Sea-Holly* moored to one of the wharves in order to discharge its presumably grateful soldiers, but *Meteor*, which had no business in town, anchored in the river at a buoy, and a boat carried me, Kevin, and Oakeshott to shore. The captain had to report his business to the Lord Captain of the Port, Kevin wished to call on some of his father's business associates, and I was free to wander over the town and enjoy myself.

I had never been in Bonille before. The inhabitants call it "the Island," deriving the name from Bonne Isle, which I consider a false etymology. And in any case Bonille is not an island, but a peninsula; and Fornland, which *is* an island, is not in their view as much an island as Bonille. It is all part of their pretension.

When long ago the first of the Aekoi regiments marched to the west coast of Bonille, they viewed the piece of ocean before them and, not wanting to travel any farther, in hope called it *Mare Postremum*, meaning the Final Sea. They did not know that Fornland was over the horizon, and the whole great ocean beyond, all the way to the Land of Chimerae, and greatly would it have dismayed them if they had known it. So, Bonille is not an island, and the sea is not the final one, but these false ideas will probably persist to the end of time.

Now that Fornland and Bonille have been united, the Final Sea is now called the Sea of Duisland, though the old name persists on maps. The Crown claims ownership of this piece of water, and collects revenue from any foreign ships passing through.

The harbor was busy with ships repairing storm damage. Some had lost yards or sails; some had dragged anchors and collided; and one large galleon, *Star of the North*, bound from Amberstone to Steggerda in the Triple Kingdom, had lost two of its four masts, and had suffered some damage to the hull as well, possibly in collision

338 † WALTER JON WILLIAMS

with another vessel, possibly from its own fallen masts turned to bat-
tering rams by the wind.

Much of the city was built of brick, as Ethlebight, and so I felt at
home, though I noted the brick was not as varied or brilliant as in my
own town. As Berlauda's outpost in Clayborne's country, Longfirth
was full of soldiers, and they had overloaded the citadel and were billeted in the town, among the people, as much an occupying army as
a garrison. When word had come that Sir Andrew de Berardinis had
secured Longfirth for the Queen, the Trained Bands of Selford had
been mustered and sent over the sea to assist the defenders, but the
Trained Bands were a militia, and were supposed to serve only for a
set time. In anticipation of a siege by Clayborne's army, these militia
were being replaced by companies of professional soldiers as fast as
the Crown could raise them and ship them over the sea along with
supplies of food and ammunition.

I climbed the city walls, which gave me a good view of the surrounding country. It was flat and watery, and the winter sun gleamed
off the quicksilver shimmer of lagoons and ponds. Behind the city,
toward the interior, was the Long Firth itself, where the River Brood
widened to a long, deep, narrow lake that disappeared into a misty
horizon. Sentries paced the walls, and I was challenged enough so
that I returned to the town, lest I be taken up for a spy.

Back in the city, I viewed the old citadel with its towering walls
of red brick, where Sir Andrew's royal garrison was quartered, and
across the main square the imposing city hall, covered with the
badges of its guilds and of prominent families. The scents of roasting
meat came from a tavern near the hall, along with the sound of many
voices singing, and I peered in the door. The singer was a young
woman with a rosy complexion and glossy brown hair that tumbled
about her ears, and she was accompanied by a young man playing a
seven-course guitar of the sort common in Varcellos. For the most
part the songs were old, and the audience was able to sing along. The

smoky common room was full, and every seat was taken. I got a mug of cool, dark beer pumped up from the cellar, and stood by the back of the room as I listened to the songs and watched the hard-working turnspit dog as he ran in his wheel, spinning the roasts and fowls before the great hearth.

After a time, the minstrels paused to wet their throats and pass the hat, and I contributed willingly, though kept an eye out for any cutpurses lurking in the shadows, as such folk were known to follow such entertainers about and take purses while the audience enjoyed the performance. The minstrels wandered out into the square to drink their barley wine before singing again, and I followed them, for the inn was hot and full of smoke, and the cold drafts of winter air, drawn into my lungs, refreshed me and made me realize that I was very hungry. The inn was more crowded than ever, and I thought it might be a long time before I would find a table, especially as there were large parties that would pay more than a single man.

There was only a little light left, and I thought it was time I made my way back to the waterfront. I could find something there to eat, or return to *Meteor* for a meal.

I approached the musicians, told them how much I enjoyed their performance, and I thought with pleasure of the young lady's rosy face I walked across the square in the direction of the river. I made my way down a dark lane when I heard a voice that sent a fear shooting up my spine like a rocket.

"It was a fine afternoon, sweetling, and perhaps I will seek thee tomorrow. But for tonight, I have business down by the river."

I know not what the woman said in reply, for I had frozen in my tracks, my right hand clawing under my overcoat for the dagger I had bought in Selford. Then I heard the sound of footsteps walking away from me, and with an effort of will I managed to free my own feet to follow.

Ahead, seen dimly in the light of the lanterns set above each door, I saw the tall figure dressed much as I had last seen him, in a long dark coat and tall hat. I knew I could not let him get away, not on a dark night where he could so easily disappear, and so I followed as silently as I could.

He reached the river and turned right, walking along the quay. He passed by a tavern where a piper and drummer played for young folk dancing, and I used the racket to cover the sounds of my approach. He heard me only at the last second, but by that time I had the dagger's point pressed against his throat from behind.

"So, Sir Basil," I said, "I find you a long way from the Toppings."

His left hand darted under his coat for his black dirk, fast as I remembered it, but I knew he would make that attempt, and I clamped his wrist hard in my strong left hand before he could draw the knife from its scabbard.

"Nay, Sir Basil," said I. "That old trick will not serve."

He straightened, my knife-point still at his throat, and stood motionless.

"I know not this Sir Basil," he said, in that rolling Northern voice I knew so well. "My name is Morland."

"Help!" I called. "Hue and cry! Help me!"

This halted the dance swiftly enough, and soon there were men surrounding us in a half circle, sailors and chandlers and longshoremen, some swaying drunk and others relatively sober.

"Bring the watch!" I cried. "Or fetch a magistrate. This man is a thief and a murderer!"

The half circle closed, and I saw from the grim looks on the faces of the men that I was not among outlaws, but men who hated robbers. The most ferocious-looking of them were the sailors, for sailors hate a thief on a ship, and often such a rogue disappears over the side on a dark night.

"It is a mistake!" called Sir Basil. "I am not the man!"

"I saw him kill two men with my own eyes," said I. "And one of them was a magistrate."

Someone ran for the watch, or for one of the military patrols that secured the district at night.

"Nay, unhand the man!" cried a voice behind me. "The man is innocent!"

I seized Sir Basil's wrist more firmly and spun him in the direction of the sound, and there I saw the old man who had been a part of Sir Basil's company, and who had captured me when I tried to gallop away from the ambush in the Toppings. He still wore the huge boots, but he had traded his flat cap for a steel morion, and he wore half-armor that glittered in the lamplight with gold inlay, I suppose part of that grand military array captured with Lord Stayne and his band. He brandished his spear at me, and his gray beard bristled with fury.

"Let go, you canker-blossom, or I'll slice your weasand!" he roared, and advanced with his weapon at the charge.

The crowd knew not what to make of this, for it now seemed as if one of the garrison was coming to Sir Basil's rescue. I could see the doubt growing on their faces.

"Bring the watch!" I cried. "Let not these men get away!"

The spear flashed at my face, and I ducked behind Sir Basil. I felt the outlaw's right hand clench the wrist of my knife-hand, and he twisted away from me. I realized that though my hand was still on his left wrist, his black dirk was free of the scabbard, and I hurled myself into him, to try to keep his knife-arm bent behind his back, and also to drive my own knife into his throat. In this last I failed.

Perhaps, after all, the black dirk had been crafted by dark Umbrus Equitus magicians who infused it with a lust for blood, or perhaps I was stronger than I imagined, but throwing my weight into Sir Basil drove his own knife not back into the scabbard but between his ribs, and put the point into his side. With a soft cry the outlaw fell to the cobbles, and I stood with my dagger in my hand, and tried to work out a way to defeat the armored spearman who had come lunging at me out of the darkness.

The old man stood there in his big boots, his eyes growing wide as he saw Sir Basil lying at his feet, and then he threw down his spear, fell to his knees, and began to weep.

CHAPTER TWENTY-TWO

The onlookers brought torches and lanterns, and Sir Basil lay pale in a half circle of light, his hand clutching at the knife that pierced his side. He gave me a dark, under-eyed look. "Goodman Quillifer," he said, "you have unhoused me."

"'Unhoused' is good," said I.

He grinned thinly. "It's a new word. I made it up." He coughed, and blood stained his teeth.

"Oh, my darling!" cried the old man. "My darling little boy!"

Sir Basil continued to direct his black, intent stare at me. "Who helped you to escape?"

"A lady," said I.

He laughed and spat blood. "Some whore helped you, and you abandoned her in the camp. For no woman was missing."

"I saw her last in Selford," I said. "She fares better than I."

"You left her. Do not deny it." He grinned again. "I know what it is to be a heartless young man."

"My poor, poor boy," wept the old man. "My beautiful boy."

Clanking soldiery approached, five men in half-armor under the command of a young officer, who frowned down at the strange scene revealed by the flickering light of torches: the man with his mortal wound, the old weeping man in his armor, I with my sword-hilted dagger in my hand. The officer touched his little mustache with his hand.

"Who is this, then?" he asked, his eyes on Sir Basil.

"That is Sir Basil of the Heugh," I told him. "An infamous outlaw. The other fellow is one of his band."

Sir Basil seemed amused by this description.

"And this is Goodman Quillifer," he said. "A young man and an orphan, heartless though no longer penniless."

The officer knew not what to make of this, and seemingly did not care. He looked down at the dirk still in the renegade's side, then bent to examine it. He gently removed Sir Basil's hand from the hilt, took a firm grip on the weapon, pulled it from the wound, and then seemed surprised and a little annoyed when blood gushed out.

Sir Basil's black eyes flashed. "Damn you, you block-headed malt-horse," he said. He snarled. "And damn all lawyers, and damn all gods." His head fell back and he died, his lips still twisted in a fierce, contemptuous smile.

The officer straightened, the dirk still in his hand. "Be wary of that knife," said I. "It's supposed to be ensorcelled, and bloodthirsty."

The officer looked at the knife and pursed his mouth in distaste. He handed it to one of his men. "Take care of this," he said. The soldier looked at the weapon uncertainly, then bent to wipe it clean on Sir Basil's coat before putting it in his belt.

The officer looked at me. "Is it your knife?"

"Nay, I have another. Sir Basil died on his own blade."

"I'll have your knife as well."

I handed him my dagger. The old man's spear was confiscated, as was the whinyard that hung at his waist.

And then he and I were marched off to the citadel, and each locked in a cell.

* * *

The citadel was under military governance, and the military being more scrupulous about cleanliness than bandits, there were no vermin in my cell. But the smells were still formidable, and I enjoyed confinement no more than I had in Sir Basil's dungeon, the more so because I had to listen to the old man weeping all night. By morning, I was impatient to secure my release. But the officer did not come on duty till ten o'clock, and then he did little but take my name. I told him to contact the owner of the *Meteor* galleon, who would vouch for me, but he said something noncommittal and had me returned to the cell.

At least the old man had ceased to wail.

By midafternoon, I was brought into the presence of a provost, and I was relieved to see that both Kevin and Captain Oakeshott were present. The provost, a lanky man with a habit of twirling his long hair with ink-stained fingers, made me undergo a formal interrogation.

"The other prisoner has confessed," he began, in a Bonillean drawl. "And he has identified the body as Sir Basil of the Heugh, which confirms your claim. This hearing is to determine whether or not you committed murder, or whether there were circumstances *extenuant*."

I thought that *extenuant* irregular, as more properly the word was the third-person plural present active indicative of *extenuo*, and not meant as the provost intended. But I chose to view the usage as an idiosyncrasy, and decided to overlook it. Instead, I got straight to the point.

"I tried to capture him, and he tried to stab me. My own weapon is unbloodied, as you may observe yourself."

The provost's pen scratched on his crown paper. "I have no way of knowing which weapon was yours," he observed.

"My friends should be able to testify to the matter," said I.

"Let us start from the beginning," said the provost.

The beginning proved to be my capture by the outlaw, my

witnessing of one murder committed personally by Sir Basil, and another at his order. I told briefly of my escape, avoiding the subject of Orlanda, and then explained my business aboard *Meteor*, and the event that led to Sir Basil's death.

The provost asked me to sign the statement, and then sighed. "I fear I must return you to your cell," he said. "While I will not recommend prosecution, I have not the authority to release you. That is in the hands of Sir Andrew, the Lord Governor, who reserves all such decisions to himself." He twirled a lock of his hair. "Indeed, justice in the Island is short these days, and Sir Andrew knows only two verdicts: death, and service in her majesty's army." He seemed amused. "You may hang, or you may trail the puissant pike. And lucky is the man who has the choice."

"As a privateer," said I, "I already serve her majesty."

"You may plausibly make that argument," said the provost, though his tone suggested that Sir Andrew was unlikely to view my reasoning with anything like favor.

Kevin joined me in my cell for a time, and had brought dinner and a bottle of wine in a basket. And so we made as merry as we could, Kevin on my bed and I on my upturned honey bucket, enjoying bread, butter, cheese, and little sweet sausages flavored with garlic, fennel, and honey, sausages I had last seen swinging from the overhead beams in Kevin's sleeping cabin.

My distress relieved by the wine and Kevin's kindness, I felt as easy as I could while locked and awaiting justice in a cold room of blackened brick. I was on my last cup of wine, and determined to savor it, and so I let it dwell on my tongue for a long moment, and then swallowed. When I looked up, I found Kevin looking at me with mingled curiosity and concern.

"I wonder," said he, "if all this is not the doing of—of the lady we dare not mention." For I had told him of my latest doings with Orlanda, and the threats she made at Kingsmere and Innismore.

"I have wondered that myself," said I. "And I know not which answer I would find more comforting—either she cares enough to put me in a cell, or she had nothing to do with it and I am here through my own misfortune."

"If misfortune," said Kevin, "that fortune may be reversed with a little effort and, perhaps, money. Whereas if you are pursued by divine vengeance, I know not what may be done."

"Find another god," said I, "who would act as my champion."

He raised a hand and made a gesture that encompassed the wide world beyond the red-brick walls. "Where should I find such a being?" he asked, half in jest.

"Don't bother asking a Philosopher Transterrene," I said. "I've already looked in that quarter." I looked into my cup of wine and swirled it in thought. "Though I do not relish the thought of two gods playing tug-of-war with my person. According to all the old stories, this sort of thing does not end well for mortals. Consider Agathe, loved by one god, and torn to bits by the hunting-dogs of another. Or Herodion, the mighty son of heaven's King, who was driven mad by the wife of that selfsame King, and drowned himself in a lake, thinking to fight his own reflection."

Kevin looked at me soberly. "I think too much musing on these subjects will do you no good."

"Nor will contemplating anything else," said I. "For consider the ancient tales, those epics and fables that have come down to us, of gods who love mortals, and who war with one another. Think of the Siege of Patara, where the gods chose sides and scarcely a mortal survived, even on the winning side. Or the War of the Champions, where the gods played with warriors as if they were chess-men, and the only victor was Nikandros the Lame, who did not fight."

"Nikandros had at least the best mind of them all," said Kevin, "and deserved to be King if anyone did. But brother, we know nothing really of that time, nothing beyond poet's fancy. If a poet chooses to say an idea, or an action, was inspired by a god, is that not merely to make human thought divine?"

"Or make human action worthless," said I. "For if we are as men in the stories, with divinities and demons whispering into our ears and prompting every action, does that not call into question our every deed? Can our lives have any meaning, if our very thoughts are not our own, and our actions prompted by others?"

Kevin's gaze was searching. "You have drunk too deep of this draught, my friend. Perhaps in your current situation it would be best to abandon philosophy for—say—the law."

"I will." And then I threw wide my hands. "And in the meantime, find me a god!"

Kevin rose and began gathering the remains of our meal. "One must hope that gods are susceptible to bribes, or at least that jailers are."

I embraced him in farewell, and then he knocked on the cell door, and passed money to the jailer on his way out. I threw myself on the bed, and abandoned myself to my metaphysical labors.

I spent another uneasy night in my cell before the thick oaken door opened, and the provost appeared to tell me that Sir Andrew had ordered my release. Very civilly he offered to share his breakfast, which consisted of raveled bread, cherry jam, salt pork, and a sweet, rather syrupy wine from southeast Loretto. "A miscellany, I'm afraid," he said. "But I wished to give you a more civil welcome to the Island than you have got till now. A deal of the food is being reserved for supporting the population during the siege, and this is the best my varlet could do."

"Give him my compliments," I said.

"I imagine your meals are a good deal less varied on shipboard."

This question gave me the opportunity of adopting the character of a much more seasoned a sailor than in fact I was. "We're not undergoing a long voyage," I said. "We're rarely out of fresh food."

"You may find that this will change," said the provost. "Now that we are blockaded."

That last word attracted my complete attention. "Blockaded? Clayborne's army has arrived?"

"Not yet," said the provost. "But one of his galleons has appeared off the coast, has already captured one of our supply ships, and will probably capture more."

"There are many ships in the harbor," I said. "Can a sally not be made?"

"It is a very large warship, greater than any of ours. I don't think our captains will want to risk a battle when we can wait safely till the navy arrives from Selford."

Indeed, the warships at Selford, which at the beginning of the war had been laid up in ordinary, were now ready to sail, and not unwilling to fight an enemy. But who would tell them to come to Longfirth, if they did not know the enemy were here?

"They will know when none of the supply ships returns," said the provost.

"But any ships coming to the city will be captured," said I. "Clayborne's forces will be enriched by supplies intended for the Queen's army."

The provost shrugged. "You are a privateer, sir. If you wish to engage the enemy, no man in Longfirth will prevent you."

I had no desire to take the little *Meteor* out to engage a great warship, but neither did I wish to be blockaded until Clayborne's army turned up and made it impossible to leave. "Thank you for breakfast," I said, and rose. "I hope to repay your kindness on some other occasion."

"I apologize for the short commons," said the provost. "And—beg pardon—I know not if you have a tender stomach, but if you have, and you want to retain your breakfast, you might not want to look up over the gateway as you leave. For that old man of Sir Basil's hangs there by the neck, and Sir Basil in a cage, as a warning to thieves and traitors."

"Who was that hoary old fellow?" I asked. "Did you find out?"

As the provost escorted me to the door, he explained that the old man was named Hazelton, and had been a servant in Sir Basil's family who had known him since he was a boy, and who out of love for him had followed him in all his adventures. Hazelton had been the only one of Sir Basil's company trusted to accompany him on *Star of the North*, the galleon bound for the Triple Kingdom, where Sir Basil had hoped to start a new life as a rich and law-abiding gentleman. But the ship had been damaged in the storm and sought shelter in Longfirth, and there Sir Basil had his fatal encounter with his own dirk, and never had the chance to enlarge his knowledge of legal systems by taking his new neighbors to court.

"What has become of Sir Basil's knife, by the way?" I asked. "Might I examine it?"

"It's been sent to the city armory," said the provost. "It will probably be issued to some soldier. But I have your own knife just here, in the gatehouse."

I was handed my knife, and I thanked the provost again and was on my way. I did not glance up to view Sir Basil and his servant, not because I would have been unsettled by the sight, but because my mind was already fully occupied by the matter of the outlaw, and his ransoms, and his escape. On my way to the waterfront, I met Kevin coming to see me, and we returned to the quay together.

"If he was planning on establishing himself abroad," said I, "Sir Basil must have been carrying a fortune with him. Have the authorities searched for it? Do you know?"

Kevin was amused. "You mean to plunder the outlaw? What does the law say on the matter?"

"Insofar as the money arrived on a damaged vessel," I said, "it might be viewed as flotsam, and thus the property of whoever finds it. However, if the money is to be viewed as a treasure trove, hidden *animus revocandi*, that is with intent to recover later, then half would belong to the finder, and half to the Crown. Though sometimes the courts have ruled that lost property *quod nullius est fit domini regis*, that which belongs to nobody belongs to the Queen."

"What of those whose ransoms made up the hoard?" Kevin asked. "Would they not have a claim?"

"In justice, perhaps, but not I think in law, for paying a ransom is itself illegal, as assisting the crime of kidnaping."

Kevin was surprised. "I broke the law when I paid my family's ransom?"

I waved a hand. "You are also in contravention of the law if you wrestle a bear, dye sheep or goats, or bury a sorcerer in a cemetery. I know of no one who has been prosecuted for such an offense, or for paying a ransom."

Kevin was puzzled. "Why would you dye a sheep?"

"To pass it off as some other kind of sheep, I suppose."

Kevin considered this, then shook his head. "We know not what claims may be made against this hoard if we find it."

"Yet"—I smiled—"there can be no disposition *unless* we find it."

"I think you may lead us into danger."

"Let us make inquiries. It will do no harm to ask questions."

"Asking questions," he sighed, "is exactly where so much mischief begins."

But he accompanied me to the gangboard of the *Star of the North*, and there asked the chief mate if the authorities had come for his passenger's belongings. They had, he said, but they found nothing, as the passenger had been unable to sleep with the constant noise of repairs, and had taken himself and his servant ashore. The passenger had called himself Morland, and was only revealed to be the outlaw Sir Basil by those who had come aboard to search his cabin.

Sir Basil had called himself Morland when he was trying to

convince me I'd captured the wrong man. I asked the mate if he knew where his passenger lodged, but he knew nothing. So, I began a search of the nearby inns, providing both a name and a description, not only for Sir Basil, or Morland, but Hazelton. I had no luck.

Then I remembered that Sir Basil had come down to the quay from the city's square, then turned right before I apprehended him. And there we had met Hazelton—which might have been pure coincidence, but also might mean that the two of them were lodging in that vicinity.

So, I retraced my steps, and found the inn before which Sir Basil had died. No one there knew him, so I went through the district, asking anyone who might have lodgers if they had a visitor.

Finally, I found a very deaf old lady who sat before her small alehouse, enjoying the sun and the traffic that bustled back and forth along the quay. The ground floor was home to a cordwainer's shop, but the two floors above seemed to be someone's residence. I bought a pot of ale.

"Good morning, mother," said I. "Have you any lodgers?" Then had to repeat myself twice before she understood me.

"I have four lodgers. Two soldiers from the garrison, my grandson, and another gentleman. And only this last pays me a rent."

"Is that Master Morland?"

"Ay," said she, "but I have not seen him today, nor his varlet neither."

"He has been invited to lodge with my master," said I, into the old lady's ear. "I am come to pay the charges, and to take his belongings."

The old lady was pleased to hear she was to be paid. "The governor's billeted two soldiers on me," she said, "and I am obliged to feed them, and not a penny comes with them. Surely not even the usurper would despoil me so."

I sympathized, and helped her rise from her chair. In a great roaring voice she called for a man named Alfred, who came out of the cordwainer's shop in his apron, the sun gleaming off his bald head.

Alfred was told to take Kevin and me upstairs to Master Morland's room, and help me pack, while she made out the bill. We went up the narrow stair to a garret, and were obliged again to explain why we were taking Morland's belongings.

"Who is your master, then?" Alfred asked, as he produced the keys.

"An old friend of Morland's," I said. "Sir Andrew de Berardinis."

Kevin gave me a look of horror at this, but the governor's was the only name I could think of at that instant. Besides, Sir Basil was in a manner of speaking the guest of the governor, even though the lodgings would not have been to his liking.

Alfred turned the keys and opened the low, narrow door. "You know my grandmother is billeting two soldiers without pay," he said. "She was depending on Morland's money to make ends meet."

"The Estates General is meeting in Selford," I said vaguely. "These money matters are their province."

Sir Basil's room was small and damp, with a fireplace that smelled of two-day-old cinders. It was probably the best place available in a city full of soldiers. The bed was narrow, and apparently Sir Basil shared it with Hazelton, for there was no room elsewhere—the place was filled to the rafters with trunks, bags, and crates. My heart leaped at the sight, and the thought of Sir Basil's treasure-trove, but I put on a face of distress and dismay.

"I wasn't told that Morland had so much gear." I turned to Kevin. "Go down and find us some fellows to help us carry this."

Kevin left, and Alfred and I started shifting boxes and bags into the hallway. There were a few loose articles of clothing, and some finely made items such as hair- and toothbrushes, and these I put in a bag. While Alfred was moving boxes into the hall, I searched the pillows, and looked under the mattress to see if anything had been hidden there, but I found nothing.

Kevin arrived with some sailors from the *Meteor*, and the outlaws' dunnage was carried down the stair. I left last of all, which allowed me to search the bed again, as well as the frame of the little hemi-spherical window, the hearth, the chamber pot, and the low rafters. Finding nothing, I went down to the ground floor, where the old land-lady presented me with her bill.

The sum was outrageous enough that I felt obliged to protest, even though it might well have been fair, given the scarcity of lodging in the city. I was eventually granted a small reduction, so I paid and insisted on having a receipt so that I could be reimbursed by Morland. After which we carried our booty to *Meteor*'s cabin and began our search.

There was, first of all, no treasure. I found a bag filled with fifty crowns, to pay for expenses on the voyage, and another bag with a few gold rings too wide for Sir Basil's narrow fingers—the general lack of gems and jewelry was understandable, since I'd already stolen every jewel I'd found in the outlaw treasury. The weightiest of the bags held beautifully crafted armor, all with the dimple-marks certifying the pieces were proof against gunshot. There were several broadswords, two with gold wire inlay, two pairs of heavy horse-pistols, and one small pocket pistol. I felt grateful that Sir Basil hadn't been carrying this last when I encountered him.

Many of the bags held only clothing, for the most part dazzling satins, silks, and velvets suitable for making a show at court, or for playing peacock among the highest in the country. Both these and the armor I assumed came from prisoners, most likely members of Stayne's party.

I also found Lord Utterback's slinkskin gloves, which I decided to return to him when I next saw him.

"Was Sir Basil tall?" Kevin asked. "Would the armor suit you?"

I laughed. "I have no plans to join the army!"

"You plan to go privateering, do you not? You would cut a great swashing figure on the quarterdeck."

"And attract the enemy's fire, no doubt."

"Which the armor would repel. Do you not see the proof marks?"

I scorned this simplistic notion. "Only a fool trusts a proof mark. I'll test the breastplate myself, with one of those pistols, ere I trust it in the war in which I have no desire to fight."

To please Kevin, I tried the armor on. Sir Basil and I were of a height, but I had broader shoulders, and the armor pinched above the arms.

"It can be adjusted," Kevin said.

"I do not see myself in armor."

"You should have your portrait painted. You look admirable, just like Lord Bellicosus in the play. Could you not utter at least a few of that worthy's lines?"

"I am not in a swaggering mood." I pulled the pintle from the gudgeon on my left side, separated the two halves of the cuirass, and let it drop to the deck. "We are allowing ourselves to be distracted. I cannot believe that Sir Basil intended to pawn his armor once he arrived in the Triple Kingdom, and live on what it brought him. He must have had a treasure with him, or something that represented that treasure."

So, we searched through everything again, very thoroughly, and eventually I found a piece of parchment stuffed into the toe of a battered old boot. It was sealed with an elaborate seal featuring whales, ships, and sea monsters, and I heated a knife over a candle and freed the seal from the document.

The parchment certified that fourteen thousand, eight hundred thirty royals were on deposit in the Oberlin Fraters Bank, in the account of one Charles Morland. I looked at the document, laughed, and gave it to Kevin.

"Do you have business with Oberlin Fraters?" I asked.

His eyes scanned the page. "I do not."

"So, you do not know how Master Morland would reclaim his money, once he arrived in Steggerda?"

"A seal and a signature," said Kevin, "and possibly a password."

The fourteen thousand royals would have supported Sir Basil in great style for the rest of his life, assuming that he didn't spend it all in quarrels and lawsuits.

"There is an Oberlin bank in Selford," said I. "We should make a deposit there, and see how it can be drawn from another branch."

Kevin carefully folded the parchment, and put it on the dinner table. "Do you seriously intend to defraud the bank of this money?"

"The bank has no more right to the money than Sir Basil."

"They may disagree. And though I am no expert, I believe the law supports them."

I shrugged. "Laws are not invariable. They are tools, not absolutes handed down from the Mount of the Gods."

"Tools may turn on their masters."

I took the document from the dinner table and put it in my doublet. "I know not what I will do with this. And should I do anything at all, I will be very careful."

Kevin looked in dismay at the riot of steel and fabric that covered his cabin. "Let us see about stowing away this rubbish," said he. "And then see about getting to sea."

I looked at him in surprise. "You haven't heard? We are blockaded."

I told him what the provost told me, that a large galleon of Clayborne's navy was taking prizes right off the mouth of the Brood.

Suddenly decisive, Kevin rose and reached for his boat cloak. "This useless hoard-hunting has distracted us from our proper duty," he said. "We must view this sea-monster."

In just a few minutes Captain Oakeshott had joined us, and we were in the sternsheets of *Meteor*'s longboat, with six oarsmen taking us down the river. It was a voyage of eight leagues to the river mouth, and though we caught the last of the ebb, the tide was making for the last part of the journey, and coming in frothing great waves up the channel. Fortunately, we were able to set a sail, and the oarsmen could rest unless they were needed to drive us through one of the oncoming waves. Still it was the middle of the afternoon before we arrived within sight of the galleon, a tall, dark shadow tacking back and forth on the glimmering western horizon.

Kevin and Oakeshott viewed the intruder with their long glasses, and murmured their conclusions to one another.

"She is a high-charged galleon," said Kevin. "But I can see only her upper works; I can't count the gunports."

Oakeshott curled his lip. "I can say with all confidence that there are more gunports than we possess, and the guns heavier. For that ship is no less than eight hundred tons, and we are but an hundred fifty."

We saw a group of gentlemen on the sandy strand, and came ashore to join them. Some were ship captains that Oakeshott knew, and others military men, among them the governor, Sir Andrew de Berardinis. He was a stout, sturdy gentleman with long white hair that flew like a flag in the fresh wind, and he was accompanied by other men who formed his military family.

I borrowed Oakeshott's glass and found the nautical stalker wearing round onto the larboard tack, the sun flashing off the high sterncastle with its diamond crosshatch pattern, lapis-blue alternating with ochre-yellow.

"Blue and yellow diamonds," I said. "And there is a device painted on the main topsail, but I can't make it out."

Kevin looked surprised, and put his glass to his eye. "That device is the blue sea-wolf," he said. "I know that ship. She was built for the Mercer Aubrey Jenkins down in Bretlynton Head, and made at least one voyage to the Candara Coast for spices before the navy bought her a couple years ago for four thousand royals. She's *Wolf Azure*, renamed *Royal Stilwell*, eight hundred fifty tons and at least forty guns, probably closer to fifty."

Oakeshott and I exchanged glances. *Royal Stilwell* so outclassed

Meteor that there was no hope of our fighting a successful engagement, nor was there any ship in harbor that could match her.

I turned to Kevin. "May we hope that *Stilwell* is a right hooker, and that we can outrun her?"

He looked dubious. "Close-hauled, may be. But she can carry such a spread of canvas that I wouldn't dare to fly before her on a wind."

And with the wind holding westerly, if *Meteor* left harbor close-hauled, we would be running toward the enemy, not away.

Oakeshott walked to the other captains to tell them the bad news, and I considered the consequences of our being blockaded in Longfirth. At best, our privateering expedition would be cut short, and there would be no income from *Sea-Holly* if she weren't carrying supplies and troops back and forth to Selford. In the worst case, we might be held here until Clayborne's army came, and lacking reinforcement the city fell, and we would be prisoners for having taken the Duke of Andrian's *Lady Tern*.

Suspicion stabbed at me, and I wondered if Orlanda was behind this somehow, and was even now prompting Clayborne to march.

But I banished such thoughts as unprofitable, and I could not in any case stop Orlanda from doing anything she cared to do.

I glanced over the flat country, the low dunes with their sparse grasses stooped in the wind, and the two lights behind. The city was well out of sight, beyond the misty horizon.

I looked at the lights again, and again out to sea where the *Royal Stilwell* patrolled, and then I returned to Kevin.

"I think I may have an idea," said I.

CHAPTER TWENTY-THREE

T he sun glowed gold on our sails, two days later, as *Meteor* and *Sea-Holly* dropped down the River Brood just before sunset. *Royal Stilwell* paced back and forth like a shadowy predator against the setting sun, a dark, ominous silhouette on a sea sparkling with diamonds. Two transports had been taken by the big galleon in the last two days, and carried by prize crews off to one of Clayborne's ports.

The anchor cables roared and rumbled as they plunged into the river, and the ships checked in their motion, then swung with the wind and tide. The wind had backed to the southwest, still blowing hard and providing a challenge for any vessels trying to leave the port. Yet we hoped to seem exactly those vessels, intent on making a dash for freedom right under *Stilwell*'s stern counter. We left our sails clewed up but not furled, ready to sheet home at a moment's notice, and hoped that the officers grouped on *Stilwell*'s poop would see what we wanted them to see.

Apparently they did, for *Royal Stilwell* moved closer to shore, ready to come down on us if they saw us running.

As the sun descended, the mist on the far horizon was turned briefly to gold, and then the winter's dark descended. Flames sprang up from the summits of the two wooden towers that served as lighthouses. The tide slapped against the sides of the ship. I supped in the cabin with Kevin, Oakeshott, and the pilot, Foster, a lank, long-shanked man who would guide us to the sea if all went well.

After supper, I put on my overcoat and went on deck with a long glass, and saw that the cabin lights of *Royal Stilwell* were just visible. At night, it was impossible to tell how close the lights were, but the ship seemed close in, two or three miles. I went below, into the warmth, and shared a bottle of wine with Kevin.

Shortly after midnight, the ship swung as the tide shifted, and I took a night glass aloft to the maintop. *Royal Stilwell* was easy to find, with some lights burning in its stern cabin, though it took some time to accustom myself to the inverted image displayed in the glass. I watched the enemy ship as it paced back and forth in the channel, like a sentry before a gate, and I studied it as it made its maneuvers, how the configuration of the masts and lights changed as it wore from one heading to the other.

"Stand by!" I called to the quarterdeck below, and I saw Kevin's face briefly illuminated as he lit a lantern. I returned my eye to the night glass.

In two or three minutes, I saw *Stilwell's* stern cabin lights disappear as she wore around, and gaps appear between the masts. "Make the signal!" I called, and Kevin ran to the larboard side of the ship and began to swing the lantern back and forth along the side of the ship, keeping it below the bulwark where the enemy would not see it.

Very quickly the flames in the lighthouses went out, and two more fires were lit, fifteen hundred yards to the north, over half a league away.

The two lighthouses were arranged so that they were in line with the safe channel that ran through the sand banks offshore. The inland light was taller than the other, so that if a ship were in the channel, they would see one light atop the other; and they might also judge how far they were out of the channel by the separation of the lights. Because the sandbanks shifted, and the safe channel with them, the towers had been lightly built of wood, so that they could be moved at need.

My plan had been to make false lights to lure *Royal Stilwell* into danger, and to this end I secured the cooperation of the Lord Governor, Sir Andrew de Berardinis, who had been inclined to douse the lights as soon as the enemy ship appeared, but who I persuaded to keep them lit. It had taken two days to measure the ground for the new lights, and to build them safely on carts—because building new towers on shore would be seen as suspicious—and then to work out with protractors and chains the sites on shore where the new lights would be placed.

I had waited until the tide began to ebb, because the time between the start of the ebb, and the moonrise at three in the morning, would have been the ideal time for *Meteor* to try to slip out to sea. I also wished the old lights doused, and the new ones lit, while *Royal Stilwell* was wearing ship, or going about, or some other maneuver, for I knew that every eye on the ship would be fixed on the sails, the tacks and braces, the sheets, the whipstaff, or the compass, and none paying any attention to the lights on shore, which were fixed, and which they had no reason to think would not remain fixed, and continue to provide unshakable confidence to mariners.

I watched as the new fires kindled, then returned to the night glass. My eye was still dazzled by looking into the light, and then it took a moment to locate *Royal Stilwell* again, but I found the great high-charged galleon in time to see the gaps between its masts narrow almost to nothing, and then the ship came on, sailing on a bearing that took her southeast, across the channel, with the wind right abeam.

In a few moments, I saw that *Royal Stilwell* wore early, as if her master thought she might have gone farther south than intended, and I saw the stern lights swing into view as she came on her new tack. The ship sailed on northwesterly, and then I saw some maneuvering that was difficult to follow in the dark, and then quite suddenly the ship was ablaze with light as lanterns and torches were kindled in the darkness. The lights ran back and forth over the ship, and some were lowered to the waterline.

"I think she's run aground!" I called, for in the darkness I still could not be certain, and a cheer came up from below.

The lights marked the *Stilwell* plainly, and as there was no longer any reason for me to remain aloft in the cold maintop, I came down the shrouds and joined my friends on deck, where I was warmed by a glass of hot whisky punch.

The ebb tide tugged at the ship. Moonrise did not make the situation any clearer, save that *Royal Stilwell* did not move, and that the lights continued moving up and down her sides. I thought she was probably aground, but there remained the possibility that she had anchored until daylight revealed a path out of the sandbanks. I went to my hammock for a brief rest, but I was far too excited to sleep, and rose before dawn.

Before sunrise, the anchor was hove short and *Meteor* cleared for action. The ship's boats were trailed astern so that an enemy shot would not turn them into deadly splinters. The crew stood by the guns, and a rank of royal soldiers, loaned us by the Lord Governor, stood on the quarterdeck with their hackbuts.

Cheers rose from the crew as the dawn revealed that *Royal Stilwell* had run clean aground, and that she had been completely stranded by the falling tide. The great galleon had toppled over to starboard, and her main topmast and bonaventure mizzen had gone over the side. Waves broke white over her larboard bow, and great sheets of spray seemed to cover nearly the entire ship. Her boats were sculling about in the water, but they were clearly unable to affect the situation.

Our seamen manned the capstan, and began their stamp about the deck. *Meteor* lurched as the anchor broke free of the river bottom, and close-hauled under the spritsail and lateen mizzen, with the spritsail yard cocked up almost to the vertical, we made slow headway against the incoming tide until we were clear of the river mouth. Then the helm was put up, and the crew manned the tacks and sheets and set the topsails. The yards were braced around hard, the sails filled with a noise like present thunder, one after the other; and then we were on our way, close-hauled on the larboard tack, the bone of foam growing white beneath the bow as we gained way.

The pilot, Foster, went up to the foretop to better see the sandbanks, which at this point was scarcely necessary, for the tide had so fallen that the reefs were all visible as vague brown forms beneath the water, with the sea frothing white over them. We steered confidently for blue water, and in ten minutes *Meteor* would range up under *Royal Stilwell*'s stern.

"Load the guns!" Oakeshott cried. "Grape on top of roundshot!"

Meteor's guns were a miscellaneous collection of weapons, almost a history of artillery, from the old iron breechloaders on the forecastle, welded iron bars hooped together like barrels, to modern demiculverins, three on each side, that took pride of place in the middle of the lower gundeck. *Meteor* carried thirty-two guns in all, but half of these were small pieces, minions, falcons, and falconets, that were known commonly as murderers or mankillers. The minions, which shot a four-pound ball, were old fieldpieces mounted on carriages with large wheels; but the smaller of these weapons were mounted on swivels and were fixed above the bulwark.

The old iron forecastle guns sat on wooden blocks that rested on the deck and would dig a trench in the planks when fired, others were field guns lashed to the ports, and some had proper naval gun carriages with four small wheels. The immobile guns had to be loaded by men hanging outboard, and this took time; so it was important that the first broadside be effective, because with the great miscellany of weapons, and ammunition and powder charges of different sizes, any subsequent shots would of necessity be more ragged.

"Run out the guns!" Oakeshott cried, and the gunports creaked open. Those guns with proper carriages were hauled up the slanting deck, and the rest made ready as well as they could. Quoins were driven beneath the breeches to bring the barrels level with the sea, and then the decks fell silent, and for a long moment we heard only the sound of the sea swirling along the ship's side, the keen of wind in the rigging, and the slap of waves on the bow.

I went to the weather side of the quarterdeck and peered out at *Royal Stilwell*. She had rolled so far onto her starboard side that her larboard battery pointed only at the sky, and the starboard guns stared point-blank at the water. Nevertheless, the crew had tried to make ready for us—the boats were bobbing unmanned alongside, the sailors having been recalled; and I could see handgunners crowding the taffrail, to welcome us with a volley of small shot.

Oakeshott put up the helm a trifle, to draw us right across the enemy's stern, and backed the fore topsail so that its canvas thundered in the wind, great cracking booms that provided a foretaste of the gunfire to come.

At the sound, I felt my own spirits give a leap, and suddenly my heart crashed louder than the canvas. I stood stock-still at the bulwark and watched the enemy ship come closer, the sun glittering on the helmets and hackbuts of the men who waited to receive us, and suddenly there seemed not enough air in all the world to fill my lungs, and the seascape seemed to whirl in my head.

There was a bang from the enemy quarter, and I gave a convulsive shudder at the sound. The lead ball buzzed like a bee over my head, and then I heard the voice of an enemy officer as he admonished the overeager marksman.

"Take your places!" This came from our soldiers' captain, and the two ranks of handgunners came to the bulwark, crowding about me in their breastplates and helmets. The brimstone odor of slow-matches spiced the sea air. I felt a hand clap my shoulder and draw me out of the press, and I turned to see Kevin.

"Be not so eager!" he said. "Let the soldiers have their turn!"

"Oh, ay, very well," I muttered, as if I grudged the handgunners their chance at glory, as if apprehension hadn't seized me in its claws and half-paralyzed me where I stood.

"Fire as you bear!" called Oakeshott. The backed foretop slowed us perceptibly, so that we would cross the *Stilwell*'s stern at a slow walking pace, with plenty of time for each gun captain to take his aim.

Now there seemed an eternity between each throb of my heart, and over the shoulders of the soldiers I could see the enemy, the pale faces that stared down from the tall canted stern, and the royal arms, the quarterings of triton and griffin, that were carved above the great glittering expanse of the quarter galleries and stern windows. One of the windows was open, and a great hawser passed out of it, leading to a kedge anchor that one of the ship's boats had dropped astern—but with the water so low, they would have to wait hours yet for a chance to kedge the ship off.

"Present your pieces!" called an officer, and for a moment I did not know whether the voice came from our ship or that of the enemy, but then I heard a rustle and clatter from *Royal Stilwell* as their soldiers' hackbuts were leveled to sweep our decks, and my heart gave a lurch as I knew that we were about to be fired upon.

Then the first of our old iron breechloaders went off in the forecastle, and I heard a crash as the ball lodged home in the enemy ship. Firing right into their stern in this fashion, our iron shot could travel the length of the enemy vessel, rending crew and wreaking havoc as they flew.

The guns went off one after the other. At this range they could not miss, and through gushing clouds of white gunsmoke I could see splinters of wood and showers of glass flying from the enemy stern. There was a rattle of enemy hackbuts in reply, and once again I was paralyzed where I stood, not unwilling to act but unable, in the din and flying shot, to think what I might do. The *Stilwell*'s response was drowned out by our own cannon fire. The first rank of our soldiers replied, then fell back to let the second rank take their shots. The wind blew drifts of cloud into my face.

Then we were past, and there was silence again for perhaps two seconds before the officers and gun captains began shouting at the crews to reload. The fore topsail filled with wind again, and *Meteor* increased speed, the water foaming under the counter. The soldiers fell back from the bulwark and began plying their powder flasks and ramrods, and men with sponges hung outboard to swab out the guns that were lashed to the ports.

I was jostled again by the soldiers, and found myself on the lee poop by the taffrail, and so I watched *Royal Stilwell* as the gunsmoke streamed away downwind, and the ship was revealed. The quarter galleries were smashed, no glass remained in the stern windows, and the royal arms had suffered badly. But flags still flew from the foretop and the stump of the main, and as the deck was tilted toward me by the ship's list, I could see the enemy soldiers busy reloading while the officers dashed about to survey the damage. I saw also limp bodies, for our murderers had wreaked fine execution with grapeshot.

We ourselves seemed to have suffered no loss, at least on the quarterdeck where I stood.

I watched the enemy fall away for at least a quarter league, and then I heard Oakeshott's powerful voice, amplified to a vast echo by his leather speaking trumpet.

"Ready about! Stations for stays!" And then, to the timoneer, "Full and bye!"

We fell off the wind about half a point and our speed increased. I tried to work out where the sail-handlers would have to run, and then to station myself so as to keep out of their way. I found myself standing next to Kevin.

"We're tacking?" I asked. "Is it not safer to wear the ship, when we have been in action and there is danger the rigging may have been damaged?"

"They fired no weapon that could damage the rigging," said Kevin. "Ay, there is a chance that we will be caught in stays, but Oakeshott is a thorough captain, and the crew is well drilled. Remember that I have been on this ship longer than you, and know well its temper."

I looked to leeward and saw plenty of blue water, and realized we were in little danger.

"Ease her down!" Oakeshott called to the helm. The timoneers drew on the whipstaff and *Meteor* began to turn into the wind. The lateen over my head was braced up to windward, to push the stern around, and I heard canvas flapping forward as the spritsail sheets were let go.

"Helm's a-lee!" called one of the timoneers, and Oakeshott immediately echoed the words through his speaking trumpet.

The topsails rattled as they began to lift, then thundered as they spilled wind. Suddenly, where I stood at the taffrail, there was no wind at all, and the lateen over my head flapped a few times and fell limp. Oakeshott stood at the break in the poop, watching the sails with a critical eye. Then he threw one arm in the air as if calling the heavens to his aid, and his voice boomed over the silent ship.

"Haul taut! Main tops'l haul!"

Men came running aft with the main braces, then stopped short as the braces took the full weight of the big yards. The sailors' bare feet dug into the planks, and they threw themselves almost level with the deck as they dragged the yards around. Orders came fast.

"Right the helm! Shift over the spritsail sheets! Shift the mizzen sheets!"

Meteor turned neatly on its heel, and suddenly the main topsail lifted and filled. The lateen yard was run 'round the mast, and the sail filled with a sharp crack. The fore yards were braced around, and now we were on the starboard tack, the water hissing and gurgling beneath the counter. My heart lifted, and I wanted to cheer.

Kevin looked at me with a bright smile on his face, and I knew he felt the same joy and relief as I. "That was well done!" I told him.

"Oakeshott is brilliant at working up a crew," he said.

"I know that we are enacting my own scheme," I confessed, "but at this moment I'm feeling rather superfluous."

"So am I," said Kevin.

"But you are part owner of the vessel," said I. "Were you to give a command, they would be obliged to hear you, if not perhaps to obey. Whereas I am of no use in this business whatever, except perhaps to take a bullet that might otherwise strike a more useful man."

"Try to stay out of everyone's way," Kevin advised.

"There seems to be no safe corner on a ship of war," I said. "For a perilous moment, I regretted my decision to forego Sir Basil's armor."

"Armor yourself with hope," Kevin said, "for I think we're going to make a great prize this day."

Oakeshott's decision to tack meant we were coming right at *Royal Stilwell* without losing way—if we had worn ship instead, we'd have had to fight our way into the wind to get close to our target, and lost time. The next broadside was a repetition of the first, *Meteor* crossing below *Stilwell*'s stern at point-blank range, and a thorough hammering to which the enemy could only reply with small arms. This time, as the murderers on the poop deck were loaded, I saw that the powder came premeasured in bags, not ladled into the mouth of the gun as the Cannoneers had with Roundsilver's guns. It seemed a practical innovation, the more so because the dangers of using powder on a crowded deck, and with all the gun-captains and soldiers carrying lit slow-matches, seemed all too obvious.

As soon as the guns were loaded, Oakeshott tacked again, and then we repeated the exercise twice more, for a total of six broadsides delivered into *Stilwell's* increasingly battered stern. *Stilwell's* small arms fire grew increasingly feeble, but scored a few hits, and some wounded hands were sent below to the orlop, where the ship's barber and the carpenter, between them, would do their best for them.

For myself, I became somewhat used to being shot at, and missed.

The tide was coming in strongly, a stir of white foam flooding up *Stilwell's* sides, but there was not nearly enough water on the bar to tip the ship upright, let along refloat her. We had hours yet.

We came about for the sixth time, and as we gained way on the larboard tack, we heard from our pilot, Foster, who had gone into the foretop early in the voyage and not come down.

"I cannot see their boats!" he called. "I think they have manned their boats, and are hiding them on the starboard side, and mean to board us as we come by!"

Which seemed to me a desperate endeavor, though I suppose desperation was all the enemy had left. An inspection with our glasses showed that the boats, which had been bobbing about *Stilwell* like a pack of hounds about a huntsman, had indeed disappeared from sight. Oakeshott laughed and let *Meteor* fall slightly off the wind, and he passed word to the gun captains concerning what was afoot. So, we crossed *Stilwell's* stern over a cable's length away, and the boats were forced to charge across a gap of open water that our shot soon filled with leaping white feathers. Half the boats were destroyed, and we left the rest far astern.

While the crew busied themselves with reloading and getting ready to put the ship about, I had nothing to do, so I took a long glass from the wreck and studied the enemy. I watched as the surviving boats pulled as many of their comrades from the water as they could, then returned to *Royal Stilwell*. Crew climbed, or were carried, from the boats into the great galleon, and then the boats, with a few men still aboard, pulled away. I thought that perhaps they would try to board us again, but instead I saw masts rising on the boats, and sails blossoming.

"They're in flight!" I cried, and everyone rushed to the taffrail to watch the boats as they scudded away to the south. Even from a quarter league away we could hear the groans and angry shouts of the crewmen who had been abandoned on the galleon, and through the glass I could see fists raised in anger.

I presumed it was the officers who were running, those who had sworn allegiance to the usurper and would face a hangman's noose if caught. Sir Andrew knows only two sentences: death, and service in her majesty's army. So the provost had told me, and I supposed the ordinary sailors would most likely be transformed into pikemen within the week.

We could not pursue the boats, as they could cross the sandbars and we could not; and in any case, *Royal Stilwell* was our prize. *Meteor* came about, sailed to within twenty-five yards of *Stilwell*'s stern and hove to, motionless in the water, our guns bearing on the enemy. We could hear angry voices on the enemy ship, and see people moving about on the stern. But no firearms were presented at us, and whatever threats were being made, they were not made at us.

"*Stilwell*," called Oakeshott through his speaking trumpet. "*Stilwell*, do you strike your colors?"

For a moment, we heard nothing but angry voices raised in argument with one another, and then one voice overtopped the rest.

"Ay!" he called. "We surrender!" And a few moments later, *Stilwell*'s flags came down.

Kevin leaped to the poop rail, took off his hat, and waved it. "Three cheers for Captain Oakeshott!"

As the cheers rang out, I saw the soldiers of the garrison shoulder their weapons and prepare to march down to the main deck and the loading port, all in preparation to board the enemy ship, and alarm suddenly flew through all my senses. And then I went to the poop rail and took Kevin by the shoulder, and drew him to where the captain stood accepting the congratulations of his officers.

"Gentlemen," said I, "I think you do not want to put any royal soldiers on that enemy vessel."

Kevin and Oakeshott looked at me in surprise. "Why not, sir?" asked the captain.

"Remember that *Stilwell* was a royal ship before the rebellion," I said. "If royal soldiers go aboard, they may retake the vessel for the Queen, and we may say adieu to our prize."

"But the ship was in enemy hands," Oakeshott said. "We have taken her as a fair prize of war."

"The status of prizes is decided by the rulings of a prize court," said I. "And courts are composed of judges—judges appointed by royal authority, and inclined (if they value their livelihood) to do as the Queen wills. If they rule the vessel was the Queen's all along, there is nothing we can do."

Kevin nodded. "We'll put only privateersmen aboard," he said.

Oakeshott looked at me for a long, thoughtful moment, and then he rushed to the entry port and began assigning our own men to the prize crew. The soldiers he sent back to the poop, to keep the enemy vessel under their guns.

In the meantime, railing voices continued to be heard from the great galleon, along with snatches of song and intimations of swift violence. When they were deserted by their captain and officers, *Stilwell*'s crew had broken into the ship's spirit store, and now they were all ranting drunk. When the prize crew arrived, they found the ship in such disorder that they had to batten the crew into the forecastle. Lest the prize crew succumb to the same temptation, our officer ordered every cask aboard to be started, and every bottle broken.

The prize crew, in their forced sobriety, found *Royal Stilwell* sound enough. She had run softly aground on the sand, and her bottom was but little damaged. Some guns and other gear had broken free when the ship fell onto her side, but these had already been secured by *Stilwell*'s own crew some time during the night.

Meteor anchored in deep water nearby, the guns were secured, and the fires were lit to prepare dinner. The tide continued to come in with great speed, and after two hours, we made an attempt to right *Royal Stilwell*, by shifting the kedge anchor out to larboard of her, and hauling on it with the ship's capstan. At first, the ship moved not at all, but as the tide came racing in, the ship's timbers gave out a series of groans, the capstan pawls clacked, at first with agonizing slowness, and then with speed as the ship began to come upright.

Stilwell did not completely right itself while it remained on the sand, but it was level enough that the prize crew could begin lightening her, first by starting all the water casks so the water ran into the hold, where it could be pumped out. While this was being done, some of the heavier guns were taken out, dropped into boats by slings, and then carried to *Meteor*, where they were hoisted aboard.

As the tide reached its height, boiling along *Stilwell*'s sides, the kedge anchor was moved aft again, and *Sea-Holly* came out to help us. Hawsers were passed between the ships, and *Stilwell*'s capstan manned again. Between the kedge anchor and the two ships hauling, *Stilwell* came off the sand—"Easy as mittens," as Captain Oakeshott put it. Afloat, the ship retained only a slight starboard list, a result of the items shifting in the hold.

The prize crew got some sail aloft, and under the guidance of Pilot Foster we came to the mouth of the Brood, and up the river to Longfirth. There we were met by the entire city thronging the wharves, flags waving from every ship in the harbor, a military band playing, and a salute of cannon-fire from the citadel.

Kevin, Oakeshott, and I had in the meantime taken counsel, and managed a plan to retain possession of our prize. We would first appeal to Sir Andrew de Berardinis, in hopes that he would use his powers martial to appoint himself, or a friend, judge of a prize court—and if the Lord Governor declined, I would take *Sea-Holly* to Selford and there recruit Lord Roundsilver and any other friends I could, to support me when I brought the matter before the prize court established to rule on *Lady Tern*.

But first there was the celebration, while the town reveled on the quay, the band played, and the prisoners were let out of *Stilwell's* forecastle and marched to prison. After which the officers of *Meteor* were treated to a torchlight procession to the citadel, where the Lord Governor treated us to a carousal in our honor, with food and wine and music, all to celebrate our courage and enterprise.

CHAPTER TWENTY-FOUR

Y ou are still awake, I see. Perhaps the tale of the sea-battle was too rousing to permit slumber. I shall proceed in a quieter key.

Four days later I was at sea again, on *Sea-Holly* carrying the last two hundred of the Trained Bands back to Selford. Sir Andrew had proved himself a great host, but was reluctant to establish a prize court in Longfirth, and so I set sail again, to play politician in the capital, while Kevin remained behind to see to *Stilwell's* repairs, and Captain Oakeshott took *Meteor* a-privateering.

The voyage to Longfirth had taken but two days, but the return would take four or five, for we set out in the teeth of the wind, which meant we could not run down to the line of Selford's longitude, but were obliged to take a zigzag course, close-hauled at first upon the larboard tack, then upon the starboard. Close-hauled, and with a high sea and a stiff breeze, *Sea-Holly's* sterncastle was subject to a corkscrew motion, first swooping up as a wave passed beneath it, then descending in a serious of sharp, angry judders that left loose objects bouncing on their shelves, and stomachs bouncing likewise. For the first time in my life I was lightly touched with seasickness, though by evening I was well enough to eat supper. Not so our cargo of soldiers, who were so ill that the main deck was filled with their vile reek, and many rolled uncaring in their own spew.

Accordingly, I took the air on deck after supper, and securely wrapped in my old cheviot overcoat and my boat cloak over it, with the brim of my old apprentice cap pulled down about my ears, I enjoyed the bracing chill wind that had crossed the entire ocean to fill our sails, the spray that came in a fine briny mist from the bows, and the stars that seemed to whirl overhead in a drunken saraband as the ship pitched and rolled beneath my feet. I was alone on the poop deck, for the watch was forward, and the ship was directed by officers and helmsmen sheltering under the break of the poop.

"Wouldn't it have been too easy," Orlanda said, "for Sir Andrew to have agreed to your proposal, and simply given you the ship?"

Possibly I disappointed her by not shrieking and leaping like a startled hind. I had drunk enough at dinner to face the nymph with something like an equable disposition, and so I blinked spray from my eyes and turned to where she stood beneath the great triangular shadow of the lateen sail. Orlanda was wreathed in a cloak of deep forest green, with a hood over her flaming hair. Starlight glittered in her emerald eyes, and drops of spray stood like jewels on her shoulders.

"Was it not difficult enough," I asked, "to have captured the ship in the first place, a vessel five times the size of our own?"

"Was that difficult?" she asked. "It seemed simple enough to bombard a helpless wreck until it surrendered. And your own part did not seem particularly courageous, or expert."

"I make no claim to extraordinary bravery, or any expertise in war."

Her lips turned up in a wry smile. "How fortunate for you, since you failed to so much as cut a bandit's throat when you had him by stealth from behind."

"Yet he died."

She reached out a gloved hand and touched me on the breast, right over Sir Basil's parchment from Oberlin Fraters Bank. "And you plundered him. Maybe you are naught but a bandit yourself, and deserve the same fate."

My blood ran cold at her touch, for now I knew that document might doom me, if Orlanda inspired anyone to question it. I decided to stay away from that ominous subject.

"Am I to understand," said I, "that you convinced Sir Andrew to refuse to empanel a prize court?"

"Why, yes," she said, her face all wide-eyed innocence. "And I may inspire others to thwart you, once you reach Selford. For the virtuous and tedious Queen has lost all her friends, thanks to you, but still must depend on others for advice, and a whisper in her ear is as good as a shout from the heavens."

"If you wished to harm me," I said, "you needn't have bothered with the Lord Governor, but merely inspired a lead ball to pierce my breast during the fight with *Royal Stilwell*. Or to strike an arm or leg, and leave me a cripple."

Scorn mounted her face. "Oh. *War.*" She put all her venom into the word. "If you wish to be a warrior, Quillifer, you will find that war is its own punishment, and needs no help from me. There are missiles enough in battle for one to have your name on it, and I need not carve it there."

Strangely perhaps, I found this cause at least for a little optimism, knowing that any death in battle would be the result of chance and not divine malevolence. Yet death in combat was still death, and I desired not to make its acquaintance either way.

"So, our contest will continue in the courts, then," I said.

"The courts, the palaces, the bedrooms," she said. "You do not discriminate, and neither shall I."

"You know," said I, "I am beginning to feel honored, that you pay such attention to me."

"See if you feel honored," said she, "when I am done."

And then she vanished into the night and spray, and left me alone on the deck, to ponder my fate.

As soon as I returned to the capital, I wrote to the duke and begged the favor of an audience. He returned that I should come to dinner the following day, and when I arrived, I found it a magnificent occasion, with the barrel-vaulted hall filled with many of the great men and ladies of the realm, all sitting at the table like an unimaginative imitation of the fresco over their heads, with all the gods and goddesses roistering with their wine-cups.

The duke's two cannons had been memorialized in sugar-paste, with all the ornaments, scrollwork, dolphins, and spells faithfully reproduced. Each gun was six feet long and covered in real gold leaf, and was displayed as a centerpiece, along with edible cannonballs, rammers, tompions, and other items of the cannoneer's art.

The two glittering figures of the duke and duchess presided from the head of the table, but as I was at the other end, in the company of secretaries and lawyers and poor relations, I could see them only by craning my neck around the sugar-paste battery, and then only when they stood to offer a toast or make a speech.

The dinner was intended to honor the Knight Marshal, Sir Erskine Latter, who had just been made the Queen's Captain General and placed in full command of her majesty's array for war. The little I could see of him did not raise my confidence in early victory, for the great veteran was elderly, with gray hair cut level with his earlobes, and he stooped as he shuffled along, between a pair of attendants who, I decided, had the duty of picking him up if he fell. He was swathed to the chin in a coat of sable fur, as if even this room, with its blazing hearths and scores of diners, was too cold for him. When he spoke in response to the praise of the other diners, I could not hear him, and I was thankful that I did not serve in his army.

I lost track of the number of dishes, with their fanciful stuffed chimeras, breads and pie-crusts in the shape of bastions and towers, marrow-bones mounted to look like cannon and stuffed with spiced mincemeat, jellies in the form of the Knight Marshal's blazon, powder-horns filled with sugared fruit, and desserts in the shape of laurel crowns. I had a bite or two of each remove, drank more fully of the wines that were paired with each dish, and asked those about me for the news.

The Estates General had concluded their business, I was told, and having done their duty, had dispersed. Now the Queen was filling vacant offices with great efficiency, having spent the last weeks judging, as well as she could, the character, talents, and loyalty of the hopeful applicants.

Those who intended to replace the Chancellor were disappointed, for he had been retained in his office and made Baron Hulme, which further outraged those among the nobility who had disparaged him for being a commoner. He would now have to guide the finances of the nation from the House of Peers, which would make it more difficult, as the power over the budget largely rested with the Burgesses. He would need a deputy in that House, and there was much speculation concerning who that worthy gentleman would be.

As I mentioned that I had been away in Longfirth, I was asked about the news there, and I considered letting my neighbors know about the capture of *Royal Stilwell*. But I decided to keep that information a secret until I had conferred with his grace the duke, and instead said that Sir Basil of the Heugh had been found there, and killed.

"Was he hanged?" asked one of the lawyers.

"I killed him myself," said I, "for I had been his captive, and recognized him on the street in Longfirth." I was then obliged to tell the whole story. This news rapidly spread the length of the table, and came to the ears of the duke, who rose and called for attention.

"I have been told," he said, "that the outlaw Sir Basil of the Heugh has been captured and executed. This report is of interest to many of us, as Sir Basil has been a plague on the realm, and has held for ransom a number of our friends. Can the bearer of these tidings kindly confirm this news?"

I rose, which caused a stir among the company, as I was known to many of them, and not all of them were my friends, while others knew me only as someone out of favor with her majesty. I waited for the murmur to die down, and then spoke.

"Your report errs in only one detail, your grace, that the outlaw was executed. Sir Basil is dead, but he was killed before he could be brought to a judge."

"Do you know the circumstance?"

"I do, your grace." I then related the story again, as modestly as I could, emphasizing the chance nature of the encounter, and the supposed sanguine history of the dirk.

There was a greater stir among the company when I finished, and then I heard a merry laugh from engineer Ransome, who as the creator of the duke's two great guns was seated far up the table.

"Quillifer it was who also brought to justice the assassin Burgoyne," said he. "Perhaps he will soon bring a like fate to all the rogues and renegadoes of the kingdom."

"I intend to leave a few for the Queen's Captain General," I said.

The Captain General nodded his gray head, and said something which I did not hear. Her grace the duchess kindly offered a translation.

"The lord Knight Marshal says that such a doughty and valiant fighter as yourself would surely distinguish himself and win renown in the army."

I smiled. "I thank the Knight Marshal for his flattering words, but I already serve the Queen as a privateer, aboard the ship *Meteor*."

Which caused more of a stir, because though *Meteor*'s capture of the *Lady Tern* was known, my connection with the former was not.

The duke smiled, raised his glass, and said, "It seems you serve her majesty thoroughly, in many spheres. To your very good health."

I thanked his grace and the others for their courtesy, and pledged them in return. After the feast ended and the diners, stuffed with glories both martial and culinary, began to totter upright, I made my way through the throng in the direction of the Roundsilvers. I viewed the Knight Marshal as the old warrior departed the feast, upheld by his two gentlemen as he shuffled along, and saw the sable coat part to reveal the broad ornate belt wrapping his narrow midsection. From this belt dangled a number of jeweled charms, and I saw also a religious medallion worn about his neck, containing a parchment with a quotation from the Pilgrim. The Captain General, I saw, was not leaving his campaign to chance, but invoking every form of spiritual aid known to man.

Were he not just proclaimed the greatest soldier in the realm, I might have considered him a superstitious, senescent fool.

As I watched the great captain depart, a hand touched my arm, and a familiar voice spoke in my ear.

"Thank you for killing Sir Basil. Did you by any chance retrieve aught of my ransom?"

I turned to find Lord Utterback offering his sardonic smile. He was dressed to take his place in this shining company, and wore the magnificent blue-and-yellow suit. Gems flashed from his collar, and from every finger.

"Sir Basil carried very little money," said I, after I had recovered from my surprise. "He either hid your ransom, or sent it ahead to Steggerda, where he was bound."

"Even dead," said Utterback, "he remains an inconvenience."

"But I rescued your slinkskin gloves, which I found in his luggage. If you call on me, I will restore them to you."

He laughed. "Thank you! For sake of the gloves, I forgive your fault in not finding the ransom."

"How does your lordship?" I asked. "Excellent well, from all I perceive."

"Well enough." He smiled. "Though my deeds have scarce equaled yours," said he. "Capture of *Lady Tern*, sticking an outlaw like you stuck that stag at Kingsmere, capture of an assassin."

"Yet strangely, the events at Kingsmere did not win me glory," I said.

"What did you expect?" He shrugged. "I would not have stuck my finger in that hell's pottage of conspiracy, and my position is far more secure than yours." He gave me a searching look. "Indeed, I expected that you would be downhearted, and instead I find you leaping from triumph to triumph."

"Hardly that," said I. "In sober fact, you might find that my life has been cursed in quite a singular manner. Let me say that, when next we have a few hours, I can contribute much to our old discussion of Freedom and Necessity."

"I will look forward to it. But I had hoped to cheer you by offering you a post, and instead you have already turned it down."

"Have I?" I was surprised. "I must be the most inconsiderate wight on earth."

"You declined the Knight Marshal's offer to join the army," said Utterback. "I am myself to be a soldier—my father has decided I am to command a troop of cavalry, which he will raise at his own expense."

"I am sure you will be a great captain," said I, though in truth I did not know what qualifications Utterback had for such a post, unless it were a rich, willful father.

"I had hoped you would join me," said his lordship. "The Utterback Troop stands in need of a secretary."

I laughed. "You'd hoped that I would be so downcast that I'd go off with you? A fine plan, were it not for the deadly war for which you are bound, and for the cavalry, which would bring into unnecessarily sharp relief my tentative relationship with the equine species."

"Ay," said he, "for knife fights with outlaws are so much more temperate and congenial than battles."

"That was as close to battle as I hope ever to be. Yet"—I took his arm and spoke into his ear—"I have more news from Longfirth, which I hoped to deliver privately to his grace before I spoke of it in public. Yet the news might concern you as well. Perhaps we should go board the duke if we can."

Lord Utterback and I made our way to the duke, who was saying farewell to a number of his guests. He saw us together and remembered, I guess, that I wished to speak with him, and he asked us to await him in his cabinet. So, Utterback and I took ourselves there, and amused ourselves by looking at the curiosities, the chalcedony statues, the enameled and gilded caskets, the ancient coins, and the carven cameos.

My lord told me of the Utterback Troop. He had raised men in Blacksykes, where his mother's family lived, and his father was Lord Lieutenant, but they were all hopeful youths with no experience, and he hoped to leaven his troop with veterans, who he proposed to find in the capital. "You will see my heralds beating drums, posting bills, and promising bounties," he said.

"What sort of bounties?" asked I.

"What do you care? You will not join me."

Lord Utterback had received martial training, as did all men of the nobility, but he had never commanded any detachment of soldiers greater than the few country lads he had led into Ethlebight after the reivers' attack. So, while Utterback would be coronel of the troop, a seasoned soldier named Snype would serve as his second-in-command, and would teach the men their drill.

This reassured me a little that Lord Utterback would not, at the first opportunity, ride straight into folly.

The duke presently joined us, and I unfolded to him and to Utterback the story of *Royal Stilwell*'s capture, and my fear that the

Crown would reclaim the ship without paying prize or head money.

"We shall go to the Chancellor tomorrow," he said. "I will send a message to him now."

He proved as good as his word. Early on a cold, wet morning in which rain clouds prowled the sky, we went to the home of the newly raised Lord Hulme. The Chancellor lived in a house very large and rambling, with thatched roofs that straggled, like unkempt hair, down to the windows—it was not grand or imposing, for the house was a place of business, not a palace. Men of affairs already bustled in and out, amid and through an amiable collection of dogs which romped about the courtyard. We met his lordship in his private study, a place as dark and disorderly as his office in the palace, and he offered each of us a tisane that filled the room with a strong herbal scent.

We informed the Chancellor of the capture of *Royal Stilwell*, and of our concerns. He listened gravely, and then leaned forward with a frown.

"My understanding of the privateering commissions is that they were intended to aid Ethlebight by allowing its seamen to make captures," he said. "How is establishing a prize court here in Selford, and awarding monies to sailors here and in Longfirth, intended to aid your city?"

"The owners and officers," said I, "and many of the men of the *Meteor*, are drawn from Ethlebight. Much of the money will come to our city because we live there—we will rebuild our homes, commission new vessels in the shipyards, and ransom our friends, who will return home and amplify the wealth of the town."

"In that case, why not apply to the prize court we have already established in Ethlebight?"

"We have two great prizes," said I. "Both *Lady Tern* and *Royal Stilwell* are too large to enter the port of Ethlebight. We would have to sail to Amberstone, then carry the ships' papers, et cetera, by land to Ethlebight for judgment by the court." I saw Lord Hulme raise a hand to begin an objection, and I spoke quickly to head him off. "Which is a mere inconvenience, I agree. But what is more to the point is that this will cause *delay*."

The Chancellor raised his eyebrows, and again I answered the question before it was asked. "Both *Tern* and *Stilwell* are great galleons suitable for war. We had intended to lease these warships to the Crown, for her majesty's use in securing the sea against any further incursion by Clayborne."

There were three classes of ships in the navy: royal ships owned by the Crown; ships owned by nobles and prominent men, who at their own expense, and from gallantry or hope of royal favor, allowed the Crown use of their ships in war; and the most numerous category, ships contracted to the Crown for the duration of the conflict. Most of these were small vessels intended to support the larger ships, and to carry supplies and troops, but it was not unknown for large warships to be made a part of the fleet in this way.

The Chancellor's eyebrows were still lifted, like the leaves of a drawbridge raised to allow a boat to pass beneath. "You propose to lease her majesty's own flagship back to her?" he said.

"A court has not yet ruled whose flagship it is," I pointed out. "According to *De Jure Praedae*, any ship taken by an enemy, and retaken before noon of the following day, is considered a recapture, and not a prize of war. But *Royal Stilwell* was held by the rebels for months, and therefore was not a recapture, and is therefore a fair prize of war."

"*De Jure Praedae* is a learnèd exposition," said the Chancellor. "A classic of legal literature and theory, but it is not the law."

"For myself," said Lord Utterback, "I like the title. *The Law of Booty* is fine, straightforward language, is it not?"

The Chancellor refused to be diverted, so I continued my exposition. "There is also the matter of precedent," I pointed out. "Soldiers and sailors both fight out of self-interest—soldiers for pay and plunder, and sailors in hope of prize money. Neither sailors nor officers will do their utmost if the Crown denies their reward."

"Yet," said Hulme dryly, "they all proclaim they fight out of purest love for her majesty."

The privateers have never made such a claim, I thought, *but I decided it is best not to say so.*

"There is also the matter of *Lady Tern,*" said I. "For if her majesty wishes to condemn that prize quickly—for reasons of state of course, as the ship belongs to one of her greatest enemies—then a prize court could be established here, and if it proceeds with despatch, the Crown will have its twenty percent soon. But if the Queen does not care to expedite that process, we will send the ship to Amberstone and have it condemned by the prize court in Ethlebight, and the Crown must wait for its money. And I will send to Master Spellman, who owns the *Meteor,* and have him send *Royal Stilwell* to Amberstone as well."

For there was little doubt that the Ethlebight prize court would happily condemn any ship brought before them, for the benefit of the city and its citizens.

"Well, well." Hulme placed his gloves hands together, his jeweled rings softly shining in the dull light coming through the narrow window, and leaned back in his chair. "Well, well."

We waited for a long moment, and then Hulme said, "Well," again. Then he looked at Roundsilver and Utterback in turn.

"I will speak to her majesty. You will support me?"

"I will do anything to bring help to Ethlebight," said Lord Utterback. Roundsilver nodded his agreement.

"Very well, then, let us go. You will allow me to sound her majesty first, to see if she is in any way inclined to receive your proposals?"

Again the two nodded. Hulme then turned to me. "Goodman, I think it best you not come to court with us. I regret extremely her majesty's prejudice, but on a matter this delicate, I think your name is best unspoken."

I said that I understood, though I found it disheartening at how my part would be underplayed. It seemed that I should be congratulated for the capture of *Royal Stilwell*, not spurned.

The three lords set off for the palace, while I slumped away toward my lodgings in a spattering rain. A short distance from the Chancellor's house, I passed by Allingham House, the Selford residence of the Marquess of Stayne. It was a fine place, of the brilliant white sandstone common in Selford, with niches for martial statues of Stayne's ancestors. I passed beneath their stern, threatening eyes and looked up at the high windows spangled with a fine jeweled scattering of raindrops that reflected the warm golden light within. I wondered if Amalie was there, and whether she was looking down at that moment. Suddenly, I seemed half mad with desire, and for a moment I dreamed of climbing the front of that building by fingers and toes and going from window to window in order to find her chamber. I stared up, rapt in this inner vision, but then the clouds opened and a hard, cold winter shower pelted down, and my fantasy dissolved like sugar-paste in the rain.

I drew my overcoat up over my ears and ran for home.

CHAPTER TWENTY-FIVE

he meeting with the Chancellor bore fruit. Whatever words Orlanda might have whispered into Queen Berlauda's ear, they were out-argued by three peers of the realm. The news of *Stilwell*'s capture was celebrated by a salute of cannon from the ramparts of the castle, bells rung in all the monasteries, and criers sent into the streets. I was heartened by this demonstration of Orlanda's fallibility, and grateful to find her less than completely omnipotent, and unable in every case to move people about like pieces on a chessboard.

On the other hand, I thought I recognized Orlanda's style in the next announcement that came from the palace, which was that Captain Oakeshott would be knighted for the action, and given land and a modest manor near Bretlynton Head. Bretlynton Head, of course, was still in the hands of the rebels, but perhaps Oakeshott was meant to fight all the harder in order to make good his new estate. I was not unhappy for Oakeshott's good fortune, but I was inclined to resent my own contribution being written out of the record.

Yet a prize court would be established in Selford, for the sole purpose of ruling on *Lady Tern* and *Royal Stilwell*. The legitimacy of other captures would still be decided in Ethlebight. I sent a message to Kevin that he should bring *Stilwell* to Selford when repairs were completed.

As for that letter of credit from Oberlin Fraters, I put it in my box at the Butchers' Guild, until I could decide what to do with it. Orlanda had threatened me directly concerning that letter, and I thought it was best to forget about it, at least for a while.

I hope you have not been too disturbed by the tale of my dalliance with a married woman. If so, you may take satisfaction in what follows, for I have come to the scene wherein I pay for my pleasures.

More news came in the form of a messenger I found at my door one morning, inviting me to the eighteenth birthday dinner of the Marchioness of Stayne. The letter was quite formal, and contained no personal message, so I responded in the like style, and wrote a polite note stating that I would attend.

I visited one of my hoards at the money-lender's, and found there a lovely pomander, gold in the form of ship, with white enameled sails, and the hull ornamented with garnet and silver wire cloisonné. A teardrop-shaped pearl hung from the ship's keel.

This I wrapped as a present, and as a private message to Amalie of my continued affection, I wore on my belt the twin of the girdle-belt I had given her, the black jet cabochons set in the same pattern as her pearls. On the afternoon appointed, I presented myself, with my invitation, at Allingham House. The place already thronged with guests, and I recognized many of them from my days at the court. Searching the faces, I recognized many aspirants to office, or the bench, or to the generalship of the army, and I knew also that most if not all had been disappointed.

I soon realized that I was attending a counter-court, a sort of political gathering in opposition to the Queen, and I wondered if they supported Clayborne, or Stayne, or had a leader at all. I wondered also if it were dangerous to be here, if government spies were present, ready to denounce the guests. But then, I thought, perhaps I should be at home here, as another that Berlauda had spurned.

I found Amalie in a drawing room, lying on a divan. She was by now only a few weeks from giving birth, and she seemed uncomfortable in her bigness, with her swollen feet on a cushion, and her two women to adjust her pillows and bring her sweet wine. A cheerful face had been painted on her strained, weary features. Yet I saw the pearl girdle-belt at her waist, and I felt a rush of great tenderness that she had worn this token for me, and perhaps missed me as ardently as I did her. I approached, took her hand, and thanked her for the invitation, and handed her my present.

"You are welcome, Master Quillifer," she said. "I hope that while you are here you will relate some of your adventures, perhaps especially that of Sir Basil of the Heugh, who held both you and my husband captive."

"I will obey, my lady."

Though I did not tell that story immediately, for a group of new arrivals came forward to wish Amalie a happy birthday, and I withdrew to engage in aimless conversation with a pair of elderly ladies who were some distant connections of Stayne, and who were overcome with joy at the imminence of Amalie's child. While I listened to this conversation, I felt my nape hairs prickle as I saw in the hall my old acquaintance Slope-Shoulder, the orgulous gentleman who I had dunked in the slop bucket in Sir Basil's dungeon. I doubted that he would make trouble for me at the party, not when it might offend Amalie and Stayne, but in case he was discourteous enough to make a fuss, I prepared some remarks that I trusted would silence him. For I knew that he would not want that story of the slop bucket known, especially in this company.

A few minutes later, Stayne came into the room to tell Amalie that dinner was about to be served. I recognized him from our brief meeting in Sir Basil's courtyard, tall and longshanked, with graying dark hair elegantly curled down past his shoulders, and a small, disapproving mouth amid his short beard. Amalie called me over to introduce me, and I bowed. He regarded me with his little mouth pursed.

"Pleased I am to meet thee," said he. "I understand that you slew that wolf's head Basil."

That "thee" marked me as an inferior being addressed by a superior, but otherwise Stayne seemed polite enough in his interest—and distant enough, for I did not desire his attention.

"I killed Sir Basil in Longfirth, my lord," I said. "He was fleeing to Steggerda along with one of his men."

"I shall be pleased to hear thy story," said Stayne. "But later, at dinner, for now we must go into the hall."

The gong was rung a few minutes later, and Stayne helped his lady to her feet, and took her into the great hall. Her ungainly walk was far from the languorous undulation that had once marked her passage, and I felt sadness touch my heart. I took into the hall an older woman, the widow of a knight, who once seated managed to keep up both sides of our conversation, scarcely pausing to eat any of the dainties laid before her.

For my part, I saw Slope-Shoulder and his friend Fork-Beard, who sat next to each other and saw me at the same moment. I saw the shock of recognition on their faces, and then at once they put their heads together, and I watched their conference with interest, wondering what feeble scheme they were hatching together.

Stayne kept the same sort of abundant table as his grace the duke, with one extravagant remove after another, though his cooks had not the same sense of whimsy as those of Roundsilver Palace. Nevertheless, there was a dish called "infant's toes," and a suet pudding called "boiled baby," which—though hardly at the epitome of taste—were probably intended to salute Amalie's pregnancy.

The dinner conversation consisted almost entirely of criticisms of the knaves who ran her majesty's government, for the guests did not dare to criticize the monarch directly, not in public. The Chancellor in particular was savaged as a thieving rogue who had wormed his way by guile into his position. The word "base" was used, and "barber-monger," and "cullion," all of which were reflections on Hulme's common birth. So persistently were these used as insults that I began to feel a considerable resentment against these well-born lubberworts and loiter-sacks.

During one of the pauses, when wine glasses were replaced and filled, I was called upon to relate the story of Sir Basil's death, which I did with a minimum of embellishment. "I failed to recover my ransom," I said at the end. "If Sir Basil was carrying a fortune with him, the governor and his soldiers must have taken it. If his hoard lies somewhere else, I know not where it is."

One of our host's friends then flattered him by saying that Sir Basil must have been fleeing Stayne's vengeance, and had probably buried the money somewhere in the Toppings before departing.

"In that case," said Stayne, "it will remain there forever, for the Toppings are such a tangle of hill and wood and dale that an army could vanish there without a trace. Indeed, I never even found the place where I had been held."

"I was lucky to have found a track leading out," I said.

Amalie gave her husband a brief consoling look, then turned to me. "We've heard of a battle at sea off Longfirth," she said. "Do you know aught of it?"

"I witnessed it," said I. "For I was in Longfirth at the time, with a ship of which I am part owner." I related the story of *Royal Stilwell's* capture, though before I got very far into my story, I recollected that I was speaking to an audience of people who were, or had been, Clayborne's supporters, and I much reduced my own part in the capture.

The party listened with some interest, then forgot my existence and returned to their business of abusing the government. For once, I was pleased enough to be forgot.

The last of three desserts arrived, and the last health was drunk. Amalie's two ladies helped her to her divan, and I thanked the voluble widow for the pleasure of her company and drifted after the marchioness. She was once again surrounded by well-wishers, so I was able to offer only a few polite compliments before her husband arrived, hovering over my shoulder.

"Master Quillifer," he said, "I quite forgot to thank thee for the return of my signet."

I donned my attentive-courtier face. "I did not wish that outlaw to abuse your ring," I said. "If he'd started using it to sign writs and loan documents, that would have been mischief indeed."

From Amalie's last visits to my rooms, I knew that Stayne's finances were in perfect disorder. He had borrowed heavily to outfit *Irresistible* and his expedition, and now owed his ransom to Amalie's father. *Irresistible* had been seized by the Crown and was being used as a warship for the duration of the rebellion, and although Stayne was being paid for the use of his ship, the payment came in the form of bills on the treasury, which would be paid only when the treasury pleased. He could not collect rents on his property in Bonille, where Clayborne ruled. Creditors had begun to hound him, and though being a great lord he could turn most of them away, he could not bar the door against his own father-in-law, to whom he owed four thousand royals.

"My friends were stripped also of their signets," Stayne continued. "Hast rings other than mine?"

"A number," said I. "But I know not to whom they belong."

"If my friends may call upon thee . . ."

"Certainly. They would be welcome." I very much enjoyed the thought of Fork-Beard and Slope-Shoulder arriving to beg their rings of me.

While I was enjoying this pleasing fantasy, Stayne looked down at my waist, and his eyes narrowed.

"I have seen that somewhere before," he said, and my blood ran chill as I realized he was referring to the pendant I wore on my belt, the black twin to the pearl-strewn girdle-belt his wife was wearing at that very moment.

"What, this?" said I lightly as I tossed the ornament in my fingers, "I hope it doesn't belong to one of your friends, since I took it from Sir Basil's strong-house. If you know the owner, I will return it."

He tilted his head, his prim little mouth pursed in thought. My nerves sparked to full alertness, and I was aware of Amalie stiffening as she realized what was at stake.

"I have seen it more recently, I think," said the marquess.

I shifted my position so that, Stayne following, he would have his back to Amalie and her girdle. My fingers still played with the pendant in hopes of disguising its true shape. "Perhaps another piece by the same jeweler? I know not who made this, but he may work here in Selford."

Stayne did not move, but his narrowed eyes followed me as I stepped around him. And then his eyes made a slow, thoughtful, deliberate track to Amalie on her couch, and fastened on the girdle-belt and its pearls, lying on his wife's brocaded gown.

"Ah," he said. "I thought I knew it."

"Your lordship has a good eye," I said, inwardly cursing that eye.

Stayne took a step closer to Amalie, viewing the girdle-belt thoughtfully. "I don't recall having seen that girdle, madam," he said. "Where did you acquire it?"

"It was a gift," Amalie said. I could hear the tension cloaked in her languid tones.

Stayne's voice was soft, barely to be heard over the buzz of the room. "It is a striking piece. Who gave it you?"

I could see that Amalie was struggling to answer the question, so I answered it myself.

"I presented it to her ladyship," I said. "I wished to thank her for having me to one of her afternoons here at your house, and having seen her at court, I knew her liking for pearls, and I thought this piece would complement well one of her ladyship's gowns. Truth to tell," I added, all offhand, "I have been somewhat free with Sir Basil's possessions, for that girdle-belt came also from the outlaw hoard, and from it I have made many presents to my friends. . . ."

Stayne's eyes moved from the girdle-belt to my own waist, to the gift's jetty twin. His voice was still soft, pitched so that only I could hear it. "You have given my wife a valuable gift, it seems." His eyes lifted to mine. "I must take care to repay the debt."

"Your lordship need not be so scrupulous," said I.

"I have always maintained that it behooves a man of high birth to be punctilious in matters of honor and dignity." Still spoken in that soft, toneless voice. His mild eyes held mine, reflecting perhaps a slight curiosity, with no obvious hint of malice. Yet I felt the malevolence flowing from him, felt the chill oppression and weight of his thought. He turned back to Amalie.

"I fear you are fatigued, madam," he said. "Perhaps we should bid our guests adieu, and go to bed."

I bade them both good-even, and made my way to the door. My imagination filled with fantasies of Stayne taking his revenge on Amalie, of oppression and brute violence, poisoning and private murder, and I could think of no way to protect her. I had no standing in the household, or in law; and even if I somehow broke into the house and rescued her, we could not fly far, for she was heavy with child, and would soon be in childbed. *Sea-Holly* was carrying supplies to Longfirth, and there was no easy way to escape by sea. My anxiety for Amalie had me clammy with sweat before I left the house.

Night had fallen as we feasted, and as I stepped through the door, I saw row of carriages lining the road before the house, their lamps glimmering. The walk was full of footmen waiting to guide the guests to their carriages, many of them accompanied by link-boys with torches, and as I looked out from the front steps, I saw the silhouettes of Fork-Beard and Slope-Shoulder outlined by torchlight, the two still huddled together, and probably plotting some mischief against me.

I walked quickly out of the gate, turned away from them, and then marched along with great strides of my long legs, dodging between the parting guests and the throngs of footmen. It was a few moments before the two conspirators saw me, and then they scurried after. I waited for them to get within five or six paces, and then I opened the door to one of the carriages and jumped inside. I crossed the empty carriage and left by the opposite door, stranding the two hapless cumberworlds on the other side. By the time they realized I was not in the carriage, and had ducked around the horses in pursuit, I had vanished into the dark, and was on the way to my rooms.

I spent a night sleepless with worry, and afterward walked armed, carrying my dagger, and with Sir Basil's pocket pistol hidden in my overcoat. Yet I did not often leave my rooms, for I remained in hope that Amalie might somehow get a message to me.

That message did not come.

CHAPTER TWENTY-SIX

The day before the Mummers' Festival, I was awakened by artillery fire from the castle, soon echoed by guns firing from the city ramparts. When I opened my window, I saw there had been snowfall in the night, and that the city was cloaked as if with stainless white samite. I could smell gunpowder, and I began to hear the ringing of bells and the bray of trumpets. I thought perhaps there had been another victory over the forces of Clayborne, and so I dressed, armed myself, and walked through the white streets to the nearest square, to wait for the crier.

The herald arrived on a horse splendid with royal livery, and was accompanied by a mounted trumpeter. The breath of the horses steamed in the morning air. After a lively sennet by the trumpeter, the crier stepped forward to announce the engagement of Queen Berlauda to Priscus, Prince of Raverro, Duke of Myrdana and Inner Trace, and heir to King Henrico of Loretto.

As part of the marriage contract, the crier announced, Priscus had agreed to lead an army over the passes in the spring, and attack Clayborne in the rear.

"He can keep his army!" shouted one of the onlookers. "Just send the ransom he owes us for his uncle!"

The herald ignored the voice and called for cheers, which were duly given though I detected no great enthusiasm for the match. The trumpeter blew another sennet, and he and the crier rode off to the next square to repeat the announcement.

"It is the surest way for her majesty to secure her throne," said the duke that afternoon. "I have urged marriage myself, as has everyone on the Council. Once her majesty produces an heir, she will be unassailable."

I had been invited to the Roundsilver Palace for an afternoon of poetry, Blackwell and a half dozen others reading their latest verses while their audience sipped sherry and sampled cheese and lacy, delicate cakes. Their graces were kind enough to invite me to gatherings involving music, songs, poetry, and the mechanical arts, perhaps because they viewed me as a superior species of mechanical, apt for killing a stag, planning a naval battle, butchering a goat, or singing a song. These events usually took place in a room they called the Odeon, which was arranged like a small theater, with an elevated stage, rows of seats for an audience, and sometimes a lectern.

At this moment, we were between poets, having risen from our stiff, creaking chairs to the comforts of the sideboard. The poets gathered in a corner and murmured among themselves, no doubt judging the audience much as we judged their verses.

"Must it be the heir to Loretto?" I asked.

"That was her majesty's preference," said the duke. "It must be said that Loretto's ambassador is a handsome young gentleman of great tact and charm, and his eloquence in detailing the advantages of the match was quite unparalleled." Leaving unsaid, I thought, the question of whether Berlauda would have preferred the ambassador to his master.

"So, now we are to have an army of Loretto march across our borders?" asked I. "Will this not unite all Duisland behind Clayborne, and against our traditional enemy?"

"The army will not fly the flag of Loretto," said the duke. "It will fly Berlauda's banner, and Priscus will fly his personal ensign, but not that of his nation, or his father. There will also be loyal Duislanders in the prince's entourage, to negotiate with Clayborne's officers and secure their surrender. For now even Clayborne's most loyal followers must admit they have no hope."

"Indeed, the odds lie heavy against them. I don't know why they aren't besieging Longfirth, and I assume it is because they cannot."

The duke smiled. "Clayborne's calling of the Estates did not go well. I have heard from my lord the Chancellor that Clayborne failed to force his will upon them."

His grace went on to explain that while Berlauda had got most of what he wanted from her Peers and Burgesses, Clayborne's subjects had been less tractable. A politician does not support a rebel unless he scents some advantage to be had in the rebellion, and for most people advantage lies in money. A fractious Mercer resentful of the taxes imposed by Berlauda's government would not join Clayborne only to vote higher taxes for himself, and Clayborne got only a part of what he'd asked for. Now Clayborne was raking out the bottom of his treasury, and since many of his soldiers were mercenaries who insisted on being paid, his rebellion was teetering on the edge of collapse.

"Perhaps Clayborne's cause will crumble without fighting."

"We can so hope," said the duchess. "But the Countess of Tern will not surrender without fighting, nor her husband the Duke of Andrian. The soldiers can, at the last extremity, loot the country for their pay. So, I fear there will be blows and terrors yet."

The duke observed a young man standing by the podium "Ah," said he. "Here is Master Robin, ready to bring us gladness."

We returned to our seats, and a poet struck a chord on a cittern and chanted, rather than sang, with a melody.

> *O cruel Love, on thee I lay*
> *My curse, which shall strike blind the day;*
> *Never may sleep with velvet hand*
> *Charm thine eyes with sacred wand;*
> *Thy jailors shall be hopes and fears;*
> *Thy prison-mates groans, sighs, and tears;*
> *Thy play to wear out weary times,*
> *Fantastic passions, vows, and rimes . . .*

I felt unease at this theme, and for a moment, I wondered if Orlanda had chosen this verse especially for me.

Yet, I thought, I was sleeping well enough, with few groans or sighs. It was my waking hours in which I waxed full of anxiety for Amalie.

Robin performed more verses, was followed by an elderly nun who wrote metaphysical verse, and then again the group met for refreshment. The duke's friends surrounded him, and he was fully taken up by a dissection of some intricate business at court, and so I took a glass of sherry from the cup-board and drifted 'cross the room to the sideboard, where her grace was chatting with several of her friends about a dinner given the previous day by Queen Natalie, the mother of the princess Floria.

"The Marchioness of Stayne attended," she said, "though great with child and her husband busy elsewhere. Queen Natalie was very kind, and made sure Lady Stayne was comfortable on her couch."

She said this last with a little under-eyed look at me, as if concerned that I knew that Amalie was well and free to move about the city. You remember that she had been present when I first met Amalie, and since that meeting she had been curious how our acquaintance had progressed. I had of course denied anything improper, but I fear I was not very convincing, for the duchess clearly suspected otherwise.

I wondered if the duchess had heard of my conversation with Stayne the other night, and what conclusion that news had led her to draw. But I was so grateful for this report, and the knowledge that Amalie was at liberty to visit her friends, that I spent the next few minutes inwardly rejoicing in this information, until the next poet took his place behind the lectern, and strove to wring our hearts with another ballad of the torments and miseries of lovers.

The Festival of Mummers lies on the first of February, halfway between midwinter and the spring equinox, and in ancient times the holiday marked the first day of spring. Though we now have a different calendar, the day is still kept, and begins with the Mummers' Parade, which marches down Chancellery Road past the castle, and from there winds into the town. I had bought a mask, that of a learnèd Doctor of Law with a long, enquiring nose to sniff out cases and fees, and in my gown and cap I joined the crowds near my lodgings as the linkboys, guisers, wren-boys, and mummers marched past, all masked, all in their brave finery, garbed as lords and knights, fish-wives and trolls and monsters. Floats were drawn past by caparisoned horses, and stopped every so often so that the mummers could enact a brief play, most of which were so full of references to local people, and local events, that I found them incomprehensible. But I cheered a play by Blackwell's troupe, which featured that famous monster-slaying Roundsilver ancestor extolling peace in the realm and killing a dragon, which was understood to be Clayborne. And there were other floats that featured comedy, with knockabout acrobats and dancers, and these I cheered with great appreciation.

One float was sponsored by the Butchers' Guild, and was apparently a satire on some recent scandal of the town. This I failed to understand, but I cheered out of loyalty.

The day was dark, but the mood of the crowd was not darkened, nor the performers silenced by occasional spatters of rain.

After the parade passed, I paused by the Tiltyard Moot, which allowed hawkers to sell their wares at tables set on the street before the building. I bought a pasty, a mug of beer flavored with rosemary and lupins, and marchpane molded in the shape of a wyvern. I tilted the mask atop my head in order to eat and drink, the lawyer's long nose thrust up into the air, as if hailing a client.

At sunset, there would be a supper at the Butchers' Guild, and afterward carousing, and songs, and merry-making till dawn. But it was barely noon, and there were hours yet before the supper began, and in the meantime the streets would be alive with celebration. If the meiny were ever to drink to Berlauda's forthcoming marriage to a foreigner, it would be on this day.

I returned the empty beer mug to the vendor and pulled my mask over my face. I had no sooner done so than I felt a blow between my shoulder blades, and was nearly knocked over the vendor's table. I straightened, only to feel a hand on my shoulder, and I was spun round to face a group of ferocious masks, an eagle, a serpent, a panther, and a boar with upturned tusks, each glaring at me with murderous, glittering eyes.

"This will teach you to play with the wives of your betters," cried the eagle. The delivery of this message took long enough that I recovered a little from my surprise, and I ducked the blow that followed, which nevertheless struck me a glancing blow on the ear. Though the fist missed its intended target, my head still rang like a bell. The eagle seized me by the nose—not the nose on my face, but the long nose of my mask—and pulled me into another blow, which I managed to parry. The others clustered around, their fists gathered to rain blows on me. Then I undid the ribbon that tied the mask on my head, and left the eagle louting back with an empty mask between his fingers.

The serpent-mask jostled closer, and I recognized the forked beard that hung below the mask and seized both tails to jerk his head down. Fork-Beard gave a cry as he stooped before me, and then I raised a knee and smashed it into his face. He recoiled upright, leaving me with handfuls of his beard, and I kicked him in the direction of his fellows and gained myself a little room to maneuver.

I turned and leaped onto the table of the beer-seller, and from the table to the butts of beer that were set on racks behind the vendor. From there I leaped for the architrave over a window, pulled myself up, and used as finger- and toe-holds a series of ornamental rosettes, an astragal, and a godroon to put me on the tiled roof of the Tiltyard Moot, two storeys above the street. From this place of vantage I turned to view my attackers, who were staring up at me—except for Fork-Beard, who was hunched over and clutching his broken nose as blood streamed from beneath his serpent mask.

The eagle gave a shout and waved on the panther and boar, and now they all leaped up onto the beer-seller's table and started a frantic climb toward me. I wrenched up a large terra-cotta tile from the roof and hurled it into the face of the boar, which sent him spilling down the front of the building and onto the beer-butts, from which he rebounded unconscious onto the road. The eagle fended off the next tile but gave up climbing and dropped to the ground, and the panther climbed down likewise. I pulled up another tile in case they came again, but instead they conferred, and then separated to run to the buildings on either side of the Moot, one of them dragging the wounded Fork-Beard with him. Both these buildings overlooked the roof on which I stood, and rather than let them surround me, I tossed my roof tile onto the building the panther was climbing, and then climbed it myself. The house was thatched, and once I'd shot my roof tile, I would have no more ammunition.

I recovered the tile and found the panther clambering up the half-timbers. He had taken off his mask, and I saw the face of a complete stranger glaring at me, a large man with a jutting underjaw and the scarred face and broken nose of a prizefighter. I had no desire to find myself within arm's reach of this hard-fisted professional, and so I marked my target and let fly. He warded the tile but slightly, and it struck him a glancing blow on the head and tore free a piece of his scalp. He paid no more attention to this than to a splinter in his thumb, and kept climbing toward me. Over my shoulder I saw the eagle mount to the roof of his own chosen building, and decided that I preferred not to be outnumbered.

Accordingly, I fled across the rooftops. The streets were narrow below Chancellery Road, and the buildings dropped steeply down the castle's hill, so it was easy to jump down from one to the next, coming ever closer to the river. I was looking for the Worshipfull Societie of Butchers, where I would be safe, but I missed my reckoning and was unable to find it. But hard on the horizon I saw the fortress-like battlements and emplaced artillery of the Companie of Cannoneers, and so I ran in that direction.

I used a cornice, a frieze, and a bolection to drop to the street. The journeymen cannoneers on the door knew me by sight as a frequent guest of Master Lipton, and so they welcomed me, and I entered. I helped myself to a brimming cup of a lively, rather lemony white wine and kept an eye to the window shutters, to see if my pursuers were still in chase. Indeed, I saw them go past, the eagle in the lead, followed by the hunched Fork-Beard and the prizefighter, who held a napkin to his bleeding head.

The hall of the cannoneers, like that of the Butchers, was ornamented with tools of their trade. With the Butchers, the tools included knives, cleavers, and pollaxes, but the cannoneers had ladles, rammers, sponges, worms, and the smaller species of artillery. I took a likely item down from the wall, and asked one of the gunners what it was.

"A linstock, sir," he said.

"Very good," said I. The linstock consisted of a wooden handle about a yard long, with a forked metal tip that would hold a slow-match, and it was intended to be used in lighting cannon from a distance safe enough that the gunner would not stand in the way of the recoil.

I left the hall and walked rapidly up behind the prizefighter, held the linstock in both hands, cocked it over one shoulder, and hit him behind the ear as hard as I could. He went down as if I'd pollaxed him, and I sprang over his body to crack Fork-Beard on his crown. That worthy gave a cry and fled as fast as he could stagger, and left me face-to-face with the eagle, who had spun about to face me. I recognized Slope-Shoulder behind the mask, and I raised the linstock as if to swing at him. He raised his hands to guard himself, and instead I dropped the point of the linstock and thrust him hard in the belly. He bent over groaning, and I hit him on the skull, a glancing blow which sent him to one knee.

"Come near me again," I told him, "and I'll serve you as I served Sir Basil."

Then—feeling alive with a perfect righteousness, and tingling with the essential fact of my survival—I returned to the cannoneers' hall and replaced the linstock on the wall.

My assaulting three people on the street attracted a certain amount of attention—there had been shouting from the crowd, and a few screams—and some cannoneers had come out to watch the fight, and so when I returned, there was a respectful half circle about me.

"Those three attacked me on Chancellery Road," I said. "I fled here, where I knew I would find friends."

And friends they proved to be, once I had explained the difficulty, and I was plied with more wine, soft cheese, and cheat bread while I told my story, and while the unconscious prizefighter was carried past the door to a surgeon.

Cannoneer Lipton approached, his white-bearded face rosy with wine, and when he had heard the story congratulated me.

"You armed yourself with a superior weapon and attacked with stealth," said he. "A useful strategy, sure, though you must beware of your foes arming themselves with weapons superior to yours, and attacking likewise from cover. Which," he continued philosophically, "will result in your getting superior arms yourself, and so on, till you come here. For there is no superior weapon than a cannon, sure."

"Difficult to use in a street brawl," said I.

"It is the simplest thing in the world," said Lipton. "A charge of hailshot will sweep any street clean of brawlers."

I laughed. "Let me take one of your guns with me, then, when I go home."

"Unfortunately, the Queen now commands them all," he said. "And the Queen commandeth even me, sure, for I am to con a battery of demiculverins in the forthcoming campaign."

"Congratulations, master." I raised my glass. "May the rebels' walls tumble before your gunshot."

"Thank you, youngster. And now, an I may not charge a gun for you, allow me to charge your glass."

We talked about the coming campaign, and I mentioned that I had seen and spoken to the Knight Marshal, who seemed rather infirm to hold such a responsible position—and furthermore prone to superstition, given all the luck tokens he'd bestowed about his person.

"He has always been lucky in war, sure," said Lipton. "And in my experience, you wish not to stand between a soldier and his luck. Yet being a great general is no great matter, for battles are but games of rock-paper-scissors, and that is a game any man can play."

"Indeed, I have played it. Shall I take command of the Queen's Army?"

"You may, once you understand the game as we soldiers play it. For look you, there are three arms—the cavalry, the pikemen, and the handgunners with their firelocks." He took a substantial loaf of raveled bread and placed it between us. "Here are the pikemen." Forks stood for the handgunners, and knives for the cavalry.

"Firelocks will defeat pikes," he said, "for they can shoot the pike formations from a distance, without the pikes being able to engage them. Cavalry will defeat firelocks, as the firelocks have no means of keeping the cavalry from riding them down. And pikes defeat cavalry, for the cavalry cannot get close enough to harm them. So you see: rock-paper-scissors."

I viewed the battle laid out before me. "And how does your artillery play in this game?"

He laughed at me with yellow teeth. "The peculiar genius of the artillery is shown best in sieges, sure. But in actions such as this we may assist in breaking up the hedges of pikes."

I deployed a pair of knives. "So the pikes being broken, the cavalry may ride the pikes down."

"Indeed."

I laughed. "Now I may be Captain General?"

He lifted a hand in a sign of blessing. "You have learned the great lesson. Be a general, youngster, and drive the rebels from the field."

I remained at the Cannoneers till near sunset, when I headed toward my supper at the Butchers' hall. The streets were still full of entertainments, including a zoo with the cages on carts, where I viewed a bear that performed a sailor's dance, seals that juggled footballs on their noses, a lion that lay asleep on straw and ignored us all, and a minikin that was said to be one of the Albiz, a native prince taken from his underground realm beneath the Minnith Peaks. I was inclined, however, to think he was a dwarf painted brown and dressed in worn velvets.

I moved on through ever-thickening, jostling crowds, among people of the city dressed as doctors and fairies and Queens and Yeoman Archers in their red caps, and stopped to enjoy a troupe of jugglers hurling torches through the air. I found myself standing behind some brawny journeyman bricklayers, and had to stand straight to crane myself up to see the entertainment over their broad shoulders. Then I noticed a small woman standing next to me—she was dressed as a bird, with the mask of a wren or a sparrow, and her hood ornamented with feathers. She was standing on tiptoe to watch the flaming torches as they flew from hand to hand. The whole crowd gave a lurch to one side, and she was knocked off her feet and only avoided being trampled because the crowd was too closely packed to allow her to drop all the way to the paving stones. Without thinking, I picked her up and set her on my shoulder.

She gave a squawk, very birdlike, and I hastened to reassure her.

"Fear not, mistress," I said, "I will not let you fall."

"Put me down at once!" she called, and boxed one of my ears.

"Mercy, I pray!" said I. There was a great moiling and shifting of the crowd, and I was too busy keeping my feet to pay close attention to my furious passenger. "It's too dangerous, mistress," said I as the torches flashed. "Enjoy the show, and I shall try to find you room to breathe."

At which point a large man in the mask of an Aekoi warrior punched me in the face, and a bright explosion flamed up behind my eyes. I reeled back, and would have fallen had not the crowd held me up. This only made me a target for the man's fist, and once again he struck me. I staggered back as I tried to keep upright, and tried not to drop my supercargo beneath the boots of the crowd.

"Help!" she cried, as she tried to fend off the blows. "Murder!"

I kicked my attacker, and he punched again, striking me on the breastbone and driving the wind out of me in a rush. We were so close, and so hampered by the crowd, that we could not miss. I kicked again and caught him on the knee. Behind my attacker I saw a man in an eagle mask wave a truncheon, and I realized that Slope-Shoulder had returned for another inning.

It had not occurred to me that he had not learned his lesson, that—having hired a pair of prizefighters, and failed in his attempt to harm me—he would simply hire another set of swashers and seek me on the street.

I saw one of the journeyman bricklayers staring at me in drunken befuddlement, and I tossed my passenger to him. He reached out his big hands and caught her, bearing her weight as lightly as he doubtless carried his hod. I rather wished he and his friends might use that great strength in my defense. The sparrow-woman, at least, did her part.

"Murder, ho!" she cried. "Help!"

I brought a knee up to my attacker's crutch, which straightened him for a knock on the chin, but there were many attackers—at least half a dozen—and the blows were raining down thick and fast. Bystanders ran, women screamed. A truncheon caught me a blow on the elbow, and the pain rose like a rocket to explode in my skull, and after that I had but a single arm to fend them off. Soon I was blind and bewildered in a circle of them, kicking and lashing out blindly.

"A rescue! A rescue!" I had heard the voices crying out, but had not sifted them from the shouts of the crowd, and then I shook blood from my eyes to see the point of a short sword emerge from the chest of one of my attackers. Red caps bobbed in the crowd, scarlet as the blood on the sword.

"Rescue her highness!" There was a whirl of weapons, and the basket hilt on one of the red caps' short, curved swords clipped Slope-Shoulder on the side of the head, and sent him sprawling.

In the joyous whirl of the festival I had not considered that the men dressed as Yeoman Archers might, in fact, be true Yeoman Archers, let alone that they were here to guard a great lady who had decided to join the throng in their Mummers' Day celebrations. A lady who, I realized, I had picked up and dandled like a puppy, and carried into the middle of a brawl.

Weariness bore me down as fighting erupted around me, and amid a bleeding rabble of dead and wounded, I sank to my knees, holding up my one good arm in token of surrender. Red caps formed a circle around us, their blades out, and among them I saw my sparrow-girl in her feathered cloak.

"Well, Pudding-Man," said the princess Floria. "Once again it seems you have made yourself the center of attention."

CHAPTER TWENTY-SEVEN

I was growing accustomed to jail cells, though I was not used to sharing them with quite so many people. My little stone room in the Hall of Justice was packed so full of drunken, disordered revelers—men, women, and children—that there was no room to sit, and no way to avoid entirely the spattering and spewing that resulted when the drunkenness rose to its inevitable climax.

Fortunately, I did not stand there for long. An ensign of the Yeoman Archers took me from the cell and brought me before a magistrate, who sat alone in the Chamber of the Siege Royal, the highest court in the land, where those accused of the high crimes of treason and forgery were tried, and the monarch herself was recorded as the prosecutor. The judge sat hunched in his fur-trimmed robe with his cap pulled down over his ears, and on the wall behind him was painted the imperial crown that signified his authority.

At least the trial was not to be conducted in a torture chamber. That, I had been told, took place on the floor below.

The majesty and importance of the court were enhanced by the two tall black candles that cast a wan light from his bench, and I was brought forward into the faint circle of light. I wished I hadn't been made so visible, for my face was bloody and bruised, and if I were to be indicted as a violent swashing rogue, my own face pronounced me guilty.

I looked up at the judge as he scratched on parchment with a silver pen. His ancient face seemed sunken into his white beard, and his dark eyes were obscured by thick spectacles tied on with black ribbon. The lines of his face were set in an expression of severity, and he looked as if that expression had not changed in forty years. I doubted that his temper was improved by being dragged out of bed in the middle of night to preside over my case.

He looked up from his writing, his pen poised over the parchment. "You are Quillifer?" he said.

"Yes, my lord."

"Do you have a surname, Quillifer?"

"My lord," said I, "Quillifer is my surname."

His pen, which had been about to write something down, remained poised over the paper.

"What is your forename, then, Goodman Quillifer?"

"Quillifer, my lord."

He peered at me through his thick spectacles. "Your name then is Quillifer Quillifer?" he asked.

I tried to clear my battered head. "Nay, my lord, I misspoke. I have only one name, and that is Quillifer."

His upper lip twitched. "Too bad for you," he said.

I blinked in some perplexity at this, for this strange scene was beginning to undermine the terrors in which the Chamber of the Siege Royal had always cloaked itself.

The judge wrote something, then put down his pen. Without looking at me, he spoke.

"Her highness has testified that you exerted yourself to prevent her from trampled by a mob, and that when she was attacked by lawless villains, you defended her."

Through my surprise I managed an answer. "I am her highness's loyal servant," I said.

"I am commanded to order your release." He signed a paper and handed it to the ensign that had accompanied me. "You may collect your belongings from the porter. It is customary to leave a tip."

I managed through my astonishment to thank his lordship, and walked in a daze to the porter's lodge. I did not forget his vail, nor to thank the ensign who had escorted me. Once outside into the night, I bathed my face and hands in the fountain in the courtyard, with its allegorical statues of Dame Justice in Triumph Over the Wicked, and went into the street. The revelers having exhausted themselves, the streets were almost empty, though filled with the spillage and wastage of the festival, abandoned and broken masks, feathers, cups, shattered bottles, torn ribbons and broken points, liquid pools of uncertain provenance, the whole of it waiting for the rain. I passed by the Tiltyard Moot, where I had been attacked that noontide. The place was shut up like a fortress, but by the light of the waning moon I marked the remains of the shattered tile with which I had felled the man in the eagle mask.

My knuckles ached, along with my face and my ribs. I walked on, and went home to my bed, where my aches and pains kept me awake nearly till dawn.

My aches had not lessened when I awoke, but at least I had grown more accustomed to them. I changed to clothing less soiled by blood, mud, and the spoutings of drunkards, and did my best to clean my gown. My breakfast was a cup of the moscatto drawn from the rundlet in my apartment. I had been doing my best in the weeks since the cask had been delivered, but I think there were still at least a dozen gallons remaining.

The wine led me straight to melancholy without passing through elation. I viewed my room with its trophies: the silver cups, Sir Basil's swords and armor in a disorderly pile beneath my table, the pollaxe from the Butchers' Guild leaning by the door, the wardrobe with my two suits, and the rundlet of wine that seemed to take up half the room. The varied keepsakes of my erratic career in the life of the capital.

I had failed as a lawyer, a lover, and a courtier, and my success as a thief-taker had resulted only in my exile from the court. While the ship with my privateer commission had done well, on an actual voyage I was mere cargo, unable to contribute to the running of the ship or to victory in battle. And now I had been the victim of a feud with a nobleman that had brought a member of the royal family into personal danger. While I seemed to have avoided prison, I hardly thought my name was mentioned in the castle with any favor.

I had failed at everything. Perhaps I was destined to rise no higher than the imaginary office of Groom of the Pudding.

So thinking, I drank myself into misery, and with aching bones and aching heart returned to my bed.

For the next several days, I remained about my rooms, save when business called me to the stockyards outside of town, where some of my cattle were being fattened, or to the lawyers, or to make arrangements for cargo on *Sea-Holly*. I armed myself when I went out, with my knife, Sir Basil's pocket pistol, and a cane with a metal tip and a heavy pewter head that I purchased in a market, and I took care as I walked, examining all about me, to make certain I was not followed, and not ambushed.

I wrote a very formal letter to Her Highness Floria, and thanked her for giving information on my behalf. I signed it "Your faithful servant," and I made no jokes about puddings. There was no reply.

I went to the Butchers' hall to withdraw a bit of money from my box, and to explain why I'd failed to attend their feast on the Day of the Mummers, only to find that they already knew. The affray had become public knowledge, and while I had been nursing my bruises in my lodgings, a series of trials before the Siege Royal had resulted in punishments for the malefactors.

For allowing their private vendetta to overflow into a public brawl that endangered a member of the royal family, all my attackers had been found guilty, including Lord Stayne, who had set them on. Stayne and Fork-Beard, being noble, were exiled at her majesty's pleasure to their estates, from which they would stray only at penalty of death. Slope-Shoulder, a mere knight, was condemned to three days in the pillory—a ghastly fate, in truth, because unless he had friends to stand by him, he would be a helpless object of violence by the mob, who at the very least would pelt him with filth, and at most bash out his brains with paving stones.

The rest, the swashers and prizefighters, being neither noble nor knights, were condemned to death.

My own part had become known, and though the castle had not seen fit either to praise or condemn me, the guildsmen hailed me as a hero and the savior of Princess Floria. Rumor had enlarged my part, and those of my assailants also, for now it was claimed that I had rescued Floria from traitors sworn to kill both the princess and her royal sister. While I denied that this was the case, and maintained it was a private quarrel, this hardly restrained their enthusiasm for my heroism. The guildsmen drank me a number of healths, and seemed to think I would be ennobled, or knighted at the very least, within the week.

I asked if anyone knew anything of Amalie, if she, heavy with child, must share Stayne's exile, but none could tell me. They seemed pleased by the thought of her bouncing down the road into exile at Allingham.

Still, I left the hall more cheered than when I arrived, and these brighter spirits lasted until I returned home, and found a messenger from Amalie awaiting me.

This latest reversal has my husband mad with rage, the letter read, *and he is determined to have you murdered. I know he is offering money for your life.*

I am safe. I was able to persuade him that I was the innocent object of a provincial flatterer, but I fear that by doing this I have put you into greater peril, for now he fancies he is protecting me from your unwanted affections, as well as avenging his own wounded vanity.

You must fly. I am in no danger, but you must leave at once, before his sure requital can reach you.

—Mrs. Freeman

The words struck me like a blow to the heart. I did not grudge Amalie her evasions; she was using the few resources allowed by her situation. But I was staggered by the knowledge that neither censure nor banishment, nor the execution of his accomplices, would keep Stayne from his murderous persecution.

Really, didn't the man have any other occupation but the heedless pursuit of vengeance? First against Sir Basil, now against me?

I considered ways of protecting myself. I could shift my residence, but then any messages from Amalie would fail to find me. I could hire my own bravos, and walk around surrounded by a swaggering bodyguard; but any guards would be mercenaries, and Stayne's silver might well persuade any of them to stab me in the back. I could take up residence in the Butchers' hall, but I would be in danger if I ever went out.

Perhaps it was time to leave Selford for the present. While I did not like the thought of fleeing before an enemy, it had to be admitted that there was nothing keeping me in the city.

Accordingly, I again paid my landlady another few months' rent, then shifted most of my belongings to the galleon *Lady Tern*, which was lying at anchor off Innismore. The ship's valuable cargo was under guard in a warehouse belonging to Customs, and while we awaited a ruling from the new prize court, the ship's crew had been reduced to an anchor watch intended only to prevent pillage. As I was one of the presumptive owners of the vessel, no one disputed my right to lodge on the ship.

I moved into the captain's cabin, enjoyed his wine and some of his choice victuals, and wrote to my Lord of Roundsilver. I explained the situation, and solicited his advice. The reply came from his lady, and was filled with sympathy.

> *There is little that can be done,* she wrote, *not when a great lord acts against one without such a high position. No one can prevent an attack, and though prosecution may ensue against an attacker, and a trail found that will lead to the instigator, that will be scant comfort to the victim.*
>
> *My lord will speak to the Chancellor, or to her majesty if he can, to point out that Stayne now takes advantage of the mercy granted him by her majesty. At the very least a warning might be sent that the Crown knows of his plans. But if Stayne chooses to continue in this mad course, I fear your life may remain in the hazard.*
>
> *I can offer you the hospitality of our house, but I fear it would become a prison for you, for you could not leave without danger. Perhaps the best course of action is to absent yourself from the capital.*
>
> *I wonder how it is that you can make so many enemies. Perhaps you should restrain your impulse to hurl yourself so wholeheartedly into situations fraught with ambiguity. . . .*

There was more along these lines, as gentle a reproach as I could imagine. In my current situation, I could not help but take the remonstrance to heart.

I wrote to thank her grace for her advice, and wrote that while I would regret being unable to enjoy their hospitality once again, as I planned to take her advice and take an immediate voyage.

But though I had no occupation to keep me in Selford, neither had I business anywhere else. I thought of returning to Ethlebight, and set in motion the ornaments and inscriptions of my parents' tomb; but I felt that if I were to return to my native city, it should be in something like triumph, and not flying from a threat like a miserable hound.

If *Meteor* were in harbor, I would join Captain Oakeshott, but *Meteor* was cruising against the enemy; and if it took a prize, it would go to Amberstone, because the special prize court in Selford was for the two large galleons only. *Royal Stilwell* was still being repaired in Longfirth, and when it returned would be caught up in the legal business of the court, and would afterward be leased into the navy, so unless I wished to serve under the Crown, I could not use either ship as a base for any further adventures.

Even *Sea-Holly* was away, which removed any temptation to plod the ocean in a slow merchantman.

I paced the deck for two days, relieving my boredom by watching the life on shore through a long glass. I saw ships busked and boun for the sea, and royal galleons flying Berlauda's long pendant, with its red horse on a white field. I saw the puffs of gunsmoke, and heard the distant thump of gunfire, as the Companie of Cannoneers tested new artillery at their emplacement down the river. I saw young folk dancing to pipers in front of taverns, sailors reeling drunk through the streets, soldiers with their pikes and hackbuts drilling on the Field of Mavortis east of the capital, whores leaning from windows and beckoning to customers below. The whole world seemed in motion, marching on to some great destiny, while I walked in circles on the quarterdeck of a near-deserted ship that swung pointlessly with the tide.

On the third day, I could bear inaction no longer. A boat carried me and my belongings up the river to Mossthorpe, and from there I took a carriage north to Blacksykes, two days on the road and a night sleeping on bedstraw at a wretched inn. On the second evening, I found the encampment of cavalry outside the city, and there sought out Lord Utterback, who I found in the stables, discussing seedy toe with a learnèd farrier. Utterback looked at me in some surprise as, stiff with two days in a carriage, I came lumber-legged into his presence.

"Quillifer?" he said. "You bring news?"

"I bring your slinkskin gloves," said I, and produced them. He took the gloves and looked at them with a bemused smile. "As for news," I added, "I report only that I have decided to follow the Knight Marshal's advice, and become a soldier."

He lifted an eyebrow. "Is it my troop, then, that will be blessed with your presence?"

"Only if the post of secretary is still open."

"It is." He frowned at me. "But tell me, have you run out of bandits to fight?"

I waved a hand. "It proved such an unequal contest I decided to give them a rest."

He bowed gravely. "In that case," said he, "I am happy to welcome you into my band of recreants, rudesbys, and runagates. And may the Pilgrim save you, for the tender-hearted Lance-pesade Stringway will not."

CHAPTER TWENTY-EIGHT

Two weeks later, I wrote to Kevin.

Perhaps strangely for someone about to join the cavalry, I had not thought to provide myself with a horse, & so my lord Utterback arranged for the veteran Lance-pesade Stringway to take me into Blacksykes & view the latest of the horses that Count Wenlock had purchased for his son's troop. One horse is not enough, it seems, & so now I have two bay chargers, with the charming names of Shark & Phrenzy. Their names provided an apt foretaste of their collective temperament, but Lance-pesade Stringway approves of their violent, belligerent behavior. "You ride these to war, not to a lawn party," said he. To achieve mastery of these beasts, Stringway advised me to carry a full leather water bottle when I ride, & at the first sign of disobedience use it to smash my mount between the ears. He assured me that when the horse recovers its wits, which may take a few minutes, it will be more compliant, at least for a while.

My riding teacher in Selford never mentioned this method.

I acquired a third horse to ride when not fighting battles, a gentle-natured mare named Daffodil. She is far more tractable, & I expect I will not have to use the water bottle method when riding her.

Horses, as you may imagine, require a good deal of work to feed & maintain, & I had no wish to do this work myself. I have now acquired a groom, a local boy named Oscar, with bushy dark hair that looks like brushwood growing from his scalp. He is country-bred & claims to be good with horses, so we will see. But of course I had to buy a fourth horse to mount Oscar, so now I have a whole string of the beasts.

As for battles, it seems I am expected to fight along with the rest of the troop. I had thought that as secretary I would manage Lord Utterback's correspondence, keep records of horses & men, & perhaps involve myself with matters of pay + supply—but it seems I am to do this, & fight as well. As the whole purpose of my enlistment was to avoid violence directed at my person, I must count myself as among the disillusioned of the world.

Daily we apply ourselves to our evolutionibus—those movements by which cavalry maneuver on the road & in the field. We practice advances, and retreats, and wheels, and changing to the flank. We form column, and from column form line. We practice inversions of the lines, and passages of the lines, and movements by twos and threes. All this under Captain Snype, a thorough soldier, who all but runs the troop himself, with Utterback as his amiable figurehead.

We have not dared to practice the charge, for there is much danger to horse & man in a mass of men galloping *across country, even when there is no enemy to fight. I am hoping that there will be no occasion to charge at all, for my own position in any fight is v. sadly exposed.*

Lord Utterback commands, of course, so in a battle he will be right in front, some ten or twenty paces before the main body. He must be so far in advance because, if he were in the line, he could not see anything but what is directly in front of him, & therefore could not maneuver his command.

But my lord will not be alone in advance of the troop, for he must have his little military family with him, just a horse's length or so behind. His ensign who carries the standard, & the trumpeter to signal the troop, & Snype to correct him if he make a fatal error.

Among this group I find myself, the poor drudge-secretary. I am necessary, it seems, in the event Lord Utterback wishes to dictate a message, or to have his thoughts recorded for posterity.

As I must fight, it seems I must practice fighting. Utterback's Troop are demilances, which is to say that we are not fully armored as the knights of old, but wear only half-armor, helmets & cuirasses & sometimes thigh-pieces, all worn over a buff coat of thick yellow suede. I do not know why we are not called "demiarmored." We fight not with lances, but with broadswords + pistols. Perhaps we ought to be called "no-lances."

I may thank the v. late Sir Basil of the Heugh for providing me with my equipment. The armor needed only a little adjustment, as you told me when I first tried it on in Longfirth. The horse-pistols I have learned to shoot as well as such weapons can be shot, for they are v. unreliable & misfire often.

I have shot at my own armor with my pistols, & the

bullets failed to penetrate. So Sir Basil's proof-marks were not feigned.

Sword practice I have daily from Lance-pesade Stringway. I have practiced till my arm is ripe to fall off my body, but my talent for swordplay is v. sadly limited. Both Stringway & I agree that I have not a genius for the sword, & he maintains that I will be cut to ribbons in my first encounter with the enemy who knows his ricasso from his knuckle-bow. My wish to carry a pollaxe a-horseback has not been granted, however, & I continue with the routine of slashing & hewing, much to Stringway's vocal & obscene amusement.

"Lucky for you," says he, "that fights on horseback are won more with the spur as with the sword." Though it must be admitted that I have no genius for the spur, either.

Stringway, by the way, is a native of Selford, & learned his art in battles fought in the streets between gangs of youths, some of them fifty or sixty strong. He says that hardly anyone was injured, for they fought to "white wounds," meaning they struck only with the flat of their swords. Many young men, he tells me, learned battle-craft in these brawls, & provided good service to the King in his wars.

"But the rapier ruined all," says he. This long thrusting blade is too deadly a weapon in a street brawl, & there are no white wounds, but fatal ones instead. Yet the rapier is nigh useless on the battlefield against an armored man, & so in the opinion of Stringway it is a weapon suitable only for mincing fashionable gentlemen in ribbons + bows, not for real soldiers.

I retain a vivid memory of Sir Hector Burgoyne nearly skewering me with his blade, so the sooner rapiers are banned from the streets, the louder will sound my approval.

The troopers for the most part live in town, being

billeted among the people who greatly resent their presence. Utterback's Troop is not the only detachment in the city, for my lord's father, the Count of Wenlock, is the Lord Lieutenant for the district, & has raised a number of regiments, both for the Queen's expeditionary force to Bonille, & for defense of the district against the onslaught of rebels who might appear, by sorcery perhaps, here in the middle of Fornland. But the Crown pays for those troops, whereas Wenlock has raised the Utterback Troop entirely at his own expense.

Lord Utterback has rented a small house for his headquarters, & I am tucked up beneath the rafters, on a truckle bed. I sup almost every day with his lordship and with Captain Snype, who relates stories of the late King's wars, & of foreign wars in which he played his part. Snype is a fierce old soul, completely bald, with a chin-beard like a goat, but he has traveled the world, & met many of the great men & ladies from the Empire to the Triple Kingdom. He also knows his evolutionibus like the back of his hand. We form a pleasant company, & discuss everything from philosophy to football, all with the inspiration of Utterback's excellent wine. We also dine with officers of the other regiments, for we are all very civil together, except when the Count of Wenlock is present.

Wenlock, you will remember, thought I had stolen his son's ring & was trying to ransom it back to him, a slight for which he has no intention of asking my forgiveness. He is brusque at the best of times, & if I am in the room his pale face grows paler still, while his blue eyes narrow with suspicion, & he barks like a ban-dog at anyone who approaches. Utterback does not take me with him when he dines with his father, & I am pleased enough to forgo these pleasures, as Utterback implies the talk is all of schemes for advancement, *for the doing-down of enemies, the looting of the rebels' land and goods, & the finding of places for Wenlock and his affinity. I have had enough of these speculations at court.*

I have also met again the three rogues who tried to knock down my door in search of Lord Utterback's signet, & it is clear from the way they view me that they wish to pay me back for the reversal they suffered at my hands. Yet I am protected by my lord Utterback, who (I believe) has also defended me before his father, who suspects I have joined the army only to steal the regimental silver.

I have been at pains to learn from Snype all the misfortunes that might befall us on campaign, in order to forestall them. He seems filled to the brim with the idiocies of generals, the badly-sited camps, the robbers & thieves who follow the army, the dishonest contractors & sutlers, the ephebes whose hunger for glory outraces their ability and good sense, & the food that spoils before the soldiers can eat it. He pointed out that cavalry were ever in the advance, & the supply train in the rear, so our supplies might not reach us during the course of a day, & our men go to bed hungry. To remedy this, I have persuaded Utterback to purchase a string of twenty mules to be kept back with the train, & to carry our supplies to us even if the wagons are bogged down somewhere in the rear.

As for the spoiled supplies, I could but recommend the commissary purchase from my friends in the Worshipfull Societie of Butchers, & I would see to it that the meat was of the finest quality. That some would come from my own beeves was unstated, but I saw no reason why I should not profit by the war, when all from Wenlock down to the lowest groom hope to do exactly that.

Anent the business of the commissary, I have met an old

friend. Below a drizzling winter sky, as the drops chimed off the peak of my helmet, I returned from an errand into town & passed by the kitchens of one of the mercenary regiments of foot, & there saw a burly Aekoi woman standing proud amid the stewpots, bellowing at her assistants in a stridulous voice that grated in a v. familiar way on my bones. I checked my steed Phrenzy & nosed the horse toward the kitchen, & when the woman looked at me, I recognized those irises like birdshot, all surrounded by white.

"Well, Dorinda," said I. "Surprised am I to see you here."

Sir Basil's cook took a while to recognize me, mounted as I was on a charger & plated in armor, & carrying one of Sir Basil's own swords with its hilt of gold-wire inlay. And when she knew who I was, I could see that for a moment she was inwardly debating action, whether to flee the camp or assault me I knew not. For though I was formidably armed, & rode a horse that overmatched even the ferocity of the cook, nevertheless I felt her to be a doughty kemperie-woman, & she stood close to any number of sharp cleavers & knives.

"Peace, Dorinda," I told her. "You need not fear me. You have not done me such harm that I need pursue you."

Though I would take care never to have a meal with that regiment, for fear of being poisoned.

She cocked her head & regarded me with her strange eyes. "You seem to have risen in the world," she said.

"And you have not," said I. "I would have expected to find you in a palace, surrounded by a circle of half-naked lads singing of your beauty & carrying you golden cups of amber wine."

She laughed at this. "If I am poor," said she, "it is entirely as I deserve."

426 WALTER JON WILLIAMS

"Your last employment did not prove as profitable, then, as you hoped?"

She glared. "You didn't help, you & your thieving." Then, coming close & lowering her voice: "After the ransoms from Stayne + his friends came, Basil decided to break up the troop. Each was to be paid according to the terms of our agreement, & the money divided before us all. But we were offered a choice—either the silver + a share of the other rings & jewels, or we could take the money as a draft on one of the Pilgrim's monasteries. This was a safe way to shift money about, & Basil had done such a thing previously when we had moved our camp, & no harm had come to us, & none of the money was lost. So I took the bill, thinking I would recover the money when I got to Selford, but Basil had cheated us, & I found the note was worth nothing. I am a fool, therefore, & deserve my poverty for failing to take the coin when it was right there before me."

So there we have the origin of Sir Basil's fourteen thousand royals, much of it money he had cheated out of his own followers. Truly it must be admitted that he was refreshingly free of principle.

"Sir Basil has paid for his crimes," said I. "He & Hazelton are both dead."

"Hah!" she said, half in surprise, but on the whole she seemed to regard this news without satisfaction. "How did they die? Some militia raised by Stayne?"

I told her that Basil died on his own dirk & Hazelton was hanged. Lest she have any remaining loyalty or affection for her former captain, I left out my own part in the business.

"So perhaps you are lucky after all," said I.

She gave me a baleful look, & gestured at the kitchen, the cold drizzling rain, the sad specter of half-rotted turnips &

half-spoiled mutton lying on the tables ready for the stew-pot. "Do I look lucky?" she asked.

"Luckier than Sir Basil's victims," said I.

"It was that bloodthirsty knife of his," she said. "It turned his mind."

So Dorinda thinks it was not the renegado's quarrels, or his vanity, or his greed, or his vengefulness that turned him outlaw, but the possession of a cursed knife.

I have no prejudice one way or another, but I am glad I never possessed that dirk. It seems to me that I am already pursued by a curse in the form of a nymph, & have no need of another.

I see that this letter has returned to a subject I seem unable to escape, that of the Lady of the Chill Waters. Yet I may at present be immune from her attentions, for she told me on our most recent encounter that her vengeance would not follow me into battle, that there was peril enough in war should I be fool enough to find it. So it seems that as a member of the Utterback Troop I may be safe from her for a while, as well as being surrounded by an armored bodyguard may save me from the vengeance of Stayne. All I have to do is somehow survive whatever battles may lie in the offing.

I find I have related all the news, & I will bring this des-patch to an end. Sooner or later we will march to Selford, & from there take ship to Longfirth, & I hope I may find you one place or another, so that we may have a night or two of merry-making before the cannons begin their thunder.

I remain, as ever, your recalcitrant servant.
(From the Ae. recalcitrare. I made it up.)
Q.

* * *

I was not to meet Kevin in Selford, as he had gone to Ethlebight to see to the laying-down of a new pinnace he was building to replace one lost in the attack of the reivers. He now had the money to do it, for the prize court had ruled on the *Lady Tern*, and the ship and cargo were now ours. The ship had already been leased by the navy, and was now abuzz with dock workers preparing her for the sea. The cargo of spices was sold very quickly, and the Crown was happy with its twenty-percent commission. My share of the money for the most part remained in the banks, though I did purchase some comforts for my journey, and invested again in some of the Crown's debt, which I purchased at a discount. As the Estates General had met and voted in the new taxes, I calculated that the government would be solvent later in the year.

Royal Stilwell sat off Innismore, swinging at its buoy, still awaiting the judgment of the court. The repair-work on the stern was plain to see, and the royal arms that graced the transom had been presented by Kevin to the Queen as a trophy of war.

The city was abuzz with the news that the young Queen Laurel, believed to be Clayborne's prisoner, had given birth to a boy, and that the infant had been crowned King Emelin the Sixth by the usurper, who then proclaimed himself Lord Regent. Queen Berlauda's government, of course, pronounced the whole thing a hoax. I sensed nevertheless that the city profoundly pitied Laurel and the babe, though such sympathy was expressed with discretion, least the speaker end up before the Siege Royal.

Utterback's Troop was obliged to wait in Selford for ten days before being carried across the sea, and I tried to visit my friends. The Roundsilvers were absent—her grace's sister was lying-in at the family home near Ruthers Gowt, and they had gone to attend the birth. I passed by Allingham House in hopes that Amalie might remain though her husband was banished, but she and Stayne were gone, and workmen moving in the furniture of the proud new tenants, a self-satisfied burgess and his plump wife. I asked one of the servants if Amalie's child had come, but he knew nothing.

I took care where I walked, but I had left the city a Butcher's son and returned a trooper in a buff coat, with a sword at his side and a plume in his hat. A paid assassin or sneaking crack-hemp might well find me too formidable to approach. The city was full of soldiers who would render me aid were I attacked, and I tried to keep soldiers always in sight as I went about the streets.

I stayed at Wenlock House with Lord Utterback, but I saw little of him, as his time was taken up with paying calls on the lords and captains who made up the army's higher tiers. So, I followed his example, though at a somewhat lower stratum, and made merry with the Cannoneers, the Companie of Butchers, and Blackwell's troupe of players.

One day we were reviewed by the Queen, and with some of the Trained Bands made a parade on the Fields of Mavortis east of the city. The Queen watched from her carriage, with some of her ladies and the handsome Ambassador of Loretto. The princess Floria shared another carriage with her mother. I doubt that they recognized me as I came trotting past on my noble and vicious charger, Shark, though I gave them a flourish with my sword as I brought it up to salute.

Then we embarked, the horses and grooms going on a ship that had been converted for the purpose. My own *Sea-Holly* had arrived, but was to carry men of the Trained Bands, who had decided to go to war even though, strictly, they were not so required. The Trained Bands were a militia intended to defend Selford itself, and not go abroad on expeditions, but their officers desired glory no less than other officers, and with some fine speeches and a little money, they convinced their battalions to cross the seas and fight the rebels. They had already been across once, after all.

The crossing was made with the protection of the warships of

430 f WALTER JON WILLIAMS

the navy, including the *Lady Tern*, now renamed the *Sovereign*, and beyond the weathering of squalls we arrived at the Island without incident, though with most of our troop being wretched and sick for the whole voyage. The wind backed just as we came to the River Brood, and so we spent a day warping up the river, capstans clanking, and arrived after nightfall, in freezing rain.

All the choice billets had already been taken up, so our horses were stabled in the prayer hall of a monastery outside the town, the troopers crowding the monks out of their cells and sending them into the world to beg for shelter. Lord Utterback and I enjoyed the quarters of the abbot, which were filled with the odor of incense, and graced with expensive hangings, with furniture imported from the Empire, and with a beautiful feather bed with a canopy, which Utterback appropriated for himself. I slept on a couch in the anteroom, and was grateful that the monks had not devoted themselves entirely to austerity.

I joined Utterback when he reported to the Knight Marshal, who had taken up residence in the citadel as a guest of Sir Andrew de Berardinis. I had nearly forgot my first impressions of the Queen's Captain General, but the memory returned at the sight of the frail old man in the coat of sable fur, his charms hanging off his belt and around his neck. At first sight of the old man, I had a presentiment of onrushing catastrophe, a storm in bright armor fast approaching, and the Knight Marshal trying to hold it back it with his frail arms. I wondered what I was doing there, and then remembered that I had nowhere else to be.

Armies were full of men with nothing to lose, and I was one of them. I had failed at everything, and if I failed at soldiering, no-one would care.

At Roundsilver Palace, the Captain General had brought two young men as his supporters, and now he had a half dozen with him. I learned they were his grandsons. The old man greeted Utterback in his mumbling voice, and offered us mulled wine. My lord introduced me, and the puffy eyes viewed me without recognition, and moved away.

"I have taken your advice, Sir Erskine," I told him.

The puffy eyes returned to my face, and as comprehension had clearly not dawned, I chose to clarify. "On the occasion, at His Grace of Roundsilver's, when I related the story of how I had put a stop to the depredations of the outlaw Basil of the Heugh, you advised me to join the Queen's Army."

"I do not recall the occasion," he said vaguely, "but I have long advised that all men should join the army and serve their Queen."

I saw in the wan light the opalescent glimmer of cataracts in both his eyes, and realized that he was nearly blind. It struck me that he was a metaphor for this entire war, and perhaps all wars, a sightless, senescent groping for glory and treasure.

CHAPTER TWENTY-NINE

I looked down from the high ground above Mankin Clough to see the army toiling up the road, pikes sloped, heads bowed, and colors furled. Volleys of April rain beat down on helmets and armored shoulders, and the long, winding serpent that was the Queen's Army dragged itself up a steep road that had become a river of mud. Mud had plagued the advance to Howel from the first day, and slowed not merely the army, but the wagons that drew the artillery and carried the victuals, plus of course the camp-followers, the sutlers, the speculators, the whores, and the officers' mistresses.

We suffered inexplicable halts followed by inexplicable marches. Half the time the army went to bed hungry, with the wagons leagues back, the oxen dragging them from one ditch to the next with mud packed around the axles. Even the string of pack-mules I'd persuaded Utterback to purchase sometimes never found us.

The siege train, with the duke's two great guns, was days behind.

We could have avoided this by taking either of the military coast roads built in ancient times by the Aekoi, but that would have allowed Clayborne to sweep in behind us and seize our base at Longfirth.

And so we marched straight for Howel, or as straight as our mire-beset road permitted.

I had also discovered why I had purchased more than one horse. My gentle mare, Daffodil, had died in Longfirth of nightshade that had been mixed in her fodder by whatever careless person had cut the grass the previous autumn, and my bay courser, Shark, had died on the march of a colic. That left me with Phrenzy, an ill-tempered animal who over the weeks I had brought to a grudging obedience, and who I hoped would be as savage to the enemy as he was to me.

The whole campaign had been a shambles from the first day. I wondered if all wars were like this, or if I were simply unlucky.

On maps, the mountains of the Cordillerie were a neat line stretching from the northern coast of Bonille to the city of Lippholme on Lake Gurlidan, but I was in the act of learning that the Cordillerie was not a single row of mountains, but many long, irregular folds of ground rising up one after the next. Each time the army climbed one pass, it was only to view another, higher pass beyond.

Today was no exception. The army had toiled up from Mankin Clough, where the lucky among us had been billeted in the town, only to top the pass and view another, higher slope beyond. The next ridge was heavily crowned by dark pines that obscured the location of the pass, and for all I knew, Clayborne's entire army might be hidden in those trees.

The dragoons, who I could see already dropping into the next valley, would be scouting the pass by sundown.

No one knew where Clayborne or his rebel army was, but it was certain that we would have to fight before the Queen's Army reached Howel. A defense of one of the passes was very possible, but Clayborne might choose to wait until the Queen's Army descended to the plain of Howel, where the many rivers and bogs formed natural lines of defense, and where our supply would have to cross every pass in the Cordillerie before it reached us.

I turned my horse's head and trotted across tall, sere meadow grass to where the Utterback Troop waited in an untidy mass by the side of the road. They were dismounted and resting their horses, which were splashed to the shoulder, and for lack of any other occupation cropping the brown grass. Lord Utterback stood apart, his eye to a glass as he viewed the ridge ahead. I drew Phrenzy to a halt and dropped the reins.

"My lord," said I. "Can you explain to me the function of dragoons?"

For certainly I did not understand their purpose. They were cavalry, but they fought not with sword or pistol, but rather with a special weapon called the dragon, after which they took their name. The dragon was either a very heavy pistol or a very short blunderbuss, with a bell mouth sometimes cast in the shape of a dragon's mouth, and intended to be used one-handed. It had a very short range and was very inaccurate, and once it was discharged the dragoons had to withdraw to reload. It seemed they would be quite useless in battle.

"The purpose of dragoons," said Lord Utterback, "is to make we of the demilances feel superior to them."

"That seems reasonable," I said. I looked over my shoulder at the valley beyond.

"We'll be made to encamp in the vale," I said. "We should go down and find a bivouac before the rest of the army arrives. Upstream of the rest of the army, to avoid the foulness they'll cast into the water."

Utterback lowered the glass and cocked an eye at me. "You are an old soldier already, then?"

"I'm old enough to prefer my drinking water clean."

"You reason well." Utterback put the glass back in its case and slung it over his shoulder, then turned to mount his bay courser. At his gesture, the trumpeter issued the call to mount, and the troop was on its way down the road.

Ere long, we were down in the valley, across the stream, and camped in one of the meads upstream of the ford when one of the camp marshals arrived and ordered us to shift to another place, because another regiment had been awarded the site. Utterback flat refused him, and said the other group could find their own bivouac, which they must have done because we never heard from the camp marshal again.

I was developing admiration for the way Lord Utterback defied Necessity. Of course, he was a lord, and had no obligation to pay attention to anyone who did not outrank him—and those who did, in fact, outrank him, did not run their own errands.

We of Utterback's household spent the night listening to the rain drum on our canvas tents, eating cheese and brawn served cold with mustard, and pottage once the cooks managed a fire, and our train of mules could find us. We ate much the same food as the troopers— Utterback cared for them as well as our supplies permitted, and did his men the courtesy of not hosting banquets while they starved— though of course the ordinary soldiers did not enjoy Utterback's excellent wines and brandies.

I was sleeping in my own tent when a messenger arrived to summon Lord Utterback to the Knight Marshal, and I was awakened to drag myself along and take notes. It was pouring, and I put on a hat and oilskins before saddling my horse, and carried my notebook inside my doublet, where it would not be soaked.

The Knight Marshal's tent was marked by blazing torches, and by men riding to and fro. Waiting inside on an ivory-inlaid folding chair, our commander looked worse than ever, much shrunken, and wore his coat of sable fur tufted up above his chin, a coat so thick and rich that it made his lean form seem thick as a barrel. Atop his head was a fur hat pulled down over his ears, and he wore mittens of marten skin.

In one corner of the tent was a little shrine, with statues and symbols of the many gods, among which the Pilgrim stood tallest. Frankincense stung the air. "Utterback," said the Marshal, as he regarded my patron with his opalescent, cataract-shadowed eyes. The eyes shifted to me. *"You,"* he said.

I bowed. "Your lordship's surmise in correct. I am indeed myself tonight."

He grunted in reply, while his staff and the other officers glared at me. The Count of Wenlock, raindrops glistening in his grizzled hair, gave me a disgusted look.

Wenlock had arrived just before the army set sail from the city to the head of the Long Firth, from which our march commenced. From what little I could discern, he spent all his time poisoning the Knight Marshal's mind against me. He was one of a pack of nobles and rich gentlemen who accompanied the army without actually having joined it, and who expected to be honored and catered to while they treated the men and officers as if they were lackeys. They were well-bred enough that the Knight Marshal couldn't get rid of them, and they buzzed about him like insects. Had it been up to me, I would have given them all to Clayborne.

The sound of clanking spurs came from outside the tent, and more officers arrived. There were more officers than were strictly necessary, and the redundancy included Lord Utterback himself. For he commanded a troop, and normally troops would be combined into squadrons, and squadrons perhaps into regiments. But the troops were for the most part commanded by nobles, and nobles could never agree to serve under one another, and the Knight Marshal did not insist. So, the cavalry were formed all of independent troops, and did whatever they pleased.

Our breath steamed in the light of the lamps. We waited, not speaking, till the tent was full, and then the Marshal heaved himself to his feet, steadied himself on the arm of one of his grandsons, and leaned on a folding table.

"The usurper's army has been located," he said. "Beyond this next pass, and the pass after that. I shall attack tomorrow."

His mittened hands searched among the papers. "He is at a town called Peckside, half a day's march away. He is fortifying the place, though the weather is hampering him, and the rain fills his trenches. Ha!"

He straightened, and his nostrils broadened, as if he was already smelling the gunsmoke. "The weather is clearing, and the march is straightforward. I will attack tomorrow afternoon."

I looked in surprise at the canvas over our head, and heard the sound of rain drumming unabated. The weather seemed not to have been told that it was clearing.

The Marshal looked again at his maps. "I am told there are two roads to Peckside. I shall take the main road directly to the town and attack the enemy on his left, where his fortifications are incomplete and partly submerged. But the other way must be guarded, lest some portion of the enemy's force get behind us."

He looked up. "Lord Utterback, I have chosen you for this duty."

This caught Utterback entirely by surprise. "Yes, my lord," he said. I looked to the Count of Wenlock and saw a satisfied expression on the count's face, and knew that it was Utterback's father who had procured this appointment.

"When we reach the crossroads," the Marshal continued, "you will take the way to the left. It leads to a village called Exton. When you come to the pass above the village, entrench yourself there. If you come upon an enemy, you will send me an estimate of his numbers and then, if he advances, fight him as long as possible."

Utterback straightened in surprise. "Yes, my lord," he said. "What force may I have?"

"Your own troop. Lord Barkin's troop. Bell's company of infantry, and Fludd's, along with Ruthven and Grace. Lipton's gunners, and Frere's dragoons for scouting."

"Yes, my lord." Utterback blinked. "May I ask where I may find my companies?"

The Marshal seemed irritated by the question. He waved a hand. "Ask about, Utterback. Come the dawn, they will be easy to find."

Utterback seemed bewildered. "Yes, my lord."

"You may apply to the quartermaster for supplies."

"Very good, my lord."

After the Knight Marshal made his other dispositions, Utterback and I splashed back to our troop. I could tell that my patron was less than pleased by his appointment.

"My lord," I said as we rode, "it seems to me the best possible outcome for you."

He regarded me suspiciously. "Yes? How so?"

"You have been honored with an independent command. Yet you will miss the battle."

Rainwater dripped off his nose. "And how is this to my advantage?"

"You run not the risk of being killed, and will therefore have full opportunity to enjoy your new command."

Utterback was irritated. "Yet will I have no share of glory."

"You will attain the glory of having participated in a victorious campaign. As you intend not a military career but a political one, any greater share of the glory will be superfluous." And then, as this seemed not to content him, I added, "Submit to Necessity, my lord. This fits well with your philosophy."

His lordship was still displeased. "You claim more understanding of my philosophy than I do," he said.

We had no further sleep that night, for soon the trumpet was blown to rouse the camp and fires lit to provide breakfast for the troopers. By the time dawn lightened the clouds, we were in the saddle and ready to move, and Utterback sent the main body ahead while he tried to find the scattered regiments which were his honor to command. He found the cavalry easily enough, but everyone else was far back in the column, and so we rode out alone on the heels of the cavalry, over the pass and down again, to where the road turned off to Exton. There

I was stationed, to find and turn aside the elements of Utterback's command as they came up.

The Knight Marshal intended the whole army to march at first light, but it took till midmorning for the Queen's force to heave itself up, like a barely conscious animal rising from its slumbers, and begin its daily trudge in the direction of the rebels. The rain clouds began to break apart shortly thereafter, and blue streaked the gray sky, with bright sun shining down through flurries of rain.

By early afternoon my task was done, and I rode on to catch up with Lord Utterback. Which I did at the top of the Exton Pass, a broad, bare, stony sett lying between a pair of high bluffs. The place was swept by wind and bitterly cold, and so wide that our little force could not hope to hold it against a more numerous foe.

"The Marshal wants us to hold *this*?" cried Lord Utterback. "The wind itself will blow us off the pass, never mind the rebels!"

"Let us go a little farther," I counseled. "There must be a more defensible place farther down—and of course there is this Exton-town, where we may place a roof over our heads."

"It grows dark," said Utterback. "We cannot march far."

I rode ahead with the dragoons, and less than two leagues from the pass we found a suitable place called Exton Scales, a narrow piece of summer pasture that sloped gently to the east, in the direction of Peckside. The pasture was cut by a crossroads, where the road to Peckside carried on straight while the track to Exton broke off to our left. The few lights of the village were just visible on the left, gleaming from behind a stony bluff, and the Exton road was bordered by hedgerows of blackthorn intended to keep flocks of sheep and cattle penned in the road until they reached their destination. The wind was much reduced here, and the hedgerows would provide a windbreak. Off on the right, shepherds had built a small earthen dam to make a pond and provide water for their flocks, and they had also built some drystone huts for themselves and stone pens for their flocks. It was already near dark, and I was unable to fully scout the place, but it was clear that no enemy force was camped in the vicinity, and I sent a rider back to bring Lord Utterback and the rest of his force. I myself rode with some of the dragoons to Exton, and found no enemy there, and few people to welcome us. These told us that they had seen no soldiers in years. I returned to the camp.

The dragoons lit fires of the sheep dung found on the field, and it was a cheerful if malodorous scene that greeted Utterback as he arrived a couple hours later. I had appropriated one of the stone huts for myself, and another for my commander, and had warm fires burning merrily in the hearths.

"A message arrived from the Knight Marshal," he said as he eased himself from the saddle. "He holds the pass above Peckside, but his attack on the usurper has been postponed till tomorrow."

"I am not surprised," I said. "Nor will the enemy be, I'll warrant."

The rest of the soldiers and their support straggled in for the next hour, and camped wherever there was room. Fires were lit and our supper cooked. Utterback fretted as he paced back and forth, looking ever to the east, and I knew he was worried that he would miss the war altogether.

I myself thought the war would be one siege after another, starting down below at Peckside, and there would be plenty of time for everyone to get killed. It seemed to me that Lord Utterback would not welcome this wisdom, however, and I kept my peace.

I spent a pleasant night in my warm shelter, and rose when trumpets called me to breakfast. I came through the low door into the morning light, stretched, and viewed Exton Scales properly for the first time.

The rosy sun hung above distant Peckside, still half a day's march away. The storm had blown itself to shreds overnight, and the sky was a deep blue that shaded to indigo in the West. The pasture was still in its winter colors, brown and faded gold. It was too early in the season for the shepherds to have brought the sheep up from their winter pasture, and the only sign of life were the crows that swooped low overhead, bright eyes alert for anything they might scavenge from our refuse piles.

The soldiers lined up for a brief parade, to be counted. The cavalry then went on watering parade to the pond, and the rest went to their messes for breakfast. Various ensigns and cornets and sergeants jogged up to report to Lord Utterback—which is to say to me, for it was I who wrote down the reports. For the first time, we now knew how many soldiers Utterback commanded, and in what order.

The two troops of cavalry, Utterback's own and Lord Barkin's, made up four hundred, with Frere's Dragoons adding another hundred sixty. The four regiments of foot soldiers massed in excess of three thousand men, and Captain Lipton's eight pieces of artillery required a hundred men to serve them.

I was able, that morning, to congratulate Utterback in commanding nearly three thousand seven hundred soldiers, not counting teamsters, sutlers, quartermasters, laundresses, camp followers, and the occasional wife. This was over twenty percent of the Queen's Army, I pointed out, a very significant responsibility for a young man on his first campaign. "The Marshal has placed great trust in you."

He frowned as he stared off in the direction of Peckside. "It's a compliment to my father, not to me. I'm sure my father argued for my command with the understanding that this errand is a needless precaution—I was never meant to use these men in battle." He looked down at the brown turf, and scuffed it with his boot. "Well," he said, "we shall do what we may."

By which he meant that he wished to get into battle as soon as possible. While Oscar and Utterback's varlet were still frying the breakfast bacon, Utterback turned to me and said, "We shall send Frere scouting toward Peckside, and get everyone else on the road as soon as we can sort them out into proper marching order. I want to support the Marshal's attack if I can."

I wished to stress caution. "Let us not get too close to the enemy. If the main army is delayed again, you don't want to attack without supports."

"The Marshal said he would attack at first light."

"He also said he would attack yesterday. We don't know his dispositions, his delays, or his problems." And, to Utterback's petulant look, I said, "At least wait for the sound of the guns."

He nodded. "Ay," he said. "But we must be close enough to *hear* the guns, at least."

He mounted and rode to Frere's camp to send the dragoons toward Peckside as soon as the men had eaten, and the horses given their water and fodder. When he returned, he found me eating the bacon along with porridge and a glass of cider.

"It would have gone cold, else," I said. "I knew not when you would be back."

Bacon was not on Utterback's mind. He dropped from his horse and had his trumpeter blow the officers' call.

"They will not love you for interrupting their breakfast," I said.

"Open your book," said he. "I want everything set down."

I finished my breakfast before I went for the ledger and my pot of ink. As the ledger had previously recorded only the information for Utterback's single Troop, I had to begin on a new page, which I headed with the words "Lord Utterback's Division of the Queen's Army."

Utterback intended but a simple march down the road, but it took some time to marshal his forces, as some of the regiments had precedence over others and would insist on having the post of honor on any battlefield, and had to be placed in the column so that they could take their place without delay. I duly recorded all this, and then it was time to don my armor, strap on my spurs, and hang my sword on its baldric.

In time, the column was duly formed, and Lord Utterback placed himself at the head of it. I rode just behind, along with the trumpeter and his lordship's standard of golden seahorses on a field of blue. I am sure we made a brave sight, all arrayed there in the morning sun, horses pawing the ground, pikes sloped over shoulders, plumes nodding over helmets, and everyone waiting the word to advance.

Which never came. For a party of dragoons had come into sight down below, and as they dashed closer to us, we saw their captain Frere was among them. Utterback rode forward to meet him, and I followed. As we came close, we saw their horses were lathered, and heard the breath rasp from their nostrils.

Frere threw an arm back and pointed. "The enemy, my lord!" he called as he reined up. "The enemy is upon us!"

CHAPTER THIRTY

L ord Utterback took the news calmly. He frowned a little, and looked off into the sun, and after a moment said, "How many?"

"We could not tell, my lord," Frere said. He was a big man, large for a dragoon, with a black spade-shaped beard. "Their column curved out of sight below us. Yet they have foot and horse, and I counted the flags of half a dozen regiments. So they have at least as many as we, and very likely more."

Utterback's calm was so absolute that it began to seem unnatural. I could see his eyes making little jumps left and right, as if he were reading written instructions hanging before him in the air.

"I shall have to fight them," he said. "I must fight them, then."

I interrupted Utterback's reverie with a question. "How long before they come?"

"Their advance guard, within the hour," Frere said. "The main body will be two hours or more. My men will try to delay them, but dragoons can't fight proper cavalry in the field."

I wondered, as I so often had during the course of the campaign, what dragoons *could* fight, since they seemed unable to match either foot or horse. Lord Utterback, however, received this latest information with another long silence.

I turned again to Frere. "Can we drive in their advance guard? Be on them with the cavalry before they know we're here?"

Frere's bushy eyebrows closed in thought. "Ay, that is possible. But we must be right speedy, and be prepared to retire smartly if those infestulous custrels prove ready for us."

Hearing this, Lord Utterback made up his mind, and turned to me. "I'll go forward with the horse," he said. "You must ready the foot and artillery for when we must fall back."

"My lord?" I said, but a whirlwind had now taken Utterback's soul, and he stood in his stirrups, turned, and waved the cavalry on. He trotted back to join them, then led the column off to the left so that all the elements could wheel and come into line, and the air was suddenly full of trumpet calls and shouted orders. "Ranks by threes! Farriers to the rear! Right wheel! Halt, dress! Walk! Halt, dress! By the standard—walk! Halt! Dress your lines!"

The Utterback Troop was experienced at this sort of thing by now, and managed the maneuver well, and as speedily as Captain Frere could have hoped. Soon, Lord Utterback had his troop formed in two lines facing down the slope to the east, with Lord Barkin's Troop just behind them. The infantry, having received no orders, stood in their column and watched these maneuvers in some surprise.

Lord Utterback, now unable to be still, trotted back and forth in front of the lines as they dressed, then placed himself in front of the standard.

"Ready to advance! Walk!"

From the sidelines, I watched in complete astonishment as the cavalry walked on down the field. In his eagerness to strike the enemy, Lord Utterback had abandoned us, along with most of his army. Frere, who stood with me, turned to me.

"I should gather up my lads. Do what you can here." His tone was not unkind.

I rode back to where the infantry stood in their marching column, and finding Coronel Ruthven and his party with their lead regiment, I asked him to have his trumpeter make the officers' call.

I looked over the ground while waiting for the officers to come up, and tried to see it as an experienced soldier might. The flat pasture was nearly as smooth as a bowling green, for any trees or bushes were grazed away by sheep while they were mere sprouts. South of the narrow field, the ground fell away into a ravine, and on the north the land rose into steep cliffs until the escarpment bent away to make a passage to Exton.

The road to Peckside ran east and west down the length of the pasture, but closer to the south side of the field than to the north. At the crossroads, the road to Exton branched off to the north.

Erosion by wagons and other traffic had sunk the roads anywhere from three to six feet below ground level, and thick blackthorn hedges, where tender new leaves were mingled with last year's black, half-rotted sloes, lined both sides of the roads, broken only occasionally by a wooden gate. The roads were intended as chutes to guide flocks of sheep and cattle to new grazing, but now after the rains, the roads were bogs of mud, and in some places were under water.

I could only think that the hedges and sunken roads that cut across the sett would aid the defense.

"An enemy force is coming on," I told the officers when they arrived. "Lord Utterback has gone with the horse to attack their advanced body, but he expects he'll be obliged to retire, and wants us to prepare to fight here."

Coronel Ruthven was a man of fifty, in elaborate armor of boiled leather sculpted to look like the muscles of an ancient hero. He stroked his gray, pointed beard as he looked with narrowed eyes over Exton Scales. "Yon thick-pleached hedge will make a fine barrier," he said. "This is a good field for defense, and no way around us."

My friend Captain Lipton took off his bonnet and scratched his balding head. "I know not where to put the guns," he said.

I ventured an answer. "In front, I suppose."

"In front of the hedge? They will be overrun." He closed one eye and looked over the sett with his remaining eye, as if pretending to view the ground with a telescope.

"We'll find a way to site your guns," I told him, "but first we must place the foot."

That business went more quickly than I'd expected. I was as inexperienced in battle as Lord Utterback, but the customs of war made many of the decisions for me. Ruthven, commanding one of the Trained Bands of Selford, had by custom the position of honor on the right. Bell, as the senior of the two mercenary commanders, took the second position of honor, on the left. That left Grace's Trained Band inside of Ruthven, and Fludd's mercenaries between Grace and Bell.

While the sergeants-major ordered their companies on the field, Lipton and I rode off to view the ground, and found a place for his demiculverins on the far left, where the ground rose as it neared Exton. Were the eight guns placed here, they would overlook the entire field, and shot would be fired over our soldiers' heads to land among the enemy.

From this point of vantage I could see the hedges and the roads winking with water, the flat brown ground, the companies marching to their places with shouldered pikes and hackbuts. Below Exton Scales, the road curved off to the right as it followed the line of the mountain, and from this point of vantage I could see well down the track, far more than I could see from the level ground.

Lipton brought out his telescope and peered down the road. "See you," said he. "Our demilances return, sure."

He offered me his telescope and I looked to see horsemen coming up the road. Not lines of disciplined troops such as Lord Utterback had led down to meet the enemy, but small groups, moving slowly. I felt my stomach clench at the sight, and I looked in some desperation for the standards and saw none.

"Is it some disaster?" I asked.

Lipton cackled. "You cannot ask too much of horsemen," he said. "It is too easy for them to run away. Not like we gunners who must stand by our pieces though hell and hailshot come at us."

I looked at him. "Do you really do that?" I asked.

"Nay," he said. "We run. But not as fast as the cavalry."

"I'll go down and speak to the horse," I said.

I rode down to the field while Lipton trotted off to bring up his guns. Passing by the soldiers, who were still deploying, I rode to discover a group of Frere's dragoons wearily riding along, their bell-mouthed firelocks lying across their saddles. They told me that they had been skirmishing with the advance guard, and were being chased away by cavalry, when Utterback's horse had arrived, and driven the enemy cavalry back. Captain Frere had then arrived and told them to withdraw and re-form behind the infantry.

The last they had seen of the fight, things were going well for Utterback.

The next groups of horsemen were also dragoons, with much the same story. It was another few minutes before I met demilances of Utterback's Troop, and these were weary men, some wounded, some with hacked swords and dented armor. Their horses were worn, and walked along with their heads drooping. These said they were driving the enemy, but were then assaulted by fresh forces and forced to fly. None of them knew what had become of Lord Utterback, Lord Barkin, or Captain Snype.

A few more interviews and I understood what had happened. Utterback's Troop had come upon the dragoons being pursued by enemy horse, who had while chasing split into small bands. Utterback ordered a charge, and faced by the formed troopers, the enemy were driven back until they came up to the first bodies of foot, who formed pike-hedges and held off the attackers while firing hack-buts and calivers into them; and as the Troop milled about in confusion, another enemy unit of horse formed and charged; and this time it was Utterback's disorganized demilances who were driven back. They fell back upon Lord Barkin's Troop—and Barkin, because he had kept his men in order, was able to countercharge successfully and knock the enemy back, and that enabled our people to withdraw without pursuit.

I was relieved at this, for it seemed the greater part of our horse had survived, but still I felt an anxious gnawing because I saw not a single officer, not Lord Barkin, or Frere, or Snype, or any of their lieutenants, nor our Captain General Lord Utterback. None of the standards had returned, and the horse were leaderless. Some had lost their horses and were on foot. I told them all to go to the pond and water their animals, and then rally behind the infantry; but I knew not what to do with them after, as they seemed exhausted and beaten.

I was wondering how we would fare without a commander, and whether I should pretend that I was in charge, and whether more experienced soldiers like Ruthven would accept my leadership. It is not without precedent for me to assume an authority that I do not possess, but there was so much at stake, hundreds and perhaps thousands of lives, that command seemed less a pleasure than a dark, approaching pall of cloud swollen with the promise of death and slaughter.

I returned to the lines to view our foot and speak with the coronels. Pikes and pollaxes lined the west side of the hedge four deep, with calivers and hackbuts in the interstices. The standards waved bravely overhead. Behind the line, a few reserve companies loitered on the grass.

In battle, the soldiers with hackbuts and calivers would descend into the sunken road, splash across, and fire through the hedge into the enemy as they approached, then fall back as the rebels came near. Any attackers would have to fight their way through the hedge, then jump down into the sunken road only to fight their way up through the hedge on the other side, with our pikes stabbing down at them.

The only exception to this was on the far right. Most of the foot were lined up behind the road to Exton, but this road ran only to the juncture with the Peckside road, which left fifty yards of clean smooth turf between the Peckside road and the ravine falling away on the south. It was such a narrow front that an advance along it couldn't be decisive, but Coronel Ruthven had put a company of pikes there, just to discourage any attempt.

I was viewing this area with Coronel Ruthven when a group of straggling dragoons was walking past, and I turned to him and said, "The enemy will attack along our main front, I assume?"

Ruthven was amused. "They can scarce attack anywhere else."

"Let's put dismounted dragoons here, ahead of the main body. When the rebels advance, the dragoons will be able to fire into their flank. And if the enemy attacks them, the dragoons can find safety behind the pikes."

Ruthven considered this. "Ay," he said. "For what else can we do with dragoons on such a field as this?"

"Or any field," said I. "For I know not what dragoons are for."

"Today," Ruthven said, "we may find out."

I rode up the scales to find the dragoons where they were rallying by the pond, and sent them down to the field. Then, from my higher position on the pasture, I could look down over the hedge, and I saw a body of horsemen approaching from the east, riding under three standards. My heart gave a leap as I recognized Lord Utterback's blue standard among them, and I urged my horse down the gentle slope to join them.

Lord Utterback rode abreast with Lord Barkin and Captain Frere, each beneath his own banner, and followed by fifty or so horsemen drawn from the three units. Utterback rode perfectly straight in the saddle, his eyes fixed to the front, lower lids drooping to show a lot of white below the pupils. He still held his straight sword in his right fist, and the steel cage that protected his face was lowered. His plume had been clipped short, and I saw fresh dimples on his breastplate where bullets had rebounded.

"You should congratulate your armorer, my lord," I said as I reined up and joined the party. "Proofs you bear now that his steel is proof indeed."

Utterback gave me a strange white-eyed look, as if he did not comprehend my words. His right hand clenched on the hilt of his sword. Perhaps, I thought, he was not in the humor for such badinage. I essayed again.

"I am heartily glad to see you, my lord," I told him. "I have tried to put the soldiers in order, and I hope my dispositions will meet with your approval."

Utterback said nothing, and Lord Barkin spoke up instead.

"We have been trying to sweep up as many of our men as we can," he said. "Have many come ahead of us?"

"Indeed," I said. "I've told them to water their horses at the pond, then rally behind the foot. The dragoons I have put on the far right, to harass the enemy as they advance. But they have had no horse-officers till now."

"We shall set them in order," said Barkin.

Coronel Ruthven met us as we rode into our lines, and saluted Lord Utterback with a cheerful smile. "Would you come and inspect us, my lord?"

For the first time, Utterback spoke. "Yes," he said. "Yes, I shall do that." He reined up. "Let me see your brave fellows, coronel."

Lord Barkin and the others streamed up the slope as Ruthven and I guided Lord Utterback over the field. He returned the soldiers' salutes with a brandish of his sword, and spoke little, but approvingly, of everything he saw.

We ended on the far left, just under the rise where Lipton had drawn up his guns. We turned our horses toward the guns, and Lord Utterback leaned toward me.

"I know not what happened when we met the enemy," he said.

"My lord?"

"I know not what happened. I could not *see*." His helmet rattled as he gave a shake of his head. "The enemy were not there, and then they were all about us. I tried to give orders, but there were precious few to hear. I fought—I struck at them. Then I seemed to be all alone, with troops of enemy horse charging, and I had to fly. I clashed with some of them, then Lord Barkin found me and took me back." He shook his head again. "I know not what happened."

"You drove them in, my lord," I said. "And most of the men have come back. So, that is a victory."

"Is it?"

I put on my sincere face. "I believe it is, my lord."

"I know not. I hope that is so, but I know not."

He rode up the slope toward the guns. They had all been placed, and the limbers and wagons withdrawn. Lipton and his men had taken off their boots, had opened barrels of powder, and were pouring the powder out onto tarpaulins.

"Captain!" said I in surprise. "What is this?"

Lipton looked up from his work, then came toward us in his bare feet, holding out his hands. "Keep back, your honors," he said. "You don't want your horseshoes striking sparks near that powder."

I hastily drew my horse back. "What are you doing with the gunpowder?"

"The powder has separated, sure," said Lipton. "Days of rattling up and down these mountains has shaken the serpentine powder in its barrels, and the nitre has come adrift from the sulphur and charcoal." He made heaping gestures with his hands. "We must remix the powder by hand and return it to the barrels before we can use it." He looked up at the sky. "Gods be thanked, it is not raining."

"Gods be thanked," I repeated. "You will finish this task before the battle begins?"

"Fear not, your honors," said Lipton. "Once the powder is remixed, you can count on each gun firing every four or five minutes, sure."

That seemed not such a good pace. "Is that the best you can manage?" asked I. "When I was on a privateer, the powder was in pre-made linen bags that were stuffed down the muzzle. Can you not use such cartridges, instead of ladling the powder into your weapons?"

Lipton put on a dignified expression. "It is part of our art to know exactly how much powder to ladle into the gun, so that the ball may land exactly where intended."

"Yet if you could more than double your rate of fire, would that not compensate for a certain amount of inaccuracy?"

"Yet the powder would still separate, whether it was in linen bags or no," said Lipton. "Can you imagine us opening hundreds of those bags, remixing the powder, and then stuffing it into the bags again and sewing them up?"

"The privateer needed not to do this."

Lipton looked over his shoulder at the powder, and then shook his head.

"A privately owned ship may buy good corned powder," Lipton said. "Corned powder does not separate. But that is not permitted to us."

I looked at him in surprise. "Why may you not have corned powder?"

"The royal army is required to purchase its powder from the Royal Powder Mill outside Selford, and the Royal Powder Mill does not make corned powder—has no reason to, you see, because they are guaranteed to sell to the army and navy whether their powder is good or no. So, they make this inferior serpentine powder, and we gunners must suffer."

Lord Utterback showed no surprise at this revelation. "Well," said he. "You may return to your mixing."

"Very well, your lordship."

When Lipton returned to his task, Lord Utterback remained unmoving, sitting very straight on his horse with his sword still in his hand.

"My lord," I said. "You can put your sword away."

He looked at the sword in his fist as if seeing it for the first time, and then drove it into the scabbard.

"My lord," I said. "You can see the enemy from here." I pointed down the slope, to where the road curved away to the right.

I had bought a cheap cardboard telescope in Selford, and I drew it from its scabbard and put it to my eye. The rebels had resumed their advance down the road, and the lead elements of horse were already filtering up onto the scales, and were in sight of our force. I could see light winking from the enemy telescopes as they viewed our line, all drawn up behind the hedge with their flags flying above.

Farther down the road was nothing but long dark lines of men marching beneath a waving succession of banners. Occasionally the sun winked off a spear-point or a piece of armor, but of particulars I could make out nothing.

"Perhaps, my lord," I said, "you can see more than I can."

Lord Utterback brought out his own telescope, a far more useful device than my cardboard toy, and tried to use it, but then realized his face-cage was in the way. He raised the cage, then applied the glass to his eye. His face remained expressionless as he viewed the marching enemy, and then I could see his lips move as he counted regimental flags. Then he stopped counting, and leaned forward.

"Lipton!" he said. "Bring us your glass!"

The gunner hastened to us, drawing his brass-mounted telescope from its case as he came. Utterback made an impatient gesture.

"Give it to Quillifer!"

I tucked my own glass under my arm, took Lipton's instrument, and put it to my eye. The enemy force appeared in much greater clarity than previously—and my heart sank as I realized their numbers were greater than I had imagined.

"Look about a third of the way back," Utterback said. "See you that white banner?"

"Ay."

"It is carried on a cart, is it not? Drawn by white oxen?"

"Ay."

"Can you see what badge it bears?"

I looked, but with the distance and the banner's rippling in the wind, I could see little. "I believe it carries a shield."

"The Pilgrim save us," Utterback breathed. He lowered his glass. "I believe it is the Carrociro."

My heart sank. "The royal standard," I said.

"It is flown only in the presence of the monarch," said Lord Utterback. "Or in this case the Regent, who is Clayborne. And Clayborne would not be here were this not his main force."

At once I understood the situation. The Knight Marshal had intended to descend from the mountains and strike at Clayborne's left, while Clayborne planned to march over Exton Pass to strike at the left of the Queen's Army. If both succeeded, they would swing round each other like couples at a dance, each ending in the other's rear. But if Clayborne broke through us while his improvised entrenchments at Peckside held off the Marshal, then he would be in the Marshal's rear and in perfect position to destroy him.

I turned to Utterback. "My lord," I said, "you must send to the Marshal for aid."

He blinked at me, then nodded. "I will write him a message. You stay here and count the enemy and see how many regiments are coming at us, then report to me."

"I will, my lord."

Lord Utterback galloped away, clods of mud flying from his horse's hooves, and I returned Lipton's glass to my eye. It was difficult to count the enemy, to distinguish regimental flags from guidons carried by individual companies, the ensigns used to mark administrative units, or from the personal banners of knights and lords and other persons of quality.

Lipton's voice came near my elbow. "It is a pity that the Captain General threw away the cavalry too soon."

I clenched my teeth. "The charge delayed the enemy. We must hope for more delay."

"Oh, ay." Lipton's voice was meditative. "But you will scarce get two charges out of cavalry in a day. Even if the troopers prove willing, sure the horses may not."

I was all too familiar with the wayward perversity of horses. I looked down at him. "You are full of cheer this day."

He grinned up at me. "Fear not, youngster. You have a fine horse, and may run away at need. Those other cavalry, their horses are tired and they will all be cut down before you."

Cut down because Utterback, at my urging, had thrown away the one charge our horse could be counted on to make.

I wondered if I had lost the campaign, or possibly the entire war, with that single suggestion.

"But this field—" Lipton waved a hand in the direction of the enemy. "This will be different. It will be decided by push of pike. For enemy horse may not attempt those hedges, and the hedges conceal our soldiers from the firelocks. The rebels must drive their pikes at us till we break, or they give up, or our succor arrives."

Our succor was at least twelve hours away, or so I calculated. "Have you any more of these cheerful little posies to scatter before me?" I asked.

He rubbed his unshaven chin with a powder-blackened hand. "You must hearten the foot, that they not run. Tell them help is on its way, and hope the gods may forgive your lie."

I raised the telescope again, and made another attempt to count the flags that swarmed before my eyes. I made my best approximation and handed the telescope back to Lipton. His men were madly refilling the powder barrels with wooden scoops.

"Do your best to kill the enemy today," I said. "And if you knock off Clayborne's head, I'll buy you a nice bottle of claret."

Lipton doffed his cap in mock humility. "I'm sure that is the best a common soldier such as I can hope for or deserve." I rode on after Utterback, and found him by the stone huts where we had spent the night, dismounted and writing on his camp table.

"I counted ten regiments of foot," said I, "and two of horse, and in addition three batteries of guns. And there are more enemy behind them."

This last statement was the only one in which I had confidence. I had done my best, but all I could say for certain was that we were severely outnumbered. For we had four regiments of foot, the equivalent of a regiment of cavalry, and Lipton's eight field pieces.

Lord Utterback duly added my numbers to his message, then sanded and sealed the paper. "I pray the Knight Marshal credits the report."

"So do I."

He gave the message to Oscar, and detailed one of his own troopers to ride alongside the boy. "As fast as ever you can, now," he said. "And give it right to the Marshal's hand."

"Ay, sir." Oscar touched his brow, vaulted onto one of Lord Utterback's spare chargers, and made off at a trot.

I turned to look at the cavalry, which were regrouping under the expert guidance of Lord Barkin. The troopers had sorted themselves out into their units, and were dismounted and for the most part spending their time caring for their horses.

"You might wish to move the cavalry back," I said to Utterback. "Here they will be exposed to artillery."

"You may order that, with my authority." So, I trotted up to Lord Barkin, and told him that he could draw the cavalry back to where our wagons had been grouped.

"You and all the horse have the Captain General's compliments!" I said, in a voice loud enough for those near to hear. "You have struck the enemy hard, and they will be a long time recovering!"

This seemed to cheer the weary troopers, and I hoped it was at least partly true. I leaned closer to Lord Barkin and said in a voice for him alone. "Move them back and put some heart into them, for if the foot give way, you must retrieve the situation."

He nodded. "Ay," he said. "I shall try to have them ready." His expression told me he didn't expect the foot to hold out for long.

I returned to Lord Utterback, who I found sitting heavily on his camp chair with his helmet in his lap. His eyes were fixed on the mountain peaks to the north, as if he were expecting something from that direction, a message or a sign or a rescue.

"Are you all right, my lord?" I asked him. "You are not wounded?"

"No, I am well." He searched himself with his hands, as if assuring himself of his own well-being. "I am ready to fight," he said. "I *will* fight. But I am a little tired right now."

"Will you join me in a glass of cider?" It was all I could think to say.

He considered my question. "Brandy would be better."

I dismounted and found the cask and a pair of silver glasses, took the stopper out of the bunghole, and poured. I handed Lord Utterback his glass, and squatted by him. I raised my glass.

"To victory," I said.

He looked at me as if the word "victory" were a stranger to him, but then he raised his glass.

"Whyever should I not?" he said. "To victory, then."

He drank half the brandy in one gulp, then sat for a moment contemplating the glass in his hand. The first stirrings of wind began to sigh down the pasture.

"This is all so unlike what I expected," he said. He looked sidelong at me. "Is it the same for you?"

"I don't know what I expected," I said. "But I rather thought war would be better organized."

He offered an amused smile. "I thought that once the fighting began, it would be over quickly. Victory or defeat, like the last act of a play. Instead, it just seems to continue."

I sipped my brandy, and the harsh fumes stung the back of my throat. "My lord, the men are standing behind the hedge with nothing to do but watch the enemy come in large numbers onto the field. They must be told what is happening."

Lord Utterback slowly nodded and sipped his brandy. "Yes," he said. "They must. I see that they must."

"They must be told that help is coming, that the whole army is coming. That they must fight on until the Marshal comes."

Utterback gave another slow nod, then drank off the rest of the brandy and handed the empty glass to me. He clapped his hands to his knees and heaved himself upright in a clatter of armor.

"Hold Amfortas for me, will you?"

I rose and took the charger's bridle. Lord Utterback put on his helmet and tied the chin strap, then got a foot into a stirrup and hauled himself into the saddle.

"I shall give the men some good cheer," he said. "You keep the rebels under observation, and report to me when necessary."

And off he trotted, while his flag-bearer scrambled to get into his seat. I pulled the flag from the ground and handed it to the ensign, who raced off after Utterback, the blue flag snapping in the wind.

Lord Utterback was developing the habit of leaving his people behind whenever he made up his mind to take some form of action.

I finished my brandy, then mounted Phrenzy and returned to the knoll where Lipton was remixing more gunpowder. I looked at the enemy with my cardboard telescope, and I could see them filing onto the far end of Exton Scales, huge dense blocks of men glittering with weapons. Rebel scouts and officers ranged forward to try to get a look at what was behind the hedges. The royal banner of the Carrociro had not yet reached the field on its cart.

The pot helmet was murdering my skull. The sun had warmed my breastplate and back, and between that and the thick buff coat, I was growing hot. I took the helmet off and wiped my forehead.

Then I heard cheering from the far end of the field, and I turned my glass to see Lord Utterback on his horse, addressing Ruthven's soldiers. As he came into focus, I saw him brandish a fist, and cheers roared out again.

He seemed to be raising their spirits. I wished someone would raise mine.

Lord Utterback progressed down the field, addressing each group of soldiers in turn. He sent the bandsmen back to the wagons for their instruments, and soon there was music, pipes and drums, sackbuts and trumpets, each of the bands playing in turn. The morning took on a jaunty air, and I thought it was well that the soldiers had things to occupy their minds other than their own present doom.

Doom, on the other hand, was very much on my mind as I watched the enemy come onto the field.

The diversions continued for another two hours, in which I relieved Phrenzy of my weight and searched the saddlebags for biscuits to gnaw on. By now, the Carrociro was on the field, and the growing breeze rippled the great white flag so that I could see the shield on it, with the tritons of Fornland quartered with the griffons of Bonille, the shield supported by the horses of the Emelins. I began to feel an echo of Lord Utterback's impatience: war seemed mainly to consist of standing and waiting.

The sun was nearing noon when a great trumpet blast echoed over the sett, followed by the boom and rattle of drums, and the first attack began to move forward: three dense squares of pikes, flags flaunting overhead, each square flanked by men carrying hackbuts. At the sight and sound a warning sensation prickled along my skin, as if my hair were rising like that of a frightened cat. My heart began to pound in time with the drums.

Our band music died away, as the musicians dropped their instruments and ran to their places in the line.

I could see the dense oncoming formations easily enough without my glass, so I put my telescope in its case, tied on my burgonet, and jumped aboard my horse. Lord Utterback's flag rippled down at the crossroads, and so I spurred down the slope to him, finding him on the far right, with the dismounted dragoons, peering through the hedge at the approaching enemy, his gauntlets holding back the thorns.

"Three squares coming for us, with the hackbuts in between," I reported.

He nodded. "I will abide here on the right. Go you to the left, and hearten the men. If things go amiss, let me know."

"Very well, my lord."

At least he was not likely to wander off and leave me behind.

While the enemy drums thundered across the field, I rode left to Fludd's regiment of mercenaries, and leaving my horse in the care of a boy I joined the commander in the muddy Exton road. He was a small, excitable man, with a close-cropped gray beard and a patch over one eye.

He had filled the mucky road with his handgunners, all armed with calivers. The first rank had thrust their firelocks through the hedge and awaited the word to fire. Fludd himself kept peering out through the hedge, only to turn his head and shout aloud to his companies.

"Hold fast 'gainst these salt-butter soldiers!" he cried in a high tenor. "Those mouse-eaters cannot stand up to our mad regiment of fire-eating bawcocks! Ha! Look you, their faces are pale as quicklime, and they will fall apart like maggot-ridden pies when they taste your fire!"

Lord Utterback had sent me to hearten the soldiers, but Coronel Fludd was doing a better job of it than ever I could. I waited for him to draw breath, then spoke. "Coronel," said I, "I am sent by Lord Utterback to make certain you lack nothing."

My last words were drowned out by a blast, followed by a tearing, shuddering sound overhead, like shrieking, chimerical fiends flying out of the western sky. I ducked, seeking shelter in my cuirass like a startled tortoise in his shell. Fludd looked at me as laughter burst from his throat.

"Take heart, whey-guts!" he said. "Have you never stood beneath a bombardment?"

For it was Lipton's demiculverins, firing over our heads into the enemy, the solid iron shot tearing apart the air. More shots followed, and Coronel Fludd again peered through the hedge.

"Fair shot!" he said. "That has opened their files, by the Pilgrim's nose!"

I counted eight shots, and knew the demiculverins would take another four or five minutes to reload. I made a hole in the hedge, wedging aside the thorns, and looked through it. The enemy was still coming on, perhaps two hundred yards away, their armor glowing in the sun, their bright banners still flying. They looked as terrifying and unstoppable as a cold spring tide rolling over the breakwater.

Fludd drew his sword. "Stand by, my keen-eyed bullies! Blow on your matches, and mark your prey! Your shot will mow 'em!"

I heard shots from elsewhere on the field, and my heart leaped. I could see very little from my hole in the blackthorn hedge, and whoever was shooting was out of my sight.

"Aim, my sweet lambkins!" called Fludd. And then, *"Let fly!"*

The calivers cracked out, white smoke gushing onto the field. Through the haze I saw a few rebels fall, and some others who clutched at arms or legs, or who let their pikes droop when struck in the hand or arm.

Coronel Fludd's high tenor voice sang over the battlefield. "First line, back! Step up, second line!

The well-drilled mercenaries did not wait for the order. Those who had fired fell back to reload, and more men rushed up to the hedge and leveled their weapons. Shots cracked out, and more enemy fell. And as the third line rushed up to the hedge, I saw, to my complete amazement, that the enemy column had come to a halt.

Another rattling volley dropped more of the enemy. And now the first rank of the enemy hackbuts dropped their pieces into their rests and returned fire, and shots filled the air like drumbeats. Leaves and twigs fell from above, and I realized that the enemy didn't understand that the Exton road had sunk below the level of the ground, and they were all firing over our heads. It was the pikemen behind us who were in danger, and anyone foolish enough to ride a horse behind the hedge.

The first row of enemy hackbuts turned and fell back, and the second row advanced to plant their rests and fire. More twigs and sloes dropped on our shoulders and helmets, and I saw that the wind was blowing the gunsmoke back into the rebels' faces. They were far more blind than we.

Fludd's men were all madly reloading. I continued to stare out through the hedge at the enemy force, which seemed so close that I could almost reach out and touch them. They continued to stand as Fludd's calivers thrust again through the hedge, and more of the front ranks of enemy fell.

Their own firearms were now all reloading. The hackbuts were long weapons that had to be fired from a rest, and because of their length, possessed greater range and were more like to penetrate armor, but they took longer to load than Fludd's calivers, and at this short range the effect of the bullets was much the same. Fludd's marksmen fired steel shot to pierce enemy armor, and even though the front ranks of the great squares were made up of the best-armored men, and much of the armor proof, the calivers nevertheless had their effect, and soon there was a line of bodies to mark the front of the enemy formation.

My ideas of warfare were formed by literature, and I had expected the enemy to hurl themselves on us in one great mass like poetical heroes; but instead they stood and let us shoot at them, replying only with the hackbuts on the flanks. While I had learned that much of warfare consisted of simply standing about waiting for something to happen, I could not imagine why this spirit of the waiting-room would prevail even under fire.

While I watched, there was another roar and shriek overhead as a demiculverin fired, and I saw a blur as the ten-pound shot plunged into the enemy mass and reaped a bloody path through its ranks. Pikes whipped in the air, and I saw arms and heads flailing as if they were saplings tossed by a tempest. More great gunshots followed, but I saw no strikes, possibly because most of the guns were firing at the enemy closest to them, the regiment to my left, and I could see but little of it through my little hole in the hedge.

The enemy line had been standing there long enough for Lipton's guns to reload. I had not thought this test of fire had gone on so long.

After the last of Lipton's battery had finished shattering the air, I heard a perfect racket of fire rising from the right, and I put my head farther into the hedge to try to discover what was happening. Such was the sea of gunsmoke that I could see very little, but at that moment trumpets blared, and drums rolled, and the rebel regiment on my right lurched forward, the flags dipping forward as if leaning into a great storm. The pikemen crossed the sward to the hedge in just a few seconds, and I could see the pikes dip to skewer anyone in the sunken road.

I pulled my head back and looked down the road, and I could

see our handgunners surging away from the attack, diving to safety through the hedge or running up the road toward me. There followed a pause as the rebels fought their way through the blackthorn and into the road, and then a clattering, thrashing din, as pikes and pollaxes and war hammers began to batter steel. The sight was horrifying, as the enemy struggled forward against the pikes stabbing down to pin them against the mud surface of the road. They had to fight their way between the pikes as if through a forest, and all the while shorten their own pikes to stab blindly up into the hedge. Our handgunners, crowded to the sides, fired point-blank into their flanks. It was like a scene from a giant abattoir, where hundreds of animals had been brought down chutes to slaughter at once, and a vast machinery of blades and death were unleashed on them. Yet the enemy came on, leaping and stumbling and falling into the sunken road, fighting their way forward until they were hacked and stabbed and pinned screaming to the mud, where they would drown in mere inches of bloody water.

I tore my eyes away from the scene and thrust my head again through my little hole in the hedge, for I could not believe that the regiment to my front would not charge to support its comrades. But still the enemy hung back, their front marked by a growing line of their fallen.

Then I heard a great cheer—*"Hur-rah, hur-rah, hur-rah. Howel! Howel! Howel!"*—and I turned to my left to see the enemy regiment on our left lumber forward into a charge. Roaring like madmen, they struck the hedge, and fought their way through the blackthorn as Bell's handgunners fled or hurled themselves through the friendly hedge to safety on the other side.

And then there was a great blow to my head, and I fell back into the road stunned. My ears rang like temple bells, and I found myself sprawled at the bottom of the road, foaming water rising to my mouth and nose. A terror of drowning seized me, and I gasped for breath as I struggled to my feet against the weight of my armor. My helmet had been knocked down across my forehead, and I could barely see; and so I wrenched the helmet off and saw then the bright crease on the crown where the bullet had struck me a glancing blow. Perhaps I'd been unlucky, or maybe an enemy had seen me peering through the hedge and taken aim with his hackbut.

I gasped for air and tried to calm the furious drumming of my heart. Bullets continued to fly overhead, clipping blackthorn twigs and last year's withered sloe, and it occurred to me to put my helmet back on.

The fighting to the left and right went on, men dying by the dozens in the sunken road. Ten-pound shot shredded the air overhead, and I heard them plunge into the enemy without any desire to peer again through the hedge and observe. That fire from Lipton's guns seems to have decided the commander of the regiment in the center, for suddenly there were trumpets and drums and roaring to our front, and Fludd turned away from the hedge with a mad gleam in his one eye.

"Back, my rampallions!" he cried. "The ill-faced cullions come, and bring their nut-hooks!"

I realized we were at last to be charged. I felt and new and desperate fear of being caught in the killing ground of the sunken road, and I turned to make my escape. Some tunnels had been cut into the hedges for just this purpose, and I was first to leap like a salmon for one of the openings. I crawled through on my belly, and then friendly hands seized my armpits, pulled me to safety, and then flung me down on the brown grass.

My face burning with cuts from the hedge-thorns, I crawled away past the forest of legs in my path, then rose to my feet. Handgunners were diving through the blackthorn with their calivers, and the roar to the front was increasing. I returned to the hedge to help draw the refugees through, pulling in one grinning soldier after another, until I grabbed the last and pulled, only to see hear his laugh turn to a shriek as he was stabbed from behind, a pike going up between his buttocks and through his bowels. I pulled him free but he left a bloody trail on the grass, and by that time the great clanging noise had gone up as the butchery in the road commenced.

I dragged the victim to safety, but his face was white and he was already unconscious, and I thought he had but moments to live. Images of the dead of Ethlebight came flooding into my mind, phantoms whose bloody aspect were strengthened by the shrieks and sounds of war. I reeled under the onslaught of remembered horror, and I realized I would go mad if I continued to stand there like a fool. I had to do something. So, I drew my sword and charged to war.

It was not an excess of courage that sent me to the slaughter, for I was driven on by fear, fear of being overtaken by my own terrors. The reality of the slaughterhouse was preferable to the phantoms of my own mind.

Battle wasn't hard to find. The blocks of pikemen had dissolved and spread across the entire front, and I ran to one area that seemed more lightly held than the rest, right on the boundary of the regiments of Fludd and Grace. I shouldered my way between pikemen till I came to the hedge and stabbed down with my sword at figures seen only dimly through the blackthorn. Thrusts came back at me, and I seized a pike and tried to cut at the hand that held it, but the blackthorn hedge itself repelled me. My sword lacked the length to reach the enemy, and all I could do was defend myself; and then one of the pikemen near me reeled back from a thrust that had gone through his armpit into his shoulder, and he dropped his weapon.

I caught the ash pole in my free hand. I thrust my sword into the turf, picked the pike up in both hands, and thrust it overhand at a barely seen enemy, almost hurling it. I felt the blade strike home, in who or what I do not know, and raised the pike to stab again. An enemy weapon grated against my breastplate, and I knocked it away with an elbow and thrust down at the man who held it. I felt the impact as the pike's twelve-inch steel blade drove through the rebel's cuirass, and the pike that had struck at me sagged from nerveless hands. To keep an enemy from using it against me, I seized it with one hand and threw it behind me.

The fighting went on, the pikemen hammering down into the sunken road while our handgunners ducked and dodged around us, firing into the enemy when they could. The sound around me was deafening, clattering and hammering and shouts and grunts and screams, and I could not hear when I struck something. I could rarely see the enemy for more than an instant, and though I could feel the impact when I struck them, I rarely knew whether I was hitting hand or foot or chest or shoulder, or whether I merely scraped the armor. As I kept on stabbing down, my untrained arms and shoulders grew tired, and I felt the breath sobbing in and out of my throat.

In time, the fighting died away. No one had called a halt, but the enemy had run out of soldiers willing to dive into the sunken road. Instead, the handgunners of both sides fired half-blind across the gap while our men jeered the rebels' cowardice, and I leaned on my pike and gasped with exhaustion, the sweat coursing down into my eyes. Eventually, the trumpets on the other side blew a retreat, and the enemy shouldered their weapons and marched away. Our handgunners leaped into the ditch and pursued them with shot, and then Lipton's guns began roaring at the retreating mass. Men swarmed into the ditch to loot the bodies.

I wished not to view this work, and began to think I should report to Lord Utterback; and so, I retrieved my sword, found my horse in the care of the boy to whom I had entrusted it, and rode to where I could see the blue flag still flying near the crossroads.

Silence had fallen over the field, though my ears still rang. It was strange to hear the thud of Phrenzy's hooves and the creaking of my leather saddle after the overwhelming noise of battle.

I found Utterback already in conference with Ruthven. "It will be an hour or more before the bastard Clayborne comes again," Ruthven said. "We should make the most of our time."

"Should I have the bands start playing again?" asked Lord Utterback. He was panting a little for breath, as if he'd run a hundred yards, and his eyes darted over the field, as if he were searching for something he could not find.

Ruthven raised his eyebrows. "Wherefore should the bands not play? Though I had in mind making sure the men had food and drink."

"Yes. Of course. An excellent idea."

Lord Utterback turned his horse and set off at once for the commissary, leaving a bemused Ruthven in his wake. I followed, along with the ensign and his flag. Utterback rode to the commissary and ordered a wagon loaded with biscuits and cheeses brought down to the field. From there we rode to the pond, where we waded our horses into the water and let them drink. Watering parties arrived from the regiments, men each carrying a dozen or more water bottles to be refilled, and so at least they had water.

I took off my helmet and rejoiced as the fresh air cooled the sweat that soaked my hair. I hadn't realized until I'd come up the slope how heavy was the murk of gunpowder below, and I joyfully filled my lungs with crisp, bracing air.

While the horses drank their fill, I reported to Lord Utterback of the fight on the left.

"Were our casualties heavy?" he asked.

"I don't think so," I said. "I think we did very well, and no one ran away."

"That's also what happened on the right." He nodded at me. "The dismounted dragoons hurt them badly, firing into their flank. That was a very fine idea of yours."

"They'll be ready for the dragoons, next time," I said. "We should try to think of a way to counter it."

We stopped by our camp at the stone huts for some biscuit, cheese, and a crock of goose-liver pâté. We each took another glass of brandy, and after we finished he took my arm.

"I know not what I'm doing," he said. "My mind is like an empty piece of paper, and I can't think what to write on it."

"You're doing very well," I told him. "No commander could do better."

I spoke with perfect truth, for I could not see aught we could do but what we were already doing. But he seemed not to credit my words.

"I wish I were anywhere but here," he said. His eyes stared into an abyss.

He went back to the lines, to speak to the commanders and congratulate the soldiers, and I returned to Lipton's battery, where I could best spy the enemy. As I rode up, Lipton walked out to meet me. There was a streak of gunpowder across his face.

"You've stopped shooting," I observed.

"The range is long," he said, "and the supply of powder and shot is limited. I can fire some more if you insist, but the results will be dubious." A grin broke across his powder-streaked face. "The shooting was fine while it lasted, sure. As a rule, after such rains as we have had, the shot would dig into the muddy ground when fired as we do from above, but the field falls away in the same degree as the course of the ball, and so we are knocking them down like lawn skittles." He offered me his glass. "As you can see."

I put the telescope to my eye, and I could see at once what he meant. Dead bodies were stretched out on the field in lines that seemed to radiate from the battery. The demiculverins were knocking them down six or eight at a time. The enemy regiment nearest the guns had suffered the most, but some of the guns at least had targeted the regiment in the center, with the result I had glimpsed from my position in the hedge.

I did not want to look at the bodies too closely, and I lowered the glass.

He laughed. "A heartening sight, is it not?"

I looked at where the enemy had stood, the lines of corpses stretching out where the artillery had found them, other rows of dead at the front of the pike formations where they had halted under fire.

"Why did they stand so long without charging?" I asked.

"Ah." His mouth twisted. "I think each coronel wanted one of the others to charge first, and watch how he fared. It was their first good look at our position, and none of them liked it." He gestured broadly with one hand. "They charged home first on our right. That was where the flank fire was galling them, and there they had to retreat or go ahead."

I put the glass to my eye again and looked farther down the sett. The disorganized mob of men that had withdrawn were sorting themselves out into their companies again. Behind them, dark masses of men stood unmoving beneath bright flags.

Time passed. I got off my horse and sat on the brown grass. The wagon of cheese and biscuits arrived for the soldiers, and later a wagon of beer. The bands played again. The great royal banner flew over the Carrociro. Lord Utterback progressed along the line, as he had before, and the soldiers cheered him when he told them how brave they were. The bright sun warmed me and made me drowsy, and the entire world seemed to be drowsing with me.

The drowse ended with motion at the far end of the field, and still sitting, I propped Lipton's glass on one raised knee and looked to see artillery coming up the lanes between the enemy soldiers. I rolled to my feet—the easiest way to rise in armor—and went in search of Lipton.

"Enemy guns," I said.

He took his glass, looked briefly, and called an order to his men. "Stand by your pieces!" Then he looked again, and frowned, and lowered his glass.

"Three batteries of demiculverins, and another battery of culverins. Those last are properly siege guns and will make things warm for us, sure, and so you may wish to stand apart."

"Can you defeat them?"

"I will try, but if those crews are trained members of my guild, most like I will have to run."

I looked at him in surprise. "Oh, ay," he said. "For what would you have, all of us killed at our stations, and for naught? We shall retire out of the enemy's sight, only to return later, when we are needed. Our guild rules permit this."

"Can you not bring up the horses and take the guns to safety?"

"Nay." He seemed amused. "Know you not that the Guild of Carters and Haulers is not obliged to endure the enemy's fire? They have placed our guns, and will retrieve them when the battle is over and the field is safe."

"And yet we pay them full guild rates? No wonder the expense of wars is so ruinous."

"I cannot speak against them. Guildsmen must stand together." Though he said it without conviction.

I mounted and rode to report to Lord Utterback, and before the words left my mouth, the first of Lipton's guns fired. It was the brave opening shot in an unequal contest, one that the rest of both armies could watch from their positions on the sidelines. For not another ten minutes had passed before the first of the enemy guns was firing, and soon solid shot was kicking up earth near Lipton's battery. I could foresee the inevitable outcome, and I clenched my teeth.

"Can these guns not be suppressed?" I asked.

Lord Utterback looked at me. "But how?" he said. "Our own guns are outnumbered."

"Rock-paper-scissors," I said, and leaving my horse with Utterback's party sought out Fludd and Colonel Grace. "Can we not send out our handgunners, and shoot us some of these gunners?"

"Those odious pizzle-brains have no supports," Fludd said. "Ay, we may pink 'em, to be sure."

"Presently, they are firing at our guns," said Grace. "Should they drive in the quoins and lower the barrels to aim at you, you must fly before they cut you up with hailshot."

I passed the word and spoke also to Ruthven and Bell, and all agreed to send their handgunners out under my direction. Captured armor and weapons, and those belonging to the wounded or the dead, lay on the grass behind the lines, and so I found a caliver for myself on the ground. I took a powder horn for priming, and a box with compartments for bullets and wads, put a bandoleer over my shoulder from which dangled the little wooden bottles holding a premeasured charge of powder, and placed myself with Fludd's men.

The hedge that stood between the road and the enemy had suffered in that first contest and, though it still stood as a considerable barrier to a louting great host of men, was porous enough to take a small number through at a time. Still, passing the hedge was the worst moment of all, for all the dead rebels, naked or stripped to their small-clothes, had been drawn out of the sunken road and left to lie before the hedge, both to get them out of the way and to deter the enemy, who would have to pass a host of their own dead before they could attack us.

I moved gingerly into the field of corpses and then froze in my tracks at the sight of a dead woman, stripped and flung out on the field with the rest. She was young, and I wondered what had brought her to this end, whether she had come for love of a man, love of adventure, or love of Clayborne. Whatever dream had brought her here, it was to end in her being stabbed in a muddy ditch by pikes, drowned in bloody water, and then flung naked on the winter grass.

One of the other handgunners brushed past me, and it broke the spell. I lifted my eyes ahead, to the rebel batteries, and kept them there as I walked through the field of dead. The enemy, standing by their guns two hundred fifty yards away, were wholly occupied with firing up at our battery, and furthermore the wind was still blowing their own powder-smoke in their faces, and so they did not see us as we loped toward them across the sward. Gunshot howled over our heads. At a hundred yards the hackbuts were laid in their rests and aimed, and the calivers brought to the shoulder. I raised my own caliver, blew on the match till it glowed red as a cherry, and peered along the smooth round surface of the barrel, to aim at an officer holding a telescope.

"Mark your men!" I called, but some were already firing, and so I pressed the trigger. The serpentine dropped into the pan, the powder ignited, and the caliver kicked like a donkey against my shoulder. I didn't see that officer again, but I doubt that it was I who hit him, as I had but little practice with shoulder weapons.

The scent of gunpowder clung to the back of my throat. I dropped the caliver's butt to the ground and reached for one of the little wooden powder bottles dangling from my bandoleer, then opened the bottle and poured the powder down the muzzle. The box for bullets had compartments for steel and lead shot, and because the gunners wore no armor, I chose a lead bullet and dropped it down the barrel, then rammed all down with a wad on top. After which I primed the pan and lifted again the weapon to my shoulder.

Being unused to the weapon, I was slow in reloading, and the other handgunners fired their second shots before me, and as they loaded again, they laughed and catcalled our targets, who crewed such mighty bronze weapons yet could not reply. The rebel gunners ran back and forth, shouting and conferring, and then I saw frantic gunners driving the quoins beneath the breeches of their guns, to push the barrels low to fire at us.

"One more shot!" I called. "Then back to the hedge!"

I fired my final shot and so far as I could tell did no execution, and then I set an example by moving away from the enemy, trotting backward while still facing the rebels, and as the others took their shots, they followed. Certainly, it was time to retire, as I saw the gunners driving into their long barrels the canvas bags of hailshot.

Once the whole mass began to retire, I turned and ran, waving my caliver overhead as a signal, and we all ran back whooping, and had overleaped the dead and were at the hedge before the first shots came after us, the hailshot making wild, wailing cries in the air. Hailshot is any kind of small iron stuff, musquet balls, small iron balls such as are fired by falconets, nails, wire, or simply odd pieces of iron cut up or broken, then stuffed in canvas bags. The sound this odd iron makes as it tumbles through the air is eerie, and it raised the hairs on my arms; but at this range, none of us were hurt, and we leaped laughing back into the sunken road, almost drunk with our adventure.

All this time Lipton's battery continued firing, the shot plunging among the enemy guns, and so we had bought him time, and had done harm to the batteries that would oppress him.

As for myself, I felt my heart afire in my chest, and my mind was alive to the possibilities inherent in the game of rock-paper-scissors. I wished I'd had the horsemen instead of the handgunners, for with a charge of our demilances I could have killed them all.

The rebel guns continued to fire at us, the weird, wailing hailshot clipping the leaves overhead. I felt in my exuberance that I was not done making mischief—I thanked the coronels who had let me use their men, and I joined Lord Utterback on the right. I reported to Utterback of my adventure, and told him what I intended to do next.

"Do you think that would prosper?" said he. "Well, go ahead."

Frere's dragoons were for the most part dismounted and in and around the east-west Peckside road, near the crossroads, ready with their bell-mouthed pistols to fire again into the flank of any attacker. Frere came with me as I took one company creeping down the road to the east, and we ended up right on the flank of the artillery line.

The enemy guns were still flailing the hedge with hailshot, and my heart lifted at the knowledge that they were not aware of their danger. "You lead this one company forward," Frere told me, "and I will have the other ready to support you."

As I and the first company bludgeoned our way through the thick-pleached blackthorn. I received more slashes on my face, and thorns even pierced the thick suede of my buff coat. I mopped away drops of blood from my cheeks, drew my sword, and led the dragoons, trotting in their heavy cavalry boots, across three hundred yards of ground toward the nearest battery.

We sped the distance so swiftly that we seemed to have taken wing, and suddenly we were there, the crew of the nearest culverin grouped around each to his task, the crew only beginning to become aware of us as the first fire from the dragons caught them. Some gunners fell, and other gunners stared at us in horror. Besides their inaccurate pistols, the dragoons were also armed with a miscellany of other weapons, hangers and bilbos, hammers and cuttles, and so without reloading, the dragoons drew these and ran at the enemy.

The surviving crew of the first gun broke and ran, and I dashed after them, and was then surprised to discover an enemy who had no intention of running. Instead, the gunner—a small, slight man my own age—had drawn his short sword and faced me with terror and determination warring for control of his features. I felt an alarm clatter in my blood.

I was running and could scarce slow down before I encountered him. I hacked at the sword that thrust at me and knocked it aside, and then I drove my armored chest straight at him. I was bigger, and stronger, and the armor added weight—there was an impact, and I knocked the man sprawling. I made a cut at him as I ran past, but I don't think I hit him. I imagine one of the dragoons behind me finished him off.

I ran on, slashing at the backs of the flying gunners, but as I ran, I tried my hardest to keep my wits. I was all too aware that we were outnumbered—my company, counting its casualties and without its horse-holders, numbered about forty, and the full complement of the battery was nearly a hundred. But we were in a group, and they were scattered among their guns and completely surprised, and so we overwhelmed them.

But I was also aware that an entire army was standing just a few hundred yards to the east of us, and that they would react once they perceived my small party through the drifting smoke. And so I kept an ear cocked for the sound of hooves, or trumpet calls, or drums, for once Clayborne's army began to move, we would have scant time to find safety.

While I listened, we overran the battery completely, cutting down anyone who tried to resist, and then ran in for the next set of guns, and now there was a pack of men in front of us, armed with short swords and their gunners' gear, the ladles and rammers and hand-spikes they used in their craft. I slowed in my career to allow the dra-goons a chance to catch up with me, so that we could attack in a mass. I took a few seconds to catch my breath, during which those who had not yet discharged their dragons took good aim and shot. Gunsmoke stained the air, men fell, and then I cried the dragoons on.

I ran right at center of the enemy, and I found myself facing a swordsman who stood in a balanced posture, knees flexed, his right arm before him cocked at an angle to direct his point at my breast, the left hand propped on his hip—the very posture that Lance-pesade Stringway had sought to instill in me during our long hours of prac-tice. And I knew, from the ease and confidence of the man's posture, and the impassivity of his features, that he was a far greater master of defense than I. And I knew as well, from the powder-stained white sash over one shoulder, that he was captain of the battery, and that his defeat might well dishearten his crews.

I slowed that I might not impale myself on his point, and brushed his sword aside as I came on. He retreated, back leg first, front leg after, and his blade came into line again in just the manner that

478 † WALTER JON WILLIAMS

Lance-pesade Stringway had recommended. Then I ducked as one of his gunners swung a rammer at my head, then took a step back to slice that gunner's arm to the elbow. The captain shuffled forward to thrust at me, and I beat his sword aside again and foined at him, then had to jump clear at a lightning riposte aimed at my throat. My heart leaped, but my enemy had in the next instant to parry a tompion that one of the dragoons had thrown at him, and before he could bring the sword back into line, I seized the enemy blade in my gauntleted hand, and stepped in to smash him in the face with the basket hilt of my sword. The impact went all the way to my shoulder. As he staggered, I hacked him in the head with all my strength, which brought him down dead or dying—for this was not a fencing match, but earnest combat, with fights broiling up all around us, and I using my sword as a bludgeon rather than a weapon of art. The enemy captain's tactics were too dainty for this field.

When their captain fell, the gunners ran, and we cut half of them down as they turned. I plodded after, for my wind was gone and I could no longer keep up such a racking pace; and it was well that I did, for soon I saw that the enemy had turned one of their culverins about, and were crowing it around with handspikes to lay it on us. I saw the gun-captain with his linstock and match hovering over the touch-hole, and I saw an intent look blaze up in his face.

"'Ware the gun!" I shouted, and darted as fast as I could to the side while ducking my head so that the bill of my helmet should cover my face. The gun roared—spat in my eye, it seemed—and I was punched in the left shoulder while the eerie wail of hailshot fouled the air. Two escaping gunners in front of me blazed up in showers of scarlet, killed by their own side.

We were too close, and the hailshot had not the room to disperse.

"Charge!" I called. "Charge, charge, charge!" I ran for the battery before they could reload, and the dragoons followed and slashed the gunners down.

But then my half-deafened ears heard a trumpet call, and I looked eastward to see plumes bobbing as cavalry advanced through the thinning gunsmoke.

"Retreat! Retreat! Follow me!"

Two of the dragoons had been wounded by the hailshot, and their fellows picked them up and helped them from the field. Frere and the other dragoons were by now too far away, and so I led the dragoons directly toward the hedge, two hundred and fifty long yards away.

We ran. Even the wounded ran. I had been out of breath in the enemy battery, exhausted with chasing down the fleeing enemy, but when the air began to rumble with the sound of approaching horses, my weariness vanished, and I felt uplifted as if by great invisible wings. The hedge grew nearer, the hoofbeats louder, and I ran all the faster. Handgunners in the hedge fired, mostly on the flanks where we were not in the way. I dared to cast a look over my shoulder, and I saw a demilance right behind me, a towering figure in armor with his straight sword aimed at my vitals. I dodged first to the right, and then to the left, so that his horse's own neck would be in the way of the rebel's blade, and the rider would have to shift his sword up for a backhand cut. I did not give him the time, for as I ran, I flung out my own backhand to slash his horse in the mouth. The horse shrieked and turned away to the right, confirming all my prejudices against horses, and the horseman lost his seat and slid down his mount's flank to strike the turf with a great clatter.

I wished I'd had time to finish him off, for I found his attempt to kill me a great offense. Instead, I just ran the faster, the hedge ahead of me blossoming with gunsmoke as the handgunners picked their targets. Bullets whirred past me, and behind I heard the cries of wounded men and injured horses. Then I was leaping over the enemy corpses stretched before the hedge, and the blackthorn whipped my face as I leaped into the sunken road.

"Lovely work, my beautiful assassins!" cried Coronel Fludd. "Pilgrim save us, but you have dealt a great knock to those soulless mechanicals!"

My knees were suddenly weak, and I leaned against the far wall of the road as the dragoons tumbled into the road around me. My heart felt as if it would burst, and my chest heaved inside my unfeeling cuirass. On the far side of the hedge I could hear and glimpse the cavalry reining up, in wrath and confusion. They milled about for a time, firing their pistols at us while the handgunners pot-shotted them, until in frustration they withdrew, leaving a score of their number lying on the field.

"My braves, that was a thing of glory!" rejoiced Fludd. "Never again will I view the dragoons as an ungainly chimera, neither one thing nor 't'other, but instead will clasp them by the neck and call them 'brother.'"

We had lost not a man, though some suffered wounds. After I recovered my strength, I led them down the sunken road to the crossroads, where Lord Utterback waited with Captain Frere. I returned to Frere his men, and praised them all as heroes.

"Are you hurt?" Lord Utterback asked me.

I'd had so much to occupy my attention that this question had not yet occurred to me, but upon inspection, I proved to be largely intact. There was a sharp pain in my left shoulder when I tried to move my arm, and my face seemed somehow constrained, as if someone had stitched up bits of my flesh that did not quite belong together.

"I seem sound enough, my lord," I reported.

"Your face is bleeding," said Utterback. I touched my face gingerly, and my gloved fingers came back scarlet. "Here," said Utterback, and very courteously handed me a handkerchief.

I dabbed at my face. "You look quite the old soldier now," Utterback said. "Bleeding, streaked with powder, and battered armor and helm."

It would seem churlish to point out that my face had been cut by the hedge, not by the enemy. Now that the high excitement was over, I had begun to feel battered indeed. My entire body ached. Captain Frere fingered the dent in my cuirass. "You should go to the armorers," he said. "Have this beaten out."

I looked at the dent and realized that the bent metal was digging into my left shoulder and restricting movement. I looked up at Lord Utterback.

"Can you spare me for the while, my lord?"

Frere spoke first. "It will be some while before there is fighting. He may as well go."

Lord Utterback gave permission, and I wearily climbed atop my horse and rode to the rear, where the armorers and farriers had set up their anvils. I was delighted to relieve myself of the weight of the cuirass, and I threw off as well the buff coat and doublet and stood in my shirtsleeves to let the mountain breeze dry off the clammy sweat that had soaked my linen. The armorers had broached a cask of barley wine which they were willing to share, and while I waited I drank at least three pints, and so spirited and high-fettled was my constitution at that moment that I felt no intoxication at all.

The repair did not take long, and so I reluctantly dragged on the buff coat and let the armorers strap the cuirass over it, and then returned to the war. I stopped along the way at Lord Utterback's camp by the stone huts, and devoured another pâté, scooping it up with hard bread and wishing I'd had more barley wine to accompany it.

During this entire time, the guns continued their work. I had overrun only two of the rebels' five batteries, and the rest had continued their duel with Lipton uninterrupted, if a bit shorthanded after my attack with the handgunners. I had been unable to damage the guns or other gear of the batteries I had captured, and they had been reoccupied as soon as we'd been forced to withdraw. Eventually, all five batteries were back in operation, though only a few guns were firing from the batteries that I had taken, and their fire was slow. Lipton seemed to have dismounted a couple of enemy guns, but their crews were detailed elsewhere, and the fire kept up uninterrupted.

Despite the damage I had done to the enemy, the numbers told. Lipton fought on until a dozen of his men were killed and one of his guns was dismounted, but then he withdrew, and he carried his flag from the field to make it clear to all that he had abandoned his battery. Enemy jeers wafted up from the field, and the gun barrels were lowered to begin firing into our men behind the hedge.

At this point I rode down to rejoin Lord Utterback, thinking I might be needed. He looked at me as I rode up. "We are about to have some pounding, I fear."

"The men in the road will be safe," I said. "But the pikemen standing behind may suffer."

"I fear so."

His fears were proved at that instant, as one of the enemy's batteries opened their fire, and I saw a ball plow through one of Bell's companies on our left, bodies and pikes flying. It struck me as a purposeless sacrifice, and I turned to Utterback.

"Why should they stand and receive the enemy's fire to no purpose? May we not have them lie down?"

Lord Utterback seemed surprised by the question. "It is not the custom," he said. "Our men take heart when they can see the enemy."

"They can see nothing, standing behind the hedge. They only know they are being killed by something they cannot fight."

Lord Utterback considered the matter, then flapped a hand. "The men may lie down."

I rode to each regiment in turn to give the order. In this I met some resistance, as many of the men—and all of the officers—considered it best to stand in the face of peril and bid defiance to the enemy. But the shot, howling through the air and beating down the hedge, made them reconsider, and in time the entire line was stretched upon the turf, and the reserve companies as well. I also bade the bands to play, as a way to keep the soldiers' minds from descending too far into a contemplation of their own mortality, and I told the standard-bearers and their escorts, who could not lie down without neglecting their duty, to march about, so as not to become stationary targets.

After seeing the order obeyed, I rode up to Lipton's abandoned battery, where I could see the whole field, and found there the captain himself with a few men, quietly loading the demiculverins one by one and training them down on the field. "'Twill save a few minutes when we return," he said.

"You are a practical fellow," I said.

"And so you are, sure. With my glass I saw you leading those attacks. It was fine work, and you saved many of my men."

"You're welcome," I said. I smiled. "Rock-paper-scissors."

He gave a weary laugh. "Never before has anyone listened to, let alone profited by, my ramblings."

I looked down at the field, the guns firing out of a pall of their own smoke, the iron shot bounding over the field, lofting higher than a man. "If you can ramble us out of this fight," I said, "I will buy you another bottle of claret."

The rebel artillery continued their barrage, the shot bashing its way through the hedge and for the most part flying far over the heads of the soldiers. The hedge suffered, but little blood was spilled. Deep in the pall of gunsmoke I could see movement, and deployed my cardboard telescope—I saw that the cavalry supporting the guns was being withdrawn, and their place taken by solid blocks of foot soldiers. The same regiments, I thought, that had attacked the line last time.

We were well into the afternoon when the guns fell silent—not all at once, but slowly, as they exhausted their ready ammunition. There was silence, and then the foot broke their formations and began to filter forward through the guns, to re-form on the other side.

It was worth informing Lord Utterback of this, so I spurred down the scales, and as I rode, Lipton called his men to the guns and opened fire, his shot plunging down into the thick hedges of forming pikes, creating bloody ripples in the swelling sea of enemy bodies. I found Lord Utterback aware of the enemy movement, and he bade me tell the soldiers to rise and prepare to repel a charge. This I did, riding down the line, but the regimental commanders had seen the enemy preparing to come on and had anticipated me.

Nor did the enemy wait long. There was a great roll of drums and blare of trumpets, and hundreds of male voices cried, "Hurrah, hurrah, hurrah, *the King!*," cheering the infant that Clayborne had placed upon the throne. This cheer was repeated thrice, and then the pikes came on.

They did not pause, as they had before, but charged straight in, the first four lines of pikemen with their weapons leveled at the charge. Our own handgunners had a chance to fire but a single shot before they were forced to fly from the sunken road. The rebel regiment on our right, receiving flanking fire from the dragoons behind the hedge on the Peckside road, shied away and sidled toward the center, but elsewhere the enemy hurled themselves through the hedge and into the road and slaughter.

It was a repetition of the first attack, but this time the enemy were more determined, and the fight went on longer, the sunken road filling with blood and bodies. I did not participate this time, but followed Lord Utterback's example and rode behind the lines, shouting encouragement.

The attackers on the right failed first, caught between our spears to the front and a hail of flanking fire, and they began to grudgingly give way, and the other regiments followed their example, their pikes dragging on the ground as they backed from the fight. We cheered then, our drums beating and our trumpets blaring out Lord Utterback's tucket while Lipton's guns saluted their withdrawal with murderous iron shot.

His lordship and I rode up the field to look over the hedges and spy what the enemy next intended. The foot withdrew past the guns, drifting into the gaps between new enemy columns that were coming on. These were cavalry, and as I watched them deploy behind the guns, they formed into a long, shimmering wall of steel.

I heard Utterback give a cry of something that might have been surprise, yet may have been despair. "It is the Gendarmes," he said.

The Gentlemen-at-Arms of the Royal Household, familiarly the "Gendarmes," were men of good family sworn to guard the sovereign, the knightly equivalent of the Yeoman Archers, and who had joined Clayborne's rebellion at the behest of Lord Rufus Glanford, their general. They were encased in steel cap-a-pie, all polished to a perfect gleam, and they rode enormous horses who were themselves plated in proof. From their lances floated pennons, each bearing the device of the rider, and they wore brave cloaks of leopard or lion skin.

Lipton's artillery began to fire, but the Gendarmes were not so thickly packed as those deep squares of pikemen, and if he struck them, I failed to see it.

I stared at the enemy. These Gendarmes were impressive, pricking along under their banners, but I found myself clinging to a degree of skepticism.

"Surely these are relics of a former time," I said. "Playing at being knights of old, like the Court of the Teazel Bird at home."

A sardonic smile played about Utterback's lips. "You may so inform *them*, if you like."

"But," I protested, "but it's rock-paper-scissors. Cavalry cannot attack our pikes."

"Again," said Utterback, "it is the Gendarmes themselves whose knowledge of this point seems to be deficient." He looked down at our soldiers, and sadness touched his expression. "I wish our men were not so tired."

"We should tell them to be prepared to receive cavalry," I said. I was about to spur down the scales to our men, but another thought occurred to me, and I turned to Utterback.

"If they break through," I said, "you must lead our own horse against them."

He looked uneasily over his shoulder, far up the sett to where our demilances had rallied. "Ay," he said. "I'll have to do that."

The Gendarmes were coming forward, breaking ranks, like the pikemen, to filter through the artillery, then re-forming on the other side. Lipton's fire kept plunging down, and this time I saw horses and riders fly. Lord Utterback and I rode down to the line to tell them what was coming.

"They send their horse against us!" Utterback scorned. "We'll turn the road into their grave, and the hedge their monument!"

In this business of raising the heart of the soldiers, it has to be said he did well.

The pikemen, who had been engaged in looting the enemy dead, clambered out of the road and readied their long spears. I rode to the far right to warn both Ruthven and Frere that Frere's dragoons might soon have to take shelter behind Ruthven's pikes. For I had seen the enemy begin to stretch out to the far right, beyond the Peckside road, and the dragoons were unlikely this time to have their unmolested flank shots into the enemy.

Frere pulled out his spyglass, and looked at the horsemen forming up opposite his men. "Ah," he said. "The Esquires."

The Esquires were the servants to the Gendarmes and apprentice knights, as well-born as the latter. The riders were fully armored, but their horses lacked the barding that protected them against shot and spear.

Two full regiments now opposed us, the Gendarmes and the Esquires, each of two squadrons composed of two troops. We had three troops to oppose them, none as well armored, and the dragoons having no protection but their buff coats, and their dragons a dubious weapon at best.

"I'll bring my men back," Frere decided. "No vantage in getting 'em skewered."

The dragoons were happy to leave the sunken lane that was no longer a sanctuary, and they retired behind Ruthven's pikemen, where the horse-holders had been stationed with their mounts. Frere had them in the saddle just as the trumpets blared, and sixteen hundred elite rebel horsemen began their advance in their shining, blinding armor, the Gendarmes in the center, and flanked by the two squadrons of Esquires.

The earth shook to the trampling hooves, and hackbuts and calivers cracked from the hedges. The handgunners leaped to safety just as the big horses broke through the torn hedge and plunged down into the sunken road. Again there rose that great hammering sound as steel met steel, but this time with the nightmare screams of horses added to the din.

On the far right, I was compelled to withdraw as the Esquires rode in to meet the company of pikes that had been standing, unmolested, since the battle began. The horsemen swarmed around the bristling square, jabbing with theirs lances or firing their pistols, while the foot fought grimly back, thrusting at the unprotected faces and chests of the horses while handgunners, sheltered in the square, shot into the mass of cavalry. I had worried that the Esquires would ride clear of the pikemen and attack our line from the rear, or ride on to plunder our camp; but Frere's dragoons, drawn up two hundred yards to the rear—and who probably looked more menacing than in fact they were—deterred any such adventures.

I rode on down the line to where Lord Utterback was shouting encouragement at the men. "Well struck! I saw that blow, there! Admirable!" As if he were cheering a game of bats-and-balls.

I rode ahead and added my own voice to the din. And then, mere yards in front of me, one of the Gendarmes broke out of the hedge, his red-eyed steed trumpeting a challenge as it heaved itself from the road in a clatter of armor. The rider swung a battle-hammer at the foot soldiers, who reeled away from the rider, or from the horse with its flashing iron-shod hooves. Spear-points flashed as they thrust at him, and either he dodged them or they skated off his steel. A pikeman dropped to the turf, his helmet crushed beneath the hammer's spike.

I felt my blood surge, and I drew my sword and dug my spurs into my courser, and the animal, responding to the neighing challenge of the rebel's stallion, leaped forward. We, Phrenzy and I, crashed into the enemy charger just behind the shoulder, all our combined weight driving into the enemy. The impact threw me forward over the saddle, but I managed to keep my seat. The rebel rider and his animal, wrapped in heavy steel, lurched to the side as the horse took a frantic step to regain its balance. The step missed. The great weight of the armor carried with it both horse and rider, and the two were dragged down like a mariner drawn into the sea by a siren. There was a vast crash, and Phrenzy made a leap, dainty as a dancer, to spring over the fallen foe.

The Gendarme was helpless now, trapped by the weight of steel and the great horse that pinned his leg. The pikemen closed in, drawing swords and daggers for the final act of butchery, and I rode on out of the press and turned about to view the line, and only then could I spare a moment for amazement, both at myself for what I had done, and at my horse for following my commands.

Fights between horsemen are won more by the spur than by the sword. I had known that—I had *heard* it, at least—but how had Phrenzy known it?

But I had little time to contemplate these mysteries, for in another part of the line I saw more armored horsemen breaking through the hedge and our line, and I rode for the nearest reserve company. They were a battered group, for they'd been pulled out of the line after having withstood two attacks, but they understood the gravity of the Gendarmes' breakthrough, and had already assumed a defensive formation, hedged in all directions with pikes.

"That way! That way! To your left!"

I did not lead them so much as drive them, but once in motion, they understood well enough what I intended, and pikes were lowered to the charge as the company came to close the gap through which the Gendarmes were vaulting. There was a crash as pikes met armor, and a steel-clad horse ran free as its master was lofted by pikes from the saddle and fell to his present doom. Pikemen swarmed the hedge and the passage swung shut, barring further entry.

But those Gendarmes who had already got through the hedge now turned to cut a new path for their comrades, and my company was beset front and rear. As the only defender on horseback, and outside the circuit of pikes, I found myself assailed and so I with a murmured apology to the horse, I slipped from the saddle and sought shelter within the company of foot. There I found my sword unable to reach the enemy, and sheathing it, found on the sward a pollaxe, and I picked it up only to feel its weight settle into my hands like an old lover. For a pollaxe was a weapon I'd wielded all my life, and I knew its usages as well as I knew the poems of Tarantua.

"Hold them! Hold them!" I cried as the horsemen swirled around us, and as one Gendarme fenced with his lance against a brace of pikes, I left the shelter of the company and swung the axe with all my strength, letting the haft slide through my top hand as the blade rose, until I held onto the very end of the shaft and the blade blurred through the air. The steel crescent on the end of the haft took the enemy in the armpit and sheared right through the armor. He gave a cry and dropped his lance, the blood already staining the shining steel of his armor as I drew my weapon back, and as he clutched at the wound with his free hand, one of the pikemen put the point of his weapon through the slit of his helmet and into his eye. The horse bounded away, its rider already a corpse, and I retired again into the safety of the formation.

I found two more opportunities to attack with the underarm strike, and succeeded once and missed cleanly the other; after which I realized the pollaxe was best used to hamstring the horses, slicing below the skirts of the armor; and so I brought a pair of enemy down, the giant noble horses lamed and destroyed by the weapon of a Butcher's apprentice.

Then I heard Lord Utterback's trumpet call, and on the echo of the tucket came another of the reserve companies led by Utterback beneath his blue flag, so that now the Gendarmes were caught between two lines of pikes. Some died, and the rest scattered. I saluted Lord Utterback from my place in the ranks, and he saw me and waved at me in the most pleasant, gentlemanly way, so strange to see on a battlefield.

The combat rattled on between the hedges for a time. A few more horsemen broke through, were hunted down or set to flight. In time, the fight reached a point of exhaustion, like a clock with its spring run down, and then the two sides glowered at each other while hand-gunners fired over the gap; and by and by, the Gendarmes and their Esquires drew back, and then rode their heavy, weary horses back the length of that long, sere field.

We were too tired to cheer. Behind the hedge, for the first time, I could see a long unbroken line of our own dead, and there was a steady swarm of wounded limping up the slope toward the tents of the surgeons. As I trudged with them, I feared we would not survive another attack.

I found my horse quietly grazing a hundred paces up the slope, and while I dragged myself after the beast, Lord Utterback came riding past, and as I mounted, he came riding back, and I joined him. I still had the pollaxe in hand.

"I've ordered up more food down to the men," he said.

"We have earned our dinner, to be sure."

He cocked an eye at me. "None of that blood is yours, I hope."

"Is my face bleeding again?"

"I can't tell what is bleeding exactly. But there is a good deal of scarlet on you. And on that poll-cutter of yours."

I took a mental inventory of my parts. "I seem reasonably intact. Though I am hungry and thirsty both, and if I may stop by our camp . . ."

"I think we may both spend a pleasant hour there, an Clayborne permits."

And so, we took off our armor and our buff coats and had more of the hard biscuit with preserved tongue and brawn, and slathered with the jelly and fat that by now we desperately craved. We opened a jar of pickles and a package of smoked sausages and a bottle of wine, and I ate ravenously, and Utterback with scarcely less appetite. I more than half expected that Clayborne would interrupt our feast with another attack, because he had little choice—he had staked the entire war on this march over Exton Pass, and if he failed here, he might be lost.

But Clayborne's men did not come, and I began to feel the wine dragging at my limbs, and my eyelids began to fall. But Utterback jumped to his feet.

"Once again I must cheer the soldiers," he said. "And my praise shall not be feigned."

"Truly," I said.

I put on my gear and rode up to Lipton's battery. The captain, drinking from a leather jack filled with what looked and scented like malmsey, greeted me.

"The enemy are doing nothing," he said, "and that suits Bill Lipton, Esquire."

"Long may they suit you thus," I said. I dropped off my horse and stuck my pollaxe in the ground. My entire body ached. When I viewed the enemy with my glass, I found nothing of note. The Gendarmes and Esquires were gathered in dispirited clumps, and I supposed they were done for the day. Some handgunners were thrown forward of the battery to protect it, but the cannoneers simply stood near their guns without firing. I suspected that the Guild of Carters and Haulers were resisting the idea of bringing up more powder and ammunition, or the reserve ammunition was caught so far back in the train that the road would have to be cleared ahead of it before it could come up.

Seeing nothing worthy of my attention, I dropped my armor and burgonet to the ground, took off my buff coat, and sat on the turf with my glass to my hand.

Now, sated, my worn body and exhausted mind could afford the luxury of emotion, and as I observed our poor battered soldiers clustered about their dinner, or tending their injured, the feeling that rose in me was disgust. What was Queen Berlauda to me, or to any of these people? What was Clayborne, or his ambitious mother? Who were they to bring about the ignoble death of thousands, death by gunshot, or pike-thrust, or by the surgeon's knife, or by drowning in the sunken road?

And who, for that matter, was I? My own ambition had brought to here, to this killing-place, and all my cleverness had accomplished was to add to the great accounting of the dead. That we had killed more of the enemy than they of us made little difference to the worms that would consume the bodies.

If I possessed true wit, I would be bent over my law-books in Selford.

The world seemed to whirl before my eyes, and I remembered Orlanda's words: *Love you will have, but it will thrive only in the shadow of death, and the grave will be its end.* I wondered if I would find my end here, and lie rotting beneath the turf of Exton Scales while the sheep cropped the grass above my eyeless head.

Weariness took me, and I stretched out on the ground, measuring myself perhaps for my grave.

"Let me know if aught occurs," I said.

"Why should *I* stay awake?" Lipton said. I did not answer him, but closed my eyes.

Hours passed. The sun was hanging low over Exton Pass by the time Lipton nudged me awake with his foot.

"Lo," he said. "The ill-fledged didappers come."

I could hear drums rattling over the sett. Lipton offered his telescope, and I saw masses of men moving forward, pikes aloft and shining in the setting sun as they arranged themselves behind the enemy guns.

I felt soreness in every limb as I donned my armor again, and the burgonet settled on my head like a permanent headache. The plates that covered the back of my neck clanked as they fell into place. I returned Lipton's glass and mounted my horse.

"Do them mischief if you can," I said, but his gunners were already busy laying guns on the enemy.

"At this range," Lipton said, with something approaching cheer, "they can see the balls coming at 'em, and it's most diverting to see them jump about."

Again I reported to Lord Utterback what he already knew perfectly well, and so we went up the scales to have a better view of the enemy. More and more men kept coming onto the field, and I saw no less than six regiments formed against us, nearly a solid block of pikes that stretched from the bluff on the north to the ravine on the south. Lipton began to fire, and indeed the enemy tried to dance away from the falling shot, and I could hear the sergeants-major bawling at them to stay in line.

"I must fight them," Utterback murmured. "I must hold here." He was giving orders to himself, and behind his eyes I could see the cogwheels of his mind spinning free, unable to find or hold or turn an idea. For he was unable to think of a way to save his army from the attack that was to come, and I, similarly bereft, could not help him.

I touched his arm. "It will be the same as before. We must hold out till night, and the sun is already setting."

"Ay," he said. "Ay, we must fight." And shaking off my arm, he rode down to the crossroads, and there we awaited the onset.

The field was in shadow by the time the enemy made their assault, but even though we were in twilight, the sky above remained a brilliant, cloudless blue, as if reflecting the majesty of an unseen god, and we were wrangling with the enemy in the great cockpit of heaven. The enemy thrice intoned their battle-cry, "Hurrah, hurrah, hurrah, *the King!*" and then the pikes came down and the great mass of men swung forward. Again our handgunners got off but a single shot before the enemy were in the ditch, and wading across that river of corpses that awaited them in the sunken road. Again the clamor rose, as steel met steel, or pike-haft clattered against pike-haft, or blade plunged into flesh, and men staggered away from the fight screaming and clutching their vitals.

Our line was breached on the left, and I rode out to bring up a reserve company and seal the rift, but the truth was that we were in danger everywhere. Our men were worn down by their long day, and they were too few.

The enemy's first true success was on the far right, where Ruthven's pikemen broke and fled. Frere's dragoons fired into the advancing enemy from the saddle, but could not stop the advance, and the dragoons fell back. Under pressure from the right, our whole line peeled away from the hedge and staggered back as the enemy cheered and came on. Drums beat, trumpets called, and I saw Lord Utterback, beneath his blue flag, galloping up the slope ahead of a thicket of pursuing pikes.

He has left us behind again, I thought. Well, he could scarcely do aught else.

I managed to rally our soldiers at the foot of the knoll just below Lipton's guns, and there we held on while the demiculverins fired their balls right over our heads. The field before us was filled with enemy troops swarming up the slope toward our camp, their eyes alight with the prospect of plunder. Few of the enemy seemed interested in fighting those of us clustered below the guns, not when there was loot to be found in the camp; but some of the enemy officers raced over the darkening field, trying to maneuver unwieldy formations of pikes so as to assault us from front and flank. These bulky squares suffered greatly from the fire of Lipton's guns, but those before us managed their change of front, and I saw the first ranks of pikes come down to the charge as they readied themselves for an attack.

"Ready, men!" I had shouted myself hoarse. "Hold them! Hold on till nightfall!"

Trumpets called, and I readied myself to dismount and fight on foot with my pollaxe. The earth rumbled, and I rose in the stirrups and readied one leg to kick over Phrenzy's back and drop to the earth, and suddenly I saw Utterback's blue flag again, this time coming *down* the slope, and behind him Utterback's Troop, a long dark line of dire troopers riding out of shadow, their long, straight swords pointed at the enemy. Captain Lipton had been wrong, and our horse were game for a second charge.

Clayborne's men had no chance, for in their triumph and their greed to get to our camp, they'd broken ranks, and they turned and ran and died howling. The enemy formations preparing to charge my position were barely aware of the approach of danger before the horsemen struck them in flank and rear, and their formation dissolved into a mob, hundreds strong, all clawing at each other in panic as they fled back across the sett.

"Hurrah for Lord Utterback!" I shouted. "Cheer, you tawdry knaves!"

As we cheered, Lord Utterback's advance continued, and left a trail of sprawled corpses behind. Utterback pushed the enemy all the way back to the tattered blackthorn hedge, and then as the enemy flight continued, our troopers crossed the road, re-formed, and pressed their advance. Behind came Lord Barkin with his own troop cantering over the grass, ready either to throw himself at the enemy, or to be a firm wall for Utterback to rally behind.

Lipton's guns fell silent, for in the growing darkness he could no longer see an enemy to fire at. Frere's dragoons, obscured by the falling twilight, advanced on the far right, and then drawing their miscellaneous cutlery hurled themselves against the enemy's flank and broke them decisively. A great distant roaring, like the tumult and thunder of a furious ocean, sounded across the field, as the thousands of fleeing pikemen overwhelmed their supports, and the entire mass of Clayborne's army was thrown into confusion, despair, and terror.

"Back to the hedge!" I shouted, and waved my pollaxe overhead. "Re-form our line! We shall advance."

Drums beating, we crossed the hedge and the road filled with dead and dying, and re-formed again on the far side. We advanced to the enemy battery, which we found deserted. There was no reason to stop there, and so we marched forward into the growing night, our banners turning black against the shrouded sky. On the ground we found nothing but corpses, some wounded trying to crawl to safety, and abandoned standards dropped by their bearers. We collected the banners as trophies, and ere long we found the Carrociro, the cart and its white oxen abandoned, the royal banner flapping listlessly overhead. I dismounted and lowered the flag, and rolling it up, tied it over my shoulder. With its heavy silk, gold thread, and bullion fringe, the standard was a weighty mass, and must have neared twenty pounds.

Captured guns and standards, the two marks of a victory. We had both in plenty.

We marched on in silence, half a league or more, as the world darkened around us. The road turned to the right and the sett narrowed. The hedge dwindled away to a few unkempt blackthorns standing alone by the road, and the pasture gave way to scrub and falls of gravel from the cliff above. Stars appeared overhead, and in their uncertain light we discovered our cavalry madly engaged in looting the enemy train. Abandoned wagons stood crowded on the road, a line of vehicles that stretched on for a league or more, all abandoned by the teamsters, quartermasters, and camp followers who had brought them to the field. All I could see was our troopers, hundreds of them, plundering the train of everything they could find.

No officers recalled the men to their duty, for the officers led the looting. And no sooner had the foot soldiers seen what was toward, than they broke ranks and ran to seize their share of the booty. I soon found myself commanding nothing at all.

I rode along the train, asking for Lord Utterback. Half the men were already drunk of wine or spirits looted from the train, and these barely understood my words. Some ill-tempered louts threatened me with violence; and the rest had no answer to my question. I wondered if Utterback had simply ridden on, so centered on the pursuit that he left his whole army behind, a possibility that did not seen entirely out of character. At last I found an old Lance-pesade, so drunk that he had to be supported by a wagon wheel, who waved an arm in the direction I had come.

"There, in the field where it narrows. Though you will not like what you find."

"What mean you by that?"

He gave me a scornful look. "I mean what I mean. I am not a man to teach a babe to suck his mammy's tit, nor a jackass to ride a pony."

In a temper, I wrenched Phrenzy around and returned the way I had come. By now, the moon had come up and cast its opal light on the field. I reined up, seeing nothing but bodies lying dark on the sere grass, and then I saw the moon glimmer on Lord Utterback's flag, which was planted in the ground near the foot of the cliff to the northeast. There I saw two horses standing, and recognized one as Utterback's courser; and as I came close I saw Purefoy, the ensign, bent weeping over the body of our Captain General.

I dropped to the ground and looked at Lord Utterback's face shining pale in the moonlight, his eyes closed, his expression suggesting that he had already accommodated himself to the demands of Necessity. I pulled off Utterback's glove, took his hand, and found it already cold. Between sobs the ensign told me that there, where the way narrowed, the flying enemy had slowed and grown close-packed, so terrified and helpless that the pursuers' arms and shoulders ached with the trouble of killing them; and that but few tried to resist, but one of these had fired a pistol and shot Lord Utterback in the throat. Utterback, choking, had then ridden madly through the press to this place of partial shelter, and here pitched out of his saddle dead. Purefoy had stayed by the body to prevent it from being looted by the baying mob that had once been our army.

Still holding Lord Utterback's hand, I sat by the body and tried to think what to do. The army was beyond control and would continue their riot all night. In the morning, a reveille might be possible.

In the meantime, the body might as well stay where it was.

Then I remembered Lipton's battery, left behind on its knoll, and thought that we might fetch Lord Utterback back to the camp on a caisson. I told Purefoy of my intention, and then I took the heavy royal flag from over my shoulder, unrolled it, and placed it on the body. I mounted again my horse, and began the long ride through the night.

I had ridden only a few minutes before I heard the pounding of advancing horses, and drew up to see a column of demilances riding in by moonlight. Our relief had come at last, exhausted men on weary horses. As they approached, I saw at the head of the column the Count of Wenlock. As he halted the column, I rode up and saluted.

His eyes glittered with what might have been anger, what might have been fierce anxiety. "Where is my son?" he asked.

"He fell as he led the last charge that broke Clayborne's army," I said. "He lies yonder, at the foot of the cliff."

"Bring me to him," said Wenlock.

I brought Wenlock to where his son lay, and we dismounted. The count looked down at the body, then bent to draw the flag away from the corpse.

"It is the royal banner," said I, "taken from the Carrociro. I thought it a fitting shroud for so brave a man."

I watched as lines of grief carved deep into Wenlock's hawk-like profile. He seemed lost for a moment in his own sorrow, and then he gave a start, as if he recollected where he was. He looked up at me, eyes glittering.

"My son needs you no longer," he said. "You are dismissed from the troop. And if I find that you have stolen aught from the troop's funds, I will slit your throat myself."

CHAPTER THIRTY-ONE

S o ended the Battle of Exton Scales, which concluded Clayborne's hopes to rule a kingdom. I was dismissed, and by next morning, Utterback's Troop had ceased to exist, and was amalgamated with that of Lord Barkin. Barkin was sympathetic, but already had a secretary, who was busy calculating his share of the loot.

I had failed to gather any loot for myself, and now would get none.

By next morning, the principal rebels were in our hands. The Knight Marshal had received our message just as he was about to launch his attack on Peckside, and he saw no sense in wasting his dispositions—he smashed his way through the entrenchments, and broke the enemy there in a single grand assault. Wenlock, the cavalry, and the reserves were turned about and sent to Exton Scales, but arrived far too late. So, when Clayborne's army fled from us, they ran right into the Knight Marshal's hands.

Clayborne; his stepfather, the Duke of Andrian; Lord Rufus Glanford; and the other leaders were executed as soon as the Marshal could call for a headsman. Queen Berlauda, who had no intention of forgiving her half brother or his supporters, had signed the death warrants in advance. The only chief rebel to escape was Clayborne's mother, the Countess of Tern, who we later learned had fled to Thurnmark.

Those not named in the warrants were made prisoner, except for the mercenaries Clayborne had employed. The mercenaries of both sides had insisted on their standard contract, which stated that any mercenaries on the losing side—whichever that was—were to be given their liberty, and so those who had fought for Clayborne were allowed to march back to Howel with our army, carrying their weapons and such gear as had survived the looting.

Even professional soldiers, it seemed, were obliged to follow the rules of their guild. All the sell-swords stood to lose was whatever monies Clayborne owed them.

I stayed with the army, but as Lord Utterback no longer provided a means of entry to the higher class of officer, I rode for the most part with Captain Lipton and the Cannoneers. These were good company, and as the April skies had ceased to spit rain at us, it was a pleasant journey, descending the Cordillerie now into the high, watery plateau that sheltered the winter capital.

A delegation from Howel offered the Knight Marshal the submission of the city several days before he arrived, which provided Lipton and me with an idea. We knew the names of the proscribed rebels, and so he and I and a few Cannoneers rode ahead of the army, past the famous water-gardens of the palace, to the capital, where we marched into the house of Baron Havre-le-Creag, told the servants that we were now billeted in the home, and ordered them to bring us dinner and wine.

The Baron, who had been executed for treason following the battle, could scarcely object.

Water-girdled Howel is a beautiful city, with its canals, fountains, bridges, and its stately, well-proportioned buildings of golden sandstone, and for a few days, that city belonged to us. There had been a great fire sixty years before, and most of the old city burned. It had been rebuilt on a more spacious plan, with wide streets, plane trees set along boulevards, and green lawns that went down to the river.

The royal palace at Ings Magna is three leagues northwest of the city, across the lake, and the high nobility have lined the road along the lake with their homes, one imposing structure after another, each with a lawn along the river and a structure to house a grand galley, so that they could be rowed to the palace by a crew of oarsmen in livery. The house of Baron Havre-le-Creag was one of these.

From our billets we went wherever we pleased with our list of the proscribed, demanded entry to the great houses, and carried off whatever we liked—coin, plate, silken hangings, jewels. If we found a strongbox, we broke it open and took what we found. I was the only one of us interested in the papers we unearthed, and I discovered myself the owner of several deeds and a number of loans and mortgages.

Officers may fight for glory or advancement, but ordinary soldiers fight for money. Wenlock had demoted me to the status of an ordinary soldier, and I felt a perfect right, indeed a duty, to fill my pockets.

We left alone the Duke of Roundsilver's fine house a short distance from Havre-le-Creag's residence. It was easy to discover his grace's house, for it had been faced with brilliant Ethlebight brick in a rainbow of colors. I wanted to go into the duke's cabinet and discover what curiosities he might keep there, but I decided it might be best to wait for an invitation.

When the Knight Marshal entered the city, the official and organized looting began. Military patrols marched up and down the street, homes of the proscribed were put under guard, and clerks began inventories of the possessions of the proscribed. Some of the loot would be awarded to the Knight Marshal, and the properties to Berlauda's supporters, but most of it would go to the Crown, to help pay for the war. Our own goods were carefully hidden from the confiscating officers.

Our house now became the headquarters of the artillery, and we put a placard on the door to that effect. When other soldiers were assigned to our house by the billeting officers, we told them the house was ours, and they should find another. No one challenged us. We ate and drank well on the late baron's largesse.

The heads of Clayborne, Andrian, and the rest were set up on pikes before the Hall of Justice, and my travels took me there one day. I looked up at Clayborne's handsome head, its glossy dark hair falling about its ears, and wondered about ambition and its limits, whether Clayborne or his supporters had ever concerned themselves with the human coin they spent, the men whose lives they were to throw away on Exton Scales in their last wager against Berlauda's army.

I thought the heads would soon have company. The Knight Marshal pursued not merely loot and property, for he also sought out Clayborne's adherents, and anyone who had sworn him an oath of allegiance or served him in any way. Those who had voted for his laws in the Estates were also in jeopardy, and it did not take long for the cells at the Hall of Justice to fill with Clayborne's friends. The remains of Clayborne's army were held in the old stadium across the river from town, awaiting Berlauda's judgment.

And as for Queen Laurel and her purported child, the infant crowned Emelin VI, not a word was spoken, and nothing was known. They were believed to have been under guard in the palace when the army marched in, but no one seemed to know anything about their fate.

April was dwindling to its close when a letter arrived for Baron Havre-le-Creag, which I was happy to take from the messenger. It stated that the baron's galleon *Constantia* had arrived at Bretlynton Head with a cargo of almond, pistachios, olive and safflower oil, and a small but valuable lading of precious myrrh, and that the master wished to know whether the cargo should be sold there, or carried somewhere else.

I was on the next barge down the Dordelle, on a boat which held a number of merchants and also, I suspect, a few refugees from the Queen's justice. Within a week, I sailed into the city of Bretlynton Head, with its castle on its scarp overlooking the bay, and set out in search of *Constantia* and its master.

I had the honor of being the first to inform Captain Newbolt that the ship-owner had been executed following unsuccessful rebellion, and that the ship and its cargo would soon be confiscated by the Crown, a sad and discouraging end to a ten-month voyage. Neither the ship nor its crew would realize a penny of profit, and Newbolt himself, though blameless, might find himself imprisoned.

His only option, I said, was to flee the city at once, before royal officers could arrive. "But unless you want to turn pirate," said I, "you should sail to Amberstone and say that you head a prize crew put aboard by the privateer *Meteor*. Report with the ship's papers to the prize court established at Ethlebight, along with a letter from me as part-owner of the privateering commission. And when the ship is condemned, you and the crew will receive your share."

"How big a share?" asked he.

So, we argued over that over the course of an hour, and in the end I wrote the letter, Newbolt took on a stock of fresh water, and was gone the next forenoon. I spent a few more days in Bretlynton Head, and acquainted myself with the city. It was in a near-lawless condition, for the Sea-Consuls who had pledged their allegiance to Clayborne had fled, the Warden of the Castle was nowhere to be found, and such aldermen as remained were not enough to establish a quorum. Privateers had been hovering off the coast for weeks, taking prizes, the news of which pleased me enormously. Eventually, I took passage back up the river. It was a slower journey, and I enjoyed the view, sitting on the foredeck with my copy of Bello's *Epics*, the stately classical hexameters running through my head while I viewed the old robber-castles on their crags, the sheep in their pastures, the vineyards that ran down to the bank of the Dordelle, cherry- and apple-trees in blossom, the hills and mountains verdant with the new spring. Bonille well lived up to the promise of its false etymology, but by the end of the journey, I was burning to get off the boat and to my business ashore.

I arrived at Howel just ahead of Queen Berlauda, who was to make a grand entry into the city to meet with her lieutenants and review her army. The artillery were busy organizing a salute of gunfire, and the courtyard behind the baron's residence was now covered with the gunpowder that had suffered the separation of its elements on its journey to the capital, and was being remixed by hand. I preferred not to be blown up, and kept my distance.

I amused myself by viewing the sights. Bonille had once been a part of the Empire, and many old imperial structures still stood. Most were temples, but there was also an aqueduct that still functioned, a theater that held two thousand people, a basilica filled with shops, parts of the city wall, and a stadium across the river. I saw everything I could but avoided the stadium, for this was where Clayborne's army was being held under guard.

The day of the review came. The enormous guns that His Grace of Roundsilver had given to the Crown were deployed with the rest of the artillery in the grand review, and between those two enormous bronze weapons I sat on my savage horse Phrenzy, very martial in my battered armor. I lifted my sword to the salute as Berlauda rode by propped up in her carriage, her blond hair agleam in the May sunshine, her handsome face displaying its accustomed serenity. The Knight Marshal rode next to her, for once without his fur coat, and dressed in a brilliant outfit of sky blue, glittering with gems and silver thread. He had arrayed his lucky medallions all over his doublet, and no doubt thought himself very blessed to have had their protection. The tale in the army was that he would be made a marquess, and receive lands from the Duke of Andrian's domaine. Neither he nor the Queen betrayed any sign they had recognized me.

Berlauda's half sister Floria followed in the next carriage, along with a group of court ladies. The princess wore a gown of dark red, piped with the bright royal scarlet, and a scarlet cap tilted over one hazel eye. Her dark hair was braided atop her head. The eye passed over me, then snapped back to my face. She stood and craned toward me as the carriage moved past, her mouth open in surprise, and then she laughed and fell back into her seat, convulsed with mirth.

Doubtless, as she rolled away, she was gasping out a joke about frumenty.

The day after the review was Lord Utterback's grand memorial. The Count of Wenlock set up the hero's casket in the city's largest temple, with its fluted pillars and boxy pediment, now desanctified and used as a setting for lectures, readings, and concerts. The royal standard I had taken from the Carrociro, the shield on white with its gold thread and braid, lay draped over the coffin. An abbot with a sonorous voice presided, the same who had addressed the crowd on the day Berlauda had been crowned. The Knight Marshal came in his sky-blue suit, with a grandson at each elbow. Her majesty attended the service for the victor who had secured her throne, as did many of the court. She wore the cream-white silken gown permitted to royalty as mourning dress.

The veterans of Exton Scales came, some of them wounded and supported by friends or by crutches. They wore their bandages defiantly, for these were the true laurels of victory. Most were not permitted in the confined space of the temple, but stood in a silent congregation outside.

I arrived with Lipton, and as he wore an officer's sash, he was allowed past the door, and he took me with him. I wore my armor, and carried my sword at my side and my burgonet under my arm. As a token of mourning, I wore sprigs of rosemary on my collar. I did not care if the sight of me drove Wenlock to a fury, for I had come to say farewell to a comrade and a friend, and to honor his courage and his victory.

I stood in the back of the dark old temple as incense and a sonorous choir wafted over me, and the abbot, the Marshal, and Wenlock eulogized the hero of Exton Scales. I did not quite recognize the man they described, this decisive and infallible titan, so intent on bringing to a fulfillment the martial grandeur of his ancestors; and I thought that the man I remembered, with his sardonic wit and his philosophical discourse, was much more interesting, and perhaps more worthy of note than the ivory statue conjured by the speakers' fulsome rhetoric.

I had not expected to be mentioned, and I was not, though I found it a strange sensation to be thus written out of history.

Trumpets blared, drums boomed, and Wenlock put on his purfled round cap and walked out the temple, followed by the casket on the shoulders of six titled pallbearers, including Lord Barkin. I don't think Wenlock saw me in the crowd of mourners.

Outside in Curzon Square, the coffin was laid on a wagon that would take it to the city's harbor, for transport down the Dordelle to Bretlynton Head, and from thence across the sea to Ethlebight, where Lord Utterback would ultimately be laid to rest at his ancestral home, some leagues up the river from the city.

I remembered the young man who had ridden to the city's defense with thirty well-armed followers, and faced Sir Basil calmly in the old fortress, and who resolved to fight Clayborne's army even though the battle was nigh hopeless. If he had been overwhelmed by his responsibility, he had never lacked for courage, and he had never failed once he understood his duty.

Queen Berlauda followed the coffin from the old temple, walking with the old Knight Marshal between two files of Yeoman Archers, and we all knelt as she passed. Lipton and I made our way out and paused on the portico, beneath the pediment with its worn, ancient statues of headless heroes. The day was bright and warm, the air fragrant with the scent of spring flowers. A line of carriages was drawn up between the temple and the group of soldiers who waited in the square. The Queen entered one of these along with the Marshal, and waving pleasantly, they left the scene. Great nobles and leaders began to fill the others.

Lipton and I turned to those leaving the building, and we greeted Frere, whose great black beard was as magnificent as ever, bald old Captain Snype, Ruthven in his muscled leather cuirass, and some of the other officers. Lord Barkin, who had helped to carry the pall, was already gone.

We held a colloquy for a while, and I think we all sensed that this would be the last time we would all be together. The war that had brought us to our rendezvous at Exton Scales was over. Ruthven would soon return to Selford with his regiment, Frere had received an appointment as Warden of the fortress of Dun Foss up on the border with Bonille, and the professionals like Snype would be looking for another war. Lipton would remain in Howel with his battery of demiculverins, and fire salutes at royal parades.

For myself, I prayed never to see another battlefield, but otherwise knew not what I would do with myself. There was nothing to keep me in Howel, not with the Queen viewing me with loathing and Wenlock wishing to hurl me into prison for theft or any other crime that occurred to him. But there was no reason to travel anywhere else, especially as Orlanda might whisper poison into the ears of everyone I met, and make any new place as inhospitable as the court. When Frere asked me what I would do next, I said that I didn't know.

"Idleness will only serve to get you into trouble," said a familiar voice. "You had best find an occupation and stick to it."

I turned and bowed to the princess Floria. She wore greens and blues, with a carcanet of emeralds. Sprigs of rosemary were pinned as tokens of mourning to her hat and her gown. Two burly Yeoman Archers stood three yards behind her, and neither eyed me with favor.

"Does your highness have a suggestion which profession I might adopt?" I asked.

"I do not," she said, looking steadily up at me with her hazel eyes. "I know only that, judging by that broil on the Mummers' Day, you make a damned poor bodyguard."

"But you, highness, make a very good one," said I. "You interceded on my behalf, and saved me from the stocks, at the very least."

"Nay," she said, "they would have cut off your head, and her majesty would have signed the warrant with a blithe heart. Yet I thought that a man who has such a useful way with bandits and assassins should not be so carelessly tossed away."

"Then I thank you for my life. I wrote you my thanks at the time."

"I read the letter. I thought that to reply might have brought trouble on you, for none of my correspondence is private."

"I thank you for that courtesy." I bowed again. "May I introduce these officers?" For the others had been standing, heads bowed, while this conversation went on, and our words must have been a great stimulus to their imaginations.

I presented the others, and said that we had all been together at Exton Scales. She looked at them with interest.

"It speaks well of Lord Utterback that you gentlemen attend his memorial," she said.

"He was our comrade," said Coronel Ruthven.

Her highness's bright eyes flicked from one to the other. "At court, Count Wenlock is like a battery of artillery when it comes to his son: he bombards us daily with his son's many virtues, and his own woes, and with the debt her majesty owes to his house. He lays siege to the throne and comes nigh to demanding honors for himself. Yet should we further ennoble an already-noble father for the sake of his dead son?"

We had no answer for that, though personally I wished Wenlock in the *Mare Postremum* without a dinghy. So, Floria turned to me.

"Was my lord Utterback the hero of the battle? Was he everything his father says?"

"My lord was the hero entire," said I. "He fought bravely all day long, he led the final charge that broke the rebellion, and he died at the moment of victory."

"But surely he was not the only hero of the day."

"There were a thousand heroes that day," said I. "But all of them are dead."

There was a moment of silence. Floria's quick, birdlike gaze settled on me. "And you, Goodman Quillifer? You are ever in the midst of quarrels and dissensions, and you have crossed swords with infamous bandits and murderous rogues. Were you not in the forefront of the battle? I see that your armor has been battered, and there is a crease across the skull of your helm."

"I had the ill fortune to be struck by the enemy, and the good fortune not to have been murdered," I said. "But as for bravery, there were many on the field more worthy than I."

She looked at me for a long, thoughtful moment, and then nodded. "Your loyalty to your commander commends you. I apologize if you find my questions impertinent—I want simply to learn things, you see. We in the palace know only what we are told by people like Wenlock, and by the Marshal, and neither of them were there."

We looked at her in silence. For my part, I would say nothing that would serve to diminish Lord Utterback's honor or memory, and I suppose the others felt much the same way.

"May the Pilgrim enlarge your knowledge," said Frere finally.

A little wry smile touched her lips. "He hasn't yet," said she. "But the world may hope."

We bowed, and she withdrew to her carriage, which soon drew away.

Lipton looked after her thoughtfully, and tugged his cap down over one eye. "That is a very strange little girl, sure," he judged.

"She wants to do Wenlock down," said Frere. "I care not what happens to the count, but I know I want nothing to do with any court conspiracy."

I had even more reason to keep away from such a conspiracy than did Frere, and so I nodded agreement.

"What was meant," asked Snype, "when you thanked her for saving your life?"

"Not so much saving as sparing." And I told her about Lord Stayne, the attack on the Festival of the Mummers, how the princess had intervened to prevent my being executed, and how I had come to join the army as a refuge from being killed on the streets of Selford.

"It ended well for you," said Frere, "so I will not say your decision was unwise. Yet it is a strange enough reason for joining the Queen's Army."

"A great many soldiers seem to have joined to flee from their former life," said I, "whether they were being hunted or no."

"You left out the reason why Stayne has taken so against you."

"Because," said I, "a great lord needs reason in nothing he does."

This they found amusing. "Is Stayne still after your life?" asked Ruthven.

"I have no knowledge one way or another, but I am sure he does not wish me well."

"Your bodyguard here is being disbanded," Ruthven pointed out. "You might wish to take care."

Lipton clapped me on the shoulder. "The Cannoneers will look after him!" he said. "Whoever wants him will have to face the great guns!"

After bidding my friends farewell, I went out into the square where the soldiers waited, and I shook many by the hand, and spoke with all those who desired to talk to me. I wished them all a safe journey home, or to their next posting, and afterward went back to the baron's house, and gazing out the windows at the pretty houses glowing gold in the noon sun, tried to decide where next my life would take me. For it seemed that since I had left Ethlebight, I had been blown from one course to the other as if by a perverse wind, and if there was any sense to it, I could not find it. Yet neither could I find a course I strongly wished to take, and so I dealt with whatever business came to hand.

The next few weeks, I spent with the documents I'd acquired when I had looted the homes of the proscribed. I had deeds to properties, and I surveyed as many as were within a few hours' ride, and decided to keep some of them. I hired a man to manage them for me, and a lawyer to help me sell those properties in which I had no interest. I also held mortgages and documents relating to loans, and these I investigated through the lawyer, kept some, and sold others to bankers. There was a branch of the Oberlin Fraters Bank in the city, and I arranged for any income to be deposited there, and investigated the means by which I might transfer the money, by note, to another branch.

While I thus occupied myself, it was announced that Priscus, Loretto's heir, was on his way to Howel to claim his bride. The marriage contract had been made with the promise that Priscus would lead an army against Clayborne, a promise that Priscus had failed in every way to fill. Even though he had done nothing, apparently Berlauda was obliged to marry him anyway.

The city was soon bustling with preparations for welcoming Priscus and his entourage, and Lipton and his artillery were sent out to practice their royal salutes. I decided I might as well stay for the celebration, as a great festival seemed a fine antidote to the great miseries of war.

Yet there were reminders of the war almost daily, for following Berlauda came her new Attorney General, Lord Thistlegorm, with a company of judges to sit on special treason courts. Anyone who had sworn allegiance to Clayborne, or to the infant Emelin VI, was found guilty, as were a number of those for whom the evidence was far less direct. Informers haunted the courts, and rumor had it they were paid by the conviction. Even Clayborne's childhood nurse was brought before the bench, and found guilty of inciting treason on the part of her infant charge.

As an apprentice lawyer, I knew that the treason laws were severe, and that guilty verdicts were all but inevitable in many cases, but that such verdicts were intended to be mitigated by the monarch's prerogative of mercy. Berlauda had the authority to pardon any of those convicted, or to alter the sentence to one less severe; but she almost never intervened in these cases, and the result was executions nearly every day. A forest of pikes sprouted around Clayborne, each with its grisly fruit.

The remains of Clayborne's army were tried by a military court headed by the Knight Marshal. As they had all been found in arms against the Queen, the verdict was never in doubt. One in ten, chosen by lot, was to be executed, and the survivors branded on the cheek with a *T* for Treason, after which they would be enslaved for ten years, to work in the Queen's silver mines in the Minnith Peaks, to maintain harbors, erect buildings, and harvest timber from the royal forests. Few, I guessed, would survive this hard labor.

Berlauda was beginning her reign with a massacre. I wondered what Priscus would think, strolling up to the Hall of Justice to find himself face-to-face with the decaying, eyeless evidence of his bride's implacable will.

If he had any sense, he would jump back on his boat and row for home as fast as he could.

Priscus was sailing in a galley along the Dordelle from Bretlynton Head, but ahead of him came the Duke and Duchess of Roundsilver across the Cordillerie from Longfirth, and bringing with them Roundsilver's Players to declaim the patriotic pageant of *The Red Horse* in the old Aekoi theater. I paid a call on their graces when I saw they'd arrived, and was invited one afternoon to what is called a banquet. A banquet is not a meal, for no meat is served, but instead nuts and sweets and cakes were laid on a board for our pleasure, and wine was served by the steward at the cup-board. Blackwell was present, but he had come down with a quinsy on the journey, and he now wrapped his throat with flannel and could barely speak. He ate nothing, drank only tisanes, and was as great a picture of misery as you could imagine. The duchess fluttered about him to make sure he was comfortable, the kindest nurse in all the world.

The duke at one point took me aside, and said, "You wrote that you were leaving Selford, but we were greatly surprised to hear that you had joined the army."

"I surprised myself in that very choice," said I. "But the army and I have now parted, and I stand before you an ordinary subject of the Crown, one who no longer rises early to the sound of trumpets, and can sleep as late as he pleases."

"You will want to hear news of Lord Stayne," said the duke. "The Chancellor and I contrived to send him a warning, that any further pursuit of vengeance by him would not be viewed favorably by her majesty. I know not whether he heeded the warning, but perhaps in the last months he has had time to reflect, and come to a more civil attitude in the matter."

"I thank your grace for your kind intervention," said I.

"You may also wish to know that Lady Stayne is delivered of a son," said the duke, with rather more care than usual, for he actually pronounced the *r* in "delivered." "Stayne has an heir, and perhaps he will refrain from any action that might tend to place his son's rights in jeopardy. Certainly, if Stayne were attainted for violence, his son would lose all property and titles."

I considered that this was as likely a settlement as I was ever to receive, and I said so. "And how is Lady Stayne?" I asked. "For she is blameless in all of this, so far as I can tell."

"Her ladyship survived the birth," said the duke. "More than that

I cannot say, but she is in the bloom of youth, and I'm sure cannot help but thrive."

"I cannot help but be glad," I said. I thought that perhaps we were speaking in a kind of code, the duke to reassure me of Amalie's health without acknowledging in speech the interest that I might have in her well-being. I was grateful for the knowledge, yet I hoped there was no great speculation abroad concerning my connection with Amalie, for Stayne's feud had no doubt caused enough interest on the part of the court.

Priscus arrived two days later, his grand galley sweeping up the Dordelle to the ponderous beat of kettledrums. The population thronged the green river-lawns to see him, but I did rather better, for I went to the boat-house of the Baron of Havre-le-Creag, fitted out the baron's galley, and crewed it with some of the Cannoneers drawn from those who would not be firing salutes on that day. So, we swept out very grandly onto the lake in a boat of bright blue, trimmed with white and accented with gold leaf, and followed the prince as he approached the water-gardens around the palace. The prince himself I viewed through my spyglass, and I found him swarthy and dark-haired, with both hair and beard cropped shorter than was the current fashion in Duisland. He had a vast, beaky nose, like the prow of a ship. He wore a glittering doublet of royal purple, slashed to allow the white satin of his shirt to gleam through the openings, and a conical hat with two feathers, the red and gold of Duisland, as a compliment to his bride. He wore a short cape of white samite trimmed with purple.

In fact, conical hats and short capes seemed to be universal among the Lorettans. Priscus and his gentlemen formed a glittering company, and seeing them all together made me realize that they stood in a somewhat different manner than we men of Duisland. For we stand square, with the weight on both feet, but these Lorettans had one foot before and the other behind, and seemed to arch forward, so that their breastbones were well to the front, with their hips, shoulders, and heads drawn back. The conical hats and short capes seemed designed to call attention to this posture. They made an elegant sight, curved like so many yew bows set up on the forecastle of the galley, and I wondered if this stance was one that would soon be adopted as the fashion by our own nation.

Among this group were monks of the Pilgrim, but monks unlike any I had seen before. The monks in Duisland wore robes of unbleached wool, but these wore robes in brilliant colors, scarlets and blues and verdant greens; and they wore gold also, belts and prayer beads and amulets. Certainly, they seem to have transcended certain notions of humility and poverty.

The Lorettan galley swept up to the quay built by the water-gardens, and a royal salute banged out from batteries set up by the lakefront. I could see Captain Lipton bustling about in his battery, and signaling each of his guns to fire at the appropriate time.

The Queen waited, serene as ever, on a white palfrey, and Priscus disembarked, swept off his hat, and kissed her hand. Another white steed was brought forward for Priscus, and the two rode off together into the water-gardens, and were lost from sight.

Days of festival followed, and the Lorettan gentlemen, with their capes and curved posture, were seen everywhere in town. There were jousts in which the knights of Duisland fought those of Loretto, and the victor was judged to be Lorenso d'Abrez, one of the prince's followers, who skillfully broke lance after lance. A water-organ was placed on a boat, and anchored in the river to play a concert for the town. There were horse-races and prize-fights, and a piper sat outside every tavern to provide music for dancing. Blackwell's masque, *The Triumph of Virtue*, was performed in the ancient theater, with the nobles of both nations playing parts in their own glittering costumes. Castinatto reprised his role as the villain, and little Floria again played Virtue, but her acting this time was more lively, as if she realized that mocking her sister, as she had at Kingsmere, was no longer wise.

All those heads on pikes before the Hall of Justice would, no doubt, agree with her.

This was the first time a masque had been performed in public rather than privately at the court, and two thousand of Howel's citizens, who were admitted without charge, watched the performance with astonishment.

A few days later, there was a regatta on the lake, in which His Grace of Roundsilver's galley took the laurel of victory from a young woman dressed as a Mermaid. The sight of a woman in Mermaid costume brought to mind the last sweet night in Ethlebight, and in an instant I felt a great swell of sadness, while tears stung my eyes. I wondered where Annabel Greyson was now, in what horrid picture of captivity I might find her, and then I thought of my family, and the thousands of others who had been carried away. I felt that no matter how well I had done, no matter what successes were laid to my account, I had lost much more than I had won.

After this, I went for a long walk to the town, drank a few mugs of ale, listened to some music, and tried to abolish the melancholy that had crept over me. I met with but light success, and when I returned, I found a carriage waiting outside my residence. No sooner had I come into sight than the Count of Wenlock burst from it, shouting.

"There you are!" he roared. "I wanted to *see* you!" He arrived in front of me, and waved a finger at my face. "I wanted to *see* the man who traduced my son! I wanted to see what sort of monster it is who steals my son's victory, and claims it for his own!"

Surprised beyond measure, I stared at Wenlock as he shouted at me, and then managed to gather my wits for a reply.

"I have done nothing of the kind! Whoever has told you this has lied!"

"It is *you* who have lied!" cried the count. He brandished a fist. "You have been spreading slanders behind my back, and trying to claim the victory at Exton Scales for your own! You will *never* succeed, do you hear me? I will *crush* you, and reveal the truth to all!"

I was on the verge of summoning another denial when he turned and marched back to his carriage, after which he spun about again. "A *statue!*" he shouted, stamping on the ground. "A damned *statue!*"

I watched the vehicle disappear in a cloud of dust, then walked into the house in a daze, Wenlock's shouts still ringing in my head. There I met Captain Lipton, who whooped at the sight of me.

"Congratulations, youngster!" he said, and waved a paper. "Your future is made, and I have made it!"

I was more intent on Wenlock's hostile arrival than on Lipton's fancies, and I tried to explain what had just occurred in the road outside the house, and Lipton thumped me on the shoulder.

"It is the honors list published this morning, and posted by the heralds!" he said. "You have been made a knight for your actions at Exton Scales, and given a manor!"

I looked at the list as he brandished it before my eyes. There I saw that for valorous and meritorious service in time of war, Quillifer the Younger of Ethlebight was to be made a knight bachelor, and awarded the manor of Dunnock, in the shire of Hurst Downs.

"Where is Hurst Downs?" I asked, completely baffled.

"I care not!" Lipton proclaimed. "It matters only that I have got it for you!"

"How have you—" I began, but could go no further. I was beyond words, for this matter was beyond all sense.

"I remind you that you twice promised me a bottle of claret on the field of Exton Scales," said Lipton. "You have never made good your promise, and I think it is time you did. For we must drink to your advancement, and this speedily!"

My head spun, but the easiest thing to do was surrender to the moment. "Let us go then to the buttery of my lord Havre-le-Creag," I said, "and I will fill my promise directly."

CHAPTER THIRTY-TWO

The buttery of the Baron Havre-le-Creag was expansive, filled to the ceiling with tuns of wine, each branded with a name and date burned into the lid of the barrel with a hot poker, and bottles piled in dusty niches, labeled with cards in a spiky chancery hand. The wine steward had deserted his post some weeks earlier, after realizing he couldn't stop the Cannoneers from drinking anything they wanted, no matter how rare or expensive. I took a pair of bottles from one of the dustier niches to the great hall, where I opened one and poured. Captain Lipton took a long drink, and with a sigh of pleasure scratched his bald head.

"Youngster, that little princess has made of you her enterprise, sure," he said.

I considered this, and felt the ghost of a warning caress the back of my neck. "I do not know that I care to be so scrutinized by royalty," said I. "I cannot see that the ending of this will bring me joy."

"You could give the manor back," said Lipton. "Or better still, sign it to me."

"Tell me first how I came to own it."

It seems that princess Floria had not understood my reticence on the day of Lord Utterback's memorial, and had thought that I was conspiring with the others to hide some great secret about the battle at Exton Scales, something to the detriment of Utterback, or the Knight Marshal, or some other great figure. Intrigued by this seeming mystery, she had contrived to interview some of the officers, including Lipton, and these had spoken of my own part in the battle.

"Deploying the men while Utterback was off meeting the enemy, rallying the cavalry as they came back scattered, fighting in the line, leading two attacks by the dragoons on Clayborne's artillery, defeating one of the Gendarmes in single combat, horse to horse . . ."

"I hardly did that!" I said.

"Youngster, I *saw* you. You bowled over that armored yaldson and danced your courser over him as neat as if you were in a horse-ballet."

"That was Phrenzy," said I, weakly.

Wine had filled Lipton with eloquence. He gestured broadly and continued his inventory of my martial achievements. "And then of course, fighting all day in the line, and bringing up the reserve company in the nick of time, and at the very end rallying the men beneath the guns to keep the cannon from falling into the hands of the enemy . . ."

Which was not why I had done it, but my own intentions scarcely seemed to matter in the larger scheme of Lipton's grand narrative.

"So, after her highness spoke to me, and to some of the others—Snype, Ruthven, Lord Barkin, even Frere after I assured him that there was no court conspiracy involved—she thought you well deserved a reward." He spread his hands. "And now you have a knighthood, as do Ruthven, Barkin, and Frere, and that—beyond exercising my genius in the serving of the guns at Exton Scales—was the best afternoon's work of my life!"

"How is it that you avoided a knighthood for yourself?" I asked.

He laughed. "I am a mere mechanical; what do I need with a coat-of-arms? I am content with my two bottles of claret, sure, though I will take the manor if you don't want it." He prodded me on the arm. "It is a gentleman who wants a shield on his carriage, and that gentleman, youngster, is now yourself."

It would be dishonest to say that I did not feel a flush of pleasure at hearing all this, but what gratified me more than anything was learning of the testimony of my comrades.

"How do I thank them all?" I asked. "They cannot all be satisfied with bottles of claret."

"They have all got their rewards. And I have got somewhat myself, for if you look toward the bottom of the list, you will see I am awarded two hundred royals. It will come as a bill on the treasury, sure, but I may hope to profit by it in time."

"I will redeem it at full value."

"Bless you, youngster!" He raised his glass. "And so we have come to the land of happy endings, sure."

I eventually understood Wenlock's strange remark about the statue. Rather than reward the count with more land, or a title ranking above that which he held, the Queen had decided to erect an equestrian statue of Lord Utterback in one of the town squares. Wenlock, it seems, had sacrificed his son, not for the advancement and riches he expected, but for a statue. That the statue would assure that Lord Utterback would be remembered for generations was of little moment. Wenlock could have bought a statue for himself for much less than he had spent on the Utterback Troop.

I heard also that he was preparing to sue for a divorce in the House of Peers. He required a new heir, and his wife was past the age of childbearing—he needed a young girl, and he was already inquiring after the daughters of his friends.

Eventually, I learned where Hurst Downs lay, which was in Bonille, along the stretch of the south coast between Bretlynton Head and Melcaster. The size of the grant, and the state of the manor of Dunnock, were unknown, and I must visit the place to discover its boundaries and condition.

Indeed, it was time to deal with a great many matters, none of them in Howel. The war being over, *Lady Tern* and *Royal Stilwell* would find employment returning troops to Selford, and then would be returned to their owners, which is to say Kevin and myself. *Sea-Holly* would have similar convoy duty, but ere long, new cargoes would have to be found for her.

I also felt that I was justified in returning to Ethlebight, not as a man who had failed at everything he attempted, but as the great hero Sir Quillifer.

But first I hunted down Frere, Snype, and Lord Barkin—Ruthven had already gone home—and I thanked them and toasted their own success. That done, there was one more person to thank. As I attended the various celebrations for Priscus and the Queen, I often saw Floria, but she was always surrounded by ladies and lords and guards, and I could not manage an interview. Eventually, there was nothing to do but put on my lawyer's gown and my apprentice cap, travel to Ings Magna, and find her in the palace.

It was a day when no celebrations were scheduled in the city, and the Queen was at home. No one prevented me from entering the Chamber of Audience, which was a beautiful, sun-filled, warm room, filled with brilliant silk hangings and carved with wonders and phantasmagoria, a delightful contrast to the cold, gloomy Great Reception Room in Selford. Neither the Queen nor Priscus were present, though I saw some gentlemen of Loretto strolling through the room, their bodies curved like willow wands. I found the princess right away, walking with some of her ladies before a tapestry of the Compassionate Pilgrim delivering his wisdom to his followers. I approached and bowed. She looked at me with a stern expression.

"Don't expect any ceremony," said Floria. "The Queen isn't about to tap you with a sword. And you're not in one of the great knightly orders or anything; you're a plain knight bachelor."

"I'm sure it's more than I deserve," said I.

"Her majesty is cross with me for adding those names to the honors list," said the princess. "I might have implied that I did so at her command—that is what is *said*, though for myself I cannot remember."

"Who was it who suggested the statue?"

A slight smile touched her lips. "My memory remains fallible on that point. Perhaps you should take my arm and remind me where to put my feet."

Having the little princess on my arm made me feel very like a broad-shouldered ban-dog trotting in the company of a spaniel. I had to shorten my steps to avoid dragging her across the floor. Her ladies fell back a few paces to give us a degree of privacy.

"I must thank you once more, highness," said I. "You saved my life, and now you have offered me honors."

"I have not heard that you have acted otherwise than to uphold the Queen's authority and dignity," Floria said. "Her majesty will realize this in time, has she a moment or two for reflection."

I thought that Berlauda did not seem to have a particularly reflective character, but did not say so.

"In the meantime," said I, "Her majesty seems to dislike me. The last time she saw me, she called for the Yeoman Pregustator."

Floria gave a sharp little laugh. "Perhaps some women are immune to your charms." She gave me a sidelong look. "Certainly, the Marchioness of Stayne was not."

I felt myself straighten. "I assure you that—"

"Oh, be silent!" she said. "I saw how she looked at you. At court we call her Lady Languid—but Lady Languid she was not, not when she gazed at *you*. And of course, there was the aftermath, with the husband trying to have you murdered." Again she looked at me side-long. "A case I have reason to remember well."

I felt my mouth going dry. "I hope the gossip of the court does not—"

"No," she muttered. "It does not. No one conceives Lady Stayne would so debase herself as to lie with a Butcher's son." She gave that sharp laugh again. "Sometimes, I think I am the only person here with eyes."

I was not quite certain what to say to this, but after some thought, I managed a commonplace.

"May the Pilgrim enlarge your sight."

"Sometimes, I think I see far too much."

Trumpets sounded a sennet from a gallery. Floria withdrew her arm from mine.

"My sister comes. Perhaps you should withdraw."

I bowed. "As you wish, highness."

"Try not to get in any brawls," she advised. "And if you do, do not involve me."

"Your highness, I shall try with all my heart to obey."

I fled the palace, very much afraid that I had become the hobby-horse of a fifteen-year-old girl with nothing better to do than to meddle with the lives of her inferiors. I was already persecuted by Orlanda, and I felt that the scrutiny of another powerful being was a great injustice.

Now there was nothing keeping me in Howel but the few tasks remaining. I called upon the Roundsilvers to say good-bye and to thank them for their kindness, and they wished me joy of my knighthood. I returned to the palace to collect the title to my manor, and to the office of the King-at-Arms to certify my knighthood and to register my coat of arms. Which, in the strange tongue of the heralds, part Loretto, part Osby Lords, part Aekoi, is this:

Azure, a galleon argent a chief fir twigged argent, in chief three pens bendwise sable.

Which is to say a blue shield with a white ship thereon, and a white stripe across the top, with a jagged border resembling in outline the twigs of a fir tree. In the white stripe are three black quills.

Which is a play on words, if you like: *Quill-in-fir.* Even the herald-pursuivant laughed.

On my final afternoon in Howel, I went to the theater to see *The Red Horse, or the History of King Emelin.* The vast theater was built for spectacle, with an enormous wall built behind the stage that featured marble columns, balconies, niches for heroic statues, and the apparatus for making actors fly. The ancient statues of gods and heroes that had once filled the niches had long been looted, but they had been replaced by figures in a more modern style, one of which had been dressed to represent King Emelin himself, caught in the act of witnessing his own triumph.

It was a revelation to see the play with the audience of more than a thousand people instead of a hundred or so folk at court, and when Sir Bellicosus and his cronies came out, the laughter seemed to shake the heavens. The clowns had sharpened and enlarged their performance since the premiere in the autumn, and the play was somewhat less of a pageant, for Blackwell had altered a few of the scenes to create more movement. Blackwell himself had recovered from his quinsy, and spoke out in a fine loud voice from amid his warrior's padding.

"You did not view *The Nymph*," said Orlanda.

"I never cared for the play," I said. The comedy had played the previous afternoon, apparently with great success.

Orlanda was seated beside me, wrapped in dark green gown that shimmered with silver stars. Her red hair was upswept into a complicated knot adorned with emeralds and pearls, and the air about her was fragrant with the scent of hyacinths.

I looked behind and along of her, and no one seemed to have noticed this verdant nymph appearing in their midst, right in the middle of a bright May afternoon. Apparently, she presented herself to me alone.

Somehow, I was not surprised. I had been expecting her any day.

"Have you come to congratulate me on my knighthood?" I asked.

"Foolishly I believed the Queen decided such things," said Orlanda. "I had thought that the hatred I had carefully nurtured in her breast would prevent her from giving you rewards."

"Neither of us, then, calculated on a meddling little girl?"

"I will not overlook her again."

She unfurled her fan of peacock feathers and stirred the warm spring air. The peacock eyes gazed at me, green and blue and indigo.

Laughter rolled up from the audience at the antics of Bellicosus. Her lip curled in disdain. "You have a gift," said she, "for showing mortals as they really are, scheming and blundering in their vain, useless way to catastrophe."

"And yet here we are," said I. "A theater full of catastrophes, all aglow with laughter." I viewed Bellicosus and his crew, begging the bandits for their lives. "Perhaps it is healthy for us to laugh at ourselves." I turned to her. "Have you ever laughed at yourself, my lady?"

She did not answer, but continued her inspection of the clowns. "You achieved honors," she said, "and it was for the one thing you did not boast of. Did you ever expect to be rewarded for modesty?"

"It is a route to fame I had not considered."

Orlanda looked at me, a shadow darkening the green eyes. "Has war changed you, Quillifer? Has it made you reticent?"

"It has made me reticent about war."

"Perhaps, then, some mite of wisdom has wormed its way into your brain?"

I shrugged. "That may be. To myself, I seem less wise than before."

I looked at the stage, at Blackwell marching onstage as the doomed prince Alain, soon to be snuffed by the hero. "Do you remember our conversation outside the foundry in Innismore? I spoke of the old epics, where the air is filled by invisible members of your tribe, all whispering into the ears of men, and laying their schemes with mortals as their pawns. If that is true—if such as you are everywhere— then how can human life have meaning? What means human ambition if it is but the prompting of a god?" I shrugged. "How can Berlauda be a Queen, a true monarch, if you or your like urge her to love and hatred, and the inclinations of her own heart are not her own?"

"You *have* gained wisdom, then. It is what I have said all along. Human ambition is worse than futile; it is delusion."

Applause roared up from the stone core of the old theater. I waved a hand. "Yet here we are, futile though we be. Watching our dreams parade themselves before us, on a stage that was dreamed by another people long ago. We are still here, after all this time, dreaming and laughing and beating our hands together in approval of the shades that play before us. Where are *your* people?"

Her expression was hooded. "We lost interest in your dreams long ago."

"Our ambitions may be futile, as you say. Our very thoughts may not be our own. We may have no more freedom of action than those actors, who speak aloud poetry written by others, and stand and strut on the stage where they are told." Orlanda looked down at the stage, her lip curled in something like derision.

"Yet," I said, "as the actors must believe the lines when they speak them, we have no choice but to act as if we have freedom. Necessity is a cold mistress, but Liberty inspires delightful bed-play."

"Finely phrased," said Orlanda, "but finely phrased delusion."

"What whispers in *your* ear?" said I. "Is there something greater than you that plays with your heart-strings?"

Orlanda's eyes remained on the stage, where Prince Alain led his armies off to their fated, doomed encounter, and King Emelin marched on to give an inspiring speech before battle.

"Master Quillifer," she said, "I propose a game. I shall thwart you, and hurl obstacles in your way, and amuse myself with your delusions and evasions and your antics. And this game shall continue till you die."

I considered this. "How is this different from the game you have played these last months?"

Her peacock-feather fan fluttered in the air. "It differs in that I play it not out of anger, but for the sake of amusement." She looked at me, and I saw that very amusement glitter in her eyes. "Come now, Master Quillifer, to defeat mortals is nothing for you. But to defeat me is achievement indeed."

"I seem to have little choice in the matter," said I.

"You can agree to play the game with a whole heart," said she. "Or you can refuse, and wither away as I send you one misfortune after another, wither until you are nothing. And what sport is *that*?"

For a moment, I said nothing, just listened to King Emelin's fine phrases as they boomed up from the stage. "I will agree to this," I said finally. "On one condition."

"Oh, ay, *conditions*," said she in scorn. "That is your lawyerly way."

"I will play your game," said I, "if you agree not to harm those I love. For if you intend to torment me by murdering my lovers or my children or my friends, then I will first end myself in order to spare them."

She gave me a look. "You are not fit for self-slaughter," she said.

I stared back at her, and let my anger show. "My family is dead," said I. "I carried their bodies to the tomb in my arms. I laid them on the cold stone. Rather than endure that again, I would kill myself. So, you will agree to my condition, or I will say farewell to this life directly, and kill myself like an ancient general in the histories of Bello."

Orlanda's eyebrows lifted. "Do you take me for a death-dealing monster? Unlike your other enemies, I have ways to amuse myself that do not involve murdering people." She nodded. "I agree to your condition, then."

I turned back to the play. "Do I now sign a document in blood?"

"It's too early in the game for blood," said she. "But I will see you another time."

I did not have to turn my head to know she had vanished.

I watched Emelin's triumph, and heard the pretty speeches, and rose with the rest of the audience in applause. I sought out Blackwell afterward, to say good-bye, and he wished me good speed.

Good speed to what? I wondered. For wherever I could go, and however speedily, Orlanda could go before me, and place one ambush after another in my path.

Early the next morning, I boarded the galley for Bretlynton Head, along with Phrenzy and my boy Oscar, and Oscar's own mount. The horses were stabled mid-deck, the boy swung a hammock with the crew, and I had a small cabin in the quarterdeck.

I stowed away my belongings and rose to enjoy the delicate dawn light as it played on the haunting mists of the Dordelle, but then I was distracted by a sight even lovelier than the dawn. She was only a few years older than me, with a lovely warm complexion, snub nose, and a mass of lilac-scented chestnut hair.

Recently widowed, I discovered, not by war or Berlauda's executions but by a flux that had carried away her lawyer husband. Her name was Lacey. Her brother had come for some weeks to Howel to help her, but his own business had required him to return home, and he had taken her two children back to Bretlynton Head while Lacey remained in the town to tie up the last threads of her husband's estate. Now she traveled south to be reunited with her family.

As a near-lawyer, I felt I should take a fraternal interest in the welfare of this lawyer's lady, and I made a point to be pleasant to her.

And that Lacey, of course, is you. And now we lie together in my cabin, your head pillowed on my shoulder while your lilac scent dances in my senses. Your sweet, regular breath warms the skin of my throat. And I see that my modest narration has eased your anxieties, and sent you at last to sleep.

For tomorrow, we will land in Bretlynton Head, and Oscar and I will take horse to my new manor, which lies some days' travel to the east, and we will discover whether it is a ruin or a bounty. You will be reunited with your family, and new lives will begin for the both of us.

Your brother, you say, is very protective and wishes you to live in his house as a sort of unpaid servant, obliged to care for his children as well as yours. He will not permit you to remarry, at the penalty of losing your babes. I fear he will not approve of your being friends with me, new-fledged knight or no. I consider this a great cause for sadness.

I have already placed on the record, I think, my opinion of brothers.

SOURCES FOR SONGS AND POETRY

"Youth will needs have dalliance . . ."
>Song, "Pastime with Good Company"

"Ah me! as thus I look before me . . ."
>Thomas Bruce, "The Summer Queen"

"What Joy or honors can compare . . ."
>Ben Jonson, *Second Epithelamium*

"O cruel Love, on thee I lay . . ."
>John Lyly, *Sappho's Song*